Praise for *The Devil's Horn*, first

'<u>Love</u> the book!'

'Will keep you gripped till the very last page.'

Rose Ferry, booktuber

'The best book set in Majorca that I have ever read. There are a number of reasons for that – a strong plot, a splendid female hero, and some surprising twists and turns. It also includes delightful evocations of the countryside around Soller and fond descriptions of village life on the island.'   Donald Trelford, journalist

'Beautifully written and intelligent, Anna paints an entertaining account of life on Mallorca. *The Devil's Horn* is poignant in all the right places and funny too, sustained by swift dialogue and detailed descriptions.'   *ABC Mallorca Magazine*

'Unputdownable. The twists and turns keep you engaged to the end.'   @booksnsunshine, Instagrammer & book blogger

'A very gripping story. It will keep you engaged to the end.'

Expert, LoveReading.co.uk

'I don't think I've read a crime story as excellent as this one. It's gripping and quirky.'

@askthebookbug, Instagrammer & book blogger

Praise for *Haunted Magpie*

'This series is one of the best I have read this year. Isabel is now one of my favourite detectives and that is saying a lot as I'm an avid crime fiction fan. I was shocked by the ending! The pacing of the book was amazing – there were lots of twists & turns... The series deserves to be a smash hit and I can see this being developed for TV very easily. I adored this book. Just go and read it!' Books By Bindu

'It's a tightly written, well-paced and highly engaging tale, celebrating the island, its people and vibrant culture.'

TheLiteraryShed

'I like a feisty woman detective and Isabel certainly ticks all the right boxes, especially with her pet ferret Furo! It has a good plot and a great twist and I really enjoyed reading it very much.'

Karenreadsandrecommends

'I love Isabel. She is the perfect sleuth. The writer has given her a great personality and made us feel that we really know her. I devoured this book in just one sitting and immediately added other by this author to my TBR list.' Little Miss BookLover

'For anyone who enjoys cosy crime, this should be added to your list!' Nightfall Mysteries

'I couldn't read fast enough at times to see what happened – I can highly recommend this book and hope to read more of Anna Nicholas' work.' Expert, LoveReading.co.uk

'I absolutely loved this book! Highly recommended.' Becca Reads

'I've loved the time I've spent in Mallorca. I didn't want the book to end. Isabel is a great character. I connected to her early on and rooted for her. Haunted Magpie is a great read.'

Thebookloversboudoir (Pamela Scott)

'The characters are inspiring and brave and the little ferret will steal your heart, believe me! This is a book to read and let you fantasise about travels to better places. I really can't wait to read the next book of the series. I am addicted!'   Varietats

Praise for Anna Nicholas's Mallorca travel series

'Terrific!'   Lucia van der Post, contributor, *FT How to Spend It*

'As intelligent as it is entertaining. From simple escapism to a much more complicated story about the difficulties of balancing life in two places...'   Leah Hyslop, *The Telegraph*

'Anna Nicholas is one of those lucky swine who has dared to live the dream and write about it.'   Harry Ritchie, *Daily Mail*

'Witty, evocative and heart-warming. Another Mallorcan pearl from Anna Nicholas.'   Peter Kerr, author of *Snowball Oranges*

'A beautifully written and highly entertaining account of the upside of downshifting.'   Henry Sutton, *Daily Mirror*

'A hugely entertaining and witty account of how to juggle life and work between two countries, keep fit and stay sane!'
Colonel John Blashford-Snell, CBE, British explorer & author

'An enjoyable read for anyone wanting to live their dream.'
Lynne Franks, OBE, broadcaster & author

'If you thought that glitz and glamour don't mix with rural country living you must read this book.' *Bella* magazine

'This is Anna's comic and observational style at its very best.'
St Christopher's Inns magazine

'Endearing, funny and poignant. What more could one wish for?'
Real Travel magazine

Anna Nicholas is the most prolific British author writing about Mallorca today. Her successful series of six travel books explores the history, culture and delights of the golden isle. An inveterate traveller and experienced freelance journalist, she is on the Telegraph's travel team, and has contributed features to FT *How to Spend It,* the *Times,* and other leading British national newspapers. Anna regularly participates in humanitarian aid expeditions overseas and runs an international marathon annually for her favourite causes.

Fallen Butterfly is her third novel in the new Mallorca crime series.

Instagram @annanicholasauthor
Twitter @ANicholasAuthor
Facebook @AnnaNicholasAuthor

Also by Anna Nicholas

Isabel Flores Mallorcan Mysteries
The Devil's Horn
Haunted Magpie

Mallorca travel series
A Lizard in my Luggage
Cat on a Hot Tiled Roof
Goats from a Small Island
Donkeys on my Doorstep
A Bull on the Beach
A Chorus of Cockerels
Peacocks in Paradise

Memoir
Strictly Off the Record with Norris McWhirter

Burro Books,
403, Union Wharf,
23 Wenlock Road,
London N1 7SJ
www.burrobooks.co.uk

Published by Burro Books Ltd 2022

ISBN: 978-1-8383110-2-5
Ebook ISBN: 978-1-8383110-3-2

Printed and bound by CPI Group (UK) Ltd, Croydon, CR0 4YY

FALLEN BUTTERFLY

AN ISABEL FLORES MALLORCAN MYSTERY

ANNA NICHOLAS

burrobooks

LONDON

Glossary

The following Mallorcan and Spanish words and expressions appear in the book. I hope these explanations prove helpful.

Acelgas – chard

Adéu – goodbye (Mallorcan)

Ajuntament – town hall

Ánimo – cheer up

Arroz brut – means 'dry rice'. A rich savoury rice dish

Autónomo – self-employed

Bocadillo – sandwich/roll

Bodega – wine cellar

Bona nit – good night (Mallorcan)

Botifarró – a local spicy pork sausage

Bruja – witch

Bu – boo

Ca rater – small Mallorcan dog breed

Café con leche – coffee with milk

Cariño – Darling

Càrritx – Mauritania grasses

Casita – little house

Castellers – human towers

Claro – sure

Coca – a popular rectangular-shaped local savoury pastry that is similar to pizza

Comandante – commander

Cortado – espresso with a dash of milk

Crema – cream (usually custard variety)

Criminalistica – criminology

Dicho – a saying

Diga – Tell me or speak!

El meu amic – my friend

Empanada – a savoury pastry

Ensaïmada – spiral-shaped Mallorcan pastry

Entrada – entrance

Feliz cumpleaños – happy birthday!

Fideua – paella dish made with noodles

Fiesta – party

Finca – country house

Funcionaria – civil servant

Furó – ferret. In Spanish 'hurón'

Galletas marineras – fishermen's biscuits

Gambas rojas – red prawns

Gató d'almendras – almond cake

Guardia Civil – the Civil Guard, Spanish military police force

Gloses – Mallorcan folk songs

Herbes – Signature Mallorcan herbal dijestif

Hombre – literally 'Man!' meaning, 'Oh, come on!'

Jefe superior – superintendent

Lotería – the lottery

Majares – cultivated plot of land

Mariposa – butterfly

Masa madre – sourdough

Menu del día – lunchtime menu

Merienda – mid-morning snack

Moix – cat

Moto – motor bike

No pasar – don't pass

No pasa nada – it's okay

Olivar – olive grove

Petanca – petanque, ball tossing game

Pica pica – cuttlefish dish

Pueblo – village

Que susto! – what a fright!

Quien es? – who is it?

Padre – father

Pasteleria – cake shop

Pequeñito – little one

Plaça – village or town square

Poc a poc – little by little

Politicos – politicians

Porc amb col – pork with cabbage

Potaje – soup

Pues – well then

Que va! – no way!

Ramallet – long-lasting local tomato

Reina – queen, term of endearment

Salvamento Marítimo – Maritime Safety & Rescue

Siesta – an afternoon rest

Sobrassada – famed Mallorcan paprika-flavoured, cured pork sausage

Torrente – river

Tomate rallado – grated tomato

Tortilla – omelette

Tostadas – toasted bread

Tráfico – traffic

Tumbet – a typical Mallorcan dish of cooked aubergine, potatoes and peppers

Uep – friendly Mallorcan greeting signifying surprise

Vale – okay

Venga, amiga mia – come, my friend

Vino tinto – red wine

Xeixa – a historic local wheat variety

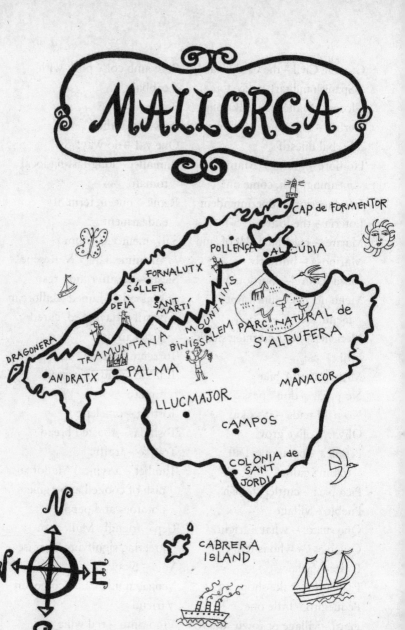

ONE

Inside the claustrophobic, heavy-duty body bag, Sebi blinked hard, trying to get a sense of place despite the impenetrable darkness. There was a sharp jolt and he groaned in agony through his gag as his body was hurled with force into the air and allowed to drop heavily onto a cold, hard surface. His hands and feet were tightly bound and on all sides something soft and damp writhed about him. What was it, earth? Seconds later he was airborne again and being rocked gently from side to side. Who were his bearers? Surely they had to be fit guys to support his weight so effortlessly? Where were they taking him?

He shook with the intense chill as rain drummed on the surface of the bag and winced when what felt like light, fluttery wings kissed his cheeks and arms. Something scurried across his legs and nipped his skin, causing him to squirm in revulsion. What was it? It had to be a rodent, something he couldn't bear to think about. Wedged inside his mobile prison and with a splitting headache, he shuddered when something heavy, wet and cold skimmed his naked body. Please God, not an eel: his childhood phobia resurfaced. He wriggled in the limited space, trying to shake it off. In relief, he closed his eyes when it landed to his right, forcing the bag to sag slightly on that side. Whatever it was, at least it didn't appear to be alive, but the fluttery things were another story. They were everywhere, tickling his bare flesh, face, abdomen and legs. He detested insects of any kind.

The rain ceased and for a while, all Sebi could hear was the eerie call of a barn owl, the methodical croaking of frogs and the sound of feet trudging forward on either side of him. The sharp plastic chord that bound his limbs was beginning to chafe and burn his skin and his heart was pounding. Never before had he felt so helpless – such sheer, unadulterated terror. He closed his eyes, trying to remember the sequence of events that had led to this ignominious point. A vague recollection of leaving the Palma office and stopping at the casino before heading home flashed through his mind. What next? A blank. Try as he might, he simply couldn't remember how he'd ended up here, trussed up and sealed inside a zip-up bag like an oven-ready turkey or a living corpse. That very word made him tremble to his core. He pushed it out of his mind. He had to stay strong, keep his wits about him. As often happened when he became completely overwhelmed by events, a cocky rationality struck him. Let's face it: he was rich and successful and a well-known and respected member of the local political elite with a gold-plated career ahead of him. Whoever these amateurs were, they'd picked the wrong guy.

Thoughts swirled about his head. Perhaps he'd been followed from the office and forced off the highway and drugged. It had been a tough day and he'd knocked back a few stiff drinks before hitting the road. His home was in a rural zone of Llucmajor, a thirty-minute drive from Palma, so there was also the possibility that his assailants had been lying in wait on a country road. Had he crashed the car, been rendered unconscious and somehow been abducted by random opportunists? Maybe he'd been transferred to another vehicle and taken to... where, exactly? More importantly, what did they want? Despite his constant shivering, he almost managed a cynical guffaw through his chattering teeth. Money, obviously. Everything revolved around money.

His limbs relaxed slightly as he contemplated his situation. Wherever these goons were taking him, some lock-up or hideaway, it was evidently in a rural place, away from prying eyes. Maybe a mountain *olivar* or *casita* hidden on a parcel of private terrain. If they were kidnappers, what would their demands be? Surely they'd make contact with his wife, but how would she handle the situation? He mulled this over. Sara would be terrified, but he trusted her to contact his office and the police. No doubt the president would get involved. These people had no idea how big a hornet's nest they'd disturbed. He congratulated himself that his sharp senses and instincts were paying off. The path along which he was being ferried appeared to be hard, maybe asphalt, and yet it was ghostly quiet, with no hint of traffic noise. Now that the rain had subsided, the ominous, insistent cries of frogs and owls seemed to accompany their every step, creating a sense of foreboding. One of his bearers tripped, cursed and sent the bag swinging to one side. As it tipped up again, loose matter scattered across Sebi's face. It smelt of rain, musty leaves and grass, but there was something else. Aside from the biting creatures and what he thought must be a large, dead fish, there were small scratchy things exploring his body. What on earth else was in there with him and more to the point, why?

His silent companions came to an abrupt stop. When they set off again, the bag tilted downward, as if heading downhill. Were they arriving at their destination? This time, his assailants began taking slower and more cautious steps on soft, squelchy terrain and now and then muttered angrily as they hit some kind of obstacle or other. Their breathing became heavier. Next came the creaking of branches and twigs and the sound of mulchy leaves and loose stones being crushed underfoot. His fellow captives were growing friskier and more restless. Like him, whatever they were, they wanted out. Maybe they sensed impending danger. He moved his head from side to side in an attempt to avoid them, feeling once again something heavy and slippery touch his stomach. If only he wasn't constrained and could shake off his unknown tormentors. Wait – was that running water? Where were they now, by a *torrente*? As his bearers plodded on, the sound of gurgling water grew louder. Gripped by rising panic, a sudden clarity hit him and his eyes widened in horror. Eels. So that was what the slithery creature had been. Once more, his body was propelled into the air, this time landing with a tremendous splash into fast-flowing water. And now he realised exactly where he was. Sebi gagged, struggling furiously against his bonds, but it was no good. He was held fast. Tears coursed down his cheeks and he spasmed as the chill of the water beneath his rubber tomb permeated his bones. Light-headed and hardly able to breathe in the dark and suffocating space, he felt his body gliding along, occasionally colliding with a sharp object before continuing on its determined watery path. Tiny droplets of moisture were forming about the zip opener and soon a thin trickle of icy water snaked across his torso. Paralysed with fear, he let out a silent scream of despair, knowing that he'd crossed the point of no return. Despite having led a charmed life, it seemed that Sebi had finally run out of luck.

TWO

Isabel sat in the village hairdressing salon munching on sunflower seeds and frowning at the reflection in the mirror before her. Her wild curly locks had transformed into a tangled heap of squid-ink spaghetti that cascaded soggily about her shoulders.

Her old friend, Marga, placed both hands firmly on Isabel's shoulders. 'What's with the face?'

'I was just thinking.'

'I've warned you about that,' she quipped with a throaty laugh. 'And stop dropping those shells all over my floor.'

Isabel winced as her friend somewhat brusquely began combing through her hair. She reached for the folded newspaper on her lap and thumped it down on the vanity unit next to her. 'Can you believe that the new motorway is still going ahead?'

'Is that what's got your goat? What's so bad about it?'

'Everything. It's going to take a chunk out of S'Albufera Natural Park, destroying so many animal habitats, and let's not even mention the birdlife. It's a catastrophe.'

'To be honest, I haven't really been following the news,' Marga replied.

'Well, you should. That Sebi Vives is a menace.'

Marga shrugged and lifted Isabel's mane of wet hair, tucking a towel around her neck. '*Pues*, at least the guy is good looking, you've got to admit.'

'He's a narcissist who only thinks about money and self-promotion. I despair of politicians.'

'The trouble is,' said Marga, waving a pair of scissors in the air, 'a lot of locals actually want another motorway.'

Isabel growled softly. 'But there are also thousands demonstrating against it. S'Albufera is the most important wetland in the Baleares.'

'Is that so?' Marga gave a sigh and began cutting Isabel's hair. 'Look how long it is. It's ages since you had a cut. I still haven't caught up with you about Colombia, what with Christmas and all the *fiestas*.'

Isabel nodded. 'I know. Life's been crazily busy since Tolo and I got back. January is usually our quiet time in the office, as you know, but we've got so many hikers and cyclists renting at the moment. Poor Pep is working flat out.'

'Don't go easy on my little brother, Bel. He needs to work hard, otherwise he'd be playing football all day long.'

Isabel laughed. 'In truth, Pep held the fort so well when we were away that he could probably run the agency single-handedly now.'

Marga chuckled. 'No way! He needs you banging the drum, trust me.'

The scissors snip-snipped and strands of dark hair fell like rain to the floor. They mingled with some of the sunflower husks that Isabel had inadvertently dropped as she cracked them open with her teeth. Despite Marga's dismissive words, Isabel knew that she was fiercely proud of her little brother. Barely a year before, the youngster had swapped tiling work to help Isabel run Hogar Dulce Hogar, Home Sweet Home, her holiday rentals agency in Sant Martí, and had rapidly learnt the ropes. The agency had belonged to her mother, Florentina, but Isabel had taken hold of the reins when it became too onerous for her. Now it was one of the most successful agencies in the Soller valley, thanks to hard work and team effort.

'How many bookings do you have?'

Isabel puffed out her cheeks. 'At least fifteen properties are occupied. Our cleaning team has been working flat out.'

'Same as always?' Marga suddenly asked, holding a bunch of Isabel's hair in her hand.

'Of course.'

'One day you might like a change, maybe go shorter?'

Isabel shook her head and looked out at the rainy January skies beyond the window. 'I like it long. It keeps my ears warm in winter and I can pile it up on my head with clothes pegs in the summer.'

Marga laughed. 'So tell me about your trip. What news of Uncle Hugo?'

Isabel had recently taken a sojourn in Colombia trying to trace the whereabouts of her uncle, who'd vanished from the streets of Barcelona three years previously, and had returned home to Mallorca more perplexed than ever. She had been accompanied on the trip by Tolo Cabot, the chief inspector of the National Police in Palma, who aside from being her old boss was a close friend. Actually, they'd become rather more than close friends of late, but they had approached their new relationship cautiously, taking it step by step, one day at a time. Soon to turn thirty-four, Isabel was aware of the ticking of her body clock, but equally she relished her personal freedom. Time would tell.

She bit hard on a sunflower seed. 'We're still in the dark. The local Colombian police received a tip-off that Hugo had been spotted in Medellín and Bogotá, but there's still no real evidence to suggest that. They showed me a few grainy images of a man they thought resembled him, but he could have been anyone.'

'But wasn't that private investigator you hired in Barcelona pretty certain the images were of your uncle when he visited Colombia?'

Isabel shifted uncomfortably in her chair. 'When Emilio Navarro visited Bogotá, he was shown several photos by Julian Mosquera, my old police contact there. They both think there's a real likeness with the man in the photos, but I'm not at all certain.'

Isabel wasn't being totally honest with her best friend, but the investigation into her uncle's disappearance had thrown up more questions than answers. One day he left the newspaper offices in Barcelona where he had worked for many years as a leading investigative journalist and was bundled into a limousine that bore a Colombian flag. The only witness had been a prostitute who shortly afterwards had died of a drug overdose in mysterious circumstances.

Isabel sent a private investigator, Emilio Navarro, to Colombia on a recce, and was suitably encouraged by his findings to visit the country herself. As a former detective inspector with the National Police, Isabel was keen to follow the trail and hopefully to find evidence that her uncle was still alive. What she hadn't told Marga was that, according to Julian Mosquera and his various informants, the man in the photos was in the company of a notorious drug baron, and the body language in the images indicated that they were on friendly terms. How could this be? Isabel had been convinced that her uncle, who had always championed the rights of the voiceless and oppressed, had been abducted for exposing drug crime linked to Colombia, but now she wasn't sure what to believe.

Marga put her scissors in the pocket of her overall and took a sip of coffee from a mug. 'Can I get you another *cortado*?'

Isabel nodded. 'Go on then.'

While Marga busied herself in the adjacent small kitchen, Isabel took out her mobile and scrolled through some images. 'You must see the resort we stayed in on the last weekend of the trip. It was magical.'

Marga placed a cup of piping hot coffee in Isabel's hands and, taking the mobile from her, began scrolling through the images. 'This looks swanky! How much did that set you back?'

Isabel laughed. 'I've no idea. Tolo organised it all. It was a complete surprise.'

'Lucky you. Is that a monkey?' cooed Marga. 'Where is this place?'

'It's called Hotel Las Islas. It's on a small island right in the heart of Corales del Rosario National Park, less than an hour by boat from Cartagena. The poor little white-haired marmoset is a protected species there. It's in danger of becoming extinct.'

'What a paradise. Look at those mangroves! Is that real coral?'

Isabel pulled the mobile towards her to inspect the image. 'Yes, the coral reefs are beautiful. The island's a little haven with just 4,000 inhabitants. We did nothing but snorkel, relax and eat fresh fish. Oh, and I finally got round to reading *One Hundred Years of Solitude*. I've nearly finished it.'

Marga returned the mobile and resumed cutting Isabel's hair. 'Gabriel García Márquez is one of my favourite authors. It's ages since I read that book, but I remember loving it.'

Isabel took a sip of coffee. 'So, are we done?'

Marga stared at her in the mirror. 'Do you want it blow-dried?'

'*Que va!* What's the point? It's pouring outside.'

Isabel sprang from her chair and thrust the bag of sunflower seeds and the newspaper into her straw pannier. Pulling off the towel about her neck, she threw on her waterproof jacket and tousled her hair. 'Good job, *reina!*'

Marga remonstrated. 'You're so impatient. I haven't put on a conditioning serum. Can't you wait a minute?'

Isabel kissed her friend on both cheeks and pushed some notes into her hand. 'There's work to be done.'

'Well, don't forget that Rafa's got smoked eel on the menu for lunch today at Bar Castell and his mother has made her famous lemon pie.'

Isabel paused at the door. 'That's tempting. If I get through my workload, I'll be there.'

Happily splashing in puddles on the wet cobbled street, Isabel pulled up her hood and strode towards the *plaça*, cheered by the golden light in the window of the Bon Día grocery that beckoned to her like a siren. Jesus, the portly owner, was smoking a cigar under the awning and staring morosely up at the opaque sky. He nodded to Isabel as she flipped back her hood and shook out her long, damp hair.

'At least we won't have to do any watering for a while.'

'A reason to be cheerful.' She winked as she strode into the store.

'There's another reason to be cheerful,' Jesus said as he followed her inside.

'Oh?' she asked.

He handed her two jumbo packs of Chupa Chup lollies that he'd secreted behind the till. 'The last two until the next delivery on Friday. Go easy on them, Bel.'

'You're a pal.' She beamed. 'And sunflower seeds?'

'Oh, we've still got loads of those. The older kids aren't so keen on them anymore. They like gum.'

Isabel plucked a fresh *xeixa* wheat loaf from the bread shelf and balanced three packets of sunflower seeds on top of the pile. In the limited wine section, she selected a bottle of *vino tinto*. At the till Jesus looked approvingly at the label.

'Ribas is a nice tipple. One to savour.'

As Isabel set off walking purposefully through the square, she heard her name floating on the still air. She turned round to find Llorenç, the village mayor, puffing towards her, his voluminous black umbrella shielding him from the drizzle and almost obliterating him from view.

'What a day! Have you a minute, Bel?'

Isabel grinned. 'For you, always, Llorenç.'

He leant forward and kissed her on both cheeks.

'I like your hair. Have you just had it trimmed?'

'Well observed. So what's up?'

Llorenç frowned. 'We're having a spot of bother at the town hall with those environmentalist types again. You know the expat people.'

She cocked her head to one side. 'What's the problem, exactly?'

He shrugged. 'They're going on about the times of day when bonfires should be burnt in the valley and making a fuss about smoke inhalation. It's not as if generations of Mallorcans haven't been burning bonfires on agricultural land for centuries and it didn't do them any harm.'

She smirked. 'Well, we don't know that for sure, do we?'

Llorenç tutted impatiently. 'The fact is that some foreigners come to the valley wanting to change everything. I always believe in that dictum, when in Rome...'

Isabel offered a pert smile. 'True, but that doesn't mean we can't hear what they have to say. They may have a point. Some mornings there has been a lot of haze over Soller town.'

'That's not my patch, thankfully. All the same, foreign residents here in Sant Martí have been grumbling about the smoke. I've tried ignoring them but they're lodging complaints daily. If they're not moaning about bonfires, they're complaining about the seawater and doing beach clean-ups. I wonder where it will all end.'

'Why not hold a meeting on the matter and invite all the locals and foreign residents to attend and voice their views? At least it shows you are listening.'

'I suppose it might mollify them,' he said.

'Maybe offer a few nibbles and wine to lighten the mood. You should have someone there to speak English, too, as few foreigners speak Mallorquí.'

'Would you come and help translate?'

She rolled her head back and laughed. 'That was a trap I walked right into.'

'You suggested the meeting, not me,' he said, with hands outstretched.

'Okay, I'll be there. Just make sure it's well publicised, otherwise there'll be complaints.'

'You're an angel.' He paused and offered her a sly smile. 'Of course, just because we hold a meeting doesn't mean we have to action anything afterwards.'

Pulling up the collar of his coat, he headed towards the huge arched doorway of the town hall. His diminutive form leant hard against the heavy wooden doors as he battled against the wind to lower the brolly and squeeze his way inside. Isabel was fond of the village's dedicated and hardworking mayor, but sometimes she despaired of his outmoded views. All the same, with patience, tolerance and gentle coaxing, she was sure Llorenç might become more receptive to new ideas. As the time-honoured local dictum went, *poc a poc,* little by little.

With the rain falling steadily about her, Isabel stood still, taking in her surroundings. The ancient and graceful Baroque-style church of Sant Antoní with its arthritic old clock was looking rather forlorn. The pretty orange trees that acted as twin sentries on either side of its front portals had been buffeted by the strong breeze and had lost many a leaf, while sunshine-hued squashed fruit rolled drunkenly about the paving stones. Café Jordi, run by Jordi, its eponymous and ebullient owner, had closed its doors and shutters, though inside a needle of reassuring light could be detected. Isabel yawned and slicked back her wet hair, smiling when she heard hysterical cackling coming from the direction of the postmistress's garden. Señora Coll, a widow with a penchant for hypochondria and hyperbole, had recently acquired a rare Ayam Ketawa cockerel, a gift from her next-door neighbour, Gori Bauzá. In truth, Gori had killed Carlos, her previous noisy cockerel, though only Isabel, Tolo Cabot, the mayor and the local Guardia Civil captain were privy to this. The culprit had been fed up with the old chap's early morning call and had finally finished him off. Through good detective work, Isabel had discovered the truth and to teach Gori a lesson, had forced him to buy the postmistress an Ayam Ketawa, a far noisier and more manic replacement. To add icing on the cake, the blissfully ignorant postmistress had named the hysterical new bird Gori. The penitent cockerel killer had subsequently become a model neighbour and now ran errands for the old lady and popped by with small gifts, much to the surprise of his long-suffering wife.

Isabel slipped through the silent, labyrinthine and cobbled alleyways towards her home in Calle Pastor. The rugged Tramuntana mountain range beyond was shrouded in mysterious low cloud and flooded with an eerie golden light. How she loved setting her eyes on it at any time of day and whatever the weather.

Clanging open the gate of Ca'n Moix, she pottered up the path, breathing in the fragrance of rosemary and thyme that filled two huge terracotta pots by her front door. As always, music emanated from her office upstairs. Pep was most likely dancing about the room or throwing paper balls for her pet ferret, Furó, to catch. She closed the creaky wooden front door and turned the lights on in her elegant *entrada*. The airy hallway was normally flooded with sunlight from the large French windows that looked onto her back garden, but today it reflected only a slate-grey sky. In the kitchen, she smiled to discover a plump plum cake baked by Florentina sitting on the kitchen table. Her mother frequently popped by the house with tasty morsels, which put paid to any thought of a diet, but then who cared about dieting? Life was for living in Isabel's book, and she ate whatever she felt like. She cut a large chunk of cake and began chomping on it as she mounted the staircase. Pep goggled at her as she walked in and turned off the music on his mobile.

'Don't mind me, Pep. Why don't you show me some of your dance moves?'

He grinned. 'Your hair looks bedraggled. I'm not sure I'd recommend my sister's salon to anyone.'

'She did offer to dry it,' protested Isabel as she peeled off her soaking jacket, 'but I just don't have the patience for hairdryers.'

He clicked his teeth. 'You don't have any patience, full stop.'

Isabel stuffed the last of the cake into her mouth and waltzed into her office. She dumped her jacket and pannier on the old Chesterfield sofa and got down on her haunches to stroke Furó, curled up asleep in his basket.

Pep stood in her doorway. 'He's slept all morning. Your early swim in the port in all that rain must have worn him out.'

Isabel sat down heavily in her swivel chair and grabbed a Chupa Chup from a colourful bowl on her desk. 'He loves swimming in the rain.'

'Really? That's not what he told me.'

Isabel laughed. 'So what news?'

He shrugged. 'The heating isn't working in Can Massia, so Idò has gone over to fix it. The renters were very laid back about it, but Idò made such a fuss about driving over there. It's only Escorca.'

'In fairness, it's not the nicest of days for a mountain drive. Have the cleaners done the changeovers?'

'All done and dusted. We got another five Easter bookings today, so nearly everything's booked up until May now.'

'Great. So we can all sit back and relax.' She winked.

He folded his arms. 'Actually, you can't. Tolo called ten minutes ago and said something urgent had cropped up.'

Isabel stood up. 'Why didn't you tell me?'

'I just have,' he replied and with a smile, closed her door.

Taking her mobile from her pannier, Isabel crossed over to the window and looked out at her garden and orchard. A few bedraggled hens were strutting about in the grass and Salvador, her cockerel, was crowing manfully at the sky. The orchard floor was littered with oranges and lemons, while flowerpots and old buckets lay on their side, defeated by the wind. The hanging blooms of the white brugmansia by the fence caught her eye as their trumpet heads bobbed up and down animatedly, as if sharing some scandalous gossip.

She wondered why Tolo was calling her. The previous summer, despite her reservations, he had persuaded her to help solve some puzzling crimes on the island. In truth, she had not wanted to return to police work after the disappearance of her Uncle Hugo. Her father, Juan, a police superintendent in Castilla-La-Mancha, had sought the help of police colleagues in discovering the fate of his identical twin, but none were forthcoming. It was as if he'd hit a brick wall and no one wanted him to dig deeper. He spent his last days trying to uncover the truth, convinced that his brother had met an untimely death at the hands of felons. Isabel, too, had sought the help of senior colleagues within Mossos d'Esquadra, the Catalan police force, for whom she'd worked in Barcelona, but she'd received a cool and hostile response. Her mother, who hailed from the north-west of the island, lost the heart to continue running her rentals agency in Sant Martí when Isabel's father died. As Isabel had felt slighted over her uncle's disappearance and had grown tired of police bureaucracy, she left her high-profile police job in Palma, instead opting for the quiet life in Sant Martí in the hills. Although he found Isabel's approach to solving crime highly unorthodox, Tolo Cabot had mourned her departure from his team as she had an impressive track record both in the Baleares and the mainland in solving baffling cases.

Now Tolo continued to lure her back into the murky world of crime, and if she were honest, she had missed the adrenalin rush and the creative challenge of unravelling webs of deception and lies. The mobile buzzed in her hands, making her start.

'Bel? You didn't ring me back.'

'Give me a break. I've only just got back from the hairdressers.'

The sound of loud chatter and laughter suddenly flooded the communal office. Isabel rolled her eyes. Her neighbour Doctor Ramis and her mother had evidently popped by.

Tolo gave a hoarse cough. 'We've got a situation. Are you free?'

Isabel sucked thoughtfully on her Chupa Chup. 'Where do you need me?'

'Son Real at Can Picafort.'

'Are you kidding? The necropolis? That's at least an hour on the road in this rain.'

'Not the way you drive,' he growled.

'Well, it's not very convenient. There's smoked eel on the menu at Bar Castell today and I was going to swing by for a bite with Marga.'

Tolo scoffed. 'I think eel will be the last thing you'll want to savour after you see this.'

'See what exactly?' she asked in some frustration.

'The corpse of Sebi Vives, the minister for transport.'

THREE

Despite the miserable weather conditions, Isabel enjoyed her cross-country drive from the Soller valley to the north-east coast. Venturing out in Pequeñito, her bright, canary-coloured vintage Fiat 500, always cheered the heart, even on a rainy day, and so with the windows rolled down, Isabel sang Mallorcan *gloses* at the top of her voice all the way to the ancient burial site. From the industrial town of Inca she took the lean country lanes of Es Pla, the agricultural heartland of the island, to the rural towns of Llubí and Santa Margalida. These peaceful communities were surrounded by lush vegetation and a bounty of carob and almond trees, and vineyards and olive groves, that always filled her with delight. Llubí was famed for its caper production, while Santa Margalida had a grand old seventeenth-century church, and on the outskirts of the village, Pou d'Hero, an ancient well dating back to Roman times.

Isabel reached the main MA-12 artery that ran from Alcudia in the north to Artà in the east and took a left turn. Rain now fell in heavy droplets and soon began tapping insistently on her arms and face through the open window as she searched for the sign to the Son Real estate. When it came into view on the right-hand side of the wet and empty road, she headed for the historic manor house with its chapel and watchtower and extensive grounds. Some years previously, the estate had been acquired by the regional government and the main building and outhouses had been significantly refurbished. It now had a visitor centre, museum and pens for various well-fed farm animals. Had the weather not been so grim, Isabel might have enjoyed a tour around the traditional Mallorcan property, but she reminded herself that this was no ordinary day out. She was here to inspect a corpse. She rumbled along the sandy and stony track flanked by wild shrubs and Holm oaks, coming to a halt at the familiar white and green tape with the words *GUARDIA CIVIL NO PASAR* stretched across the road, supported on either side by orange reflective cones. Isabel nodded at two green-uniformed officers and pulled out the police badge which Tolo insisted she use when assisting his team with investigations.

A young officer examined it carefully. 'National Police? Your police chief, Tolo Cabot, is already here. Just follow this track up to Son Real.'

The other officer shivered in his heavy-duty jacket and gloves. 'Got something warm to wear? It's bleak over there.'

She smiled. 'Sure. I've even brought coffee and cake.'

The two men smirked and pulled one of the cones aside, waving her through. It had been some years since Isabel had visited the ancient talayotic burial ground of Son Real, and at the time she had reached it from the beach of Son Bauló, leaving her car near the *torrente* of the same name. She loved this stretch of coastline that was so wild and untamed in the winter with its soft undulating sand dunes and natural beaches framed by Aleppo pines and the low hills of the Llevant. In summer it was a different place, groaning with sunbathers and tourists strolling along in the sunshine, enjoying the bustling holiday atmosphere. Pequeñito juddered as the track became stonier and less accessible.

'You can do it!' whispered Isabel, as she peered at the scowling skies and tutted to see whirls of sand settle on the bonnet. As rain pelted down the windscreen wipers creaked and spluttered, vainly attempting to hold back the flood.

'Well, Pequeñito, this is nice weather for an outing by the sea,' she muttered. 'We'll need to give you a good clean tomorrow.'

Soon she spotted a cluster of Guardia Civil and National Police vehicles parked up on a sandy verge. A mobile *criminalística* laboratory van was already on the scene and police officers stood around with sombre expressions. For a moment she scanned the mature pine and juniper forests about her and the criss-crossing woodland trails. In the sunshine it would be a magical place for a picnic, but with a leaden sky above, it took on a sinister mantle. In the heavy rain a familiar figure trudged towards her, shrouded in a massive rain jacket. He opened the passenger door and jumped in.

'Thanks for coming, Bel,' said Tolo, his wet hand briefly gripping one of hers as he planted an icy kiss on her cheek.

'You know I can't resist a day at the seaside,' she replied.

'It's filthy out there. We managed to set up a tent at the crime scene but the conditions aren't ideal. Nacho's already on the case and is examining the body.'

Isabel shivered in the chilly air. 'It's definitely Sebi Vives?'

He pulled back his dripping hood to reveal a shock of damp, greying hair. 'He's not looking his best, but it's definitely our esteemed minister for transport.'

'Drowned?'

'It's a homicide, no accident at sea, but you need to see it for yourself.'

'It?'

'He was trussed up inside a body bag. In all my years of police work, I've never seen anything so weird. It looks ritualistic.'

Isabel frowned. 'Is Gómez here?'

'What do you think? The good *Capitán* is in his element and none too pleased that my boys are on the scene, but the president wants all hands on deck. This is going to have the media in a frenzy.'

Isabel stared out at the distant sand dunes, watching the long grasses dancing wildly in the harsh wind. A search and rescue helicopter buzzed overhead. Maybe a bit late for that.

'Where was the body found?'

'On rocks, just beyond the burial site. A fisherman spotted the bag at around ten o'clock this morning and notified the Salvamento Marítimo. That's one of their helicopters.'

'Is the fisherman here?'

'The Guardia Civil have already interviewed him. I've asked him to be here in the next hour to talk with us too.'

'Great.'

Tolo yawned and rubbed his eyes. 'Given the weather, it took the dive team some time to recover the body bag and floats.'

'Floats?'

He shrugged and blew on his hands. 'That was strange. A bright yellow body bag with orange floats attached as if screaming for attention.'

Isabel reached down by Tolo's feet and pulled a flask and foil-wrapped object from her straw pannier. She passed them to him.

'Coffee? You're a mind reader as well as being a first-class detective.'

'Mama's plum cake too,' she replied. 'So, was the body deliberately dumped here or it came from elsewhere?'

Tolo poured himself a cup of coffee and began munching on the cake. 'There's a criminologist named Borja Ruiz here from the Guardia Civil in Madrid. He was attending a conference in Palma so they dragged him in. The guy's convinced it's a ritualistic killing and that the body was deliberately placed at the site.'

'Based on what evidence?'

'You'll find out soon enough. He's not floating my boat, nor Gómez's in fairness.'

'Did you tell Gómez you'd asked me over here?'

He nodded. 'Don't worry about him. The National Police has got the same jurisdiction as the Guardia on this case, so he'll have to put up with us all.'

As the rain gave way to a bright and luminous sky, Isabel steeled herself for an encounter with Capitán Gómez. He was one of the leading local lights for the Guardia Civil, the green-uniformed military force in Spain, which traditionally presided over rural crime. All the same, there were often blurred lines when it came to homicide, and the national government's Ministry of the Interior encouraged cooperation and accord between its two forces. It had taken Capitán Gómez some time to accept that Isabel was now assisting Tolo Cabot with some of the island's tougher cases, thanks to her track record in crime-solving during her time in the force.

'It's stopped raining so shall we brave it?' she suddenly asked.

Tolo zipped up his jacket and pushed open the car door, wincing when the cold wind raced about his head. Isabel made her way to Pequeñito's boot and pulled on a thick jumper and rain jacket. Securing a large rucksack on her back, she trudged behind Tolo through the silt and wet sand towards the isolated, rocky outcrop of Son Real. It stood on a small, desolate headland in front of the sea and was formed of huge, eroded slabs of limestone fashioned into circular and square tombs. Lashed constantly by waves and unprotected from inclement weather, it was a miracle that the bleak site had stood the test of time. Isabel watched as white-suited figures slowly moved about, cautiously stepping over the wet rocks as they took photographs and placed samples into polyethene bags. As they neared the necropolis, she turned to Tolo.

'You know this is the largest prehistoric cemetery in the Baleares?'

He raised an eyebrow. 'I knew it was a significant historic site, but that's impressive.'

Isabel strode on. 'More than a hundred tombs containing three hundred bodies have been discovered here. The site dates back to the seventh century BC and is a fine example of talayotic culture. Archaeologists found all sorts of artefacts such as jewellery, ceramics and glass vessels in the tombs.'

'Funerary offerings?'

She nodded. 'During the talayotic period, the corpses would have been buried in the foetal position in small spaces. Stone slabs would then be placed on top in the style of a talayot or naveta.'

'A bit bleak.'

She nudged him. 'They'd have been dead, so I doubt they'd have minded too much. Most of the skeletons they've recovered show scant signs of hard work, so the assumption is that they were from the ruling classes. Much later, the Romans used it as a common burial ground.'

'Thanks for the history lesson,' he said with a grin.

'One more thing. See that little island to the right? That's S'Illot des Porros, where another talayotic site has been found.'

'The island of leeks. A good name. Can you visit it?'

Isabel shook her head. 'I think only archaeologists are permitted access. I've always wanted to row a boat over there.'

'Not today, please,' he replied.

As they reached the barren site, Tolo pointed to distant rocks and the white investigation tent that was being buffeted by the wind. They carried on to the crime scene, where various brightly coloured and numbered markers had been placed. It looked bizarrely festive.

'This is where the body bag was found,' Tolo said. 'The floats were pretty well secured between the rocks, but whether the bag was deliberately placed here or just washed up from the sea, is hard to say.'

Isabel squatted close to the water's edge and looked out onto the choppy waves. 'You'd either have to have dumped it by boat or driven up to the necropolis and carried it from there. Both options would be risky. When we know estimated time of death, it'll give us a better idea.'

Tolo rammed his hands into his pockets. 'True. A boat could get into trouble coming in this close to the rocks, and driving up to the burial site from the *finca* could attract unwelcome attention, especially as it's illegal to bring unauthorised vehicles here.'

'On the other hand, it was presumably in the early hours, so the area would have been devoid of life.'

She rose to her feet and they walked back towards the tent.

Tolo shivered. 'You've got your kit?'

'Of course.' She patted the rucksack. 'Have Vives's next of kin been informed?'

'Yes, a Guardia Civil officer has already interviewed his wife Sara, and Mateu, the son, is returning home from the University of Barcelona today.'

'We'll need to speak with them too.'

Tolo nodded glumly and led her over to the tent. At the entrance, Isabel spied a flash of pristine green uniform and gloved hands and braced herself. Capitán Gómez turned and offered a thin smile.

'Ah, the cavalry has arrived. What would we do without you, Bel?'

'I'm sure you'd cope splendidly, Alvaro. I'm only here for the sea air.'

He ushered them both inside. Isabel pulled on her white forensics jumpsuit and surgical gloves and took in her surroundings. The tent was bigger and airier than she'd expected and in the centre she saw her friend, Nacho, the head of forensics at the National Police, leaning over a bright yellow body bag. When she was ready, Isabel turned to them both.

'I'm assuming you've already seen enough?'

'Enough for today,' Tolo mumbled.

Capitán Gómez nodded curtly. 'When you're done I'd like you to meet Borja Ruiz, one of our criminologists from Madrid who by serendipity was at a conference in Mallorca.'

Isabel caught Tolo's eye. 'Ah yes, you mentioned him to me.'

'Ruiz is highly respected.' The Guardia chief rubbed his gloved fingers together in the chill. 'I think you'll find his hypothesis compelling. He's making some calls in his car, but I'll go and fetch him.'

He strode out of the tent with Tolo following slowly behind. Nacho smiled as Isabel approached. He was masked up and his long hair was captured under a surgical cap.

'We meet at the most thrilling of places,' he said. 'This case is going to fox you.'

She stepped towards the gurney on which the bright yellow cadaver bag rested, its zipper opened to reveal the ashen and battered body of Sebi Vives. Black and greenish bruises had formed around the wrists and ankles that were bound with tight plastic ties, while the head was matted with blood. The body was covered in scratch marks and lesions that had the appearance of bite marks. Isabel's gaze drifted to the dead creatures, insects, plants and mud that surrounded the corpse. She stared up at Nacho.

'What is all this?'

He shrugged. 'You tell me. We found them zipped up inside the bag. Like Sebi, the mice, rats and insects appear to have been alive before entering the water. Most wouldn't have survived for long, though, and the large eel and fish were probably already dead.'

Isabel started. 'Vives was placed in the bag alive?'

He eyed her steadily. 'It looks that way. Not a fun way to go, even for someone like Vives. The poor guy was only forty-four. I'll be able to tell you more when we've done a full post-mortem.'

Isabel frowned. She was no fan of the transport minister, but she would never have wished him such a fate. Her eyes fell on the thin muddy form of a viperine snake. They were harmless to humans but quite common in local ponds and rivers. Of the dead fish, she was able to identify a perch and mullet.

'No birds.'

Nacho cocked his head at her. 'Should there be?'

'Just thinking out loud.'

Nacho stifled a yawn. 'We'll need to get him back to the lab for analysis, but at this stage I'd estimate death occurred approximately eight to ten hours ago. He died of asphyxiation and hypothermia, not through inhalation of water.'

Jorge, a young male assistant from Nacho's department, appeared at her side. 'These heavy-duty Australian water-resistant cadaver bags are so cool. Dual external one-way vent valves and a waterproof zipper. They're double-sealed and have internal particulate filters to allow bodily gasses to pass easily out of the bag. Come in great colours too.'

Nacho and Isabel exchanged looks and began tittering.

'Want one for Christmas, Jorge? It can be arranged,' Nacho replied. 'We'll even give you a trial run out in the open sea.'

Jorge gulped. 'Sorry, it's just not often you get to see such a quality cadaver product. I worked in a hospital in Melbourne one summer and they used the same brand there. They're really resistant, much stronger than the usual European ones.'

'Actually, where might you buy one of these?' Isabel asked.

He pulled a face. 'Not sure, maybe a surgical store online. It's not a cheap brand and I doubt they're available to buy in Spain.'

As he scurried off to pack up some samples, Isabel turned to Nacho.

'An Australian cadaver bag? That gives us a head start.'

'Maybe.' He shrugged. 'One thing worth noting is the propensity of butterflies in here.'

'Any particular species?'

He used tweezers to pick up a wilted specimen. 'Well, I'm no expert, but these are mostly the kind you'd find all over the Baleares. For example, there are a lot of clouded yellows.'

Isabel sighed. '*Colias crocea*. I love this golden butterfly. It always seems so happy, flitting about the forests in the spring and summer.'

Nacho eyed her gloomily. 'Those left to a watery fate in here probably weren't too happy.'

Capitán Gómez suddenly appeared at her side. 'May I introduce you to our criminologist, Borja Ruiz?'

Isabel nodded politely and inspected the slightly built bespectacled man before her, noting that he had a rather uncompromising mouth and lacklustre eyes.

'Capitán Gómez tells me that you have a fascinating theory about our corpse?'

He hugged his chin with lean white fingers. 'It's quite clear cut. I believe that we're dealing with a very disturbed sociopath with occult ideologies. In the trade, we would call this a ritualistic crime.'

'Tell me more.'

He beckoned her over to the corpse. Nacho caught Isabel's eye and winked.

'You will observe that the body has been impacted by natural objects. Ritual homicides nearly always occur outdoors and the creatures here are symbolic, a form of sacrifice along with the human victim. The placing of the body by a neo-pagan site is indicative of sacred violence.'

'Do go on.' Isabel fumbled in her bag for a Chupa Chup, which she unwrapped noisily and shoved into her mouth.

'In Voodoo rituals or indeed in religious belief systems such as Santeria…'

'What's that, exactly?' asked Capitán Gómez, a tad irritably.

'It's an Afro-Cuban religion,' Isabel replied. 'Santeria means "way of the saints".'

Borja Ruiz folded his arms. 'That is correct. As I was saying, such religions believe that living creatures absorb the negative vibrations of a human. It's a form of ritualistic cleansing.'

'So, the body was deliberately left here as part of a ritualistic rite?' quizzed the Guardia captain.

'Indeed,' Borja Ruiz replied solemnly. 'The question is why this man was sacrificed and whether the killer will strike again.'

'You think we could have a serial killer on our hands?' Capitán Gómez barked in some alarm.

Isabel pulled the lollipop from her mouth. 'Of course, the body bag might just have been placed in the water elsewhere and drifted to the site and got caught on rocks.'

Borja tutted impatiently. 'Highly unlikely. In this kind of scenario, you must suspend belief and abandon Western paradigms and values. This is a disturbing case, in my view. A realm that could involve Satanism, invocations, incantations and magic.'

Isabel smiled. 'A very interesting hypothesis. I suppose we must wait for the post-mortem results to be sure of what we're dealing with. Excuse me, gentlemen.'

Capitán Gómez narrowed his eyes. 'Where are you going?'

'To meet the fisherman who discovered the body.'

'My team spoke with him earlier. I very much doubt you'll find his account adds much to the investigation,' he replied.

Isabel smiled enigmatically. 'One never knows.'

She found Tolo standing facing the agitated sea, puffing on a slim cigar, while the wind whistled about him.

'Even in the gale, you can still keep that cigar wedged in your mouth.'

'That applies to Chupa Chups too,' he retorted.

Isabel laughed. 'Has our fisherman turned up?'

'Pere Marques?' He nodded. 'He's waiting for us in his vehicle. So what's your take on Borja Ruiz?'

'He seems obsessed with rituals and magic.' She zipped up her jacket. 'I'd say he probably overdosed on Harry Potter as a child.'

He scrunched her arm and guffawed. 'You're cruel.'

'Not at all. Just honest.'

As they reached the car park, a burly, elderly man threw open the door of his ancient pick-up.

'You wanted to see me, Chief?'

Tolo shook his hand and led them to a sheltered zone in the nearby woodland.

'We won't keep you long. This is my colleague, Isabel Flores Montserrat.'

Isabel offered a reassuring smile. 'Pere, thanks for coming over. I've seen where you discovered the body. What was the wind direction at that hour?'

The elderly man pulled his woolly cap down over his ears. 'A strong westerly wind has been blowing since last night. I took the boat out from Alcudia Bay at around eight o'clock this morning and the breeze fairly carried me all the way.'

'It took you two hours to sail here?' she teased.

'*Que va!* I stopped to fish and have my *merienda* along the way.'

Isabel grinned. 'Food first, that's my motto too. So, in your opinion, could the body have drifted here from the north? Maybe from S'Albufera?'

He pulled on his bushy grey beard. 'Yes, although with those floats, this close to the coast, it could have snagged on rocks en route.'

'But with a fair wind and out in open sea, it could have reached here quite swiftly unencumbered, and then become ensnared on rocks on the headland.'

He gave a hearty cough. 'That's very possible.'

'Did you see any other boats in the area or anything out of the ordinary?'

He puffed out his lower lip. 'It's been wild so there were few boats out early this morning. I can't say I saw anything suspicious.' He scratched his head. 'Thinking about it, if the body bag came from S'Albufera, it would most likely have been placed in the

Gran Canal as the water's fast flowing at this time of year and it would just drift into open sea.'

Isabel fixed her gaze on him. 'True. You could slip it into the canal from the park end. There'd be no one about there at night.'

'Funny thing to do, though,' the old man muttered. 'Simpler just to push the blighter off a boat out at sea.'

'You've been very helpful,' she said with a flicker of a smile. 'Tolo, do you have any other questions?'

Tolo shook his head.

'Wait!' said Isabel. 'What did you have for your *merienda*?'

The fisherman laughed. '*Sobrassada*, bread and red wine, as you'd expect.'

'Perfect. Thank you, Pere. You're free to head off.'

They watched as the man jumped into his van, churning up mud and mulch as he headed back along the stony track to the main road.

'He's made me hungry. To think I missed the *menú del día* at Bar Castell today. Are you going to treat me to a bite?'

Tolo rolled his eyes. 'Come on, we'll find somewhere.' He paused. 'So you're thinking this murder has something to do with S'Albufera?'

Isabel cracked her teeth down on the last sweet remnants of her Chupa Chup. Tolo winced at the sound.

'Put it this way: from what I could see, many of the creatures in that body bag are native to S'Albufera, the proposed site for Sebi Vives's motorway. I'd hazard that it was most likely launched from there and carried here by the wind. The creatures may be symbolic, but our friend Borja Ruiz is wide of the mark. This isn't about ritualistic crime.'

'So environmentalists could be to blame? Tensions have been running high over this motorway and there are demos every day.'

Isabel shrugged and took out her car key. 'What's certain is that whoever did this wanted the corpse of Sebi Vives to be found. Otherwise why on earth would they have attached floats to the body bag?'

FOUR

After a late lunch of *calamares* and *tumbet* followed by *gató de almendras*, Isabel and Tolo drove off in different directions, agreeing to speak later in the day. They were so at ease in one another's company, both professionally and personally, that there was never any awkwardness between them. Isabel acknowledged that their peers must find them an eccentric pair, but what of it? For now they would take their fledgling romantic relationship step by step, and if for some reason it wasn't to be, Isabel felt sure that they would remain close friends as before.

As Isabel parked Pequeñito in front of Ca'n Moix, she saw her ebullient neighbour, Doctor Ramis, and her mother standing by his gate, which sat plumb next to her own. They were wearing jogging gear and chatting loudly. Isabel was pleased that a close friendship had recently blossomed between them. As a widow, Florentina had been lonely and had little zest for life. Now she attended village yoga classes run by Juliana, Isabel's recently installed Brazilian neighbour on the other side of her house, and had been persuaded by the good doctor to join a cinema club in Palma that showed vintage films.

Before Isabel had gathered up her pannier and jacket, Florentina began knocking on the car window.

'Bel! Where have you been?'

Isabel opened the car door and pecked her mother on both cheeks.

'Mama, do I have to tell you everything I'm doing?'

Florentina tutted. 'Pep told me you'd gone off to meet Tolo somewhere and I was just concerned about you driving in all that rain.'

'It was a cultural trip. We visited the Son Real necropolis together.'

Her mother frowned. 'Near Cala Rajada? That's miles away. Is Tolo getting you involved in another police investigation? A fine boyfriend he's turned out to be.'

Isabel laughed. 'Murder and mayhem unite us, I'm afraid, but he did at least buy me lunch.'

Doctor Ramis stepped forward and kissed her hand. 'Another grisly murder, Bel?'

'Now, that would be telling,' she replied. 'So what have you both been up to?'

He gave a theatrical sigh. 'It's been a whirlwind, dear girl. We had an early morning stroll by the river, followed by an energetic yoga class, then sampled the *menú del día* at Bar Castell. Jolly good it was too.'

'You would have loved the lemon pie,' said Florentina. 'Rafa's mother still makes one of the best. To think she's in her eighties.'

'Nineties, I'd say,' said Doctor Ramis, guffawing. 'She's quite deaf now but still as fit as a fiddle.'

'I hope you'll still be making me cakes and pies in your dotage,' Isabel baited.

Florentina gave her an affectionate nudge. 'We'll see about that. Dotage indeed! By the way, we're popping by Bar Castell for a drink later. Pep's going to join us.'

'Is he not in the office?'

'A water pipe burst at Can Rivera in Fornalutx, so he's meeting the plumber directly there. That rental property is always a problem.'

'Ah, but it dates back three hundred years. Think of the stories it could tell.'

Florentina gave a sniff. 'I'd rather not. Anyway, now we're off to a new painting class given by Alfonso. He's hired a room in the town hall.'

'You two never stop. I'll see you at Bar Castell.'

As they set off arm in arm, Isabel smiled and sauntered up her garden path.

In the silent *entrada*, she looked out at the damp patio beyond the French windows. The residents of Sant Martí always complained about rain during the winter months, but they knew very well that without it, there'd be trouble come the summer when hordes of visitors arrived for their holidays. The last few years the three hundred-odd residents of Sant Martí had needed additional water trucks to supplement their supplies from the local reservoir and valued every drop.

Upstairs in the office, Isabel found Furó still asleep in his basket, though when she dropped her car keys on the desk, he stirred and pattered over for a cuddle. She whipped him up into her arms and stroked his whiskery muzzle.

'Are you the most beautiful ferret in the world?'

Furó issued a few grunts.

'Come on, louder! I can't hear you.'

As he nuzzled into her, her mobile rang. Her heart sank when she heard the honeyed tones at the other end.

'Dearest Bel. How are you? I've been meaning to call, but between my mayoral duties and work at *El Periódico*, it's been impossible. I'm a man in constant demand.'

Isabel rolled her eyes. Josep Casanovas, editor of the leading newspaper on the island, had recently become mayor of Forn de Camp and his overinflated ego was now in real danger of drifting away in the current high winds. He strongly disliked Tolo Cabot and was still in denial about there being more to Isabel's relationship with him than just police work.

'Well, Josep, what a joy it is to hear your dulcet tones. And to what do I owe this unexpected pleasure?'

A pause. 'Purely a social call, but as it happens, I did want to verify an unconfirmed story with you.'

Isabel had to admire the sheer chutzpah of Casanovas. When it came to news, he had the nose of a truffle hunter. She said nothing.

'It's about a corpse discovered this morning off the coast of Cala Rajada. There have been unconfirmed reports that it is Sebi Vives. Would you know anything about it?'

In some irritation, Isabel bit hard on her lip. She wondered who the mole was within the National Police or Guardia Civil, slipping such confidential morsels into the ear of the obsequious editor.

'Remember, I run a rentals agency, Josep.'

He snickered. 'But you are also unofficially on the homicide team of the National Police and in cahoots with Cabot.'

'I'm sure if the story has any foundation, there'll be an official statement issued shortly. Now, sadly I must leave you as I have a meeting.'

'Imagine! Sebi Vives, the golden boy, murdered. If true, it's shocking, don't you think?'

'I don't like to speculate on gossip, Josep.'

'Well, when you want to talk, call me. You know it's all about team effort, Bel. We can help one another.'

She culled the call and stared into Furó's eyes. 'Why does he always have to be so irritating?'

Yawning heavily, Furó wriggled off her lap and returned to his basket and began playing with his favourite toy, a grubby white woollen rabbit. He'd bitten off its fluffy scut, but the long ears and embroidered eyes were still intact. Isabel checked through her emails, made a couple of calls and surveyed her watch. It was seven o'clock. Where did the time go? Slipping on her rainproof jacket, she walked back through the main office and marvelled at the neat appearance of Pep's desk. He had colour-coded folders for each property and a 'to do' list sitting centre stage, ready for the morning. Maybe she could pick up some tips from her fast-learning apprentice.

Although the rain had stopped, she found the cobbled pavement of Calle Pastor slick and slippery. Stepping onto the less hazardous narrow tarmacked street, she briefly admired her black Chelsea boots from Carmina, the exclusive shoemaker in Mallorca. Isabel was a self-confessed fan of British style, and her boots were no exception, though they were handcrafted on the island and made from soft, French Funchal full-grain leather. The history of the local family business harked back to 1866, and although Carmina had expanded successfully with flagship stores in the likes of Madrid, Paris and New York, the company continued to craft its footwear using authentic wooden lasts and refined Goodyear stitching in Inca, a town famed for shoe manufacturing. A British friend living in Sant Martí had told her that in the nineteenth century, Joseph Sparkes Hall, the shoemaker to Queen Victoria, had invented the iconic footwear and that its popularity had been revived in the 1960s when the stylish London Chelsea set wore the boot and inspired its name. When Carmina began crafting the low-heeled black boots for women, she was quick to purchase a pair of their 1896 Madisons and they hadn't disappointed. They were chic, semi-sporty and fitted like a glove, allowing her to run distances in comfort.

By the time she had reached the *plaça* it was dark and a light drizzle had begun to fall. Isabel pulled up her hood and walked towards the bright lights of Bar Castell. Upstairs, the balcony overlooking the square was bereft of customers, but small wooden tables huddled together, glistening with rain. Running up the stairs two at a time, she threw open the door to find Rafael at the bar drying glasses, an old apron tied around his waist. Loud conversation and raucous laughter spilled out from the rooms beyond.

He flicked the tea towel over his shoulder. 'Ah, look what the cat's dragged in. The usual?'

Isabel nodded and inhaled deeply. 'Rafa, is that *paella* cooking?'

'I hope so. I've got the Soller *petanca* club in tonight and so it's a *paella* for twenty.'

'Lucky them,' she said. 'I missed your mother's lemon pie at lunchtime.'

'That's because you're always off gallivanting. Luckily for you, I saved you a big slice to take home. If you're very nice, I might find a portion of *paella* too.'

'Rafa! But I'm always nice.'

She popped round to the other side of the bar and offered him a hug. He laughed and handed her a glass of *vino tinto*.

'You'll need this. Llorenç and the rest of them are all here. Pontificating as always.'

She slipped through to the warm interior and spotted her mother, Doctor Ramis and Llorenç in deep and animated conversation. Uncle Idò and Pep sat at the same table, evidently discussing some weighty matter. She assumed it would be about the plumbing issue at the rental property in Fornalutx. They all looked up as she weaved her way through the occupied tables, greeting locals on the way.

'Come and sit next to me,' yelled Uncle Idò. 'Pep and I are discussing the plumbing problem at Can Rivera. That house is…'

Llorenç waved a hand in the air. 'Actually, Bel, can you sit here as I need to discuss a confidential matter with you.'

Doctor Ramis chuckled as he raised his glass of wine in her direction. 'Always so popular, Bel. No peace for the wicked!'

Pep's eyes were trained on her as she squeezed onto the banquette next to the mayor.

'How was the necropolis?'

'Still there,' she replied.

'The story's already online,' he blurted. 'Your chum, Casanovas, has just uploaded a piece about a corpse discovered at sea that's presumed to be the transport minister.'

Isabel shook her head. 'Little snake. I knew he'd do that.'

'That bloke's got a real shine for you, Bel. He'd be heartbroken to hear you call him a snake,' goaded Idò.

Isabel issued a low growl and gave her uncle a warning look.

Her mother leant forward confidentially. 'Is it true? Is that poor young man dead?'

Isabel inhaled deeply as all eyes were fixed on her. 'I can't tell you more than you already know. Yes, it is believed to be the body of Sebi Vives. It's an ongoing investigation and until the post-mortem is completed, it's not worth speculating.'

'Did he drown or was he murdered?' chipped in Uncle Idò. 'I don't know anyone who liked the fellow.'

'Idò, that's a terrible thing to say!' exclaimed Florentina. 'I can't believe any brother of mine would say such a thing.'

Pep tried to mask a guffaw but was poked in the ribs by Idò, who gave a snort of laughter.

Isabel took a long sip of wine and licked her lips.

'I'm not saying another word about the case. It's unfair to ask me.'

Llorenç crunched on a nut. 'Indeed it is. Besides, we have far more pressing matters to discuss close at hand.'

'We do?' asked Isabel warily, as she pulled a bowl of plump black olives towards her.

Llorenç looked stern. 'This morning, the mayor of Soller called me to say that an American hiker had badly fractured a leg, close to Puig de Massanella. He was apparently an experienced climber and lost his way in the early morning mist and went plummeting.'

'Blithering idiot,' mumbled Uncle Idò. 'Who goes hiking in this weather?'

Llorenç crunched on an almond. 'The point is that he claims a wooden sign threw him off course and was the reason for his fall.'

Pep narrowed his eyes. 'Maybe he wants compensation. I've heard in America that they sue for millions these days. If you trip on a loose paving stone, bam, you've hit the jackpot and can sue the city council for thousands.'

Llorenç shifted in his seat. 'Well, we'll have none of that nonsense here.'

Isabel patted his arm. 'Don't worry, the paving stones in Sant Martí haven't budged in about three hundred years. Tell me about this sign.'

Llorenç took a swig of his beer. 'All I know is that our wooden trail signposts are not remotely misleading. The man said it was misty and he got disorientated. A female hiker was some way ahead of him and he called to her, but she didn't hear him. He said he saw a cairn and a wooden arrow, followed it and went right over a cliff edge.'

'How did he get help?' asked Idò.

'Luckily, a rock climber was on a lower path and found him. They had to get him out by helicopter.'

Isabel helped herself to some salty almonds from a bowl and chewed thoughtfully.

'Why did the American not follow the female hiker?'

Llorenç shrugged. 'Apparently, the mist was so thick he could only see her silhouette and long brown hair, but she was way ahead of him and he simply lost sight of her.'

'Poor man!' exclaimed Florentina. 'I hope he'll heal quickly.'

Doctor Ramis clicked his teeth. 'That all depends on the extent of the fracture. Sounds like the chap just got unlucky.'

'As long as he doesn't sue,' Pep teased.

Isabel turned to him. 'He can't sue unless there's hard evidence of a council signpost being dangerously placed and forcing walkers off course. That isn't the case. If a cairn was misplaced, that isn't the council's responsibility either. I know that climb well and have never seen any ambiguous wooden signs.' She paused. 'All the same, we should keep an eye on the situation.'

'What do you mean, Bel?' asked Llorenç.

'Just in case this should happen again.'

'How can it? The mayor of Soller even got the forest wardens and local Guardia to check the route and they found nothing untoward.'

She shrugged. 'I'm sure, but I'd like to see the full report from the incident.'

'I'll get it to you tomorrow,' Llorenç replied.

'And now let's have another drink,' said Pep.

Llorenç blew his nose. 'A good idea, and while we're at it, this is the perfect opportunity to finalise plans for the *fiesta* of Sant Antoni and Carnival next month.'

Isabel drained her glass. 'I've got to finish some work, so I'll leave you to it.'

'But Bel, we need your input,' he cried in dismay.

'Pep will bring me up to speed.'

Isabel wished them all a good night, but as she passed Pep, he grabbed her arm, whispering, 'You owe me' in her ear. She grinned and set off to the counter where her prize of a generous portion of *paella* and homemade lemon pie awaited her.

Isabel arrived home to find Furó pattering about the *entrada*. She whisked him up in her arms and danced with him about the room until he wrestled himself free and led her to the back door of the kitchen. She turned the key and allowed him to run freely into the darkness.

'Have fun, but don't kill anything tonight!' she called after him.

Isabel's pampered pet had a rich diet of fresh meat, eggs and his favourite kibble, but she had to accept that as a predator, his natural hunting instincts came into play on his nightly prowl. No rat or mouse was safe with Furó on the loose and even the geckos would give him a wide berth. Fortunately, he showed little interest in the hens as they strutted about the orchard during the day, but she made sure to lock them up safely at night.

After heating up half of the *paella*, she helped herself to a glass of red wine and tucked into the dish at the kitchen table, saving enough room for the slice of lemon pie. With a full stomach, she pottered into the garden and cast her gaze up at the white moon that floated like a smooth, round Eucharist wafer above the jagged ridge of the Tramuntanas. Isabel was instantly transported back to her childhood holidays in Sant Martí and the ritual of attending Sunday mass. At the time, her family lived on the mainland and yet she and her brother, Eduardo, were still forced to attend the weekly mass when visiting family in the village. At Holy Communion, Father Agustí, who even then seemed ancient, would pop the dove-white host on her tongue at the altar, muttering sombrely as he first raised it above her head. Her mother had told her never to bite or chew the host as it was the body and blood of Christ. A shrewd child, Isabel regarded this as a preposterous fib and took her mother and grandmother to task on the issue, only to be accused of sacrilegious behaviour and sent to bed with no supper. Nowadays, she popped by the church for key religious events in the calendar if only to see the look of relief in the old priest's eyes.

Shivering in the frosty air, Isabel returned inside only to hear the mobile ringing. She knew it would be Tolo.

'So how was your evening?' His voice sounded weary.

'Good,' she replied. 'And yours?'

'Don't ask. I've just got home to find a shrivelled lemon and a mouldy piece of Manchego in the fridge. I might pass on supper.'

'Drive over here. I've got *paella* and *vino tinto*.'

'If only, Bel. I'm up at six o'clock tomorrow. There's an early briefing with the regional president and representatives from the Ministry of the Interior who flew over today. The Guardia interviewed Sara Vives again this afternoon. She's still in shock but told officers that Sebi was going for a drink after finishing at the office on Monday night. She said he always went to Gran Casino Atlántico in Santa Ponsa.'

'So he disappeared on the way home?'

Tolo coughed. 'Sara Vives phoned him at the casino around eight o'clock, and he claimed to be leaving soon after. She said he often stayed out late so she went to bed early and discovered him missing the next morning.'

'So something untoward happened either at the casino or on the way home.'

'The couple has several cars, but Sara Vives confirmed that Sebi was driving a black Audi R8 V10 sports car on Monday, so we're checking CCTV now.'

'Who'd have thought government ministers earned so much,' Isabel scoffed. 'Maybe he'd won the lottery at some stage.'

'Just what I was thinking too. By the way, there's some good news that backs your theory about S'Albufera. A windsurfer called in tonight after reading the article posted online by that buffoon, Casanovas. He said he'd seen something orange bobbing on the waves close to Muro beach at around seven o'clock yesterday morning.'

'He didn't think to report it?'

Tolo yawned. 'He was some distance away and believed it to be a group of escaped buoys. It was only later that he questioned what he'd seen and wondered if it might be related to the body that had been discovered.'

'I take it that S'Albufera has been sealed off?' she asked.

'Do you think Gómez was born yesterday, comrade?'

'Of course he would have done that. I shouldn't underestimate him.'

He gave a snort. 'Don't overestimate him either. Listen, I need you at S'Albufera pronto in the morning. Gaspar and the forensics team will arrive before eight.'

'No problem. Try and get some rest.'

He gave a hoarse cough. 'Just to warn you, Borja Ruiz is pitching up at S'Albufera tomorrow too. According to Gómez, he's still adamant that this is a ritualistic murder.'

Isabel clicked her teeth. 'He can believe what he likes, as long as he doesn't get in our way.'

'Well, if he gives you any trouble, just push him in the canal.'

Isabel laughed. 'Don't tempt me.'

She finished the call and took her glass of wine and copy of *One Hundred Years of Solitude* upstairs to her office. She still had one hundred pages to go.

FIVE

By the time Isabel pulled into the wooded parking area by the entrance to S'Albufera Natural Park, an anaemic sun had appeared like a phantom in the pale pewter sky. Attaching a lead to Furó's collar, she patted the bonnet of her cherished Fiat and strode off towards the park's entrance. She was pleased that it wasn't raining and that only three National Police vehicles and a Guardia van were parked up in the same spot. Two of the cars would belong to Nacho and his forensics officers, and the other to Gaspar Fernandez, Tolo's deputy at the Palma precinct. The Guardia van would have earlier ferried its officers to the park. Hopefully, that meant that they had a head start on Borja Ruiz who, she assumed, would arrive in a rental car.

Isabel paused to greet the two uniformed Guardia officers at the entrance and continued the short distance to Pont dels Anglesos. She looked down at the fast-flowing water of the Gran Canal that coursed under the five elegant arches and out into the open sea. The bridge had been constructed by a British company in the mid-nineteenth century, hence its sobriquet, and two enterprising engineers had drained a vast section of the wetlands in order to create agricultural land. Hydraulic pumps powered by steam engines had been used to clear 2,000 hectares of land and 1,200 local workers had been drafted in for the task. Major water channels had been dug and various cultivated plots known as *marjares* had been created. Unfortunately, due to the constant presence of seawater, only about 400 hectares of the drained land could be made fertile. The British company went bankrupt in 1892, a rather sorrowful end to a story of great enterprise, though all was not lost. Thanks to the campaigning efforts of international conservationists and an enterprising local British environmentalist named Pat Bishop, the Balearic regional government had declared the reserve a natural park in 1988 and it had since become a sanctuary for birds and wildlife with its lagoons, marshes and wild terrain.

It was still only eight o'clock and the early morning traffic was light on the MA-12. Deep in thought, Isabel crossed over the narrow bridge with Furó at her side. She looked down at the swirling, murky waters that rushed to kiss the sea, imagining the terror that Sebi Vives must have felt inside his icy, rubberised prison. It seemed inconceivable that eco-zealots would go to such lengths to make a point, but from experience, she knew that unbridled rage and a sense of injustice had proven worthy triggers for countless murders. Her gaze fell on the towering, mature and bushy Aleppo pines that rose majestically on the west side of the bridge. This road led to Alcudia, with its popular sandy bay, whereas to the east was Muro, an authentic rural town famous for its pumpkin festival, an event faithfully attended by Isabel annually. Furó sniffed the wild grass that bordered the bridge and whimpered when Isabel pulled him away.

'I'll let you loose in a minute,' she said. 'Once we're away from the road.'

As she retraced her steps back to the park's entrance, she saw the handsome, honey-toned face of Gaspar. He enveloped her in his arms and gave her a kiss on both cheeks, much to the amusement of the Guardia officers on duty.

'Is this normal police procedure?' quipped one.

'Sure. We kiss everyone, including the suspects,' he replied.

They all laughed.

'So has anything interesting turned up so far?' Isabel asked.

The officers shrugged. One shivered inside his jacket and pulled up the zip.

'Our team did a preliminary search at first light and secured the site. They found a lot of conflicting footprints along the banks that they marked for your forensics team. There are so many visitors walking along these tracks that it's hard to know how useful they'll prove.'

She offered a sympathetic expression. 'Let's not forget the birds and wildlife either.'

As Isabel donned her white overalls and rubber boots, she gave Gaspar the once-over. He was still sporting a smooth bald head but now had a dark cropped beard. His black vintage leather jacket was zipped up to the neck and had a lambswool lining against the chill. He wore dark jeans and trainers.

'Looking very cool.' She winked. 'It must be your Guinean roots.'

'Someone has to act as a style reference in the office. The boss is just a crumpled version of his former self.'

Isabel giggled. 'So true, but he likes to think he's shabby chic.'

'Shabby, certainly.' He grinned.

Gaspar pulled on his own forensic gear and they set off along the gravel track that ran parallel to the Gran Canal. Isabel allowed Furó to run free. She scanned the wet, lush foliage about them. It was difficult to imagine that this peaceful sanctuary could be the setting for so dark a crime. Lost in her thoughts, she jolted when a fast-moving, piping flock of starlings formed peppery loops in the sky and the urgent quacking of raucous ducks sounded from the nearby canal.

Isabel stopped to face Gaspar.

'What's your take on all this?'

He eyed her seriously. 'I've seen a lot of grisly murders, but this takes some beating. I don't want to think about the guy's last moments. Who'd do such a thing?'

'Someone who hated him?'

'You think?' he replied dryly.

They walked in affable silence following the track and listening to the morning birdsong. It seemed so at odds with their grim mission and yet it cheered Isabel's soul. Thick reeds and shrubs covered the banks, including brittle juniper trees and pines. Isabel wondered what secrets the undergrowth might offer the forensics team. As a regular visitor to the nature reserve, she knew the terrain well. She was an amateur twitcher and a lover of the natural world so came to the park frequently to witness the changing seasons and to identify the migratory feathered visitors that flew into the serene refuge for sustenance and rest. In the summertime, she would look out for little bitterns, ringed plovers and yellow wagtails, and listen for the cry of the nightingale. Now the park was shrouded in its winter cloak and yet at least 10,000 birds flocked in for a brief respite on their journey. As they walked along, she spotted a great cormorant among the tall reeds of the canal and a pure white egret wading in shallow waters.

She looked up at Gaspar. 'Do you like birds?'

'The feathered variety? Sure, but don't ask me to name any. Remember, I'm an urban boy. I can just about recognise a gull.'

Isabel laughed. 'There are more than three hundred different species in this park, so it's not easy. I spend time here in the hides with an ornithology tome checking the birds against the pictures. I get a lot wrong.'

'Shame you weren't in one of the hides on Monday night. Sebi Vives might have made it.'

She gave a sigh. 'Where's Nacho?'

'He and the forensics team got here a while ago and have been collecting soil samples along the lower banks of the Gran Canal. If there are identifiable shoeprints, they can run them by the National Footwear database, but with all the recent rain, I don't hold out much hope.'

Furó disappeared into the undergrowth, appearing every few minutes in an excitable state.

'Your ferret's a real character.'

She nodded. 'He has the makings of a good detective too. He has an amazing sense of smell and finds things that could otherwise be overlooked.'

'Maybe we should get him a badge,' he said.

Isabel thought about the weight of the body bag. If it had been carried into the park, it would have needed two or possibly three strong people to navigate it along the gravelled track. At night and in the rain, the bearers would have been in little danger of meeting anyone on their deadly sortie. Although the park was out of bounds after five o'clock at this time of the year, it wouldn't have been difficult to climb over the simple, low wooden barrier. On the other hand, the body bag could have been launched from the bridge or just beyond at the entrance to the sea known as S'Oberta. She shook her head. That would carry too much risk as anyone could be driving or walking past, even in the early hours of the morning.

Gaspar cocked his head. 'Penny for them?'

'The body was most likely ferried along here for some distance and then presumably carried down one of the paths on the right bank to the lower canal path and launched into the water, but where?'

Gaspar rubbed his hands together. 'They'd have wanted to be out of sight of the main road. We need to walk a little further.'

They trudged on for a few more minutes until Gaspar broke the silence.

'I guess they'd have left the vehicle in the car park.'

'Or would they? Maybe there was a getaway driver.'

Soon they both stopped and looked back towards the entrance, which was obscured from view. They'd walked about half a kilometre. Isabel pulled out a pair of latex gloves, anticipating that they might find potential evidence as they headed right towards the first muddy path that led down to the canal. A little way ahead was a pretty wood-decked path leading to a lookout terrace over the water. Isabel set off there with Furó hot on her heels and looked up and down the canal. She returned to Gaspar. As they began their descent and explored the scrubby terrain, Isabel heard Nacho's voice close by. They edged their way carefully further down the bank, as their light rubber footwear had little grip. Nacho was squatting by the canal, his hair pulled back into a tight ponytail. Forensic officers in white garb were taking samples in the dense and shrubby area close by.

He smiled up at them. 'Morning. Anyone got coffee?'

'I wish.' Isabel grinned. 'How's it going?'

He nodded towards a collection of lidded specimen containers.

'We've got a good selection of soil and water samples, so hopefully we'll soon be able to confirm whether or not this is the spot where our victim was launched on his watery voyage.'

'One of the Guardia said there were shoeprints,' said Gaspar.

Nacho shrugged. 'Not on the gravelled track, obviously, but down here. Our photographers were busy earlier. They think we're on to something. Come and take a look at this.'

He rose and stretched his back before leading them to a zone close to the edge of the canal where discernible prints still remained despite the recent rain.

'There are three different sets of prints here. They appear to be from the same brand of footwear judging by the markings, in sizes forty-three, forty-four and forty-six. I'd guess they were wearing rubber boots with heavy soles, but we'll confirm all that back in the lab.'

'Be even better if we can match them with a brand,' said Isabel.

He nodded. 'We'll check back with the international database. What's curious is that there are clearly two sets of male prints in size forty-three and forty-four going down the bank, but on the way back up, only forty-four and forty-six prints are visible.'

'That's a big shoe size for a man. He'd probably be more than six feet tall,' she replied.

Gaspar turned to Nacho. 'You're saying that if this proves to be the place where the body bag was launched, a third male, and a tall one at that, was already down here?'

Isabel frowned and fumbled for a Chupa Chup in her pocket. 'That can't be right. If true, we'd still see his footprints both ways, unless he came from another direction along the bank.'

Nacho shook his head. 'The Guardia checked the entire bank along the canal before we arrived. These sets of prints don't match any others and these are the only ones close to the water at this point. Judging by their state of degradation, I'd estimate they all relate to Monday night.'

'So where did the guy with the forty-three prints go?' asked Gaspar.

Isabel smirked. 'Maybe he was thrown into the canal along with the body bag by the people with the forty-four and forty-six prints and will wash up shortly.'

Gaspar scratched his head. 'How about the third party with the forty-six footprints was in a wetsuit and swam up the canal to join the other accomplices who were carrying the body bag? When all three of them had disposed of it in the canal, the guy with forty-three prints, also wearing a wetsuit, took over and got in the water to guide the body bag along until it reached S'Oberta and the open sea.'

Isabel sucked on her lollipop. 'You'd have to be one heck of a strong swimmer or have a death wish to attempt that on a filthy night in January, and let's not even mention the dangerous currents and obstacles en route in the dark. Even with a headtorch it would be impossible to navigate safely.'

'She's done enough canyoning to know,' drawled Nacho.

'Besides, Gaspar,' she said, 'why swim up the freezing canal in the first place when you could just walk along the gravelled path with your chums? Be a lot more pleasant.'

'It's a mystery.' Gaspar shrugged. 'Maybe a motorised boat?'

'He'd have the same problem with rocks and currents on this stretch,' said Isabel.

Nacho eyed Gaspar steadily. 'It's all a mystery, *amigo*, but that's the thrill of our work, isn't it?'

Isabel frowned. 'Where's Furó gone?'

She put her thumb and forefinger in her mouth and let out a shrill whistle. Seconds later, Furó emerged from the tall reeds.

'How do you do that?' Nacho laughed.

'Just buy a ferret. You learn quickly enough.' She winked.

Leaving Nacho and his forensics team to their task, Isabel and Gaspar headed back up the bank and strolled along the track as far as the visitor centre, which sat in a tranquil spot among pine and juniper trees. A middle-aged man in gardening overalls approached them in a defensive manner until Isabel flashed her police badge at him.

He eyed them mournfully. 'More police. It's been quite a circus since first light.'

Isabel pulled back a rogue strand of dark hair. 'I can imagine. You work here?'

'Yes, for more than twenty years. To think such a crime could take place here. It's awful.'

'Is anyone on duty here at night?' Isabel asked.

'We're a small team and knock off around six o'clock in the winter. It's dark so there'd be nothing to do anyway.'

'Are you here every day?' asked Gaspar.

He nodded. 'Before you ask, no I haven't seen anything out of the ordinary these past weeks apart from demonstrators hanging about the place with placards. I told the Guardia officers the same.'

Isabel smiled. 'You must recognise some of the regular twitchers and demonstrators?'

He shrugged. 'There's a fair few of them. If you showed me some mugshots, I'd probably be able to identify most.'

'Good to know,' she replied. 'What do you think about the proposed motorway?'

He folded his arms. 'It's an abomination. It will slice off a third of this park, so it's game over for a lot of the wildlife here.'

'Did Sebi Vives pay many visits here?'

'He came with the local press and grinned at the cameras, claiming that the birdlife wouldn't be affected. Typical politician. He just rolled out statistics that made no sense.'

Gaspar rubbed his chilled hands together. 'Tempers must have been very frayed of late. Have any of the environmental groups become violent or threatening?'

The man shifted uneasily on his toes and ran a fretful hand through his hair. 'Look, I've got to know some of the guys who demonstrate here. They just care about the park and want to preserve island wildlife. GOB is obviously vocal on that front, but they're quite an academic lot.' He paused. 'The ones that have got a bit physical and clashed with the constructors coming here have been from TAA.'

'Terra: Acció Ara, you mean?' asked Isabel.

He nodded. 'That Pablo Pons, the leader, is a huge guy. Wouldn't want to get on his bad side. He stands at the entrance most days with his supporters. The Guardia officers have banned all of them from coming inside the park now after he took a swipe at Sebi Vives.'

'When was that?' asked Gaspar.

'A few weeks ago. Sebi Vives came here for a tour of the area allocated for the motorway and that hothead Pons punched him as he entered the park. Vives told the Guardia to let the matter drop.' He suddenly frowned. 'Is that a police ferret? I've heard they're used for drug busts now. How do they get on with the police dogs?'

Isabel smiled. 'Like blood brothers. They share food bowls and watch cat movies together.'

'Who'd have thought it,' he muttered as he lumbered off with a sweeping brush in tow.

'You're incorrigible,' said Gaspar.

As they headed back to the car, Isabel's mobile rang. It was Tolo.

'How's it going?'

Isabel smiled. 'It's a perfect day for a stroll with one of the force's most stylish detectives.'

'Maybe he should take up modelling instead?' he growled.

Gaspar laughed. 'I heard that. It would certainly pay better and I wouldn't have to put up with you all day.'

Tolo sniggered and then sighed heavily. 'So, a quick update. The Guardia is still trying to track down Vives's black Audi R8 V10. Still no sign. We've identified two key agitant environmental groups and of course there's GOB, so we need to set up interviews. There's also a local university professor worth visiting. He's a butterfly specialist at CMIB, Conservación de las mariposas de las Islas Baleares. Never heard if it? Neither had I.'

'Presumably Pablo Pons of TAA is one of the leading hecklers?' asked Isabel.

'Spot on. There's another smaller outfit called Feel the Earth. I think you'd be best interviewing Pons and also Professor Vilalba from CMIB. They both sound like complete oddballs. Right up your street.'

'I'll choose to take that as a compliment,' Isabel replied.

'Gaspar and I will deal with GOB and Feel the Earth. What kind of name is that?'

Isabel smirked. 'Meanwhile, what is the Guardia doing locally?'

'The usual, carrying out patrols around Alcudia coast, setting up roadblocks and interviewing locals in the area. The team at the precinct is trawling through Sebi Vives's hate mail and general correspondence. You should read some of this stuff. It's incendiary.'

'Yes, he doesn't appear to have been Mr Popular. As we're done here, I might as well head over to see Pablo Pons. If I have time, should I touch base with Sara Vives later this afternoon?'

Tolo clicked his teeth. 'That would be helpful, but let me check back with the Guardia first. If we get the go ahead, I'll ask one of my team to set up the meeting.'

'Perfect, let's check in later.'

'Wait, Bel, can you put Gaspar on the line?'

Isabel passed the mobile to Gaspar.

'Hey boss, have we got to hang around for Borja Ruiz? He hasn't shown up yet.'

As they chattered, Isabel took some images of her surroundings and quietly contemplated the long stretch of gravelled track. Normally it would be alive with day-trippers. She imagined there'd be many disappointed bird watchers and families unable to access the park due to the incident. Who knew when it would be re-opened to visitors. The forensics team would need to make several more forays.

Gaspar handed Isabel back the mobile and smiled.

'Tolo says we don't need to wait for Ruiz. That's a relief. When the guy came into the precinct he looked like a ghoul and gave me the creeps.'

Heading back along the track at a fast pace, he suddenly let out a silent curse as they approached the entrance.

He whispered. 'Look who's turned up.'

In seconds, the pinched and pallid face of Borja Ruiz appeared. Isabel offered a well primed look of surprise mingled with disappointment.

'What a shame, Borja! We're just leaving, but do take your time to familiarise yourself with the potential crime scene.'

Gaspar nodded curtly and shook the man's hand. 'You'll find Nacho and the team on the right bank as you head along the main track. Take the first accessible path.'

Borja Ruiz looked about him, his pale eyes inside heavy spectacle frames reflecting the blanched sky.

'I am not convinced that this was the departure point for the body bag. The Guardia is conducting a complete search of local waters and crafts to determine whether a boat was seen in the vicinity late on Monday night or in the early hours of Tuesday morning. I maintain that the body was deliberately secured close to the Son Real site.'

Isabel offered an encouraging smile. 'In that case, we look forward to your final report.'

As they reached the car park, Gaspar offered her an exasperated look.

'How did you keep your patience with him? Let's hope he hops back to Madrid soon.'

'Anyone can expound a theory about a murder but without offering a clear motive, it's pretty worthless. Still, at least he's an enthusiast.'

They turned as Furó appeared from the park's entrance and came bounding towards them. He had something wedged between his teeth.

'What have you got there?' she asked, crouching down to pull it from his mouth.

He wriggled and gave a low growl as she held it up to Gaspar in her gloved hand.

'An old chewing gum wrapper with used gum. Not such a prize, my chum,' he said, tousling the ferret's fur.

There was a sudden clap of thunder and rain began pouring from the sky. Isabel waved to Gaspar as he quick-footed it to his car and drove away. Once in Pequeñito, Furó shot into the passenger seat where he snuggled into his favourite pink woollen blanket and licked his wet paws. Isabel took a clear plastic bag out of her pannier and sealed the gum and wrapper inside it. She used the sleeve of her jumper to wipe the rain from her face.

'Well, partner, who knows whether your little find will bear any fruit but better safe than sorry.'

Furó eyed her brightly and issued a contented grunt. As the rain tumbled, Isabel turned onto the empty road, not surprised to find it devoid of life. She drove slowly across the Englishman's Bridge, distracted momentarily by the vision of a tall, black-hooded figure peering into the canal. A sudden, involuntary shiver ran down her spine. When she looked again, the bridge was empty.

SIX

A golden sun hung low in the sky as Isabel coursed through the narrow country roads to Muro in the north-east of the island. After leaving S'Albufera, she had popped into Can Picafort for a *cortado*, a glass of freshly squeezed orange juice and *pa amb oli*, while Furó dozed in the car. She had been mindful to leave a bowl of water and the window partially open to ensure that he had a ready source of fresh air. In her early life as a rookie police officer on the beat in Madrid, she had often come across dogs left inside stifling vehicles during the summer months. Their thoughtless owners would go off for hours, leaving them with neither water nor proper ventilation. Often she and her colleagues would force entry in order to save the badly dehydrated pets. As an animal lover, it still incensed her to think about it.

Despite the nip in the wind, Isabel lowered her windows and smiled. The rain had subsided. It seemed inconceivable that only an hour previously a scowling sky had unleashed lashings of rain. This was the beauty of the island, with its various micro-climates. There could be a storm brewing in the south while in the north, the sun might be shining brightly.

It wasn't often that Isabel had the chance to visit the pretty, understated village of Muro with its imposing 400-year-old church, vast *plaça* and labyrinth of narrow streets. Many of the sandstone buildings harked back to a bygone age and the place had a relaxed and sleepy feel. All that changed in the autumn with the Fira de Tardor, a colourful *fiesta* whose highlight was the annual pumpkin competition. These mighty homegrown squashes were duly paraded outside the church and locals would inspect each closely, trying to guess which of the hard-skinned beauties might win the annual crown. Isabel relished this festival, especially as the streets were filled with food stands and the cafés full of fun and laughter.

The town had another jewel in its crown and this was Gori de Muro, the makers of *galletas marineras,* the wheat, salt and olive oil biscuits favoured by old sea dogs in days of yore. The company was established in 1890 and offered its small oval biscuits in various flavours. Isabel always kept a supply of the rosemary and spicy varieties at home for moments when she felt peckish at her desk and would smear them with fresh green olive paste. In Isabel's book, frequent nibbles kept hunger at bay and aided concentration. It was the same with her Chupa Chups and sunflower seeds and no one would convince her otherwise.

Beyond the village, she discovered Gymnasió Pons, housed in an old stone house on a quiet rural lane. She parked in the verdant courtyard next to a vintage white van with a battered bonnet and took in the peaceful surroundings, water feature and antique well. Bending over the sleeping Furó, she stroked his warm pelt.

'Fancy a workout, Furó?'

The ferret offered a sleepy eye and covered his face with a paw.

Isabel shrugged. 'Suit yourself, but that furry belly could do with some toning. I won't be too long.'

She grabbed her pannier and jacket and strode up to the arched doorway. A youth eyed her sleepily as she stepped into the *entrada* but with a sudden burst of energy jumped up from his chair, seemingly aware that she was no local.

She offered a reassuring smile. 'I'm here to see Pablo Pons.'

'Are you with the police? He said a cop would be visiting here this morning.'

Isabel was pleased that someone in Tolo's office had rung ahead. She nodded. 'Is Señor Pons here?'

The young man scuttled off into a back office, closing the door firmly behind him. Isabel looked about her. A wooden sign to her right indicated changing rooms and the gym itself, while on the other side of the room, a door appeared to lead to a sauna and steam room. As she contemplated peeping along one of the corridors, the door banged open and a tall, meaty man sprung out of the office with the youth following in his wake.

'Isabel Flores?' he barked.

'Correct.'

He frowned. 'I'm Pons. Your office said you had some questions?'

'A nice gym. How long have you owned it?'

He folded his arms and frowned. 'Three years. The house was in a bad state, but I've renovated it gradually and put in a small spa. I had to get change of use too.'

'You've done a great job. Can I look around?'

A tad defensively, he shrugged and whisked her off on a tour of the premises. When they stepped into the large gym space, she smiled to see a peaceful rural scene beyond.

'What a view! That was a smart move, putting in a glass wall.'

He nodded. 'It wasn't easy to get a planning permit, but it's been a big selling point. That's the trouble with most hotel gyms.

They're nearly always in dingy basements. It's wasted space, so the architects tend to stick spas down there.'

'You're so right. I've often noticed that. They can be quite soulless places.'

He gave a gruff laugh. 'I doubt you came here to talk about gym design.'

'I just want to ask a few questions about Sebi Vives. Shall we go somewhere more private?'

Pablo Pons offered her a chair and sat down heavily on a piece of gym equipment. 'This is as good a place as any. We only take private appointments here and no one's booked for the next hour.'

Isabel smiled and took a seat. 'So, aside from running this gym, you are the founder of the environmental group, Terra: Acció Ara?'

'I created TAA five years ago with a group of like-minded others. There are four founders and we all share the decision-making and of course we have a lot of volunteers and supporters. We don't get any funding so rely on donations.'

Isabel pulled out her notebook and pen. 'Can you give me the details of your three close associates and any other key members of TAA?'

'I'll print all that info off for you.'

He grabbed his mobile and tersely issued instructions to someone.

'What do your co-founders do?' Isabel asked.

'They all work. Manolo is a builder, Antonio is an agronomist and Fernando is a mechanic.'

She winked. 'A macho team.'

He grinned. 'We have female members just none call the shots.'

Isabel felt the need to crunch hard on a sunflower seed and wrestled a few from the bag in her pocket. She toyed with the idea of lobbing a few at him.

'I believe you've been very vocal about the proposed new motorway?'

He emitted a cynical grunt. 'Someone has to be. That scheme by Vives would destroy the most cherished reserve in the Baleares.' He stopped. 'If it's true that it was his body that washed up at Son Real yesterday morning, then I'm not surprised.'

'Word gets around fast.'

'It's no secret. It was reported online in *El Periódico* yesterday. People here have been talking about nothing else.'

'If it's true, how do you feel about it?'

'Honest answer? I'm not going to shed any tears.'

'And where were you on Monday night?'

He pushed a hand through his thatch of thick, black, wavy hair. 'That's easy. The four of us had a TAA meeting here from eight o'clock until eleven. The others left and I locked up and went to bed.'

'Would anyone else be able to confirm that?'

'My two cats.'

'Have you ever threatened Sebi Vives?'

Pablo Pons rubbed his eyes. 'A few weeks ago, I was demonstrating with our group outside S'Albufera and punched him when he made a joke about using dynamite to blow up wildlife on the marshes. I lost my temper.'

'Do you lose your temper often?'

He gave her a surly look. 'Only when I don't find a bad joke funny.'

'Have you ever been to the construction site for the motorway at Búger?'

'Of course. We have demonstrators hanging out there every day. Anything to slow down the work.'

'Who else is campaigning?'

He shrugged. 'GOB supporters are there and small environmental groups such as Feel the Earth, which is run by two women, a Brit and a Swede. There are concerned locals too.'

Springing up from his seat, he paced the floor of the gym. 'Do you realise that this new motorway will carve a path between Muro and Sa Pobla, upsetting the biodiversity over a huge area of rural terrain?'

Isabel split open a sunflower seed and crunched on it thoughtfully. 'There are a lot of things damaging the local biodiversity, but I always find it pays to keep a cool head.'

As they returned to the *entrada*, the young man handed her a file. 'Here are the contact details for the TAA members and key volunteers.'

'Perfect,' she replied. 'And can you get me the shoe sizes of Fernando, Manolo and Antonio, please?'

Pablo scowled. 'I suppose you want mine too? It's forty-six. Are we eco-warriors proved guilty by our feet size now?'

'Only if they smell bad,' Isabel quipped.

In the courtyard, Pablo Pons walked Isabel to her car.

'Is that yours?' he asked, pointing to the sleeping ferret curled up on the passenger seat.

'I hope so because I rarely welcome random ferrets into my vehicle.'

Despite his mood, he offered a fleeting smile.

Isabel looked up at him. 'Can you think of anyone who might want Sebi Vives dead?'

With his hands thrust in the pockets of his sweatpants, he threw her a mocking glance. 'Are you serious?'

'Well?'

He shook his head. 'Listen, *señorita*, I can't think of anyone I know who didn't want Sebi Vives dead.'

Isabel sauntered through the sunny *plaça* with Furó scuttling along behind her. Pau, the village's police officer and Enric, one of the local mountain guides, were in deep discussion under the awning of Bon Día, surrounded by crates of fresh oranges, onions, potatoes and peppers.

'*Uep!*' Pau yelled when he saw her, beckoning her over. Enric bent to stroke Furó, who rubbed against his legs.

'We've been talking about these cliff falls,' said Pau. 'There's been another one near Llucalcari this morning.'

'A tourist?' she asked.

Enric nodded. 'An elderly English walker who lost his footing on loose rocks and fell about three meters. He was alone but luckily a couple found him and raised the alarm. He's badly bruised and shaken but nothing was broken.'

Isabel sighed. 'It happens every year. Hikers underestimate the power of the mountains and the dangers.'

Pau raised an eyebrow. 'True, but this guy maintains the cairns were misplaced and disorientated him.'

'I doubt it,' replied Enric. 'I hike that route with groups often enough and the cairns are always in the same place. He's probably just embarrassed that he made a spectacle of himself.'

'All the same,' Isabel replied, 'that's the second time we've heard this. Did he mention a woman with long brown hair on the track?'

'Not to my knowledge.' Pau puffed out his cheeks. 'Maybe some kids are being mischievous and moving cairns as a joke.'

Enric frowned. 'Not so funny if someone gets killed and they end up in the dock. I wish tourists would hire us guides. Sure, it's to our advantage, but we have GPS and know the hills like the back of our hands.'

'Some people might not have money to hire a guide,' replied Isabel. 'Besides, I quite like hiking on my own.'

'You don't like my company?' he joked, placing an arm around her shoulder.

'Not when we go canyoning together and you take me to flooded caves.'

'Come on, that was only once and you loved the adrenalin rush!'

Pau laughed. 'You two are nuts. I'd never go canyoning. Too much risk involved for me.'

Isabel made to leave. 'It's nearly one o'clock. I've got to catch up with Pep and then leave for Llucmajor.'

'How's the Vives' investigation going?' he asked.

'It's still early days, but it won't be straightforward.'

'It never is,' he replied.

The old church clock boomed a single chime.

'One o'clock,' yelled Enric. 'How do you do that?'

'She's a witch.' Pau winked. 'Never needs a watch.'

Isabel playfully punched his arm and set off with Furó back to the office, where she found Pep hunched over his desk, evidently on a long call with a client. She settled Furó in his basket and after catching up on some emails, flicked through a document left on her desk by Pep. It was the report about the first hiking incident that Llorenç had promised to give her. She thoughtfully cracked open a few sunflower seeds and rang Gaspar.

'Good timing, Bel. We've just confirmed your meeting with Sara Vives. Is six o'clock okay?'

'Perfect. It gives me some time in the office. Any news?'

'Tolo has just briefed local press following his meeting with the regional president this morning. Casanovas was like the cat who'd got the cream, having broken the story online yesterday.'

Isabel could imagine how infuriated Tolo would have been to see Josep Casanovas in preening mode. There was little love lost between the two.

'Poor Tolo,' she murmured.

Gaspar chuckled. 'He's got broad shoulders. Meanwhile, we're still waiting on the post-mortem results. Nacho and his team will brief us late morning tomorrow so I trust you'll be here.'

'You bet.'

'How did the meeting with Pons go?'

'He was defensive, but that's not surprising. Unfortunately for him, his shoe size is apparently forty-six. I've also asked him for the shoe sizes of his three co-founders.'

'For his associates' sake, I hope theirs don't match the other prints. Mind you, it would be an easy wrap-up: Pablo and two of his associates dump Sebi in the canal and one acts as the getaway driver. Case closed.'

Isabel laughed. 'If only life were so simple.'

When she'd finished the call, she popped back into the central office where Pep was sitting listlessly at his desk, flicking rubber bands at the nearby wall.

'Am I paying you to do that?' she asked.

He rolled his eyes. 'You've no idea what kind of morning I've had.'

'Try me.'

'We've got two houses with leaking gutters and the plumber can't fix them until tomorrow. Meanwhile, the Swiss couple in Biniaraix have lost the key to the house and left the spare inside so Idò has gone over to sort it out.'

'That all sounds straightforward.'

'That's not all,' he replied ominously. 'Angélica wants us to go on a diet.'

Isabel reeled back in horror. 'Now that is serious. Just say no.'

'I wish it was that easy. Even her father and mother are joining in. She got Llorenç to visit her nutritionist in Palma, who suggested we work as a family to get healthy.'

'You are healthy. I shall have to have a word with Llorenç.'

He yawned heavily. 'Good luck. All I know is that we're only going to be eating salads for the next few weeks.'

Isabel winked. 'Well, there's an easy solution. You can eat Mama's dishes here during the day and just play the game in the evening when you get home.'

He brightened up. 'That's a thought, but Angélica and her parents must never find out.'

'Your secret's safe with me. Now, how about making me a *cortado* with a big piece of Mama's plum cake on the side?'

The sky had darkened by the time Isabel drew up outside the gates of Sebi Vives's home on the outskirts of Llucmajor. It was a traditional stone *finca* with a broad drive of chunky white gravel, surrounded by orchard land. She guessed that there would be a significant garden at the rear and the customary pool and outhouses. This was a substantial property, afforded complete privacy by dint of it being on a private track and surrounded by a high wall. How the other half lived! Pressing the intercom, she announced herself. The tall iron gates slowly peeled back like the unfurling wings of a butterfly. Isabel parked up and walked over to the porch where a willowy blonde awaited her. The woman wore a white neck brace and had sad, restless brown eyes. Isabel noticed that they were bloodshot.

'Isabel Flores? I'm Sara Vives. Come inside.'

She found herself in a brightly lit kitchen-cum-diner with double sets of French windows that looked out over a perfectly manicured rear lawn and pool. It had grown dark, and tiny lights twinkled among shrubs and trees and pretty garden lamps lit up the pathways.

'It looks like a fairyland out there,' remarked Isabel.

The woman offered a wan smile. 'Yes, it's beautiful. We have a first-rate gardener. Sebi insists on a neat garden and a sparkling pool.' Her voice tailed off and she blinked hard. 'Can I get you a drink? We're having wine.'

'A *cortado* would be great, thanks.'

Isabel turned at the sound of footsteps behind her. An elegantly attired woman with the frame of a model approached. She was holding a near-empty glass with long, pale fingers. Isabel recognised her immediately as she often featured in the social pages of *Ultima Hora* magazine.

'Please, let me introduce myself. I'm Mariana Blasi. My brother, Teo Puig, is the president, and my husband, Felip, is the tourism minister.'

'Yes, of course. And what do you do?'

She laughed. 'I'm just a boring old cardiologist, I'm afraid.'

'Where are you based?'

'Clinica del Rei in Palma.'

Isabel nodded. 'Impressive. My father was treated for a deteriorating heart condition there. The service was impeccable.'

The woman looked concerned. 'Is he doing okay?'

'No, sadly he died a few years ago. More from a broken heart than his medical condition. So do local politicians and their partners usually socialise out of work?'

Mariana helped herself to white wine on the kitchen counter. 'Adelante Mallorca is like a family. We look after one another.'

Isabel wasn't a great fan of AM, the incumbent ultra-conservative party running the regional government, but she accepted that no political party was ever perfect.

Sara handed Isabel her coffee and led them both into a large drawing room with cream sofas and contemporary, stylish furniture. The polished oak floor had a herringbone pattern and was offset by chunky, cream lambswool rugs.

'I like your flooring. It has an English clubby feel.'

Sara shrugged. 'My husband loves the English style.' She paused, her voice breaking. 'Loved.'

Mariana sat close to her friend, protectively patting her arm and supplying her with tissues as both sipped on their wine.

'Sara, what happened to your neck?' asked Isabel as she settled in an armchair.

'It was a shunt. Last Friday, I was coming up to a junction on a nearby country road and from nowhere a large white van smashed into the rear of the car. Thankfully, the road ahead was empty, otherwise it could have ended badly. By the time I'd clocked what had happened, the van driver had sped off.'

'Did you see who was driving?'

She shook her head and dabbed at her eyes. 'No. It was all a blur.'

'Has anything like this happened before?'

'Never, but I sometimes get abuse in the street from activists about the motorway. Just because I'm Sebi's wife. I guess I'm fair game.'

Mariana set her glass down on the coffee table before her.

'We didn't bother to report the shunt to the Guardia because what could they do? It was obviously one of these wretched environmentalists.'

Isabel sat poised over her notebook. 'It's always wise to do so. Vehicles can be traced. Has any particular activist threatened you or your husband?'

Sara shared a glance with Mariana.

'That aggressive man, Pablo Pons from TAA. He has constantly threatened my husband and even struck him at S'Albufera a few weeks ago. It was horrible. Sebi was so calm about it, but I was in pieces.'

'Can I see your car? There may be traces of paint from the other vehicle.'

Sara shook her head. 'It's all fixed. I took it into our local mechanic on Friday afternoon and it was good as new by Monday.'

'You're lucky. Our village mechanic, Bernat, takes his time, though he is good at his job.' She took a sip of coffee. 'Have you any idea where your husband was heading the night of his disappearance?'

Sara sighed. 'He called me from the office to say he'd be popping by the Gran Casino Atlántico on the way home. He often stops by there for a drink after work.'

Mariana gave a brittle laugh. 'It's a regular hang-out for local politicians, particularly our party elite. The owners have a private bar and salon away from the other punters reserved for them and other VIPs.'

'So what time did you expect him home?' asked Isabel.

Sara took a deep breath. 'To be honest, Sebi could be back at any time. I called him just before eight and he told me he was having one more for the road. So I went to bed around ten o'clock and was surprised that he still wasn't home by early morning. Sometimes he'd stay at a colleague's place if he drank too much, but I rang round all of his colleagues and no one had seen him.'

Mariana interrupted. 'As we're close friends, Sara called me and I rang the casino. The owners, David, Rocci and Toni Mestre, all remembered that he'd left the premises just after eight o'clock. They have video footage of the car exiting the forecourt, which they've shared with the Guardia.'

Isabel fiddled with her pen. 'It's possible CCTV in the area might have picked up images of where his car was heading.'

Mariana looked glum. 'We can only hope, but of course in the rural areas there's little in the way of cameras.'

The front door opened and a young man with jet black curls and large dark eyes walked into the room. His face was flushed and he looked startled to see Isabel. He unzipped his jacket and offered Sara a hug.

She turned to Isabel. 'This is my son, Mateu. He's just returned from the University of Barcelona.'

Isabel stood up and introduced herself, shaking his hand.

'I'm so sorry for your loss.' She hesitated. 'I think I have all I need for now, so I'll leave you all in peace.'

He nodded, offering her a tense smile, and bounded up the stairs.

At the front door, Isabel took Sara's hands in hers. 'Take good care of yourself. I hope your son is okay. Does he need counselling?'

Sara rubbed her eyes. 'He's just in shock like me. If he needs help, our doctor can organise it.'

As Isabel opened her car door, she turned to her. 'Just one last thing. Did Sebi have any enemies aside from those who opposed the motorway?'

Sara was silent for a moment. 'Surely all politicians have enemies? Sebi was no different from the rest.'

Later that night, as Isabel sat in bed reading her novel with Furó sleeping at her side, Tolo called.

'It's nearly midnight. Can't you leave a girl to get some beauty sleep?' she scoffed.

'Sorry, *cariño*, I've been meaning to call you all day. I've finally got rid of the guys from Madrid. Tomorrow the media will be full of the murder, but better it's made public now.'

'I think so. We may get some helpful leads from the coverage. Did you know that Sara's car was shunted by a white van on Friday? She's in a neck brace.'

'Really?' He exhaled deeply. 'Let's discuss it tomorrow when you come into the precinct. Meanwhile, I wanted to let you know that the Guardia has just located Sebi's Audi not far from his home in Llucmajor. It seems like he was heading home from the casino and either got ambushed or followed. Who knows.'

Isabel sat up and listened intently. 'Where was it found?'

'In woodland, off a narrow country lane. The car was locked so the Guardia had to force entry. You won't believe what they found.'

'Don't keep me in suspense.'

'A kilo of cocaine and a pistol were taped under the back passenger seats.'

Isabel let out an expletive. 'What on earth was going on in Sebi Vives' life?'

Tolo breathed heavily. 'I've no idea, but we've got our work cut out. Maybe he was being threatened or was part of a drug deal gone sour.'

She tapped her chin thoughtfully and a sudden bright spark came into her eye.

'Bel? Are you still there?'

Isabel started.

'Sorry, Tolo, I just had a sudden thought. Anyway, onto more important matters. Shall we do dinner tomorrow night?'

He laughed. 'It's going to be a fraught day, so that will give both of us something to look forward to.'

'One last thing,' she said. 'Were there any fingerprints on the cocaine stash and gun?'

'The whole car was wiped clean.' He gave a grunt. 'Of course, if Sebi's death is connected to the drug world, it might at least narrow the field.'

'Or quite the opposite. I think this is just the beginning.'

'Of what?'

'Something menacing and strange.'

Tolo said his goodbyes and Isabel lay down and placed her hands behind her head. In deep thought, she stared up at the old wooden beams that ran along her ceiling. She felt a weird fluttering sensation in her stomach and turned to Furó.

'Butterflies. That's what I'm feeling, my furry friend. And butterflies, I feel, may hold the key.'

SEVEN

A big commotion was going on in the kitchen downstairs. Pots and pans clanged and windows and doors banged open and shut. In some frustration, Isabel stomped through the main office, noting that Pep was absent from his desk, and yelled down the stairs.

'Mama! What on earth is going on? I can't hear myself think.'

Her mother's cheery voice pounded her ears. 'Come down, Bel. We need you!'

Isabel felt a pang of hunger and wondered whether Florentina might have brought round a delicious morsel or two. It might at least justify all the activity at such an early hour. Doctor Ramis greeted her at the bottom of the stairs.

'Bel, there you are. We've just had breakfast, but we've left you *ensaïmadas* and fresh orange juice. Pep is preparing you a nice *cortado*.'

Isabel shook her head. 'Do make yourselves at home.'

'Oh, we are!' he bawled jovially without the slightest irony.

As Isabel followed him into the kitchen, he clapped his hands together excitedly.

'By the way, Florentina and I are off to Palma this afternoon to see a cinematic masterpiece called *Dial M for Murder*.'

Florentina looked up from the sink, giggling. 'Oh Miguel, you must tell Bel what you re-christened it.'

'Ah yes, Bel, in light of how Tolo Cabot and the National Police are always seeking your help, I suggested it be called instead, "Dial Bel for Murder!"'

Pep turned from the coffee machine and winked at Isabel.

'I like that. It's got a certain ring to it.'

Isabel jokingly banged her fist on her forehead. She grabbed a fluffy *ensaïmada* pastry from a plate and began chewing on it.

'Bel, do sit down like a civilised creature,' said Florentina. 'Here, take this fresh juice. By the way, in the fridge I've left you stuffed aubergines, *frito mallorqui* and artichoke soup. In the larder there's a fresh lemon meringue pie, *xeixa* loaf and *gató de almendras*.'

Isabel's heart pumped with pleasure and gratitude. 'Mama, you shouldn't have.'

Florentina flipped a tea towel over her arm. 'Nonsense! Now that Tolo is involving you in another terrible murder, you need to eat. And poor Pep is starving. Heaven knows what has got into Angélica with this new-fangled diet.'

Doctor Ramis folded his arms. 'I would always recommend a good, balanced Mediterranean regime, and I will have strong words with Angélica and Llorenç. He above all should be setting the right example for his daughter. In the meantime, I suggest that Pep eats his fill here.'

'Indeed, Miguel,' replied Florentina. 'Diets are a nonsense.'

Pep grinned. 'So our secret is safe? I gorge myself here and eat salads with Angélica and her family by night?'

'*Claro*,' replied Florentina.

'And maybe fit in a little work in between feasting,' said Isabel.

Doctor Ramis sat down heavily in a chair at the table. 'Dear boy, would you kindly bring me a coffee?'

Pep nodded and soon placed a steaming cup in front of him. Doctor Ramis took a long sip and turned to Isabel.

'Now, Bel, the plot of this film we're going to see is very intriguing. It was released in 1954 and starred Grace Kelly and Ray Milland.'

Isabel licked her sugary fingers and nodded enthusiastically. 'It's a classic Hitchcock.'

'You know it?' he said, a tad deflated.

'*Dial M for Murder*? Of course! I'm a fan of Grace Kelly. Isn't the husband a famed tennis player whose wife is having an affair so he has her murdered?'

'Oh, don't spoil it!' yelped Florentina.

Isabel frowned suddenly. 'Life can be complicated.'

'What do you mean?' asked her mother.

'Things aren't always as they seem, I guess,' she replied.

Doctor Ramis pressed a napkin to his lips. 'By the way, did you hear about the hiker?'

'Is this one of your jokes?' said Pep.

'Far from it, my boy. A German hiker has fallen from Sierra de Son Torrella and been helicoptered to hospital. Early this morning, after shopping at Bon Día, I ran into Llorenç in the *plaça*. The man is apparently still unconscious.'

'When did this happen?' asked Isabel.

'Yesterday afternoon, I think. Luckily the chap was found by a mountain guide,' he replied. 'It's odd because his wife told Llorenç that he was an experienced climber.'

Isabel drummed her fingers on the table. 'This is becoming too common. A pattern seems to be developing.'

'You think so?' asked Doctor Ramis.

'Too many people are having falls in the Tramuntanas. This is now the third incident.'

'Come on, Bel,' Pep replied. 'It happens every year.'

Isabel was quiet for a moment. 'I read the report Llorenç left me about the first incident and there's something odd about it. I'd like to question this man when he's conscious. We could have a serious problem on our hands.'

Doctor Ramis looked up and sighed. 'Well, that won't be music to Llorenç's ears, especially on an empty stomach.'

Isabel gulped down the rest of her juice and stood up. 'Sadly, I need to leave you all. I have meetings at the precinct. I'll take Furó along.'

'Anything you need me to do?' Pep asked with bright eyes.

Isabel paused in the doorway. 'Actually, there is. Can you compile a list of mountain guides, landowners and environmental groups in the area?'

'Whatever for?' asked Florentina.

'We need to find out what's going on in the hills and talking with these people will be a good start.'

Pep beamed. 'I like playing private investigator. I'll get cracking right away.'

'Good,' said Isabel with a grin. 'Anything to keep you from dancing.'

Isabel sat on a plastic stool in the stark laboratory listening to Nacho in rapt attention. Tolo and Gaspar leant against one of the stainless-steel surfaces that ran along one side of the room, with arms folded and brows furrowed.

Nacho held up a handful of dried vegetation in a gloved hand. 'So from the fragments of samphire, reed and succulents that we found in the body bag, we're confident that the victim was launched from the Gran Canal in S'Albufera. The water and soil samples are an exact match. You see the water is a mixture of fresh and saline water and the soil has unique mineral traces.'

'So there's no chance that the body was deliberately secured at the Son Real necropolis?' asked Gaspar.

'Don't forget that a windsurfer believes he saw the body bag near Alcudia Bay around seven o'clock on Tuesday morning, so nowhere near Son Real at that time,' said Tolo.

'That aside,' replied Nacho, 'I double checked our findings with Cofib, the consortium that protects fauna and flora in the Baleares. They identified the invasive *Cotula coronopifolia*, which they've all but obliterated in the park, along with *Cladium mariscus*, a swamp grass, and sago pondweed. Both are aquatic herbaceous plants that are very common in S'Albufera and respond well to saline conditions.' He paused. 'Of course, another theory might be that the body bag was filled with fauna and flora from S'Albufera and then driven or brought by boat to Son Real, but that would make no sense. It would take far too long and would carry the risk of detection. On the exterior of the body bag there were traces of native aquatic plants from the canal that had become entwined with the cords of the floats.'

Gaspar grinned. 'That'll take the smile off the face of Borja Ruiz.'

'Just as well he's returned to Madrid. He can go and crawl back under his rock,' said Tolo.

'What about all the creatures in the bag?' asked Isabel.

'We identified quite a variety of S'Albufera residents. Many insects, beetles, moths and butterflies, of which the clouded yellow was most prevalent. There were maybe one hundred in there.'

Isabel shifted on her stool, a frown embedded on her forehead.

'How would they have caught so many clouded yellows? They must have bred and incubated them from egg or larvae stage.'

'I agree,' Nacho replied. 'Maybe they were bought online. They feed well on clover so it's easy to breed them in the right conditions.'

'If the moths and butterflies were still alive when entering the bag, would they have been able to flit around?' she asked.

He nodded. 'For a short while, yes. They'd have had enough space just about. It would have been an unpleasant experience for Sebi Vives, I imagine.'

He placed the dried plants back in a specimen tray and turned to them all.

'Aside from insects and rodents, there was a large eel, three *Natrix maura* – viperine snakes – and a few mullets. Mercifully the eel, fish and snakes were already dead before being placed in the bag and can be identified with the park fauna.'

'Whoever did this was putting out quite a clear environmental message,' replied Gaspar sombrely.

'No birds?' Isabel asked. 'You'd think with so many species in the park, they'd have included a few in the body bag.'

'Thankfully, no. Nor were there any horses or bulls,' Nacho replied dryly.

Despite the charged atmosphere, they all laughed.

Nacho continued, 'The victim was alive and placed in the water between approximately two and four o'clock in the morning. He was bound so wouldn't have been able to move much, but he would have been drowsy anyway as there were traces of propofol in his system. I found a puncture wound on the right arm, which indicates that he was subdued before being enclosed in the bag. Judging by the bruises and wounds around the wrists and ankles, he was shackled for some time before being transported to the canal.'

'Interesting that the killers used propofol,' mused Isabel. 'They knew what they were doing. It can knock a victim out pretty quickly.'

'Very true,' Nacho replied. 'I get the feeling that this was a well-organised, almost military operation by a group of cool customers. A quick and well-planned abduction.'

'So what finally killed the poor guy?' asked Gaspar.

'Although water from both the canal and sea managed to seep through the bag, he actually died from hypothermia and shock. Mercifully, he would have at least drifted off into unconsciousness quite quickly in the severe chill. I did notice a bad knock on the back of the head, which might have disorientated him further. It was probably as the bag was swept along in the Gran Canal and collided with protruding rocks and branches before it washed out to sea.'

'What a way to go,' said Tolo quietly.

Nacho cupped his face in his hands. 'It's safe to say that whoever did this really wanted Sebi Vives to suffer. I wonder what he did to deserve such a cruel fate.'

As Isabel stood looking out of the grubby office window at the busy street below, the door banged open and Corc, Tolo's erratic and clumsy assistant, walked in. He was balancing a tray of coffees and sugary doughnuts, which he dumped unceremoniously in front of Tolo. He shot a nervous glance over at Furó, who was busy snuffling under a chair.

'Can I get you anything else, boss?'

Tolo thanked him and waited for the door to close.

'Do help yourselves. I'm still feeling squeamish.'

Isabel grabbed a doughnut and a coffee. 'Poor Vives. I keep wondering about the eel and the yellow butterflies. Surely they have significance?'

Gaspar took a bite of his doughnut and shrugged. 'Everything might have significance.'

'But there were a lot of this particular butterfly and the eel seems to be making some kind of statement,' she insisted.

Tolo sat at his desk and ran a hand through his wild locks. 'The S'Albufera connection does point the finger at local belligerent environmentalists, but then how does that square with the cocaine and gun found in the victim's car?'

'Perhaps it's just a coincidence. Maybe they're totally unrelated,' suggested Gaspar.

Isabel tapped her chin. 'Why did the killers want Sebi to be found? They deliberately placed him in a bright yellow body bag with floats that would be located quickly. They are obviously quietly confident that they've got away with this. They almost seem to be mocking us.'

Tolo took a long sip of coffee and warmed his hands on the sides of the cup.

'So how was your meeting with the wife?'

'She was distracted and jumpy and evidently still in a state of shock,' Isabel replied. 'As I mentioned to you, she was wearing a neck brace from a recent car shunt. I had hoped we could run her vehicle by forensics, but she'd already got it repaired.'

'Who might have been responsible?' quizzed Gaspar.

'It sounds like they were attracting enemies like flies,' Tolo replied.

Isabel wafted her doughnut in the air. 'Her son, Mateu, arrived home while I was there but darted upstairs. I'll need to talk with him at some stage when he's had time to absorb news of his father's death.'

'Poor family,' said Gaspar. 'Does the wife have any support?'

Isabel nodded. 'Her friend, Mariana Blasi, was there. She's a cardiologist and the tourism minister's wife. The AM party seems very close-knit. She mentioned that a lot of the local politicians drink after hours at the Gran Casino Atlántico in Santa Ponsa.'

'If Vives had a regular routine after leaving the office, the killers could have been monitoring his movements closely and then pounced,' Tolo replied. 'I think we need to check out the owners of the casino too and also look at those in Vives' close circle of friends.'

'So what about Pablo Pons at Terra: Acció Ara? Surely he is a likely suspect?' Gaspar said.

Isabel sighed. 'He's got no real alibi for the night Vives went missing and neither have his three close associates. His foot size is a perfect match for some of those found at the crime scene, but what does that prove? Two of the co-founders have size forty-four feet and the other has size forty-three, as do countless others. Pons's assistant has sent me through a list of TAA members which I'll be checking through too.'

'Where were the founding four on the night of the murder?' asked Tolo.

She gave an impatient tut. 'Apparently altogether at Pablo's home with no alibi, but why leave themselves open for investigation? Mind you, people can surprise you.'

Isabel heaved on her jacket. 'I have an appointment to see Tomeu Vilalba, professor of biology and entomology, at the Balearic University.'

'Is he the butterfly man?' asked Gaspar.

She smiled. 'Yes, he's the president of CMIB, Conservación de las Mariposas de las Islas Baleares.'

Tolo groaned. 'Rather you than me. Some of those academics can be so dreary.'

'I'm looking forward to it,' she replied with a wink. 'I love butterflies. They embrace freedom and pack so much into such a short life.'

Tolo accompanied her to the lift. 'You and Furó are still coming over tonight?'

'Of course. We're both expecting a *degustación* menu.'

'Sure, you know I'm a dab hand in the kitchen, especially with takeaways.' He gave her a hug. 'What time can I expect you?'

'Well, after the university, I'm going to pop along to that strip of forestland in Llucmajor where the Guardia found Sebi Vives's car. Gaspar gave me the directions.'

'Do you need to do that today, Bel?'

She offered an enigmatic smile. 'Don't worry. I won't be late.'

Isabel found herself in a large office, crammed with glass cabinets full of hefty tomes and moth and butterfly specimens. It had been a lengthy walk from the university car park to the biology department. She had left Furó sleeping in the car and hoped he wouldn't wake in her absence, wondering where she had gone. Professor Vilalba sat behind his desk, appearing somewhat bemused by her evident interest in the artefacts about her.

'After so many years, it's incredible what you amass,' he said with a sigh. 'I believe you know Toni Bauzá, one of my colleagues here in palaeontology?'

Isabel nodded enthusiastically. 'I do indeed. He helped me with a difficult case recently that involved a myotragus specimen.'

'So he told me. As you know he's a leading expert on that singular prehistoric goat. You know he's been trying to retire for years, but none of us will let him.'

They both laughed. Isabel looked out at the hills beyond.

'You have a lovely view.'

'It's one of the advantages of being old. You get a nice office with vistas to the foothills of the Tramuntanas.'

Isabel tutted. 'I think it's more to do with your expertise and your colleagues' respect for you than age. So do you class yourself lepidopterist or entomologist?'

'A bit of both. I embrace the insect world, but butterflies are my passion. I love them all – cardinals, swallowtails, red admirals, clouded yellows and my favourite, queen of Spain fritillary, or rather, *Issoria lathonia*.'

'I'm not familiar with it.'

His eyes blazed with excitement behind gold bifocals as he leapt to his feet.

'Here it is in this cabinet. It's beautiful. Golden orange with pearlised spots on the underside of its hind wings. What do you think?'

'Gorgeous. Such delicate markings. It has a violet hue too.'

'A remarkable creature.' He smiled. 'But then butterflies have had many years to perfect themselves. Of course, you'll know that they evolved from moths and that *Lepidoptera* date back to the Triassic-Jurassic period.'

'I didn't know that. And what about butterflies?'

He looked up at the ceiling as if for inspiration. 'Butterflies were around fifty million years ago. An extraordinary thought, isn't it?' He gave a cough. 'Now, how can I help you? Can you give me details of the case you're working on?'

'I'm afraid not, but there is one aspect I can discuss with you.' Isabel took out her notebook. 'We found a number of dead clouded yellow butterflies at the crime scene. I'm curious to know why.'

'Ah, yes! *Colias croceus*, from the *Pieridae* family. It's a very special little creature that hails from North Africa and Southern Europe and is a summer migrant in Europe. It is quite distinctive, with a broad, black margin on all four wings and a black spot near the centre of the forewing. The females have yellow spots along the black borders. Quite different. Odd that you should find so many at this time of year.'

'If you wanted to get hold of a large number of living clouded yellows, where would you buy them?'

Professor Vilalba frowned. 'I'm really not sure, but I do know that a recent fad has been to buy living butterflies to release at weddings. It's a deplorable activity and I've even heard that people can buy pupae online to be bred and released as butterflies at celebratory events.'

Isabel nodded. 'I imagine that could cause problems if certain species were invasive and brought into another territory.'

'Unfortunately, any exotic, invasive species can have a bearing on the population dynamics of the native variety. Take the butterfly moth, *Paysandisia archon*. It hails from Uruguay and Argentina and has made its way to Spain, which isn't good at all as its larvae are palm borers. Plant invasion is always the problem with the introduction of new species to certain regions.' He cleared his throat. 'But you wanted to know about clouded yellows.'

Isabel smiled. 'I suppose what interests me most is to know if they have any significance.'

The professor ruminated on this for a few moments. 'Not that species as such, but the ancient Greek word for butterfly is *psyche*, and of course Psyche was the goddess of the soul. The colour of clouded yellows is important, though. In the old world, yellow butterflies were associated with death, whereas in Greek culture, seeing multiple yellow butterflies represented the soul of those who had died young. It was a sign of renewal and rebirth. In native America, yellow denoted hope, and it's widely associated with happiness and joy.'

'I'm re-reading *One Hundred Years of Solitude* by Gabriel García Márquez, and yellow butterflies are a powerful symbol,' Isabel said.

He clapped his hands together. 'Ah, one of my all-time favourite books. You will know that the author adored yellow and thousands of yellow paper butterflies were released at his funeral at the Palacio de Bellas Artes in Mexico City.'

Isabel nodded. 'It must have been such a visual feast and what a tribute. Of course, one of his key characters in the book, Mauricio Babilonia, is always surrounded by golden butterflies.'

'Indeed he is,' he replied with a grin.

He rose from his chair and began sifting through a stack of large, black portfolios that rested against a bookcase. Finally, he selected one and dusted it down. He laid it flat on his desk and peeled back the leather covers. A stack of unframed watercolours lay within.

'Here are some glorious old illustrations of endemic and foreign butterflies. There are many beautiful clouded yellows in here too. One of my gifted students drew them years ago and offered me a set of originals. I have always treasured them. Look at the detail.'

Isabel flicked gently through the illustrations. 'They're all beautiful. What a talent.'

He nodded. 'Indeed, and such wonderful subjects to paint. I really should get round to framing them.'

Isabel's eyes rested on an iridescent, multi-coloured butterfly. She had never seen such a dazzling and unworldly creature in her life. 'What is this?'

He gave a strange little chuckle. 'You'll never guess. The ancient Moors apparently named it the mighty mountain meh. There are those who believe it was endemic here during the Islamic period but disappeared soon after the Christian conquest by James I of Aragon in 1229.'

Isabel eyed him curiously. 'How do they know? Was it recorded in ancient documents? Why did it vanish?'

'All good questions,' he replied with a wink. 'Maybe it was a pacifist and simply flew away to a more blessed land once the Moors were defeated.'

'Can I take an image of the mighty mountain meh and the clouded yellow?'

For a moment he hesitated, but then he waved a hand at her. 'Go ahead.'

Isabel took a few images on her mobile and stood up. 'Thank you for your time, Professor. It's proved very helpful.'

'Has it really?' he said in some surprise, running a frail hand through his snow-white locks.

As Isabel walked into the corridor, he popped his head round the door and looked at her over his bifocals. 'I nearly forgot. Yellow was also associated with Judas and his betrayal of Jesus Christ, so it has a negative connotation, signifying duplicity and cowardice.'

Isabel stood still for a second, absorbing his words. She thanked him and headed for her car.

EIGHT

By the time Isabel arrived in the quiet rural lane in Llucmajor close to where Sebi's abandoned Audi had been found, it was already growing dark. Furó stood on his back legs and looked out of the window and began chuntering. Isabel turned off the engine and rubbed her eyes.

'Listen, my little friend, if I let you out for a wander, no funny business, okay? We've got dinner with Tolo tonight. If you want some steak, don't make me late.'

Furó yawned and closed his eyes for a moment as Isabel stroked his sleek fur and kissed his head. She leant across and opened the passenger door and laughed as he dived off into the scrubland bordering the road. Placing a powerful torch in her rucksack, she pulled on a pair of latex gloves and set off across the road to the adjacent forestland. She had followed the Guardia's map to the letter, and after a short walk along an overgrown track arrived at a perfectly secluded spot surrounded by unruly scrubland, bracken and wild shrubs. There were traces of Guardia police tape hanging forlornly off trees; it no longer served a purpose now that the abandoned vehicle had been removed and the area searched.

It was obvious that this stretch of land was rarely visited and had become a natural playground for wildlife. Gaspar had said that the landowner had died some years previously and that relatives were still contesting his will, leaving the land in a state of neglect. With help from the sharp rays of her torch, she carefully examined a scramble of tyre prints left in the caked mud. One very faint set most likely belonged to Sebi's Audi, while the others seemed to be quite fresh. Evidently, they were left by the Guardia vehicles.

For a few moments she stood stock-still. Trees creaked eerily in the breeze and a barn owl called in the distance as dusk gathered. Something scampered in the long grasses nearby, maybe a rodent or weasel, but she resisted the urge to investigate. It wasn't the familiar tread of her beloved ferret. Where was he, anyway? This place was so remote, despite it lying so close to the road. Whoever had abducted Sebi must have been an industrious scout, finding the perfect hideaway for his car before the Guardia eventually located it.

So what had happened? Isabel sat on a tree stump, her mind working on overdrive. The Guardia had confirmed that according to his wife, Sebi never took this route home. Why on Monday did he choose to drive to this remote zone? Had there been an assignation that had gone wrong? After all, the Guardia had found cocaine and a gun under the back seat of the car. Isabel frowned. Something didn't add up. There were neither prints on the package nor the gun. As she ruminated, a twig snapped close by. Isabel jumped to her feet and shone the torch in the direction of the sound. The hairs on her arms rose and a prickly sensation coursed through her limbs. She wasn't alone. Bending down slowly, she grabbed a small rock, ready to lob it if danger should present itself, but her ears were assaulted by another sound as Furó, whimpering and snuffling, came skidding towards her.

With her torch trained on the impenetrable tangle of overgrown shrubs beyond, Isabel turned quickly to Furó.

'Let's go!'

Furó sniffed the air and suddenly puffed up his tail and hissed. Her instincts were right. Someone was there, unseen, watching her. Quickly, she turned tail, and with a hissing Furó hot on her heels, she jogged along the uneven forest track back to the car and opened the driver's door.

'Come on!' she called, but Furó had other ideas. He ran ahead of the car and began circling a patch of road just beyond, sniffing frantically. Isabel shone the torch wildly about her and kept an eye on the dark track as she set off to join him.

'What's so special about this?' she whispered.

She got down on her haunches on the lane and inspected the asphalt surface. There was nothing unusual, but then she noticed something glinting in the torchlight. A small silver ball of paper lay on the grass verge. It was a piece of foil, most likely discarded chewing gum. Carefully, she picked it up and placed it in a plastic sample bag in her pannier. Much to Isabel's chagrin, Furó circled the patch again and dashed across the lane to the start of the track, sniffing enthusiastically at the caked mud. He romped back to the roadside spot again and lay panting at her feet.

'You're making me dizzy. What are you trying to tell me?' she asked. 'We should go. I don't feel comfortable here.'

Safely inside Pequeñito, Isabel felt relief as the engine sprang into life and the headlights lit up the dark countryside surrounding her. She hadn't seen a vehicle on the road the whole time she'd been there. As she headed rapidly in the direction of Palma, she suddenly thumped the wheel.

'I get it, Furó. You think Sebi was lured to that stretch of road and parked up on the spot you indicated. He must have got out of the Audi and been incapacitated and was taken away in another vehicle. One of the abductors must have then driven his vehicle into woodland, locked the doors, and either taken or thrown away the key. He surely had to have known his abductor or abductors? Had they used propofol to subdue him?'

Furó curled up on the seat beside her, his head hidden by his blanket, and closed his eyes. His fervour for the investigation had seemingly waned.

Isabel tutted. 'And where is the key? The Guardia didn't find it in woodland.'

As she joined the busy road back into the capital, she gave a sigh. For all her conjecture, this bizarre and troubling case seemed to be throwing up far more questions than answers.

Isabel squeezed Pequeñito into a parking space in front of the sea on the Paseo Marítimo and attached a lead to Furó. He grunted and wheezed in protest, but when she offered him a handful of his favourite kibble, he nuzzled her leg.

'There, not so bad. You don't want to get run over, do you? The traffic on this road is so fast.'

'Hey, Bel?'

Isabel turned round sharply and broke into a smile when she saw a young uniformed officer squatting next to an old car close by. She remembered her from her time as a detective at the Palma precinct.

The woman pushed her short, dark hair back behind her ears.

'Bea! Long time. How's life?'

The slightly built girl shrugged. 'Still waiting for a promotion, but I'm okay. I hear you're running a rentals agency these days in Sant Martí?'

Isabel nodded. 'And why are you squatting next to a civilian car at this time of night? Hope you're not trying to break in?'

The girl gave a long sigh. 'I'm searching for a Lada which supposedly contains a case of cocaine. We have a drug mule in custody and he claims that his dealer always keeps a stash in the boot. The mule is trying for a plea bargain so he could be spinning us a yarn. I've been here an hour looking at cars and this is the only Lada, but the boot is empty.'

Isabel got out her own torch and inspected the vehicle. 'Best to look inside.'

Bea laughed. 'Yeah, well, I don't have a set of skeleton keys and I'm not authorised to smash a window.'

Isabel unlocked her car and returned with a metal coat hanger, which she pulled open. 'Here, this should do it.'

'Bel, I'm not authorised to break in.'

Isabel shrugged, pulled on latex gloves and flipped the lock on the driver's door in a matter of seconds. 'Seems like it was already open.'

Bea grinned. 'Just as well you're no longer on the force, Bel.'

Isabel let Furó loose in the car and soon he was pawing at the back seat. She flipped open the back doors from inside and examined under the seats with her torch while Bea acted as involuntary lookout.

'My ferret has a good nose. There's a big cavity under here.' Isabel pulled at a strip of black tape and felt a heavy package loosen. More followed. She dumped each one on the back seat and watched as Bea's eyes opened wide.

'Incredible, Bel. The mule seems to have been telling the truth. I need to call my boss.'

While Bea spoke on her mobile, Isabel opened one of the bags, dabbed at the white powder and put it to her lip.

She stroked Furó. 'It's the real deal. You could give those police dogs a run for their money.'

Bea returned, a smile of relief etched on her face. 'I owe you, Bel. You're a rule breaker, but you always get results.'

'So who is this drug dealer?'

Bea pulled a face. 'Come on, Bel. You know I can't share that kind of confidential stuff now you've no longer got the badge.'

'Of course.' Isabel smiled. 'We have to go as it's nine o'clock and we're expected for dinner.'

'Are you meeting up with friends?'

Isabel paused. 'Actually, Tolo Cabot is cooking me dinner.'

Bea stared at her in some shock. 'I take it that's a joke?'

With a mischievous giggle, Isabel turned to her. 'I'll leave you to decide.'

Moments later, Isabel and Furó walked through the narrow, atmospheric streets of La Lonja to Tolo's apartment. Even though it was a cold night, groups of locals sat outside cafés, snuggling in blankets under the warm blaze of patio heaters, enjoying wine and *tapas*. They reached an historic stone property, a former seventeenth-century palace. Isabel removed Furó's lead. She pressed one of the buzzers and pushed open the ancient arched mahogany door. Tolo's flat occupied the whole top floor. She set off two steps at a time up the grand, sweeping marble staircase with Furó pattering behind her. At the top she stopped to catch her breath. Tolo was leaning on the polished wooden balustrade, awaiting her arrival.

'What's wrong with the lift?'

'You know I hate them. Mobile metal coffins. I avoid them when I can.'

He laughed. 'You read too many crime novels.'

'You think?'

She grinned impishly and stepped into his embrace. Furó issued a low growl. Tolo broke free and bent down and ruffled his fur.

'Don't be jealous. I've prepared you an exclusive gourmet treat all to yourself. Chopped up beef and a big juicy bone. Let's go!'

Furó pricked up his ears and pottered after Tolo into the kitchen, where he began tucking into a bowl of meat. Within seconds he was sneezing and chasing his tail.

'That's his ferret *fiesta* dance. It means he's really happy,' said Isabel. 'You've scored a ten, Tolo.'

He laughed. 'Well, let's keep it that way. And for you, a cool glass of Veritas rosé *cava*.'

'You know how to capture a girl's heart. Can we sit out on the terrace?'

'Of course.' He popped the cork and poured her a glass. 'I've set the table out there so you can admire the *casco antiguo* and the cathedral. It can't beat your views of the Tramuntanas, but it's not bad.'

She took her glass and walked through the oak-beamed, open-plan living area to the huge terrace overlooking the old quarter. She loved Tolo's flat, which had retained many of the ancient property's original features yet had an airy and uncluttered feel similar to a modern New York loft apartment. She'd seen some in American décor magazines and always thought they looked classy and serene. Tolo had inherited the place from his grandparents many years before and had made it his home. Although many an opportunistic estate agent had tried to persuade him to sell up for vast sums, Tolo had steadfastly refused. He loved the old apartment with a passion, its history and family associations something that money could never buy. Isabel's gaze fell on the white walls adorned with works by local contemporary artists. She had always coveted the canvas of three flautists by Juli Ramis, a twentieth-century home-bred artist with an international reputation. Tolo stood behind her.

'You should have that work.'

'Nonsense. Your father left it for you and it looks perfect here. You know that Ramis was born in 1909, the same year that the ancient Mallorca mouse-goat, myotragus, was discovered on the island?'

'You love that prehistoric goat.'

'Of course I do. It's part of our rich heritage.'

'My father left me three works by Ramis. One is a classic from the thirties, but the others produced at a later date have a very different feel. They are reminiscent of Paul Klee and of course Ramis met both Klee and Vasily Kandinsky around that time.'

'You're quite the collector,' Isabel replied. 'This charcoal and oil work is beautiful too.'

'Ah yes, *Love and Death* by Joan Bennàssar. The song of life. He is the master of capturing the human soul. I once had the pleasure of meeting him at a vernissage. A nice, down-to-earth guy.'

'You're worryingly aesthetic for a homicide chief,' she teased. 'Aren't those female busts up at your *casita* by Bennàssar too?'

'Well remembered. Actually, last week, Gaspar and two of my nephews helped me to bring them over here. It took some effort as they're cast in stone.'

'They're beautiful works.'

He nodded. 'They embody nature and primitive desire. We placed them on the terrace so that they can admire the view to the floodlit cathedral and to the sea, where surely they belong?'

Isabel savoured her first sip of sparkling *cava* and stepped out onto the candlelit terrace. The city glittered before her like a rare jewel set against the charcoal sky and the whisper of a briny breeze caressed her lips. She sank into a comfortable wicker chair and closed her eyes, revelling in the peace. Tolo soon reappeared with a tray of dishes and basket of crunchy, fresh bread balanced on top.

'Time to eat, *cariño*. We have grilled seabass, *tumbet,* asparagus spears and my own special spicy salsa and *alioli.*'

Isabel sat up in her chair and grinned. 'An aesthete and an impressive chef. I must work harder at finding your Achilles heel.'

He scrunched her hand. 'I have enough to furnish many feet, but I celebrate frailty and fallibility. It is, after all, what makes us human.'

Isabel brushed his face with her hand. 'Well said, dear Tolo. Let's drink to that.'

He smiled. 'But you are my Achilles heel, of course, and I am happy to admit it.'

It was late and a hazy moon cast silver light over the sea. Isabel sat cross-legged in her wicker chair, the remnants of a glass of red wine in her hands. Breaking her gaze from the exotic scene beyond, she turned to Tolo.

'So, what next in the investigation?'

He yawned heavily and ran a hand through his hair.

'Tomorrow morning I have a press conference, but we can't divulge your thinking about the abduction yet. If, as you have hypothesised, Sebi was lured to that quiet road in Llucmajor and abducted, we need to know the whys and wherefores.'

'Maybe his phone records from Monday night might hold the key?'

'Gaspar should know more about that tomorrow. We're also both re-interviewing staff in Sebi Vives's department. They've been a bit tight-lipped so far, which makes us both feel they're hiding something. Silvia Porres, his deputy, is very defensive. What are your plans tomorrow?'

'I'm going to visit Marc Castell, the motorway contractor. I called his office yesterday and he'll be at the site tomorrow afternoon. We need to know how his company, Construcción Castell, was awarded the contract and whether that has any bearing on Sebi's seemingly luxurious lifestyle.'

'A backhander from the developer, you mean? Sebi Vives's ministerial salary certainly wouldn't have paid for his palatial property and car. His elderly father lives with a carer in the family home near Colonia Sant Jordi but leads a simple existence. Sadly, he has Alzheimer's. Gaspar wondered whether the family of Sara Vives might have money. He's doing checks, but by all accounts, they are humble people.'

Isabel eyed him keenly. 'I'll pop by Gran Casino Atlántico later. As the three brothers who own it have ties to Construcción Castell, maybe there's a connection. We know that Rocci, the youngest, has a thriving drugs racket on the island.'

'True, and frustratingly we've never been able to nail the crook. He's a piece of work.'

'You'll recall that I once had a nasty encounter with him when I was in the force. It was at a drugs bust in Magaluf, but his lawyers got him off. He's a violent and vindictive thug.'

'I do remember. Two Albanian traffickers found shot dead in a barn groaning with cocaine and we never got the killer. It was most likely Rocci.'

'I'll find out what I can,' Isabel replied.

'Something doesn't add up. Finding that haul and gun under the backseat of Sebi's car was all too easy.'

She nodded. 'Agree.' A moment later she eyed him brightly. 'I nearly forgot to mention that before I got here, I helped one of your officers to break into a car on the Paseo Marítimo. It got me thinking.'

He choked on the dregs of his wine. 'What car? Which officer?'

She waved a hand in the air. 'Calm down. It was just young Bea who used to be in *trafico*. It was an antiquated Lada and you know how easy it is to open them.'

'That's not the point, Bel,' he replied. 'You're far too cavalier. Did anyone see you?'

'Of course not. I'm a pro and Bea played no part in it, so you can spare her a grilling. The point is that Furó discovered packs of coke under the backseat.'

'You've even got your poor ferret breaking and entering.'

She laughed. 'Stop it, and listen. I need you to get Nacho to analyse the black tape used. I think we'll find that whoever planted the gun and cocaine in Sebi's car could be responsible for the drugs haul we found in the Lada. I'd guess Rocci Mestre is behind this.'

He stared at her with a furrowed brow. 'Bea took the tape and coke packets straight back to the precinct?'

'I'd hardly have stashed them away in my pannier.'

'Nothing would surprise me with you.' He chuckled. 'At least Gómez is off our backs for a while. He's still interviewing members of GOB and Feel the Earth – a waste of time – and seems to have some other urgent casework that needs his attention. And that ghoul, Borja Ruiz, is thankfully back in Madrid but still rattling on about ritualistic killings, which is unnerving the minister of the interior. I've had to assure his team that Ruiz is barking up the wrong tree.'

Isabel exhaled deeply. 'In that case, let's hope we're right and he's wrong.'

He suddenly smiled. 'Anyway, we have your birthday to look forward to on Saturday. A quiet supper over at your mother's place.'

'Yes, I suppose so,' she replied wistfully. 'Thirty-four. I'm getting older.'

'We all are, dear Bel, and I'm way ahead of you, so stop making me feel bad.'

'Time is marching on.' She pulled a face. 'And there's still the mystery of my Uncle Hugo. Our trip to Colombia achieved nothing, though it was lovely being with you.'

He shrugged. 'Don't dismiss it. We are now fairly certain that he's alive. We just need to understand why, if that man in the images was him, he was filmed in the company of a known drug baron. There could be a very rational explanation.'

She let out an exasperated sigh. 'That he's become a criminal, you mean?'

'Not at all,' he replied gently.

'In the images he was smiling and the drug baron even had a friendly hand placed on his shoulder in one snap. What could it all mean? I can never let Mama know about it. She'd be heartbroken.'

'Let's not worry about it for now. Emilio is on the case. Let him do some more digging before we jump to conclusions.'

Isabel rose to her feet. 'It's midnight. We should get some sleep.'

He nodded and followed her back into the apartment. 'By the way, how is that American hiker who fell from Puig de Massanella?'

'He's fine, but there have been two more mountain falls. I've got a bad feeling about it.'

Tolo carried the wine glasses into the kitchen.

'Come on. Hikers often overestimate their abilities on tough new terrain, especially in this wet weather. Most likely there won't be any more incidents now. Like buses they come in threes.'

Isabel eyed him with a serious expression. 'My gut tells me otherwise, but I really hope you're right. Frankly, Tolo, we've already more than enough on our plate.'

He sighed. 'I know. We've another media circus on our hands and three days into the investigation we're no closer to finding answers. Let's hope for a breakthrough and fast.'

NINE

The early morning sky blushed a soft lilac, reminding Isabel of the pretty wisteria that hung in heavy clusters from her garden pergola during spring. Furó scurried about Can Repic beach, occasionally darting into the cold, briny water and hurtling back onto the powdery, golden sand and shaking himself down. Wrapped in a cosy bathrobe following her swim, she took a final sip of coffee and smiled. The beach was devoid of life at such an hour, but a graceful eagle soared in the sky and gulls chatted raucously as they screened the calm waters for prey. She and Tolo had risen at five-thirty and gone their separate ways. While he had set off to the office to prepare for his televised press conference, she had driven straight to Soller port, a mere thirty-minute drive from Palma at that hour.

Isabel turned when a delivery van stopped close to the esplanade and the driver jumped out and deposited crates of bottles outside a local café. They made a pretty clinking sound as he set them down. He waved across at her and she smiled. All the early birds got to know one another on this stretch and she enjoyed the sense of camaraderie. As she stood up to towel-dry her hair, a few uniformed staff were making their way into the Pure Salt Hotel. The chic four-star property had recently changed hands and she was keen to try the coffee, a sure sign of whether a hotel was really worth its 'salt'. It occupied an enviable spot close to where she swam most days, away from the hubbub on the esplanade and with some of the best views of Soller bay. As she packed her coffee flask and towel into her pannier, Furó appeared, his fur covered in wet sand.

'Look at you! Now you'll make a mess of Pequeñito and he won't be happy. Come on, I need breakfast.'

They walked back to the car, which she'd parked on a yellow line close to Agapanto restaurant. One of the windscreen wipers was resting at a strange angle. While Furó jumped into the passenger seat, Isabel wrestled with the wiper outside, returning moments later with it in her hand.

'You see how flimsy these things are, Furó? It just snapped off. I'll have to pop by the garage and get Bernat to fix it.'

The ferret offered her a doubtful glance and with a yawn, promptly fell fast asleep.

An hour later, Isabel walked into Bar Castell and greeted Llorenç, who she found chatting with Rafael at the bar.

'How was your swim?' he asked jovially.

'Cold but a wonderful way to start the day. I've not had much sleep. Tolo and I were talking late and up at the crack of dawn.'

The mayor tutted. 'We all need our beauty sleep, Bel... even you! Also, good nutrition is so important. These days I am shunning bakes and bread in favour of a new diet that Angélica suggested we all follow as a family. I've already lost a few kilos.'

Isabel smiled. 'Good for you. So what are you having for breakfast?'

'Scrambled eggs, tomatoes and mushrooms.'

Rafael offered a cynical grunt. 'I'd like to see how long this lasts.'

'I'll have the same, Rafa,' replied Isabel. 'But also toast with salt and lashings of olive oil for me.'

Rafael laughed. 'Here's your *cortado*. I'm off to the kitchen.'

When they were sitting down, Llorenç leant forward confidentially. 'I've just had a report back from the Guardia about the hiker who fell from the Sierra de Son Torrella. Thankfully he's now conscious, but he is adamant that the cairns he followed looked freshly made. He mentioned that he'd seen a woman with long dark hair on the path shortly beforehand, but she was walking quickly and he didn't have a chance to pass the time of day.'

'What about the Englishman who fell in Llucalcari? Did he see anyone in the vicinity?'

Llorenç shrugged. 'Capitán Gómez only mentioned that he'd grumbled about the cairns misleading him. I believe the Guardia will be interviewing him further.'

Isabel pushed her damp hair back behind her ears. 'I've asked Pep to form a list of all the guides and landowners locally. I think we need to talk with them and find out if they have noticed anything untoward lately. Is it just a coincidence that a similar-sounding woman with long hair was on the path in two of these episodes?'

'I don't think we should read too much into it, but all the same, maybe I should call a meeting of all concerned.'

'A good idea. What about any local agitants?'

'What do you mean, exactly?' asked Llorenç.

'Do you know of any environmentalists or activists who might be unhappy about tourists hiking in the Tramuntanas?'

Llorenç guffawed. 'Where do I start? I've told you about the foreign residents complaining about bonfires and holding beach cleans.'

Isabel tutted impatiently. 'I'm talking about those who believe visitors shouldn't be allowed to hike in the Tramuntanas for fear of damaging the fauna and flora.'

Llorenç pulled a glum face and banged his fist down on the table.

'What about that potty artist, Frans Bordoy, who lives in a run-down mountain *casita* near Fornalutx? He's got a real beef about hikers.'

Isabel nodded slowly. 'Yes, of course. He staged an exhibition on the theme a few years ago. Lots of pictures of weeping rocks and bloodied mountain scenes.'

Llorenç took a sip of coffee. 'He's very peculiar. Half mainlander, half German. The Guardia had to stop him from attacking a group of German hikers last year – his own people. He was angry that they had poles with spikes. He said they would wound the rocks and plants. I ask you!'

Isabel sniffed. 'Well, he has a point. Besides, we don't want the Tramuntanas overcome by tourism. The reason it's so peaceful is because it's a wilderness with few people about. He's right that the rocks and the wild mountain flora should be respected.'

'Shall I get the Guardia to pay him a visit?' Llorenç asked.

'Let's not be hasty. Frans Bordoy may have an axe to grind, but I've always thought him pretty harmless. On Saturday I'll go up Son Torrella following the route that the hiker took. Furó will enjoy the exercise.'

'Be careful, Bel. We don't want you coming a cropper.'

She laughed. 'Don't worry. I know the range well and will have GPS.'

'Now, while I have you here, when can we discuss plans for the Sant Antoni *fiesta*? Father Agustí is getting very agitated about it all.'

'What about at our next village committee meeting?'

Llorenç nodded.

Rafael appeared with two plates of scrambled eggs and grilled mushrooms. He placed the larger in front of Bel and set a basket of crusty toasted sourdough bread next to her. He returned with olive oil, sea salt and a pepper mill.

'Rafa, you're a marvel!' exclaimed Isabel. 'I'm so hungry.'

'What about mine?' puffed Llorenç. 'And why is my helping smaller than Bel's?'

'You told us you don't eat bread anymore and I assumed portion control was a fundamental part of your new regime.'

Isabel could barely stifle a grin as she smothered a piece of toast in olive oil and crunched on it.

'Indeed,' replied Llorenç with furrowed brow. 'I'll soon be the envy of the other mayors in the valley when I've lost ten kilos.'

'Sure I can't tempt you?' asked Isabel, wafting the basket of hot toast under his nose.

He dismissed it with a wistful expression. Rafael gave Isabel a surreptitious wink and set off to the bar, shaking with mirth.

Isabel stood by her open window, absorbed with the antics of her frisky hens. Salvador was strutting about majestically under the lemon trees, muttering to himself, while his feathered harem followed in his wake. The office door banged open and Pep walked in, one hand gripping an *ensaïmada*, the other a file.

'Penny for them?' he said.

'I was just thinking how simple the animal kingdom is. There are no complications. It's all about just eating and living in the moment.'

Pep winked. 'Sounds just like you.'

'Ha, very funny. What's with the *ensaïmada*?'

'You said I should keep up my strength while Angélica has me on this stupid diet.'

Isabel smiled. 'Ah yes, of course. I think your future father-in-law's resolve is slipping. We had breakfast together and his eyes were boring through my basket of bread.'

Pep tutted. 'Stop calling him that! Angélica and I aren't going to marry any time soon.'

'Sorry, couldn't resist.'

Pep chewed cheerily on a morsel of the pastry.

'Well, let's hope you're right. It's making life very boring at home. Mind you, my Angélica could lose a few kilos.'

Isabel narrowed her eyes. 'A word of advice. Don't ever say that to her or you'll be toast. I think she's perfect as she is.'

He licked his sugary fingers and grinned. 'You're right. She's voluptuous and curvy, which is how I like women. All the same, she did start piling on weight recently. She said it was the stress of starting work in the local nursery. I mean, that can't be too hard, can it?'

'Yes, I think it could be very stressful and tiring looking after other people's precious kids and having to be on your toes all day long.'

'In that case you'd think she'd lose weight.'

Isabel flicked her eyes heavenwards. 'Maybe you could try engaging your brain some time, Pep. Why not bother to find out if she's okay with the job and offer some support?'

He eyed her in some alarm. 'You want me to help out at the nursery?'

Isabel groaned. 'I mean, ask her about what's worrying her. Even if you can't do anything, she'll appreciate you listening.'

'Okay. I'll try it tonight.' He handed her the file. 'Anyway, I'm working on that list of landowners and guides you wanted. It'll be done soon.'

'That's great. I think we need to find out if something is amiss or whether these cliff falls really are just accidental.'

'You seem convinced that they're not.'

'Two of the hikers mentioned seeing a woman with long dark hair far ahead of them on the path. What if she deliberately placed signs in the wrong place or created new cairns to confuse them?'

'What on earth for?' he asked.

'It could be a local activist who's against tourists hiking in the Tramuntanas. Llorenç suggested someone like Frans could be behind it. He has a group of activists that he often deploys at demos. They often complain about valley buses that fill up with hikers and prevent locals getting on. Maybe this woman is one of them?'

Pep shook his head. 'He's a bit crazy, but I don't think he'd go so far as to hurt people. Mind you, you never really know anyone.'

Isabel clapped her hands together. 'Very true, Pep. Often suspects can seem genuine and convincing but turn out to be seasoned murderers. You're becoming a fine investigator.'

Pep blushed and faltered by the door. 'So what are you going to do?'

'I've suggested to Llorenç that we sound out the landowners and guides. He's going to call a meeting.'

Pep laughed. 'Oh, he loves meetings! It'll be the Sant Antoni *fiesta* next. Hopefully I can help run the bar in the *plaça* again.'

'You're spot on. He mentioned Sant Antoni this morning. Let's get the details finalised at the next committee meeting to keep him happy.'

'Meanwhile, we've got loads of renters off hiking. A young couple in Soller are going to Mortitx soon, but they are really experienced and know the area quite well.'

'I hope so,' Isabel replied. 'We don't need any more accidents.'

'By the way, the plumber has fixed the gutter problems at two of our properties and the burst pipe at Can Rivera.'

'Excellent.' She hesitated and then took the broken windscreen wiper out of her pannier.

'That reminds me, would you mind taking Pequeñito over to Bernat and getting this fixed before I leave for Búger later? It just fell off at Can Repic this morning.'

He gave her an old-fashioned look. 'Just fell off! What is it with you? Can't you just try being less impatient and less like a raging bull.'

Isabel growled. 'You'll do it?'

'I suppose.' He grinned. 'Oh, and one more thing. I suggested to the Swiss family staying at Can Rivera that they cut down on the number of baths they have and try showers instead. The wife told me they have six between them every day. I explained to her that we're going to have a problem this summer with so little rain and are all trying to conserve as much water as we can.'

Isabel frowned. 'You're right, but be careful as we can't dictate the rules to clients. I'm assuming you were your usual diplomatic self?'

'Of course. The wife seemed to have no idea about our water shortages and promised they'd have showers instead. She even gave me a big bar of Swiss chocolate.'

'That's odd. Maybe she mistook you for one of her kids?'

Pep giggled. 'It's my magnetic personality.'

'Seems to me, Pep, you're racking up the calories. At this rate, Angélica really will need to put you on a diet!'

A radiant blue sky accompanied Isabel all the way from Soller to the tiny village of Búger with its outlying fields and orchards rich with almond and carob trees. The rural Raiguer area in the north presented many a pastoral scene that included fields of gambolling lambs and sheep, and ancient stone windmills. Every May, Isabel and her friend Marga, whose grandmother hailed from the village, liked to pop by the artisan market that accompanied the Fira des Jai, a *fiesta* that was revived in the 1970s and which celebrated grandparents. Búger was famous for being the smallest municipality in Mallorca, crafting cowbells and having some notable talayotic burial sites close by.

As Isabel had thirty minutes to spare before meeting with Marc Castell at the starting point of the new motorway, she took a stroll in the village square. The *plaça*, with its pretty fountain, was empty and the town hall, housed in a grand, green-shuttered stone mansion, appeared to be closed. Isabel wasn't surprised as it was still the *siesta* period. She wandered around the quiet streets and was struck by a sudden twinge of rage. The new motorway would scythe a path north of the peaceful municipality, cutting through the tranquil villages of Sa Pobla and Muro. It would then bulldozer its way through the southern extremity of S'Albufera, re-emerging onto the MA-12 highway, close to Muro beach. The project made no sense to Isabel. The new motorway, MA-13A, as it would be known, would enable those drivers heading east from Palma to Artà or Capdepera to turn off the MA-13 motorway just before reaching Búger and reduce their journey by about twenty minutes. Currently, without the new motorway, they needed to go cross-country from Inca or follow the motorway to Alcudia and then take the MA-12 eastwards. Why had the project even been hatched? What had been the motivation?

Isabel walked to the eighteenth-century church with its clock tower and wondered how the fortunes of the area might change with the extra traffic and pollution. As she headed back towards the car, a woman emerged from the church and waved at her. Isabel smiled with delight. It was Marga's grandmother. The frail elderly woman offered her a kiss on both cheeks, remarking on Isabel's hair.

'You were always such a pretty girl, Bel, with that beautiful mane of yours.' She paused. 'I suppose you know that we are all very upset about this new motorway. It will change all our lives forever.'

Isabel touched her arm. 'It's awful. I just can't understand why it was proposed, let alone approved by the regional government.'

'They say the president has a *finca* off the MA-12 near Artà and so wanted to reduce his journey time from Palma.'

Isabel puffed out her cheeks. 'I hope that's just tittle-tattle.'

The woman shrugged. 'Who knows, but none of us here can see any reason for it. We live in a rural paradise and now they want to destroy it, and for what?'

Together they walked back to Isabel's car.

'We had posters up in all the windows opposing the motorway and we held many demonstrations, but no one in the regional government took any notice, even when the TV channel IB3 covered the events. The president seems soulless.'

Isabel gave her a heartfelt hug. She had never met Teo Puig, the president of the regional government, but in media interviews he appeared aloof, unsmiling and cold. The rural lanes were empty as Isabel headed from Búger and the dusty slip road for the new motorway just a few minutes away. She navigated around the orange cones and barriers on the hard shoulder where countless diggers and vehicles were parked and turned off the engine. She sat in her car for a few moments, taking a few deep breaths in an attempt to calm her mind until a fist banged on the window.

'You can't park here. Only authorised personnel are allowed. This is a building site!'

'Tell me about it,' she said under her breath.

Isabel opened the car door and looked up at the belligerent man in the hard hat. She whipped out her police badge and shouted to him above the noise of the traffic and hubbub.

'I have a meeting with Señor Castell.'

The man's expression changed. 'Sorry, officer, I thought you were a driver that had got lost.'

'No problem.'

'I'll take you to him. He's driving that digger.'

She followed the man along the untarmacked road, the traffic rumbling along the motorway close by. Along the hedgerows lay rotting posters, all angrily protesting about the motorway.

'No protestors today?'

The man shrugged. 'Since the murder of Sebi Vives, they've mostly kept away. The police are here every morning and evening. You picked a slack time of day.'

'How is the motorway going?'

He gave a cynical laugh. 'In stops and starts. We'd only just begun bringing in the equipment when Vives was found dead. It's going to be a long project at this rate.'

They reached the digger and waited for Marc Castell to dismount. A stout man with lean lips and a chin of black stubble, he jumped to the ground and nodded in Isabel's direction.

'You're the copper?'

She showed her badge. 'Is there anywhere we can talk privately?'

Dismissing her companion, the man indicated for her to follow him, and after a short meander past vehicles and piles of gravel and cement, they entered a prefabricated hut on the side of the road. He offered her a white plastic chair and pulled up another in front of her. Chewing frantically on a piece of gum, he leant back heavily in his chair with legs akimbo.

'So what do you want to know?'

Isabel resisted the urge to ask if he was as boorish at home, instead offering him a smile.

'Tell me about your working relationship with the owners of Gran Casino Atlántico.'

He frowned. 'What's that got to do with anything?'

She waited.

'I've done the odd bit of construction work for David, Rocci and Toni Mestre. My firm added an extension onto the casino last year and we've helped them with refurbishing their own properties around the island.'

'Do you socialise together?'

He laughed. 'In this job I don't have much time for socialising. We've had the odd beer at the casino.'

'And when did you get to know Sebi Vives? With the brothers?'

'Can't quite remember. I meet a lot of people.'

'Surely you'd remember those offering you lucrative motorway contracts?'

He cleared his throat. 'Look, Construcción Castell won that contract fair and square. I had to go through the selection process like everyone else. I nabbed it based on our company's expertise with road construction and for offering a competitive price.'

'I'm glad to hear it. When was the contract confirmed?'

He shrugged. 'Two years ago. It's taken time to get things going with all these idiot protestors and injunctions. Then Sebi had to get himself killed.'

'What an inconvenience for you. How do you know for sure that he was killed?'

'Don't be daft. The newspapers are full of it.'

'It's just conjecture at this stage. Don't believe everything you read.'

He shook his head and spat his gum into one of several used plastic cups on a filthy table. He pulled a cigarette from the pocket of his work overall and lit it slowly.

'Listen, Sebi Vives would never commit suicide. Those bastard protestors did for him, that's for sure.'

Isabel breathed heavily, her hand tapping her knee in irritation. 'You have proof?'

'It's obvious, isn't it? If you lot did your jobs properly, you'd have rounded them up by now. You need to arrest that Pablo Pons guy.'

'Well, rather boringly, we prefer to make arrests based on evidence, Señor Castell.'

'Pity,' he hissed.

The door of the hut suddenly burst open and a mousy, middle-aged, bespectacled woman looked from one to the other in surprise.

'I'm sorry to interrupt.'

Isabel stood up. The woman's face had turned pale.

'I'm Isabel Flores Montserrat. I'm working with the homicide team at the National Police.'

The woman shot a nervous look in the direction of Marc Castell and offered a tense smile.

'Silvia Porres. I worked with Sebi Vives. It's been a terrible shock for all of us in the office.'

Isabel shook her hand. 'My condolences. This must be such a difficult time for you all. Had you worked with Sebi Vives for long?'

She nodded and distractedly pulled a packet of cigarettes from her handbag. 'We were political colleagues for a few years. He invited me to become his deputy when he was appointed transport minister. Have you any more news about the nature of his death?'

'I'm afraid not. We're still at an early stage in the investigation.'

'Best to get a move on, then,' snarled Marc Castell.

Running a shaky hand through her cropped red hair, the woman frowned at him. 'I'm sure the police and Guardia are working around the clock to solve this tragic case.'

Isabel smiled. 'Indeed we are. And are you here for a meeting?'

Silvia Porres lit a cigarette and inhaled deeply. 'Yes, Señor Castell and I need to discuss the works. As you can imagine it's proving a difficult time all round.'

'I can imagine. Did Sebi Vives ever mention feeling threatened by anyone?'

'Every day protestors sent him threats. It was part of our daily lives in the office. Your colleague, Gaspar Fernandez, has copies of all the correspondence we received.'

'Did Sebi ever mention anyone following him home or approaching him in the street?'

'No.'

'Did his wife ever feel threatened?'

Silvia Porres looked non-plussed. 'Not that Sebi ever mentioned.'

As Isabel took her leave, she turned to her.

'Have you ever visited Gran Casino Atlántico? I believe many of your colleagues hang out there after work.'

The woman flicked some ash into one of the empty plastic cups and shook her head. 'Never.'

'So you've never met the owners, David, Rocci and Toni Mestre?'

She shrugged. 'Sorry, no. I'm a bit of a home bird. I don't socialise much.'

Isabel eyed them both. 'So how long have you two known one another?'

Marc Castell stubbed his cigarette out underfoot. 'We met two years ago when my company won the motorway contract. Sebi introduced us.'

'And how did Construcción Castell get to tender for the motorway project?' Isabel asked.

Marc threw a swift glance at Silvia.

'The relevant people in our department drew up a list of the key contractors on the island and we took it from there. Construcción Castell offered the best terms and has a certain reputation,' Silvia said.

'Ah, I'm sure that's true,' Isabel replied with a faint smile.

She thanked them both and returned to Pequeñito. She patted the steering wheel.

'Well, Pequeñito, I'm certain of one thing and that is that both Silvia Porres and Marc Castell are lying through their teeth.'

TEN

As Isabel squeezed into a slot in the large car park of Gran Casino Atlántico, she sized up the expensive cars parked on either side of her. She drummed her fingers on the steering wheel.

'Well, Pequeñito, you may not be a cherry red Ferrari or an azure Rolls Royce, but you are tasteful and understated and have a vintage pedigree. Your previous owner loved you unconditionally and so do I.'

She gave the bonnet a friendly pat and turned to the Ferrari.

'What are you staring at? You're vulgar and showy, which makes me think you're very insecure. Please don't even think of insulting Pequeñito while I'm away because he'll ignore you. As Shakespeare once said, "Never did mockers waste more idle breath."'

Isabel swivelled round at the sound of laughter and clapping behind her. A debonair man eyed her keenly. To her embarrassment, she recognised him as the regional tourism minister.

'I agree with you wholeheartedly. There are so many flashy cars parked here. Hopefully, I shan't incur your wrath as my vehicle is a modest Audi.' He held out his hand. 'I am Felip Blasi, and you are?'

She faltered then smiled and shook the man's hand. 'I am Isabel Flores Montserrat. By coincidence I recently met your wife, Mariana.'

His eyes opened wide in surprise. 'Do you have a friend in common? Or perhaps you're a doctor at her clinic?'

Isabel guffawed. 'Luckily for any patients, I'm not. I own a rentals agency in Sant Martí, but I'm a former detective. I met Sara Vives the other day with your wife.'

He stared at her for a few minutes. 'Now I know who you are. Mariana mentioned a female detective visiting Sara. My wife is a close friend of hers and is trying to offer as much support as possible in the tragic circumstances.'

Isabel nodded. 'It's a puzzling affair and indeed a tragedy. Did you know Sebi well?'

He shrugged. 'I thought so, but now I'm not really sure.' He hesitated. 'I probably know more about the circumstances of his death than I should, but Sara has naturally confided in me and my wife. My brother-in-law has also shared some details with me.'

'Ah yes, Mariana's brother is the regional president, Teo Puig. What a family!'

'In truth, this is why Mariana doesn't use her family's surname. She likes to keep out of the limelight. It can become a little too political at times.'

'In what way?'

'Just because we're family and in the same political party doesn't mean we have to agree on everything. I am totally opposed to the motorway, for example, while Teo, my brother-in-law, pushed it through in his capacity as regional president.'

'Presumably because he has a home on the new route?' she replied with a grin.

He folded his arms and sighed. 'I don't want to go there. You'd need to ask Teo directly.'

'Somehow I doubt I'll get the chance. Do you know if Sebi had any enemies?'

'All politicians are hated by someone or other, but his zeal for the new motorway created tensions. Maybe one of these activists took revenge. I'll leave it to you and your colleagues to find out. Nice meeting you.'

'One last thing. Was Sebi friendly with the casino owners here?'

He pushed out his bottom lip. 'No more than the rest of us, I'd say. Still, Sebi was quite a gambler. He spent a lot of time here. The brothers also introduced him to the motorway constructor, so they had things in common. Speak to David Mestre. He's the eldest and the shrewdest of the brothers.'

He offered a polite smile and wandered off to his car. Isabel headed towards the casino's entrance. A second later a shiny gold sports car roared into the drive, missing her by a whisker as it thundered past and parked with a screech in a large bay. She issued a low growl and shook her head as a preening young man, clad head to toe in black, emerged from the driving seat. He ran a hand through his glossy, dark locks and, looking about him, surreptitiously undid the top buttons of his shirt.

As Isabel walked up the casino's carpeted red staircase, she pondered why Audis held such an attraction for local politicians. The modern, stone-fronted building was emblazoned with gold light. Isabel winced before taking refuge in the dark interior. A toffee-coloured marble-floored entrance hall led directly onto a vast red-carpeted space with a glitzy, underlit circular bar flanked by black, cushioned high stools. Two heavily made-up hostesses in towering heels approached. One eyed her warily.

'Do you need some help?'

Isabel offered a stiff smile and produced her police badge. She was amused to see both their smiles fade quickly.

'Could you let the Mestres know I'm here? My name is Isabel Flores Montserrat. I'll be in the bar.'

'Are they expecting you?' the same young woman asked a little pointedly.

Isabel smiled. 'No, it's a surprise.'

She wafted into the area beyond as the woman made a call at the front desk. Her companion stood in the doorway, swishing back her mane of peroxide-blonde hair. It was still only six-thirty so there were few patrons about and all the discreet booths that housed small tables and plush, black leather armchairs remained unoccupied. Isabel sat up on a stool listening to the bland muzak and was immediately greeted by a smiling young barman.

'A mineral water, thanks.'

'Can't persuade you to try one of my special cocktails?'

'Maybe another day.' She winked.

He placed a bowl of salted almonds and green olives in front of her. Isabel tried one and, deciding that they were delicious, wolfed them all. The barman returned and with raised eyebrows asked if she'd like the bowls re-filled.

She nodded. 'How kind, thank you. It's my late lunch.'

As she munched on more nuts, she made a quick call to Tolo. 'Guess who I just bumped into?'

'The King of Spain?'

'I'd have liked that, but no, Felip Blasi.'

'Then I take it you're already at the casino, favourite haunt of Adelante Mallorca.'

'Correct.'

'Good luck if you meet the youngest brother, Rocci. He's no charmer.'

'In fairness, the brothers have good taste in nuts and olives. I'm on my second helping.'

'I can always rely on your professionalism on the job.'

She gave a guffaw. 'Be grateful I haven't already sunk a few cocktails too.'

As she put her mobile back in her pannier, footsteps sounded and she turned. One of the giraffe-like hostesses appeared in the company of a lean and tanned bespectacled man. His platinum hair was closely cropped and as he drew nearer, she observed that he had a slight but discernible twitch above his left eye. His tanned face portrayed deep lines, showing his age and love for the sun.

'How can I help you, Miss Flores? I am David Mestre.' A slight smile crossed his face. 'I see you like our bar fare.'

'Yes, I have to compliment you. These Sevillian Gordal olives are spectacular. What is the other bright green variety?'

'Olives cassées de la vallée des Baux de Provence.'

'Ah, of course, it was on the tip of my tongue,' Isabel teased.

He laughed. 'I'm sure you didn't come here to discuss my olives.'

Isabel nodded. 'Sadly, I am here about Sebi Vives.'

'Indeed. Please, let's sit at a private table.'

They headed to one of the quiet booths, where to Isabel's relief, the music was hardly audible. She deposited the bowl of mixed olives in front of her and popped one in her mouth. David Mestre observed her for a few seconds. He chewed slowly on what appeared to be gum.

'So are you a detective, Señorita Flores?'

'I work in a private capacity with the homicide department, but yes, I have been a detective inspector with the National Police.'

'How fascinating,' he replied. 'It must be an exciting job.'

'All depends on if murder gives you a thrill, I suppose,' replied Isabel smoothly. 'I take it you've been abroad recently?'

He nodded. 'You're referring to my tan? It accentuates my lines perfectly, don't you think? At the time of Sebi's unfortunate death, I was in Cancun on vacation. My younger brothers were holding the fort here. I only returned this Wednesday, so the news came as some shock.'

'So were you and your brothers, Rocci and Toni, close to Sebi?'

His face took on a pinched aspect. 'We did business together.'

'And I believe you introduced Sebi to Marc Castell, the contractor of the new motorway?'

'I think I know where this is heading. My youngest brother, Rocci, facilitated an introduction here but nothing more. Marc is a regular client and a good friend of Rocci. Castell Construcción won the contract, deservedly so, but my brothers and I had no involvement in that.'

'And I believe Sebi was a regular client here and quite some gambler.'

He breathed heavily. 'He came here several nights a week to relax after work. He'd have a few drinks with his political chums and sometimes enjoy the tables.'

'Was he in debt to you, thanks to his gambling habit?'

'That is confidential information.'

Isabel chose another olive. 'Suit yourself. We'll find out anyway.'

'Look, Sebi sometimes needed a small bridging loan for a few weeks. We were happy to help as he was a trusted club member.'

'How decent of you. Did he repay you handsomely?'

'He always paid back what he owed. He has no further debt with our casino.'

'Just as well, in the circumstances. So I wonder how he magicked the money to pay you back?'

He offered a whinny of a laugh. 'I'm not at liberty to speculate on that.'

'Fair enough. So tell me about the drugs scene here.'

He rapped the table. 'Drugs are banned in our casino.'

'Since when? You've had various drug busts over the years. Rocci has quite a reputation.'

'Nothing has ever been proven.'

She smiled. 'Full marks for getting off the hook. I hear you've all got a great lawyer.'

He offered her a hollow stare.

'On the night of Sebi's disappearance, he came here after work. His staff say he left the office around seven o'clock. The CCTV footage that you handed to the police shows Sebi leaving here at 8.35 p.m.'

'That's correct. He had a few drinks and left. He told our barman that he was going straight home.'

'Why would he feel the need to tell that to your barman?'

'He was friendly with the staff. There's nothing odd about that.'

He rose and beckoned over the young barman.

'Can you confirm to Señorita Flores here that on Monday night, Sebi Vives told you that he was going straight home?'

The young man gave a nervous nod. 'He was at the bar when he took a call, I presume from his wife. A little while afterwards, he finished his drink and said he was going home. I remember looking at my watch soon after he left. It was around eight-thirty.'

'Did he mention going anywhere else first?'

'The last words I heard him say to his wife were, "see you soon".'

'What kind of mood was he in that night?'

He looked at his boss and then back at Isabel. 'He seemed in good spirits. Whenever he came here he was in a cheerful mood.'

Isabel smiled. 'Did he gamble that night?'

'No, he just enjoyed a few whiskeys at the bar. Jack Daniels.'

The barman left and Isabel turned to David Mestre. 'I won't take up any more of your time, but as this is an ongoing investigation, we'll no doubt meet again.'

He rose to his feet and gave a courteous bow. 'I look forward to the pleasure. Just a moment.'

He walked swiftly over to the bar and disappeared into a back room, returning with an elegant heavy-duty paper carrier bag. He passed the weighty item to Isabel.

'A little gift from the club.'

She peeked inside to find a selection of bottled olives and packets of smoked and salted almonds.

'Bribery and corruption starts in small ways,' she said with a sigh. 'All the same, at least I'll be able to eat the evidence.'

The casino owner rolled back his head and laughed. 'Come again soon and I'll offer you a game at the tables.'

Isabel shook her head and smiled. 'Thank you, but I'm not a gambling girl.'

As she walked towards Pequeñito, an engine revved and the gold sports car reversed with a screech out of a parking bay and promptly smashed into a stationary vehicle to its rear. Amid the sound of tinkling glass, the same young male Isabel had seen earlier emerged shakily from the car. He swayed slightly and cursed loudly when he saw the damage to the headlights of the other car. Isabel hesitated a moment, but when she saw the doorman running towards him, she shrugged and started her engine. She gave an involuntary smile and patted the wheel.

'That surely couldn't have happened to a more deserving person, Pequeñito. It's what I call karmic justice or perhaps, swaggering young cockerels getting their just desserts.'

Isabel sat in the centre of the busy bar, flanked by Marga, Idò and Llorenç, enjoying a large plate of *paella*. She helped herself to another glass of robust red wine.

'It's hard to beat Rafa's *paella*,' mused Llorenç, taking another large mouthful of rice.

'True,' replied Isabel. 'Though Fabian's comes a close second. I'm glad that your new diet allows you such a treat.'

'But *paella* is so healthy!' exclaimed Llorenç.

'*Si, si!*' Marga giggled. 'All that olive oil is very slimming.'

Idò gave her a wink. 'Indeed it is. I find chocolate and *ensaïmadas* also carry the same health benefits and have few calories.'

Llorenç observed them all and lowered his fork. 'You may all joke, but come spring, the men of this village will all be envious of my svelte profile.'

'I'm sure you're right,' said Isabel soothingly. 'Just ignore us. All the same, I shall not be following a diet myself, especially as it's my birthday tomorrow. Mama is cooking a simple supper, but I'm hoping she'll bake one of her special cakes.'

'Good for you,' said Llorenç. 'You've been working so hard on this new murder case that it'll be nice for you to have an evening off. Any plans during the day?'

'Of course. I shall be climbing Sierra de Son Torrella tomorrow. I want to sniff around the area where the last hiker fell. Later, I have arranged to speak with him at the hospital. Apparently he speaks good English, which is fortunate as my German is basic.'

'So much for time off from work,' grumbled Idò.

'Do be careful, Bel,' added Marga, wiping her mouth on a napkin. 'I'd come with you, but I'm working in the salon all day. Besides, I think I'd expire on the first uphill slope.'

Isabel scrunched her arm. 'I appreciate the thought, but I'm best on my own as I can keep up a fast pace. I'll have GPS and a mobile plus all my supplies.'

Idò slurped at his beer and wiped his mouth on the back of his hand. 'Now don't be late home. Your mother will be beside herself with worry.'

Isabel sat back in her chair. 'Don't worry. I'm setting off early and will be back late afternoon.'

'What are you hoping to find, Bel?' asked Llorenç.

She shrugged. 'I won't know until I find it. We need to rule out foul play in the hills so that oddballs like Frans Bordoy aren't under scrutiny. Until we can prove that someone deliberately misrouted those hikers, we have nothing to go on.'

'He's very *raro*, that guy. I wouldn't trust him,' opined Idò. 'His old father was as mad as a raging bull. He used to shout at tourists getting off the Soller train. Chip off the old block.'

Isabel drained her glass and nudged him playfully. 'There are many eccentrics in this valley, but that doesn't make them all criminals. Imagine what people might say about you, my dear uncle.'

'Eh?' he shouted.

As laughter erupted, Isabel said her farewells and went to pay Rafa at the bar. He raised a hand.

'Llorenç is picking up the bill, so save your money for a birthday treat.'

Isabel kissed his cheeks and made her way home through the dark and chilly *plaça*, smiling when she heard raucous activity going on at Café Jordi. Barcelona was playing against Sevilla so the television was blaring and even with the doors and windows closed, whistling and clapping spilled out. Calle

Pastor was eerily silent and Isabel gave an involuntary shiver as she passed the row of naked plane trees that lined both sides of the street. The poor things would have to wait some months to cover their modesty with new coats of young spring leaves. Yawning heavily, she clicked open her garden gate and made her way through the front garden. A light was on upstairs in Doctor Ramis's house. Perhaps he was having an early night. Furó was staying with her mother for the night and so she resolved to pick him up in the morning as he loved to go hiking. As Isabel went to open her front door, she found it already ajar. The hairs on her neck rose. Stepping back, she fumbled in her pannier for a torch and gloves. With the beam of light in front of her, she kicked open the door, only to find the *entrada* silent and undisturbed. Flicking on the main light with a gloved hand, she listened carefully for some seconds and strode into the kitchen. Nothing was out of place, but in the office upstairs she found files opened, papers littering the floor and her office turned upside down. She sighed heavily and explored her bedroom and salon on the upper level, yet nothing appeared amiss. Descending the stairs, she called Tolo and braced herself for his reaction.

'Can you be sure there's no one still in the house? You should leave now. Can you stay at your mother's?'

'Of course,' Isabel replied, stepping onto her porch. 'Any chance of Nacho or one of the forensics team doing a quick sweep early tomorrow morning?'

'Sure, Nacho is on duty. The key is still under the frog statue near the front door? Great security, by the way.'

She tutted. 'We rarely have thefts in Sant Martí.' She walked over to the stone frog and discovered the key intact. 'It's still there.'

'All the same, maybe you need to find a less obvious hiding place. The thief could have used it to access the house and politely popped it back under the statue.'

'A well-mannered thief. That would be curious. I'll stay at Mama's tonight and pop by early before I go off to Serra de Son Torrella, so hopefully I'll see Nacho.'

'Is it wise to go hiking alone, given what's just happened? It's your birthday dinner tomorrow too.'

Isabel gave a groan. 'Wisdom doesn't come into it. I'm going and that's that. Besides, I also need to visit the hiker who fell. It could prove useful. I'll see you at seven tomorrow night at Mama's house.'

'Please keep in touch during the day.'

'Of course.'

Isabel stood glumly in her doorway, her eyes fixed on the swollen moon hanging bewitchingly above the Tramuntanas.

Tolo was still talking. 'Bel, who do you think did this?'

She blinked and cleared her throat. 'I haven't a clue, but I think it's a good idea if we make it our business to find out.'

She finished the call, locked her front door and external shutters and made her way briskly through the quiet, sombre alleyways to her mother's house. She was deep in thought and agitated. Who had violated her space and why? What were they hoping to find and had they got what they wanted, whatever that might be? She felt a sense of dread and started when a barn owl flitted across the sky, emitting a shrill cry. In a sober mood, she arrived at Florentina's welcoming home, relieved to see it emblazoned with golden light. The front door was open as was customary and her beloved ferret came pottering excitedly over to see her from his favourite chair. She hugged him tightly, allowing the warmth of his fur to chase away the chills. The kitchen door banged open and Florentina stood before her with eyes narrowed and hands on hips.

'And what, may I ask, has happened now?'

'It's a long story,' Isabel replied. 'Give me a glass of red and I'll tell you all.'

ELEVEN

A pink blush appeared in the pale sky as Isabel sat outside on her patio, sipping a cup of strong coffee. The hens were busy pecking corn around her feet and Furó stood behind them, gauging their every move. Isabel glanced over at him.

'You know the rules. Kill one of my hens and you're in the ferret house.'

Furó padded over to her and lay in sulky mode under the table, chuntering to himself. It had taken Isabel many months to train her ferret not to hurt her beloved hens. He was, after all, a carnivore with all the cunning and instincts of a weasel. The key to creating harmony was to ensure that he always had a full stomach, and Isabel never left him for too long alone in the orchard in case temptation might get the better of him. She heard the front door open and followed her inquisitive ferret into the *entrada*, where Nacho stood holding a large box. He opened it to reveal a freshly baked *ensaïmada* topped with one white candle.

'*Feliz cumpleaños*! I drove over to Morells this morning to get this for you. It's full of *crema*, just how you like it.'

Isabel gave him a hug. 'Let's have some for breakfast. I saw you'd been here earlier. What on earth time did you arrive?'

He yawned. 'Six o'clock. I was up before five this morning and it's going to be a long day, but I'm off work tomorrow. I'm taking Patrice to see the bears at La Reserva Puig de Galatzó.'

'He'll love it. That place is so good for kids.'

Isabel cut them each a large slice of the gooey *ensaïmada* and placed a hot coffee in front of him. Nacho and his long-term French partner, Alice, doted on their mischievous three-year-old son and always tried to find local adventures for him at the weekend.

Isabel looked about her. 'Did you find anything interesting here?'

He shook his head. 'My feeling is that whoever broke in was looking for something specific in your office. What could it be? Something to do with this case?'

Isabel munched thoughtfully. 'I have no idea.'

'It looked like a professional job. There was no forced entry, so perhaps they used a skeleton key. Or, of course, they just found the spare key under your frog statue.'

'Or my door was already open?' She grinned.

Nacho let out a sigh. 'You trusting village people. You never learn.'

She paused then rose quickly to her feet. 'One minute. I've just had a thought.'

She raced up the stairs to her office and dived under her desk, where she used a pen to upturn a wooden floorboard. She pulled out a small transparent plastic bag and skipped back downstairs, presenting it to Nacho.

'Two nights ago in Llucmajor, Furó found this chewing gum in its wrapper close to the site of Sebi's abduction, but to be honest I didn't put much store by it. All the same, I hid it in a secret place in the office and have been meaning to bring it into the precinct.'

Nacho took it from her. 'I'm glad you remembered. Didn't he find another at S'Albufera?'

She nodded. 'He's got a thing about chewing gum wrappers.'

He laughed. 'It might not be relevant, but it's still worth checking out. To be honest, even if we find DNA on either wrapper, they'd have to match existing DNA on the database, and with other samples we found at the abduction site, nothing showed up.'

Isabel cut another slice of *ensaimada* for Nacho and for herself too.

'I can't think of any classified information that I might be harbouring in my office that could be of interest to anyone involved in this case apart from this.'

Nacho licked his fingers. 'Anyway, on Thursday night, you went to Llucmajor on your own and no one was about, right? So how could anyone know that you found that wrapper?'

Isabel frowned. 'Actually, I did hear some strange sounds in the forest while I was there and had an uncomfortable feeling that someone was watching me. I might have been imagining it, but I left quickly.'

'That puts a different perspective on the matter. Have you discussed this with Tolo?'

Isabel pulled a face. 'No, I didn't want to worry him.'

'You should have told him. Your break-in could be directly related.'

Isabel sighed. 'I'll mention it tonight over supper.'

There was a sudden urgent rapping at the door. Nacho flinched. 'Are you expecting anyone this early?'

Isabel laughed. 'In this village, you learn to expect the unexpected.'

She opened the front door and was greeted by a huge bunch of sunflowers. A face peered through the leaves.

'Delivery for Señorita Flores.'

'That's me.'

She took the flowers and laid them on a chair in the *entrada*.

'From an admirer?' asked the cheery deliveryman.

Isabel opened the accompanying note and gave a slight groan. 'Hm, you might say that.'

She returned to the kitchen. 'Flowers from the esteemed mayor of Forn de Camp.'

'Josep Casanovas? Is that rat still on your back?'

Isabel laughed. 'Do me a favour, don't mention this to Tolo.'

He nodded. 'No love lost there, I know. He's such a pain. Everyone at the precinct dreads his calls.'

'All the same, journalists have their uses. *El Periódico* has done us some favours.'

The front door banged open and Marga appeared with her daughter, Sofia, who rushed to embrace Isabel.

'*Feliz cumpleaños*!'

'Thank you, Sofia. You know you're my favourite goddaughter.'

'But I'm your only goddaughter,' she replied, giggling.

'Exactly!' Isabel said, ruffling her hair.

The little girl handed her a present. 'It's an orange with cloves to hang in your kitchen. I made it at school.'

'Let her unwrap it first,' Marga remonstrated.

Isabel beamed. 'It's perfect. My kitchen will smell amazing.'

She gave the child a big kiss on both cheeks.

Marga headed for the door. 'I've got to open the salon, so I'll give you my gift at supper tonight.'

'It's a green shawl,' said Sofia gleefully.

Her mother rolled her eyes. Isabel grinned. 'Nothing like a surprise.'

Nacho heaved on his heavy rucksack and kissed Isabel on the cheek. 'I'm getting out of this madhouse while the going's good. Have a fantastic birthday party tonight.'

'It's just a simple supper at my mother's house.'

'Ah, yes, Tolo did tell me. Enjoy.'

Isabel stood at the open door, happy to see a slice of sun in the sky. Moments later, a voice rang out from the gate. 'Coooeeee! Hello birthday girl!'

Isabel smiled as her neighbour, Juliana, headed towards her with a lavish red pot plant and stylish brown bottle with shoelace tie on the stopper. Isabel whooped.

She was already familiar with CapuCana, the famed 1886 tipple, and knew that it meant 'house of canes' in Brazilian because it used three different sugar canes, all grown on sustainable land. It was her favourite *cachaça* for making caipirinhas. Juliana had told her that it was matured in bourbon oak barrels on the Scottish island of Islay.

'CapuCana! What a treat.'

Juliana thrust the bottle into her hands and hugged her. 'Only the best for you, dear Bel.'

Isabel kissed her. 'I will treasure the beautiful bottle once we've exhausted the contents.'

As Juliana left, Doctor Ramis appeared, wearing his exercise gear and carrying what appeared to be a chilli pepper plant in a terracotta pot. She gave a small sigh, touched by the kindness of her friends and neighbours, yet wondering when she and her beloved ferret might ever set off on her promised birthday hike.

A sharp wind whipped around the sparse shrubs as Isabel and Furó sat in a hollowed-out rock, enjoying a snack. They had finally set off from Sant Martí at nine o'clock and driven up the winding mountain road towards Pollença, where Isabel had parked Pequeñito in a lay-by close to the Monnaber Tunnel. She and Furó had hiked up to the rocky ridge of Serra de Son Torrella, heading south along the same route that the German tourist had taken before his fall. Isabel knew the Tramuntanas like the back of her hand, having climbed many of the *miles*, the peaks over 1,000 metres, with her brother and father as a teenager. They'd master different hikes during their long summer vacations on the island when they visited relatives from her mother's side of the family. Finally, Isabel's parents left the mainland to settle there permanently. Son Torrella was an arduous climb, but the views to the Cuber Reservoir, Soller and Fornalutx were mesmerising. She smiled at Furó as he crunched on some kibble.

'Look at that vulture! Isn't it beautiful?'

The majestic bird had taken advantage of a thermal column of air as it soared effortlessly above them. Isabel had handled a vulture at a local sanctuary in Campanet. They were very weighty birds that skilfully used wind power to gain extra height. She always felt that they undeservedly had bad press as vicious birds of prey when really they kept the world's ecosystems healthy by offering a voluntary clean-up operation of carcasses. In fact, she mused darkly, a few vultures would come in handy at homicide scenes. Wiping crumbs from her face, she rose to her feet, slung the rucksack back on her shoulder and carried on clambering over the cool, grey rocks towards her prize. She was aiming for the western slope where the hiker had fallen, apparently misdirected by false cairns. That side of the ridge presented a sheer drop, but fortunately, the man had slipped onto a rocky shelf not far from the crest, which had at least broken his fall. His rescue still involved an emergency helicopter as he was unconscious and in a bad way. The cairns that marked the route had seemed in order all the way along the ridge, but as Isabel progressed westwards, there was evidence of scattered rocks. Had they been fake cairns at the time the unfortunate hiker ventured along this path? She examined her GPS and soon arrived at the exact spot where the man had fallen. She looked up at the sky and exhaled deeply.

'It's almost eleven-thirty, I'd say. We've been going about two or more hours, so that would make sense, Furó. I'll just explore this site and then we'll set off for the hospital. Okay with you?'

The ferret performed a dainty circular dance and began chortling and squeaking.

'You're in a happy mood. Looking forward to Mama's meatballs when we get home, I bet.'

As Isabel crouched down to examine the loose gravel and rocks about her, she frowned. Lying on its side, obscured by stones, was a rudimentary wooden arrow sign with a butterfly motif etched on it. She pulled on some latex gloves and turned it around in her hands. The etched butterfly made her uneasy. Could the new menace of the mountains have any connection to the death of Sebi Vives?

'So, dear Watson. What do we make of this?'

Furó sneezed.

'My thoughts entirely. It's highly suspicious. What if someone really is placing false signs and cairns around the hills, and does this butterfly motif have any significance? We've got a potentially very serious problem on our hands, but what is the motive?'

As Isabel carefully placed the wooden sign in a bag in her rucksack, she looked over the edge of the mountain and whistled. Far below were bushy trees, lush woodland and craggy rocks jutting out like old men's chins. She winced. Anyone falling from this height would have little chance of survival, meaning that the false cairns and signs had a deadly purpose. This was no playful mischief, but rather an intent to kill or badly maim. She spent some time taking images and began making her way back over the rugged stretch of rock for home. Llorenç and indeed Capitán

Gómez, whose force had jurisdiction in the area, would be far from happy to learn of her findings. She resolved to call the military captain as soon as she returned to the car and allow him to suggest next steps while she quietly conducted her own investigation. Isabel yawned, pulled out a Chupa Chup and sucked thoughtfully on it. She would drive over to Son Llàtzer Hospital and visit the recovering hiker. With any luck he might recognise the wooden sign.

Once back, Isabel enjoyed a hot shower and a piece of almond cake. She had spoken at length with the injured hiker at the hospital and he had immediately recognised the butterfly arrow sign. It matched the wooden signs that he had followed, and he verified that he had seen a slim and athletic-looking woman with long dark hair ahead of him. She sent a polite email of thanks to Josep Casanovas for his bunch of birthday sunflowers. Much as he could be a nuisance, he at times displayed a streak of kindness and gallantry, and of course had his uses in investigations.

She strolled over to her mother's home with Furó. As it was her birthday, she had made the effort to wear one of her favourite hippy-style, colourful dresses that she'd picked up on a weekend break in Ibiza and had matched it with dangly earrings and a pretty bracelet. She opened Florentina's front door only to be greeted in breathless fashion.

'My *reina*! Before you get cosy, could you just pop over to Bar Castell and collect Sofia for dinner? Marga got held up at the salon and she left her with Rafa. She'll be here as soon as she can.'

'Is Tolo not here yet either?' asked Isabel, trying to hide her disappointment. She knew by her uncanny instinct that it was seven-thirty or thereabouts.

'Not yet, but I'm sure he'll be here shortly. Miguel is still with a patient but is on his way.'

'And where's Pep?'

'I think he had to pick something up for Angélica, but by the time you're back, they'll have arrived.'

Isabel and Furó set off for Bar Castell. She was slightly suspicious of her mother's assurances and wondered what could possibly have delayed Tolo. He had a heavy workload, but it was, after all, her birthday and he hadn't called to say he'd be running late. Odd, too, that the others still hadn't turned up for supper. She gave a philosophical shrug and reaching the bar, threw open the door to huge whoops and cheers. Isabel gave a gasp. Before her stood Tolo, Marga, Llorenç, Doctor Ramis and many neighbours and friends. A grinning Rafa stepped forward with a glass of *cava*.

'You didn't think we'd let you have a quiet supper over at Florentina's?'

'Well, this time you've all caught me off my guard, but what a fantastic surprise.'

Isabel stepped forward into a warm embrace from Tolo followed by kisses and greetings from the merry throng inside the bar. The door behind her swung open and Florentina burst in and gratefully accepted a glass from Llorenç.

She giggled. 'I thought you might have suspected something was going on, Bel!'

'I did wonder why everyone seemed so busy... but where's Pep?'

Tolo squeezed her arm. 'Ah, he's outside. You need to come to the balcony.'

Mystified, Isabel followed Tolo to the bar's terrace overlooking the *plaça* where Pep now stood next to a dazzling red Ducati

Monster adorned with multi-coloured ribbons and balloons. Several locals and children stood by admiringly.

'What?' yelped Isabel, her eyes bright with excitement.

Tolo smiled. 'It's my birthday gift to you. Poor Pep has been at the end of his tether with you borrowing and breaking his *moto* and Pequeñito is a pensioner and needs some rest now and then. I know your penchant for Italian brands.'

'I simply cannot believe it,' she murmured, clasping him tightly. 'But it is far too generous a gift, Tolo.'

He tutted. 'Not at all, but you must be careful. It's the 1200 R model that you love so much. That engine is powerful. Do you want to give it a whirl?'

'What, now?' Florentina wailed. 'Aren't we having dinner soon? Rafa has prepared a feast of *gambas rojas, porc amb coll* and his mother's lemon pie.'

Rafa bustled through the crowd of cheery locals. 'We've got a good hour before we sit down to eat. Go on, Bel. I can see you're dying to give her a spin, but whatever you do, please don't fall off!'

With a skip in her step, Isabel raced down the stairs and accepted a bear hug from a grinning Pep. Hitching up her dress, she straddled the bike and tutted as Pep leant forward, issuing her with instructions and handing her a helmet. Running her hand over the controls of the gleaming motorbike, she shook her head in disbelief. Now she understood why Tolo had taken her for a test drive of various Ducatis when they were in Colombia. It had been a fun experience organised by one of his police contacts there and she had fallen in love with the V-twin engine Monster R version. After all, what more could she want? Sleek Italian design, excellent handling and incredible power and control. She smiled up at the onlookers, all the people she loved most in the world, and blinking back tears of joy, fired the engine.

'If I'm delayed, don't eat all the *gambas*!' she hissed at Pep.

The *moto* gave a healthy and powerful snarl.

'That's my girl,' whispered Isabel. 'I shall christen you Boadicea, the British warrior queen. Together we will achieve great things.'

And with a loud roar, she set off at speed along Carrer del Bisbe, to the sound of clapping and cheers from the bar.

TWELVE

A bright sun cast a golden halo on the glass table that was loaded with *tortillas*, fat green olives, crusty bread and *tomate rallado*. A flacon of rich virgin olive oil jostled for space with two glasses of freshly squeezed orange juice and coffee cups. Isabel looked up when Jordi approached, full of his customary bluster and humour.

'So you've finally jumped ship? What's that old goat Rafa done to lose such a VIP client?'

Isabel savoured a piece of omelette. 'I like to share the love, Jordi. Tolo and I thought it would make a nice change to dine at your illustrious café this morning. Besides, poor Rafa is still clearing up from the festivities last night.'

'That was one memorable party,' Tolo declared. 'The pièce de résistance was Pep dancing on the balcony to the Gypsy Kings with all the local girls swooning in the *plaça* below.'

'Heaven help us!' roared Jordi. 'And what was that old rogue Idò doing? Snaffling everyone's glasses when they weren't looking?'

Isabel offered a mock frown. 'That's my uncle you're talking about, a fine figure of sobriety and wisdom at all times.'

Jordi wiped his hands on his apron and gave a hearty laugh. 'Well, enjoy the sunshine. Hopefully you're not nursing hangovers.'

'As if,' she replied with a wink. 'We only had one caipirinha with Juliana when we got home.'

Tolo smiled across at Isabel. 'It's Sunday. Do you have plans aside from giving the Ducati another spin?'

'I'm still pinching myself. The Monster is such a beauty and so smooth to ride. Furó will enjoy it too, thanks to the carrier you thoughtfully bought him.'

'It's simple to use. You just strap it securely over the sissy bar and keep him on the harness inside. That way he can move about and pop his head out without any danger of falling.'

'Sissy bar? You're becoming a *moto* expert. Who'd have known?'

He laughed. 'Not at all. The sales guy gave me the spiel and demonstration of how it worked so I'm just parroting what he said.'

Isabel scrunched his hand. 'I can never thank you enough, Tolo.'

'I'm glad it makes you happy. Just be careful and don't take risks.' He chuckled. 'Why did I even bother saying that? So, tell me about that wooden sign you found yesterday. You want me to check it out at the lab?'

Isabel nodded and took a last sip of her coffee. 'I'd quite like to show it to Ruben, our local carpenter, first to see if he can identify the wood used. It's a long shot, but he might know someone that carves them locally.'

Tolo nodded. 'Much as I'd like to hang out with you today, I think I'd better head home to do some paperwork. You can bring the wooden sign into the precinct tomorrow once you've talked with Ruben.' He reached into his rucksack and pulled out a file.

'Tomorrow we're going to be checking out other political contacts and friends of Sebi and his wife. It's a list drawn up by the Guardia. There are a few of his old school friends that you might think worth approaching.'

Isabel took the file and flicked though the contacts. 'Jaume Perez and Eli Castano? A lawyer and an accountant. So these guys are a couple?'

Tolo nodded. 'Married. They all went to school together, but importantly Perez and Castano are godparents to Sebi and Sara's son, Mateu. They may know if Sebi had any enemies or talked about threats to his welfare.'

'I'll speak with them.' She scribbled down their details and handed back the file. 'I'm yet to get to know Mateu. They might be able to shine some light on him too.'

As Tolo rose, Padre Agustí appeared, his fine white hair rising and falling like a soft feathery plume in the gentle breeze.

'How lovely to see you both enjoying some winter sunshine,' he said, beaming. 'What a marvellous dinner it was last night.'

Tolo touched his arm. 'It was good to see you there, Padre. It's a shame you had to leave early as you missed seeing Bel dancing on the tables.'

The elderly man looked momentarily alarmed and then shook his head. 'I think you might be teasing me.'

'Just possibly,' replied Isabel.

'I wanted to remind you, Bel, that Sant Antoni is fast approaching and we have so much to sort out on the events committee. There's the village supper, animal blessing and the children's parade. Ah, here comes Llorenç. How timely.'

The mayor walked quickly in their direction, a serious look on his visage. Nevertheless, he greeted them all cheerily.

'I've just been speaking to the mayor of Escorca and he's expressed grave concern over the hiking accidents, if that's what they are. We're holding a meeting soon to discuss the situation with our counterparts in the area.'

Isabel sighed. 'As I mentioned last night at dinner, there is definitely something amiss. The sign I found up on Son Torrella yesterday points to that, though it could be youths being mischievous and not realising how dangerous their actions might prove.'

'It's highly irresponsible and the culprit must be stopped before someone gets killed,' Llorenç said.

Padre Agustí cut in. 'And meanwhile, how are plans progressing for the *fiesta*?'

Llorenç frowned. 'Ah yes, don't worry, Padre. It's all in hand. We have already placed an order at the bakery in Morells for *gató* and *empanades*. The celebrations for Sant Antoni will be a triumph this year, rest assured.'

The elderly man nodded. 'Still, before long we need to have a meeting, and looking further ahead, we need to discuss the Easter procession and parade.'

'All in good time,' replied Llorenç a tad impatiently. 'We'll convene another event committee meeting in the coming week, won't we, Bel?'

Isabel smiled reassuringly at Padre Agustí. 'Yes, of course.'

She and Tolo took their leave, followed by a sleepy Furó, who had been enjoying an early *siesta* beneath their table. As Tolo sat in his car outside Ca'n Moix, he looked up at her.

'So, where will you be taking Boadicea for a ride?'

She looked up at the blue sky for inspiration. 'Hm, I have an idea but may not know until I get there.'

He shook his head and laughed as he drove off. Isabel stared after the departing car and turned to Furó.

'Let's drop off that wooden arrow at Ruben's house, and then how about an exhilarating trip to Son Real?'

The ferret sneezed excitedly and danced about her feet, a sure sign that he heartily approved.

Isabel enjoyed her ride across country to the Son Real estate. She was cautious, keeping to a safe speed in case Furó found the ride unnerving. She needn't have worried. Whenever she turned round to check on his welfare, she found him contentedly peering out from his carrier at the back of the bike, enjoying the rural views. At times, he'd bob back down and curl up on the soft black fleece inside. Isabel called to him above the grinding sound of the *moto*.

'That's the Rolls Royce of pet carriers, Furó. You see how Tolo cares about you?'

As she turned into the entrance of the Son Real estate, she wasn't surprised to find it deserted but for a Guardia officer sitting in a vehicle at the entrance. He nodded at Isabel and passed a lazy eye over her police badge.

'They've removed the forensics tent now. Nothing much to see except crumbling talayotic tombs and the sea.'

'How I like it,' she replied with a pert smile.

'Just one thing. There's an archaeologist working on the necropolis. He has a government permit.'

Isabel shrugged. 'That's fine by me.'

She roared off along the sandy and bumpy track, parking up just beyond the site. She unfastened Furó and put him on his lead and together they ambled over the rocks towards the necropolis. A man was squatting by one of the funerary constructions, observing it closely. He looked up when Isabel approached.

'*Uep*. You're the first person I've seen for hours.'

Isabel nodded. 'It must be lonely work being an archaeologist.'

'Sometimes,' he replied. 'News travels fast. I take it you're with the police?'

'Well, we're the only ones permitted here aside from you it seems. What are you working on?'

He rose and pointed out to sea. 'I'm actually taking a boat over to that little island. There's an interesting necropolis there too. I'm writing a paper about it.'

'S'Illot des Porros. I've always wanted to go there. Can I hitch a lift?'

The man laughed. 'Do you trust me not to capsize the small boat?'

'I'm a good swimmer.'

'Just as well,' he quipped. 'I'm Antonio, by the way. I am also a professor at the university.'

Isabel shook his hand. 'Well, this is Furó, my second in command, and I am Isabel. I'm assisting the National Police with the Sebi Vives case.'

He grimaced. 'The local Guardia chief was here yesterday and asked in confidence for my take on the ritualistic nature of the killing.'

'Capitán Gómez?'

'Yes, indeed. I explained to him that a ritualistic killing might not be quite as straightforward as it appears to be.'

'Nothing about this case seems straightforward to me,' she replied.

He was pensive for a moment and then surveyed the necropolis with a glint in his eye.

'Did you know that this talayotic site was excavated back in the fifties and sixties under the expert direction of Guillem Rosselló-Bordoy? He is one of the island's most esteemed experts in prehistory and the Arab-Islamic period.'

'I know of him. He wrote an important paper about ancient Islamic ceramics in Mallorca, an essential reference for historians and archaeologists everywhere.'

'Spot on. The fact is that more than one hundred tombs and the remains of three hundred people were unearthed here. All sorts of ritualistic artefacts were found buried with them such as jewellery, animals and metal utensils. You must remember that in the seventh century BC, those buried were aristocrats, though in later centuries such as the Roman period, that all changed. These objects were often left with the departed after funerary celebrations in their honour.'

'Go on.'

'Ritualistic items placed in the tombs signified respect and love for the departed. It wasn't about hate and revenge, as Capitán Gómez and his colleague implied with this death.'

Isabel frowned. 'So you're saying that the creatures locked inside Sebi's body bag might have been placed there out of respect? A funny way of showing it.'

He gave a cough. 'Love, maybe, more than respect. I can't help but feel that the choice of any predominant creature is highly symbolic. The bag was above all filled with butterflies.'

'Clouded yellows, to be precise.'

He scratched at his stubbly chin and offered a glimmer of a smile. 'So I heard. It's quite puzzling, but I'd hazard that despite the shocking nature of the death and yes, the probable inclusion of vengeful motifs, there is a love story in there somewhere.'

Isabel frowned and looked out to sea. The waves splashed and hissed noisily against the rocks and gulls whirred above a patch of choppy water. No doubt they had discerned the presence of fish. Lost in her thoughts momentarily, she blinked when Antonio spoke softly to her.

'So shall we visit Porros? The boat's moored close by. Better now before the weather turns.'

Antonio got down on his haunches and gently stroked Furó's creamy fur. 'So *mi amic*, are you coming too?'

Isabel smiled. 'He'd love to go. Furó and I are always game for a seafaring adventure.'

It was evening by the time Isabel arrived in the environs of Colònia de Sant Jordi. She had spent an hour with Antonio roaming the scant remains of an ancient talayotic necropolis on the tiny, barren island and discussing ancient burial rites. Thanks to his insights, she had felt a seismic shift in consciousness and an inexplicable excitement; a feeling that she was now back on the scent. And why had she decided to get on her Monster and ride over to a remote area of Colònia de Sant Jordi so late at night? It had been a spur of the moment decision to observe the home of Sebi's father and for the life of her, Isabel couldn't even explain to herself why she had felt such an urgent need to do so. She was pumping adrenalin and her instincts were on high alert. Turning off the engine, she got off the bike and stretched. It had been a long day and despite the relaxing, short boat ride with the archaeologist, her body was taut and wired. Standing on a dark and deserted country lane by a clump of cypresses, she scanned the shadowy white façade of the sprawling *finca* in the near distance. A scruffy saloon car and a *moto* were parked on the drive and a solitary light shone from the porch. Furó yawned and scratched about in the soil at her feet.

'Shhh! We won't be long. Just give me a minute.'

He lay down at her feet and uttered an indignant whine.

Minutes went by, but Isabel waited doggedly... for what? As if her instincts were being tested, she remained in situ, binoculars trained on the silent house, hoping that she hadn't made a wasted trip. Suddenly, she detected activity. The front door opened and a light illuminated the *entrada* and drive. Isabel held her binoculars steady, homing them in on the young man exiting the house, carrying what appeared to be a heavy box. He seemed furtive and after looking about him, he headed for the *moto*. He spent some time attaching the load to the rear of the motorbike. Moments later, he pulled on a helmet and roared off at speed. She lowered the binoculars and looked down at Furó.

'I may be wrong, but I'm fairly sure that was Mateu, Sebi's son. The question, my friend, is why did he come here and what was in that box?'

Furó gave a grunt.

'Indeed, I agree. He appeared shifty. Perhaps he came to see his poor, ailing grandfather, but there was something apprehensive about his movements as he left the house. This is becoming a disquieting case and instinct tells me that we haven't a moment to lose.'

THIRTEEN

U nder a cornflower-blue sky, gulls hovered above the still waters of Can Repic in Soller bay. Sitting on a rock wrapped in a towel, Isabel sipped on a mug of coffee and breathed in the saline air. Furó was still paddling along the shoreline on the empty beach, chortling to himself and occasionally glancing up at Isabel. She waved to him.

'I'm still here. You won't have to run back to Sant Martí.'

Moments later her mobile rang and the name Capitán Gómez flashed up on the screen. She frowned.

'Alvaro, to what do I owe this early pleasure?'

He gave a dry cough. 'I heard that you were back at Son Real yesterday. It would be good to know your movements in advance, Isabel. I thought we were sharing information on this case.'

'So did I. I haven't heard much about your own movements, Alvaro.'

'I don't think I have to answer to a consultant for the National Police,' he scoffed.

'Ditto. I don't have to answer to you either. My boss is Tolo and as you know, I'm a free spirit. My trip to Son Real was purely

163

spur of the moment. I fancied a trip over to S'Illot de Porros with that nice archaeologist, Antonio.'

'What did he tell you? Borja and I didn't find him very helpful. He seemed to discount Borja's ritualistic killing theory.'

'So I heard. In the spirit of cooperation, I think he may be onto something. He said the death of Sebi was about love as much as hate or vengeance. A few other things you might like to know. I drove by the house of Sebi's father late last night and saw Mateu carrying a large box to his *moto*. It looked suspicious.'

'You enjoy lone nocturnal activities, don't you?' He gave a hyena laugh. 'I carried a large box to my car yesterday morning too. Does that make me seem suspicious?'

'All depends on what was in the box, Alvaro.'

'A pile of old junk to donate to Fundació Deixalles.'

Isabel grinned. 'I believe you.'

A sigh. 'Okay, Bel, is that your only intel so far on this case?'

'I'm still joining the dots. How about you?'

'I've packed Borja off home to Madrid. He was becoming a bit of a sticking plaster. Something odd about that young man.'

Isabel decided not to offer her pearls about the ghoulish character.

'You may be interested to know that we have discovered multiple threatening emails to Sebi Vives from members of Terra: Acció Ara, particularly Pablo Pons. Some are actual death threats. He therefore remains our number one suspect and his foot fits, as you discovered.'

'I think you're barking up the wrong tree. He's a hothead, but he's no fool. I don't think he'd leave a murderous paper trail if he was involved.'

The police captain snorted. 'Time will tell. We are still information-gathering, but we are confident that we have our man. I think Tolo is coming round to my way of thinking.

Remember, he has a gym and is as strong as an ox. He could snuff someone out with his little finger.'

Isabel shook her head. 'I don't think we should make any assumptions at this stage.'

He gave an impatient sigh. 'Meanwhile, any thoughts on the Tramuntana falls? The regional government has instructed us to do regular patrols of the areas of concern.'

Isabel beckoned to Furó, who had begun burrowing in the sand and was sneezing loudly.

'Areas of concern? How can anyone know where our culprit or culprits will strike next?'

'I agree.' He clicked his teeth. 'The Tramuntanas are a vast area to police, but we at the Guardia have to be seen to be doing something.'

Isabel felt a twinge of sympathy for him. It would be a thankless and impossible task.

'I climbed Serra de Son Torrella on Saturday and discovered a discarded wooden arrow that I'm bringing into the precinct today for Nacho to analyse. It had the motif of a butterfly on it. There was also evidence of fresh cairns that had been deliberately dismantled.'

'A butterfly? Could the two cases be connected?'

'I don't think so. Probably an unhappy coincidence.'

'Let's see.' He sniffed. 'Meanwhile, we have brought Frans Bordoy in for further questioning. He's a radical nut who is anti-tourists.'

'That doesn't mean he's trying to maim hikers, Alvaro. My worry is that whoever is doing this is growing bolder. Next time, we could have a fatality on our hands.'

Capitán Gómez sounded gloomy. 'My force is going to have to give this its full attention, but I will rely on you and Tolo's team to keep me apprised of any developments on the Vives case.'

'Fair enough.'

He hesitated. 'By the way, I went to interview the British walker who fell at Llucalcari and he mentioned seeing a slim young woman with long, brown hair on the track ahead of him.'

'What? Are you sure? The American who fell at Puig de Massanella saw a similar woman, as did the German hiker who took a fall at Sierra de Son Torrella.'

He coughed. 'Maybe just another coincidence.'

'Or maybe not,' she said quietly.

Isabel replaced the mobile in her pocket and exhaled deeply. Capitán Gómez could still be obnoxious, but at least there appeared to be a gradual thawing of ice between the two forces. Or was she fooling herself? In some ways she was relieved that the hiker falls would become the focus of his attention, leaving her and Tolo to pursue the Vives case without his constant intervention. However, she was unnerved by the possibility of a mysterious long-haired female stalking hikers. She stood up, yawned and whistled to Furó.

'It's eight o'clock, time for breakfast at Bar Castell. Come on, I've got a busy day ahead.'

The ferret shook the golden sand from his damp body and followed her up onto the esplanade. A local valley police officer was standing by her Ducati.

'Hey Bel. Is this Monster yours?'

She grinned. 'A birthday gift.'

He folded his arms and frowned. 'Now why don't I get birthday presents like that?'

'Maybe you haven't met the right man yet.'

Laughing, he wished her a good day and strolled back to his patrol car. She had parked illegally, of course, but what did that matter between friends?

After a scrumptious breakfast of scrambled eggs, *tostadas* with *tomate* and fresh orange juice at Bar Castell, Isabel sauntered back to Calle Pastor. As she turned into her street, she was flagged down by Señora Coll.

'Bel, if you see Doctor Ramis, can you tell him that I've had quite a fever this morning and would appreciate his popping by some time. I've asked Gori if he can man the post for me today.'

'Sorry to hear that. You should go back to bed. Is Gori not working?'

She shrugged. 'He did several shifts at his construction company over the weekend so today is his day off. He's become such a good neighbour.'

The postmistress scurried away and Isabel smiled to herself. A short while ago it would have seemed impossible that Gori and she could form such a friendship. As for her fever, Isabel had severe doubts that she was in any peril. It was well known in the village that dear Señora Coll was an inveterate hypochondriac.

Isabel entered Ca'n Moix and discovered Florentina and Doctor Ramis in her *entrada*. They were huddled over a map.

'Sometimes I wonder if you two have your own homes,' she quipped.

'Well, that's a nice thing to say when I've just packed your fridge and pantry with my homemade goodies!'

Isabel gave her a hug. 'Only kidding, Mama.'

'We're very excited, Bel,' boomed the doctor. 'A new cinema has just opened to the west of Palma. It's called Cine Paraíso and it shows vintage films in different languages. You can even order drinks and *tapas* at your seats which, by the way, are reconditioned comfy armchairs.'

'It sounds heavenly,' she replied. 'So are you planning a visit?'

'Indeed we are. This afternoon it will be premiering with *La Lengua de las Mariposas*, a masterpiece directed by José Luis

Cuerda in 1999. It's a coming-of-age film set in late 1936 when the Spanish Civil War was looming.'

Isabel nodded. '*The Tongues of Butterflies*. Believe it or not, I have the DVD upstairs. It's a bittersweet and poignant experience.'

'So true, dear Bel. I laughed, cried and cried again when I last saw it,' he said.

'Am I the only one not to have seen it?' asked Florentina. 'We could just watch Bel's DVD at home and save money.'

'Nonsense! We are invited, free of charge, to the cinema's launch party, Florentina, and seeing the film on the big screen will be much more enjoyable.'

'I hope it's not too miserable,' she replied. 'It's a very strange title. Do butterflies even have tongues?'

Isabel was pensive. 'In the film, the butterfly is a symbol of freedom and transformation. The butterfly has an *espiritrompa*, a proboscis, which is like a tube for sucking up nectar from flowers. It's not a tongue, but it looks like one as it is long and rolls up when not in use.'

Florentina shrugged. 'My biology days are long gone, but it's coming back to me now.'

'Fernando Fernán Gómez, who plays the old Republican school teacher, won a Goya, and deservedly so,' replied the doctor.

'Oh Miguel, don't spoil it for me! Shall we set off?'

He looked at his watch. 'Heavens, *si*!'

'You'll find all the bakes in the pantry and a pot of *arroz brut* on the stove. I've given scraps to Mrs Buncle and the girls in the orchard.'

'You're a wonder. The hens will love you,' Isabel replied, kissing her on the cheeks. 'Oh, by the way, Miguel, Señora Coll stopped me. She thinks she has a fever and wants you to pop by.'

He furrowed his brow. 'I'll visit her when we return. It's all attention-seeking, you know.'

No sooner had they left than there was knocking at the door. Ruben, the carpenter, stood on the doorstep clutching the transparent bag with the wooden arrow she had left with him. He handed it to her.

'I can't stop long, Bel. We're frantic today. I didn't open the bag in case of prints, as you instructed, but I can tell you that it's a cheap plywood sign, knocked up in bulk with the butterfly symbol stamped on. It's probably one of many banged up in Asia and bought online.'

'Why do you think that?' she asked.

'It's crude and flimsy. I've ordered cheap signs before for manufacturing clients and the best value is from places like China and Singapore. This is typical of those on offer. You normally buy them in big packs. Dirt cheap.'

'How many would be a minimum order for something like this?'

He scratched his head. 'Maybe one hundred?'

When he'd left, Isabel walked upstairs, ruminating on his words. If those placing the fake cairns and signposts were ordering in bulk from Asia, it sounded like they were only just kicking off their campaign of terror for hikers. Pep looked up as she entered the room.

'I've just taken bookings for five houses this morning. I'm on a roll.'

'*Enhorabuena*, Pep, shame you're not on commission, but don't put your feet up just yet. We need the cleaning team to do the laundry pick-ups today, and what about the broken gate at Can Teix in Biniaraix?'

He nodded. 'All in hand. By the way, I've compiled that list of landowners and mountain guides you wanted. It's on your desk.'

'That's impressive. Thanks.'

She walked into her office and found Furó asleep in his basket. Pep stood behind her.

'He crept in here when you were talking with Florentina. Was that Ruben's voice I just heard?'

'He brought the wooden sign back that I found on Son Torrella. He thinks it could be mass manufactured in Asia. If that's the case, whoever planted these could be planning to place a lot more in the hills.'

He groaned. 'Let's hope not. I've had a thought. I could show it to the Chinese family who run that bargain store in town. They're always friendly and might be able to suggest a source in Asia.'

'Excellent plan, although you'll have to wait until Nacho has finished with it.'

Isabel checked her emails and called Tolo at the precinct. He fairly barked.

'Sorry, Bel, a fraught morning first with the president and then a load of annoying journalists. The phones never stop.'

She laughed.

'You love it all, really.' She paused. 'A couple of things. I wanted to let you know that I was over at Sebi's paternal home late last night and spied Mateu leaving with a large box which he strapped to a *moto*.'

Tolo let out an exasperated sigh. 'I suppose there's no point in my asking why you were there in the first place?'

'Just had a strange feeling that I should be.'

He guffawed. 'And you wonder why your colleagues used to call you a *bruja* when you worked in the force. You found it suspicious?'

'Don't you?'

'Not particularly. It could have been anything. He might have been collecting nostalgic items connected to his father, such as old stamp albums. Poor kid must be in shock.'

'True, but he seemed furtive. Meanwhile, I wondered if Gaspar had confirmed my meeting with Jaume Perez and Eli Castano this afternoon?'

'Yes, he was about to call you.'

'Great. I'll pop by the precinct en route with the wooden sign I found on Son Torrella. I'd like Nacho's thoughts.'

She finished the call and sucked thoughtfully on a Chupa Chup from the pot on her desk. She was keen to speak with the couple as they had known Sebi since childhood and perhaps could offer some insights to his character and his current roster of friends and contacts. They might also offer some nuggets about Mateu. The image of the youth struggling with the box the previous night at his grandfather's home flashed before her. If only she could discover its contents... but to do that, she'd need to break in to Sebi and Sara's home, providing he'd stashed it there. She threw her car keys in her pannier along with a bag of sunflower seeds and set off for Palma.

'Taking Boadicea with you?' asked Pep.

'No, I'm driving my old friend, Pequeñito. I would never want to make him jealous.'

Having dropped the wooden sign off for Nacho at the precinct, Isabel parked up on the Paseo de Mallorca. She strolled past Es Baluard modern art museum and cut through the old town to Calle Sant Feliu. It was rare to find anyone with an apartment in this prestigious street as the cost of real estate was high. It was the preserve of politicians, bankers and wealthy foreigners looking for a sound investment, although a few ordinary mortals born and bred in Palma still clung to inherited properties bought when prices were affordable for locals. Isabel thought about Tolo's large apartment only a few minutes' walk away. He would never have been able to buy such a property had it not been inherited from his grandparents. If ever he grew tired of his onerous job, he could sell it for a small fortune and become a hick with her in the mountains.

Isabel reached the elegant historic building and examined the gleaming mahogany front door. A cleaner had evidently toiled hard to achieve such polish. She pressed the buzzer and a quiet male voice instructed her to take the lift to the second floor. Isabel took the stairs, two at a time, and arrived just as a door creaked open.

'Isabel Flores, I presume? I'm Eli Castano. Please come in.'

She shook his hand.

'What a convenient spot you have. Just near some of my favourite shops.'

Inside the bright and minimalist apartment, Isabel nodded politely as she was introduced by Eli to his husband, Jaume Perez.

Eli directed her to a plush cream sofa while Jaume got busy in the open kitchen area.

'Jaume and I got married four years ago and moved here from Llucmajor as it's close to our places of work. The prices have shot up so it turned out to be a shrewd move. All the same, this street can be noisy at night with revellers.'

'Can I get you a coffee?' Jaume called to her.

'A *cortado* would be fantastic.'

Isabel took out a small black notebook and pen and turned to Eli.

'I'm so sorry about your loss. By all accounts, Sara and Sebi were old school friends?'

He sat back in a voluminous leather armchair and puffed out his cheeks.

'We were very close. Our families lived in properties close to Llucmajor on the Algaida country road and all of us went to the same local primary and secondary schools. Mind you, Sebi's younger brother, Gabriel, was five years younger than the rest of us, as were both of my sisters. The younger kids, which included Sara, were in the same class.'

'Would you say Sebi had a happy upbringing?' asked Isabel.

Jaume retuned with steaming cups of coffee and a plate of delicate iced biscuits.

'Do help yourself. I made them myself,' he said.

Isabel's eyes lit up. She leant forward and crunched on one.

'Almond and vanilla. Delicious.'

Eli laughed. 'He's quite the chef when not being a boring lawyer.'

'I think being an accountant can eclipse that,' Jaume quipped. 'You were asking about Sebi's upbringing. He came from a normal family, but things were tough. At nineteen, his younger brother, Gabriel, tragically drowned after a drinking misadventure, then his beloved mother died of cancer a year later. His father, Martín, was a successful agronomist but withdrew into himself when his wife died.'

Eli nodded. 'It was a horrible period for Sebi. He missed his brother and mother hugely and his father was too traumatised to help him. I suppose he went off the rails for a bit with soft drugs and drink and later gambling. In fact, Sebi never really stamped out the latter habit.'

'How old was Sebi when all this happened?' Isabel asked.

He took a sip of coffee. 'Sebi was twenty-four when Gabriel died. As Sara was close to Gabriel, she and Sebi comforted one another and soon became an item. Sara helped him to clean up his act. She's a good person and did her best to make their marriage work.'

Isabel chomped on another biscuit. 'When did they marry?'

Jaume pulled on his neat black beard. 'About a year or so after they got together. Sara was already pregnant with Mateu. Eli and I weren't together then, but we both became godfathers to him.'

'Mateu is like a son to us and we're so proud of him. He is extraordinarily talented,' enthused Eli.

'Here's one of his paintings,' added Jaume.

Isabel rose to inspect the watercolour of a dreamlike rural scene on the nearby wall. 'Is that Llucmajor?'

'It's a woodland area near to Algaida. His grandmother was a well-known artist too, as you probably know. He's definitely inherited her gene. She trained in Paris and London and had exhibitions all over the world.'

'Margalida Manu?' volunteered Isabel.

'That's right. A terrible loss to the art world. She was only forty-nine when she died.'

'And what about Martín Vives? I believe he has Alzheimer's?'

Eli nodded. 'That came on about three years ago. He has a wonderful full-time carer from the Philippines named Agila, but he is in a bad way. Sebi had told us that his father was no longer able to hold a conversation and got very impatient and confused.'

His husband admonished him. 'Come on, it's a horrible disease. It must be a living hell for Martín.'

'Of course, but I'm just stating fact. Mercifully, he appears not to have fully understood that Sebi has died. Agila says that he just potters about the gardens and stares for hours at his wife's paintings and those of his dead younger son. Gabriel had shown real promise as a student and could have become a great artist, but it wasn't to be. As for Sebi's father, before long he'll probably be in a care home.'

'Agila presumably lives in?'

Jaume nodded. 'It's essential now. Mind you, I believe on her day off, which is a Monday, Martín stays in a private home overnight in Palma. She's very good with him and takes him to a care centre there a few times a week where he can socialise with other sufferers.'

'Does Mateu visit him often?' she asked.

Jaume shrugged. 'He's studying art at the University of Barcelona and rarely mentions popping by the family home when he's back here, but his grandfather's mind has gone. I doubt he's visited him this trip, but you can't blame him. He's so traumatised by his father's death.'

'Has Mateu many friends here and in Barcelona?'

'Very few that we know of,' Eli replied. 'He's a bit of a loner and always has been.'

Isabel drained her cup. 'At least you presumably all had fun together, growing up.'

Jaume smiled. 'We were always off camping and cycling at weekends and hanging out in a gang. Happy days.'

Eli nodded. 'A long time ago, but we like to share those cherished memories with Mateu.'

'Do you still have such fun?'

Eli laughed. 'I just about get to the gym once or twice a week and Jaume runs, but we don't have much free time for weekend camping trips anymore, I'm afraid.'

Isabel thanked them and headed slowly for the door. Eli asked her to wait as he rummaged about in a drawer.

'Here we all are as teens,' he said, thrusting two grainy images into her hands. 'That's Sara making the peace sign and Sebi and Gabriel are holding beer bottles. They were so close. Jaume and I are both just looking geekish.'

Isabel felt a stab of sorrow seeing the big smiles of the teenagers, their arms slung casually over one another's shoulders. She recognised a younger Sara and Sebi, both looking so happy and carefree. She handed them back to Eli.

'I wouldn't have recognised you two with those heavy specs,' she said.

Eli grinned. 'Thankfully, we've upgraded our frames since then.'

'And Gabriel was such a handsome boy. I see the family resemblance.'

Isabel reached the street and leant pensively against a wall for a few moments. Her hands shook and she had butterflies in her stomach. She took a few deep breaths and strode off in the direction of Pequeñito.

It was late and Isabel sat on her patio in jeans and heavy jumper with a blanket wrapped about her legs. There was a chill in the air, but she was engrossed in *One Hundred Years of Solitude* and enjoying a glass of Sela. It was a *rioja* she particularly savoured, and best of all she could buy it by the case at the Aubocassa farm in Manacor run by her good American friend Tiffany. As she took a long sip, her head filled with images of the unfortunate Mauricio Babilonia and the butterflies that were drawn to him. She reminded herself that his inventor, the author, Gabriel García Márquez, was a Nobel Prize winner. It was Márquez who proclaimed that 'fiction and reality are inseparable in our lives' and she heartily agreed. Where did fiction end and reality begin, or were they not forever caught in an eternal cycle? She jolted when her mobile rang. Surely it was too late for a call from anyone but Tolo, and that meant trouble.

'Tolo? It's gone midnight.'

'And you're still up. Reading?'

She yawned. 'Good guess. I was about to head off to bed, but that's not going to happen, is it?'

Tolo let out a long sigh.

'They've just discovered the body of Silvia Porres at the site of the new motorway. It's not pretty. I'm on my way there now.'

Isabel blinked hard and sat upright. 'What happened to her?'

'Run over time and again by a heavy vehicle. The first officers at the scene discovered a note pinned to the corpse. It read, "You had it coming."'

She gave a cynical grunt. 'That's convenient.'

'So, can you drive over here?'

'I've had a few glasses of wine.'

He hesitated. 'In that case, I'll send over a car. Maybe make yourself a strong coffee. It's going to be a long night.'

FOURTEEN

In light drizzle and under cool, dark skies, Isabel emerged from the police car that had ferried her from Sant Martí to the murder scene. The motorway was practically deserted save for a few bulky lorries thundering by. The construction area was flanked by orange cones and cordons, and bright LED lamps had been rigged up by the investigation team that cast anaemic white light on the dismal scene. Investigators in white garb were carefully combing the entire zone with hand-held flashlights, while a clutter of police cars and Guardia vehicles ran along the hard shoulder. Isabel took a deep breath, slipped into her white forensics suit and rubber boots and pulled on her latex gloves.

She had seen countless dead bodies in her time while serving with the National Police in Madrid, Barcelona and Mallorca, but the initial sense of shock never went away. Isabel still made the mistake of viewing corpses and imagining them as live beings with loving families and friends who would likely grieve them. She would always steel herself for the task of identification, but it never got any easier. Her thoughts were interrupted by a sharp cough. Gaspar stood eyeing her intently. He betrayed a weary aspect and rubbed his forehead.

'Bel, thanks for coming. Tolo's with the forensics team. I hope you haven't eaten.'

Isabel appreciated the attempt at levity, the coping mechanism of her police colleagues, but this time it felt forced.

'No problem. Let's go.'

They walked silently through the semi-constructed site, carefully stepping over debris, piles of sand and chunks of concrete and stone.

Isabel broke the silence. 'When was this road actually scheduled to go live?'

Gaspar shook his head. 'Originally, it was planned to open in two months' time, but that's not going to happen.'

'In the circumstances, I wonder if it will open at all.'

'Just what the environmentalists wanted.'

Isabel shot him a look. 'True, but that doesn't make them murderers. Is Gómez here?'

Gaspar shook his head. 'He's leaving this to us. Things are hotting up with his mountain stalker and he's got the tourism department and central government on his back.'

'I actually feel for him. It's impossible to man the whole Tramuntana range. The next hiker fall could end with a fatality.'

'More eco-zealots, no doubt.'

'Be careful, Gaspar. I'm a bit of an eco-zealot myself.' She grinned. 'I want clean beaches, fewer developments and the Mallorcan countryside free of rubbish.'

'So do I, but I'd draw the line at murdering people.'

As they neared the crime scene, Isabel winced in the bright lights cast from the powerful temporary lamps. Beyond tape and bollards, she could see Tolo and Nacho hovering over the corpse. As she joined them, they both looked up.

'Not a pretty sight,' opined Nacho with a frown.

Tolo offered her a fleeting smile. 'Sorry to drag you over here at this hour, but I'd like your opinion.'

Isabel got down on her haunches and examined the grotesque and mangled form before her. Fragments of clothes still clung to pieces of flesh, but it was impossible to identify the inert, semi-naked figure that lay face down in the mud. Isabel felt a stab of anger at the undignified nature of the woman's death. Who would contemplate such a vile killing and why had Silvia Porres been dealt such a vicious punishment? She slowly scanned the corpse and homed in on the matted hair, remembering the woman's bright red crop. Now it was difficult to distinguish the colour with so much dried blood.

Someone had evidently driven over the body time and again as multiple tyre marks were discernible in the caked blood. The back of the woman's broken neck had taken on a purple and black hue and a distinct crimson line was visible. Isabel carefully examined the fingers and skin and the rain-splattered ground around the corpse. With a loud sniff, she sat back on her heels.

'She was dead when she was dumped here. The blood's caked hard so I'd hazard intervention with a vehicle happened a day or two ago. Looks like some kind of ligature was used on her neck. The fingertips are missing on both hands, presumably to erase any DNA under the nails as she struggled with her assailant or assailants. The body is ice-cold and has a chemical odour, so whoever did this must have used an oxygen-based cleaner before bringing her here. I'd guess she was throttled in her own property or abducted and her corpse taken elsewhere. Whoever did this ran over the body multiple times, made a hasty clean-up operation and possibly stored the corpse in a freezer or lock-up. It looks like a heavy-duty vehicle was used, possibly a tractor or pick-up truck? It was most likely performed on a remote piece of rural land away from prying eyes. I'm assuming dumping the battered body on this site was a heavy-handed attempt at being symbolic. So, Nacho, what are your thoughts on time of death?'

Nacho raised an eyebrow. 'Impressive analysis, Bel. We estimate that she was killed yesterday in the early hours. It looks like she was strangled with some kind of plastic ligature and run over by a substantial vehicle and brought here by road.'

'Any chance of identifying the vehicle used?' she asked.

'We may be lucky enough to find some paint flakes on her clothing or identifiable residue. We've bagged the note found next to the body. It's formed of cut-out letters from a newspaper. I'll show it to you back at the precinct. There's a faint chance it contains DNA.'

'I wouldn't count on it,' growled Tolo.

'Remember that time we found one partial latent print on a piece of rubbish? All it took was some magna powder and a wand to reveal it and we got our killer. *Ánimo!*'

'*Si*, Bel, where there's death, there's hope,' he remarked dryly. 'Meanwhile, members of our forensics team visited Silvia Porres's house outside Palmanyola and found it trashed. Her computer, laptop and phone have all gone. They'll be there another few hours. Let's hope they'll give us a few fresh leads.'

'Did she live alone?'

'She had a cat,' Gaspar interjected. 'It's being picked up later tomorrow by a neighbour.'

'I'll go over there early in the morning,' Isabel replied. 'By luck, I'm seeing Pablo Pons later too.'

'This isn't going to look good for him,' replied Gaspar. 'Both the Guardia and our team have got a stack of evidence against him.'

'Still no DNA,' Isabel replied.

'Maybe not, but we do have motivation and he still can't prove his whereabouts the night of Sebi's murder,' Tolo replied crisply.

Isabel stifled a yawn. 'True, but you know as well as I do that there's more to this. We've got to close in on Marc Castell and the Mestre brothers. This has to be tied up with Construcción Castell and Sebi's awarding Marc the contract. Silvia Porres was involved somehow.'

Tolo lit a slim cigar and took a long drag.

'We need proof, so let's get onto it. Gómez wants Pons behind bars and he'll get his wish if we don't come up with something concrete.'

Tolo swivelled abruptly at the sound of footsteps and his face turned to thunder.

Isabel followed his gaze and was shocked to see Josep Casanovas sauntering towards them with a big smile, his blonde highlights glinting under the harsh spotlights.

'What the hell do you think you're doing? This is a crime scene!' boomed Tolo.

'Just doing my job.'

'How did you get wind of this?'

Casanovas grinned at him. 'We all have our private sources. Happy to see you here, Bel. Can you confirm that the deceased is Silvia Porres?'

He attempted to get a glimpse of the crime scene but was prevented by Isabel, Gaspar and Tolo, who formed a hostile wall with Nacho in front of the police tape.

Isabel stepped forward and was about to remonstrate with Casanovas just as two breathless Guardia and one of Tolo's own officers jogged over and roughly grabbed the editor's arms.

The officer caught his breath and offered Tolo a doleful expression. 'Sorry, sir. This chap just drove fast through the cordon on his *moto* and refused to stop. We'll remove him from the site.'

Tolo's face was white with rage. 'I'm taking this further, Casanovas. For now, you will be escorted to the precinct for questioning.'

'Is this a joke?'

Puffing on his cigar, Tolo quickly regained his equilibrium.

'That all depends on how humorous you find time spent in a police cell.'

Isabel folded her arms tightly as a protesting Casanovas was briskly led to a police car.

'He does chance his arm, but at least he's dedicated to his newspaper. How the heck did he find out about this, though?'

'It's the elephant in the room,' replied Tolo.

Gaspar gave a frustrated groan. 'We have a mole in-house, Bel, and the sooner we find him or her, the better for us all.'

Having snatched a few hours' sleep back in Sant Martí, Isabel rose at eight o'clock to find Pep making an omelette in the kitchen. Isabel offered a lazy smile from the doorway.

'Help yourself, Pep.'

'But you said I could eat here now that Angélica and her crazy family are on this diet. I'm starving.'

'Ah yes, of course. Well, you can make a larger one for us both while you're at it. I'll do the coffees.'

'Late night?' He smirked, cracking more eggs into a bowl.

'Another murder.'

He turned and dropped the whisk onto the floor.

'Careful, Pep.'

He gawped at her. 'Who?'

'Silvia Porres. She was discovered run-over at the site of the new motorway last night. Flattened like a chicken escalope.'

'I'm not sure I want to eat now,' he mumbled, tipping the mixture into a hot frying pan.

'You'll never make a private investigator with a weak stomach. Get a grip and finish making the omelette. Thank your lucky stars you didn't have to examine the corpse.'

He picked up a wooden spatula and busied himself at the stove.

'But why her? What's she got to do with anything? She's just a *funcionaria*. I can see why environmental groups might want to harm Sebi Vives, but she was just his sidekick, wasn't she?'

'Never make assumptions, Pep.'

He divided the omelette between two plates and cut thick slices of fresh brown bread. They sat down together at the kitchen table.

He shook his head in confusion. 'So let me get this straight. Sebi Vives was sent off to a watery death from S'Albufera most likely by those opposed to the motorway, and now Silvia Porres, his deputy, has been murdered by the same people. What I don't get is why Pablo Pons or other suspects haven't been arrested yet.'

Isabel cut her omelette and waved her fork at him. 'Where's the evidence, Pep?'

'You said that Pablo Pons didn't have an alibi for the night of Sebi's murder, presumably nor do his three TAA associates, and his footprints are a match to those at the crime scene.'

'The other three don't all have matching footprints, and besides, each has an alibi for later that night after they left Pablo's home. They were checked out by the precinct.'

'Fair enough, but Pablo Pons also sent death threats and once attacked Sebi Vives at S'Albufera. Maybe he involved other members?'

Isabel tutted. 'Grabbing at straws, but I'll give you the list of Terra: Acció Ara members and you can do some digging, if you like.'

'Great!'

'Here's another scenario. How about Sebi Vives and maybe his deputy, Silvia, were both mixed up in something murky with David, Rocci and Toni Mestre, owners of Gran Casino Atlántico. Possibly even Marc Castell from Construcción Castell?'

'Where's the evidence, Bel?'

She laughed and poured olive oil on a chunk of bread. '*Touché*!' She stared at him. 'When I spoke with Silvia Porres at the construction site, she seemed very ill at ease and was quick to tell me that she'd never been to the casino. I think she was lying.'

Pep gave a long sigh and sipped on his coffee. 'It's always like a messy jumble of jigsaw pieces, but then you always solve the case.'

Isabel smiled. 'Well, dear Watson, I really hope you're right.'

The drab house belonging to Silvia Porres sat on the edge of a huddle of unattractive detached properties on the outskirts of Palmanyola. The dormitory town belonged to the municipality of Bunyola yet had enjoyed the status of 'minor local entity' since 1985. This sobriquet offered the town few advantages save to appear less of an adjunct to Bunyola and more of a *pueblo* in its own right. Many residents worked in the capital and had an easy commute to nearby Palma while enjoying the benefits of living in a more rural setting. According to Gaspar, Silvia had apparently inherited her childhood house from her mother after spending some years living away. It would have proven a convenient bolthole for her government job in Palma.

Isabel left Pequeñito close to the front gates, stepped over the police cordon and walked up the drive. The front garden was overgrown and mature cypresses surrounded the property, making it secure and private. If Silvia had been attacked in her own home, she would have stood little chance of attracting her closest neighbours' attention. The nearest house was a few minutes' walk away and obscured by huge metal gates. As Isabel looked around her, a voice called out.

'Hey, this is a crime scene. You're not allowed on the property.'

Isabel turned and flashed her badge at the young police officer.

'Hm, and why were you not on duty at the front gates?'

He turned red. 'I'm sorry, *señorita*. I needed a pee and my senior officer has just gone off to get coffees and *ensaïmadas*. We've been here all night.'

She smiled. 'Don't worry, but maybe next time coordinate so one of you is always on duty.'

'You won't tell him about this when he gets back?'

'That all depends. How about you call him and ask for an extra *ensaïmada* and a *cortado* and we'll call it quits?'

He nodded, unsure how to respond, but he quickly called his colleague.

'He was just in the café so I caught him in time.'

'Lucky for you.' She grinned.

On the doorstep, she donned her forensics suit and shoes.

'Can you let me into the house?'

'Of course.'

The young man unlocked the front door. 'Shall I accompany you?'

'No, thanks.'

'There's a cat somewhere. Not sure where. Big hairy thing. I'm a dog man myself.'

'I love all animals but a ferret has stolen my heart.'

'Really?' He smiled awkwardly and with a look of confusion, nodded and quickly departed.

Isabel stood in the silent, dark abode. The air was dank. Turning on the dull hall light, she raised an eyebrow at the devastation around her. Cupboard doors had been wrenched off their hinges, the bellies of cushions gutted so that their contents spilled out onto the tiled floors and drawers had been upturned. The English expression 'leave no stone unturned' came to mind. She learnt it from her fastidious father during his interminable English lessons as a child. With a gloved hand she began to examine the walls and surfaces. The forensics team had evidently done their bit, but small details could sometimes be overlooked.

Upstairs, in the master bedroom, soft, white feathers lay scattered about the floor, the casualties of pillows that had been ripped apart. The mattress stood upright against a wall, its belly savagely torn open to reveal foam and springs.

'What were you looking for, I wonder?' said Isabel out loud.

Her attention was diverted to a fur fabric cat basket, accompanied by toys and a scratching post. Silvia evidently loved her cat. The two smaller bedrooms had also been violated and the bathroom's mirrored cupboard smashed and hurled into the bath. Coloured towels had been pulled out of a cupboard and lay in a disorderly heap on the floor.

In the kitchen, she bent down and explored the contents of a cleaning cupboard under the sink. She found bottles of *amoníaco*, an ammonia-based cleaner, and also *agua fuerte*, two fiery products she had banned her mother using in her home. The contents of the bin had been taken away, presumably by the forensics team. She smelled all the surfaces, got down on hands and knees and sniffed the floor. She was interrupted when an officer appeared with a coffee and an *ensaïmada* pastry wrapped in tissue paper.

He grinned. 'Having fun down there?'

'Oh yes, just doing my early morning yoga moves. Is that for me?'

'Sure. I take it you're Isabel Flores? Tolo Cabot asked us to look after you. I'm Pere.'

Isabel stood up and shook his hand. 'Your colleague outside was very helpful.'

'Good to hear. He's new to the force.'

Isabel took a sip of coffee. 'Thanks for breakfast.'

'My pleasure. Anything you need?'

'Have you met the neighbours?'

'There's a weird old guy living in the closest house. Didn't seem to know Silvia Porres at all and hadn't seen or heard anything. A young woman a few doors down hadn't seen Silvia's car for a few days but said she kept to herself. Most of the other houses are vacant.'

'Really? I thought this was a commuter town.'

He nodded. 'True, but a lot of people in Palma have weekend places here too.'

When he'd left, Isabel opened the French doors to a walled garden and looked up at the leaden sky. Hungrily demolishing her pastry, she inspected the miserable turf. Even with a recent shower of rain, it was stubbornly dry and ill-nourished. There were few plants in the borders and those that did grow, mainly ivy, were yellowed and frail. Leaves clogged the drains, and old and cracked terracotta pots stood empty. Bending down, Isabel discovered a wet cigarette butt and a biro lid under a plastic pot and as was routine, sealed them in a bag to take back to the forensics team.

'Not much of a gardener, were you, Silvia?' she muttered.

There was a meow and a large, grey Persian walked along the high wall. She called to it and it jumped down, seemingly keen for company. Isabel inspected its collar and read the name 'Lobo' out loud.

'Wolf? Well, you're certainly a beauty. Hairy thing, indeed!' She paused. 'I'm sorry for your loss.'

The cat accompanied Isabel as she walked slowly around the garden. At the far end of the patchy lawn was a clutter of aged and broken brooms, spades and pitchforks and a small barbecue on wheels. She opened the lid; the remnants of recently burnt coals lingered inside. Why would Silvia be preparing barbecues for herself in the winter? Or had it served another purpose? Carefully, she sifted through the ashes with a gloved finger until a tiny fragment of glossy card caught her eye. It was scorched but still held its red colour and displayed a single typed digit. What was it? Maybe a matchbook? The figure nine was clear, but would it prove any kind of steer? She slipped it into a clear bag and sat on a damp bench, sipping her coffee. The cat rubbed against her legs and finally jumped onto her lap, purring when she stroked its long, damp hair.

'Are you hungry, Lobo? I thought someone from the force was supposed to have fed you.'

The cat mewed pitifully.

'I'll find you something in the house.'

As she rose, she noticed an upturned bin and, lying next to it, a large crumpled piece of decaying tarpaulin. She tutted. What a sad and joyless garden this was, and yet it had such potential. Maybe Silvia had prioritised scaling the greasy rungs of the political career ladder over allowing herself time out in the natural world. Stretching, she yawned and strode over to the tarpaulin and kicked it over. A host of beetles, slugs and bugs clung to the underside and recoiled at the light and sudden exposure.

'Sorry, old chaps, but there's something odd going on here.'

She got down on her haunches and ran a hand over the soil. It was different from the rest of the earth in the garden and looked as though it had been freshly dug. Isabel plucked one of the old spades languishing against a wall and pushed it into the turf. It was soft and compliant and before long the spade hit something metallic. In some excitement, Isabel squatted down and cleared away the surface soil and began removing it with her hands until the lid of a large container became clear. She pushed a tendril of dark, curly hair back from her forehead, took a few deep breaths and prised it open. Inside were countless tightly rolled bundles of 500-Euro notes, always the choice of the criminal fraternity. She gave a low whistle.

'Well I never! What had you got mixed up in, Silvia?'

The cat came over to inspect her prize and, unimpressed, padded off towards the French doors. Isabel stood up and brushed the soil from her jacket.

'Sometimes, Lobo, you hit the jackpot, and today is one of those days. Now for your breakfast.'

It was five o'clock by the time Isabel reached Muro. As she approached the house of Pablo Pons, she contemplated what she might learn from him about his relationship with Silvia Porres. Her death had yet to be announced and with Josep Casanovas currently languishing in a police cell, there would hopefully be no news leakage. All the same, Gaspar had mentioned a mole in the force. Who might that be?

She was hungry, having driven straight from the precinct after delivering the metal container of bank notes and other items of potential interest that she had found at Silvia Porres's home. She had spent a long time going over the forensics with Nacho, frustrated that there was still little to go on. Tolo and

Gaspar had been jubilant about her discovery at the home of Silvia Porres, convinced that her assailants had known about the hidden treasure and murdered her when she refused to divulge its location. Isabel felt there had to be more to it than a simple robbery. Why had Silvia's killers risked transporting her corpse to one unknown location and then all the way over to the site of the new motorway? More to the point, where had the money come from? According to Tolo, the motorway project had now been frozen by the regional government until the police investigation was complete. Gaspar and the team had traced offshore payments made to the Mestre brothers from a personal account held by Sebi Vives and were keen to question them.

To her disappointment, before she left the precinct, Nacho had returned the wooden butterfly sign that she had found in the hills, telling her that it bore no DNA. She would need to pursue another avenue with Pep's help.

Pablo Pons opened the front door before Isabel had reached the porch. He was pale and agitatedly flexing his fingers.

'I'm glad you're here. That Guardia captain came by earlier. He's trying to pin the murder of Sebi Vives on me. I had nothing to do with his death. You have to believe me.'

Isabel wearily rubbed her eyes. 'Can I come in?'

They entered a back office. Pablo closed the door and she took a seat by the window. A pretty garden beckoned from beyond.

'Can I get you a coffee or water?'

'A *cortado*, if that's on the menu.'

He nodded and got busy with a coffee machine.

'That Guardia captain…'

'Capitán Gómez?'

He nodded. 'He said that they will shortly arrest me if I cannot confirm an alibi for the night of Sebi's murder. He said the evidence against me was overwhelming. It's absurd. I didn't move from here that night.'

Isabel took the coffee he proffered and regarded him seriously.

'You don't do yourself any favours, Pablo. There's a stack of hostile correspondence from you to Sebi. It's all on file. There are death threats.'

He threw his hands in the air. 'It's just angry rhetoric. People write insane things in diaries, but it doesn't mean that they'll realise those fantasies and thoughts.'

'It's been known, though,' she replied with a thin smile. 'Why don't you start by telling me if you had dealings with any other people in Sebi's office.'

He frowned. 'Such as?'

Isabel pulled a packet of sunflower seeds from her pannier and began cracking them open with her teeth. 'His deputy, for example, Silvia Porres.'

Pablo Pons gave a cynical guffaw. 'That woman is vile. A few months ago, we organised a peaceful demo outside the transport offices in Palma and she came downstairs to lambast us. I decided to find out a bit more about her background and even followed her a few times.'

'Do you fancy stalking charges too, Pablo?'

He shrugged. 'Okay, it wasn't clever, but I made a discovery.'

'Care to share?'

He formed a pyramid with his fingers. 'I ran a Google search on her which didn't offer much information, but by chance I tried its image bank, and bingo. I discovered an old image of her in an El Corte Inglés uniform with some colleagues. It came from a food trade magazine celebrating a promotion in the store's gourmet department. Therefore, the woman was poorly qualified to work in the regional government.'

Isabel munched on a handful of seeds and placed the husks in her saucer. 'The gourmet section has got some great products, so don't knock it.'

He took on a confidential air. 'Look, I haven't told anyone in authority about this, but she visited the Gran Casino Atlántico on two occasions last month. I followed her from the office and have the dates in my diary. It was at night and she was carrying a rucksack.'

Isabel yawned. 'Lots of people do, including me. It's not an offence.'

'But to a casino?' he yelled.

'Okay, Pablo. Is that all you've got?'

He cleared his throat. 'One more thing. Just two weeks ago, I followed Vives and Porres to S'Albufera.'

'This sounds like obsession. Do you ever do any work?'

He issued a tut. 'Hear me out. I'd been parked at their offices all afternoon waiting for either to leave so I could confront them about the motorway. I wanted to plead with them to shelve it pending an environmental report from GOB.'

'A little late for that, I'd have thought.'

'As it happened, at about eight o'clock they emerged together. I was on the point of getting out of the car but saw that they were yelling at one another. Moments later they drove off at speed in their two cars, so I followed them all the way to S'Albufera.'

Isabel shook her head. 'Why didn't you mention any of this before?'

'Can you imagine how it would look? As you say, stalking is an offence.'

Isabel swigged the last drops of her coffee. 'So what happened next?'

Pablo rubbed his chin and exhaled deeply. 'They met a man on the Englishman's Bridge and walked together to the park. They were furtive and seemed to be arguing as they went inside.'

Isabel plonked her cup down on a desk. 'But who was the man?'

'It was Marc Castell from Construcción Castell.'

'It was dark.'

'No. There was enough light on the bridge. It was Marc.'

'You're absolutely sure?' asked Isabel, offering him an intense stare.

'Without a shadow of a doubt.'

By the time Isabel had returned to Pequeñito, her stomach was rumbling furiously. She patted the dashboard and gave a sigh.

'We're both hungry, my little *amigo*. You need petrol and I need a plate of something warm and delicious, perhaps *arroz brut* or something fishy.'

Her mobile rang. It was Tolo.

'How did it go, Bel?'

'I've just left Pablo Pons. If what he told me is true, we have something to get our teeth into. He's agreed to make a statement at the precinct and have a DNA swab.'

'Excellent, but I'll have to inform Gómez as he's been gunning for Pons and is convinced he's our man.'

'I think he's got enough going on with the mountain menace for now,' she replied.

'Maybe, but better to keep the beast on side. Meanwhile, are you free to visit Sara Vives? Our protection officer at the house says she's been strung out over the death of Silvia Porres. She specifically asked if you might pop by.'

Isabel frowned. 'As long I can cadge a late snack somewhere on the way. I'm starving.'

'Nothing new there.'

'I might shock you and join Llorenç on his diet.'

He chuckled. 'Heaven forbid.'

Moments later, Isabel set off from Muro in the direction of Llucmajor. Despite keeping her eyes trained on the near-empty country road, she'd occasionally glance furtively to one side or another in the hope of finding a restaurant still open for a very late lunch. A sign offering a *menú del día* caught her eye and she pulled over. By chance, a man in an apron was standing in the doorway of the restaurant, enjoying a cigarette. Isabel leant out of her window.

'Are you still open?'

He nodded. 'What do you want, *reina*?'

Isabel smiled. 'Any chance of hot food? I've been on the run for work and haven't had a chance to eat much today.'

The man ground his cigarette underfoot and disappeared into the building. Moments later he returned.

'*Pues*, the lunch menu is finished, but cook says she still has some spinach *croquetas* and baked cod with a spicy tomato sauce and potatoes. She's also got a delicious *crema Catalana* and baked apples for dessert.'

'Fantastic,' Isabel replied.

Parking the car, she walked briskly into the restaurant and sat at a cheery table with a blue checked cloth. The man brought her some water, a basket of fresh bread, olives and *alioli*.

'So what can I get you?'

'I'll have what you suggested.'

'What, everything, *reina*?' he asked in surprise.

'Yes, everything.' She beamed.

Isabel enjoyed her drive to Llucmajor. She had a full stomach and so all was well with the world. There were still many puzzling aspects to the Sebi Vives case, but she had begun to feel a new confidence as threads slowly began to unravel. She parked in the drive of Sara Vives's *finca* and took stock. Three sleek black Audis were parked close by, all beautifully maintained. The protection officer was already walking towards her, a grin on his face.

'If it isn't our Bel. How are you doing these days?'

Isabel hugged the uniformed officer.

'Manel! It's been so long. How's life?'

He shrugged. 'All good. I'm married now and have a nipper. Swapped to protection work a year ago and am loving it. I heard you were back on the force.'

She laughed. 'Just dabbling on the odd case.'

He lowered his voice and checked they were not in earshot.

'Señora Vives seems in a bad way. She's got two of the politicians' wives with her today. I think the latest murder has really got her on edge.'

'You can't blame her, really. It's been a torrid time.'

He nodded. 'Horrible goings-on. Any leads yet on Sebi Vives's murder?'

She sighed deeply. 'Nothing concrete just yet.'

The front door opened and Sara stood in the light of the hallway, a wistful expression on her face. She was no longer wearing her neck brace and a pale blue scarf was slung about her neck. Her fair hair fell about her lean shoulders. Isabel nodded to Manel and set off towards the porch.

Sara offered her hand. 'Thanks for coming, Bel. I'm sorry to have dragged you back here.'

'Not at all. It's my job.'

They walked into the kitchen where Mariana Blasi, looking effortlessly elegant, leant against a kitchen counter, a glass of white wine in her hand. Standing close by was a trim, petite woman with a glossy dark bob and sparkling eyes. She was wearing Lycra and chewing on what Isabel assumed to be nuts.

Mariana smiled. 'Hello, detective. Good to see you again. Can I get you a glass of something?'

'Just water, thanks.'

The other woman stepped forward and with a grin shook her hand. 'I am Fran Grau Puig, Mariana's sister-in-law. Nice to meet you. I've just come straight from my Pilates studio and I'm starving. I'm on the hunt for nuts or something healthy.'

Isabel laughed. 'I was ravenous today too. I've just had a late meal at a country restaurant.' She paused. 'You are the wife of the president, Teo Puig.'

The woman rolled her eyes. 'Indeed I am. One of the crosses I have to bear. We girls are all politicians' wives.'

'Well, I'm not anymore,' replied Sara quietly, clutching a tissue.

Fran scrunched her shoulder and whispered, '*Ánimo*!'

Isabel smiled at Fran and attempted to lift the mood.

'You look very fit. Do you attend many Pilates classes?'

The woman burst out laughing. 'I have no choice. It's my studio, so I have to set a good example to my clients. We have an exclusive gym and a nutritionist, physio and personal trainer on the premises. I'm also an experienced reflexologist.'

'It's in Palma?' quizzed Isabel.

'*Sí*, just off Jaime III. You must come for a complimentary session, though you look like you work out.'

'I swim in the sea most mornings and I like to run and hike.'

Fran looked at her in approval. 'Wow, a real action girl.'

When they were all sitting in the living room, Isabel turned to Sara.

'I can imagine that the murder of Silvia Porres must have unnerved you.'

The woman snuffled into her tissue and cleared her throat. 'It came as such a shock. I knew Silvia well and she and Sebi worked closely together. These eco-warriors are completely insane. How can they justify murdering two people so horribly while parading their green credentials? It sickens me. Who's next? Me?' She burst into tears.

'We don't know yet who is responsible for these deaths, but we will find the killers and they will face justice. As for your own safety, we will continue to ensure that you have around-the-clock protection.'

The other women listened intently. Mariana sighed.

'Teo tells me that Pablo Pons and his dubious associates at TAA are the main suspects. It is despicable that poor Silvia and Sebi should be the unwilling martyrs for their deluded cause.'

Fran nodded as she munched furiously on some smoked almonds.

'I hope they are swiftly arrested. Is there still not sufficient evidence to charge Pons?'

Isabel took a sip of water and surveyed them all.

'Ladies, I appreciate your concern and sense of frustration, but this is privileged information that is not yet in the public domain.'

Fran nodded. 'I'm sorry. You're right. My husband probably shouldn't have shared such sensitive intel, but as you know we are all very close and we girls are best friends.'

'I understand,' Isabel replied.

Sara gulped down some tears. 'Have you no leads at all about how these monsters managed to lure poor Sebi off the road? What about CCTV or witnesses that night?'

Isabel chose her words carefully. 'When we know more, I'll be able to give you a clearer picture of how things stand.'

Fran licked her salty fingers. 'But was there no evidence left at the crime scene? In these police dramas they usually find DNA or something.'

Isabel tutted. 'Sadly, police dramas are works of fiction. Reality is a different matter altogether.'

She turned to Sara. 'Meanwhile, I would appreciate having a few words privately with your son. Is he here?'

Sara's eyes opened wide. 'Whatever for? He's grieving his father and is in no way involved in this tragedy.'

'It's purely routine. Mateu is not implicated in any way.'

The women all exchanged tense expressions before Fran spoke.

'I think it would be good for you to speak with him. He's been very quiet with all of us and might like to be able to confide in someone outside of our circle.'

Sara rose stiffly and called to Mateu from the bottom of the grand staircase. A door banged open and he jogged down the steps, looking wan and nervous.

Isabel offered him her most reassuring of smiles.

'Mateu, might I have a quick word with you privately in the garden? It's just a routine chat.'

'None of this will be official?' his mother asked.

'Not at all,' Isabel replied.

Isabel followed the tall, hunched youth out onto the back terrace and together they walked away from the house. She stopped next to a bench and indicated for them to sit. He eyed her warily as he dug his hands into the pockets of his hoodie.

'So, Mateu, I know this must be painful for you, but could you tell me about your relationship with your father?'

He shrugged. 'We got on okay, but I never saw him that much. He was always so busy in his political work.'

'And of course you have been away at university the last year.'

He gave a brittle laugh. 'I've always been away. They sent me to boarding school in Madrid when I was eleven, so I've only been here during holidays since then. Most summers, Mum and I went abroad for a few weeks, sometimes to the Caribbean or the United States. My dad never joined us as he was always working. Just as well.'

'What do you mean?'

He looked uneasy. 'Put it this way, they were always bickering about one thing or another. Much like most married couples, I guess.'

'Did he ever do fun things with you such as fishing or going for country walks?'

'No way. Anyway, my dad hated insects and fish of any kind, especially eels. It was a kind of phobia.'

'What about the rest of your holidays?'

He sat back and folded his arms.

'I spend a lot of time working on my art projects and still have a few old friends on the island. I hang out a lot with my godfathers and try to see my grandfather a bit, though he's unwell.'

Isabel nodded. 'Yes, I heard about your grandfather's Alzheimer's. Have you seen him since you got home?'

He hesitated and looked her firmly in the eye. 'No, not yet. It's been a really upsetting time and I've tried to be at home as much as I can to support Mum.'

'Of course.'

Isabel rose from the bench. There was a bite in the cool night air. 'Is that one of your Audis parked in the drive?'

Mateu gave a scoffing laugh. 'No, I've got a *moto*. Those cars belong to Fran, Mariana and my mum. My dad has a few old cars in the garage, but I prefer motorbikes. Every Adelante Mallorca politician has an Audi. Maybe they got a discount from the local dealer.'

Isabel laughed as they strolled back across the lawn. 'So what do you think about the new motorway?'

He stopped to look at her. 'I am totally against the new motorway and it made me mad that Dad went ahead with it. We argued about it all the time and now it's killed him.'

Isabel frowned. Fran's husband was the president, Teo Grau, and he gave the project his approval. 'Do you feel anger towards Fran and her husband?'

He gave an impatient shake of the head. 'Of course not. I've known Fran since I was a kid and the same goes for Mariana. They are like family and have always been there for Mum. It's not their fault that they married those...'

He gave an exasperated groan and strode ahead. Once in the house, he said a curt goodbye and went straight to his room. In the living room, Isabel was surprised to find Sara lying on the sofa with her eyes closed and bare feet extended. Fran sat massaging them gently and offering soothing words. She smiled across at Isabel.

'I'm giving Sara a little reflexology. It is so relaxing.'

'It looks it. Did you have to train for some years?'

She nodded. 'Actually, feet are my thing. I have a lot of experience working with them. It's amazing what you can discover about the human body from a foot.'

Mariana giggled. 'I could do with one of your massages after my mammoth cycling session on Sunday. My feet are still feeling it.'

'Where did you go?' asked Isabel.

'I'm preparing for a three-hundred-kilometre island race in April and a tougher one in the autumn. It'll be a five-hundred-kilometre challenge over two weeks. I'm raising money to help build a hospital for a small indigenous community in Bolivia. In truth, with my work schedule I'm not sure I'll get in enough training.'

Sara's eyes popped open. 'Don't listen to her. She's done loads of triathlons and races. She's one of the most competitive people I know.'

The women laughed as Fran poured them all another glass of wine. Isabel gave a discreet yawn and, heaving on her warm jacket, headed over to Sara.

'Don't get up. I can easily see myself out.'

Sara smiled. 'Thanks so much for coming over. You make me feel so safe and reassured.' She paused. 'Was Mateu helpful?'

'Very. He filled in some gaps,' she replied.

Isabel took her empty glass and wandered into the kitchen while the women chatted in the other room.

Mariana tutted when she returned. 'You didn't have to do that.'

Isabel hesitated briefly as she bent to say goodbye to Fran. Sara's pale feet bore two small tattoos and her toenails were painted a glossy red.

'Nice nails,' she said with a wink.

Sara sighed. 'Thanks, it's the simple routines and pleasures that get us through each day.'

Isabel took her leave and quietly closed the front door behind her. Manel was standing by the entrance gate and gave her a wave. She opened the car door and, biting a fingernail, stared up at the emerging white stars. They seemed cold, sharp, fragile and just a touch hostile. With a shiver, she started the engine, happy to be heading home.

FIFTEEN

A bright orange sun glimmered in the sky as Isabel sat on the balcony of Bar Castell, munching on a fluffy *ensaïmada*. Rafael suddenly appeared with a copy of *El Periódico* and a fresh *cortado*.

'You're not going to like the headline,' he drawled. 'Mind you, what can you expect from the Sunflower King.'

Isabel's brow furrowed as she pulled the newspaper towards her and cursed loudly.

'Told you,' he said, flipping a crumpled tea towel over his shoulder. 'He's really got it in for the National Police.'

Isabel swore under her breath. 'No, Josep Casanovas just loathes Tolo. It's an old enmity.'

She began reading a line. '"The police investigation into the shocking death last Monday of respected transport minister, Sebi Vives, appears to have yielded no answers to date. At a press conference held at the National Police precinct in Palma on Monday, eccentric chief of police, Tolo Cabot, was clearly under pressure, stating only that he and his team were following several lines of enquiry."'

Isabel looked up at Rafael.

'What was Tolo supposed to say?'

He shrugged. 'It'll all come right in the end.'

Isabel was relieved to see that there was no mention of a corpse found at the Búger motorway site. Maybe the editor and esteemed mayor of Forn de Camp was still languishing in a cell at the precinct, though she doubted it. All the same, she imagined that Tolo would not have allowed Casanovas his liberty without somehow preventing him going public on the discovery of Silvia Porres's body. She called his mobile.

'How's your day?'

He gave a gravelly cough. 'Oh, just dandy. I've had to release that squirming little worm, Casanovas, from his cell. I let him sweat there for most of the day until he signed a legal document agreeing not to report on the Silvia Porres murder until tomorrow when we release our own statement.'

'Ouch. I'm sure you two are now closer than ever. Listen, I've got a meeting with Llorenç and Gómez midday, but I have a lot to report back. I had an interesting encounter last night with Sara Vives and the wives of the president and transport minister.'

Tolo sniggered. 'You do like to keep elevated company.'

'I managed to have a private word with Sebi's son, Mateu. He told me that he didn't see eye to eye with his father about the new motorway. More importantly, he lied to me about visiting his grandfather's house on Sunday night.'

'That's interesting. I wonder what was in that box you saw him carrying.'

'I intend to find out,' Isabel replied. 'We need answers.'

'Should we get a search warrant?'

'I'd rather not. We don't want to arouse any suspicion.'

Tolo gave a grunt. 'Okay, your call. Meanwhile, Nacho needs to get you up to speed on the latest forensics report. He now has the analysis of the footprints found by the canal at S'Albufera on the night of Sebi's death.'

Isabel clicked her teeth. 'There's a switched-on forensic podiatrist in Barcelona who Nacho rates. A brilliant woman,' she replied.

'It's she who has done the analysis with estimates of the height, weight and physical state of the assailants.'

Isabel knocked back the dregs of her coffee. 'Forensic podiatry is an extraordinary science.' She thought back to her time as a rookie at the Madrid police academy when they studied one of the earliest instances of its use at a crime scene in Glasgow in 1862. A woman named Jessie McLachlan was accused of bludgeoning a female servant friend to death and the police used photographic evidence of her footprints in court. It was a celebrated case, and although McLachlan was found guilty, public opinion was divided. In the end, she avoided being hanged and served fifteen years in prison. She always maintained her innocence and blamed the elderly father in the servant's household.

'In 1862, a Scottish woman was found guilty of murder based on her footprints but it wasn't conclusive.'

Tolo laughed. 'How do you remember all this historical stuff?'

'Because it's fascinating. Anyway, after serving a prison sentence, she ended up remarrying and emigrating to America.'

'But do you think she was guilty?' he teased.

'Ah, who can say, but her feet certainly tripped her up.'

Tolo guffawed. 'So when can we catch up at the precinct?'

'Today is difficult. I need to get to grips with this worrying case closer to home.'

'The hiker falls?'

'Exactly. That's why we're all meeting later. I think Llorenç would appreciate my input.'

'As would Gómez, if he'd care to admit to it.'

Isabel looked up. Pep was heading towards her table wearing a perplexed expression.

'I've got to go, Tolo. Let's catch up at the precinct tomorrow morning. Dinner at mine this weekend?'

'You bet, *cariño*.'

Isabel put her mobile in her pannier and stood up. 'Everything okay?'

Pep frowned. 'I've just taken a call from one of the young German couples renting Can Vidal here. They say that their friends, Susanne and Klaus, have gone missing.'

'When?'

'Yesterday morning Susanne and Klaus said they were going to hike to the ruins of Pla des Porxo near the Puig de Moncaire and haven't returned. Their bed has not been slept in and both their mobiles are dead.'

Isabel shook her head impatiently. She went to the bar and paid. With Pep on her heels, she hurried down the steps to the *plaça*.

'And their friends have only just noticed?'

Pep remonstrated. 'In fairness, they had gone to Palma for the day and stayed overnight in that swanky Sant Francesc Hotel. They only returned to the house this morning and discovered that Susanne and Klaus were missing.'

'Were they not in touch with them by phone yesterday?'

He shrugged. 'Apparently not. They left for Palma around lunchtime and spent the day there visiting the sights.'

Isabel fixed Pep with an intense stare. 'Have you called Llorenç or the Guardia yet?'

'I've only just found out. I tried to call you, but your line was busy, so I thought I'd run over to get you at Bar Castell.'

They walked through the quiet *plaça* towards the town hall. Isabel and Pep bounded up the main staircase only to find Llorenç's office abandoned. Even his faithful secretary, Maria, was absent. Josep, the morbid caretaker, approached them with a long face, his matted, greying hair askew.

'Llorenç is at a meeting with all the local mayors until this afternoon and Maria is off sick. She looked terrible this morning before she left.'

'I'm sorry to hear that. Thanks, Josep. I'll call him later,' Isabel replied.

He gave a sniff. 'I was here late last night and heard a fearful bang from the mayor's office. It was him again.'

Pep's eyes opened wide. 'Who again?'

'Antonio Ribes, of course. The phantom of the town hall. I opened the door and there he was floating about, not a stitch of clothing on him and covered in boils as big and purple as plums.'

'Yuck!' Pep pulled a face. Isabel stifled a yawn, having heard about the alleged sightings of the seventeenth-century aristocratic and plague-ridden ghost many times before from Josep. She turned to the elderly caretaker.

'I hope you didn't frighten Maria with the story this morning.'

He offered her a lugubrious expression. 'Well, I felt duty bound to inform her. After all, the poor woman is stuck in that office all alone for much of the day.'

He wandered off muttering to himself, his gait slow and laboured.

Isabel beckoned to Pep and they set off back to the *plaça*, where Isabel called Capitán Gómez.

'A mountain search and rescue operation? Come, Bel. Could it just be that this couple returned to the rental property last night and left early this morning for another excursion?'

'I did think of that, Alvaro. However, their bed has not been slept in and their mobiles are dead. I'm concerned that our mountain menace could have something to do with this.'

'That's all we need,' he replied glumly. 'Very well, we'll organise an initial search party in the area. I'll go up there myself with a Guardia team and alert mountain rescue. Why on earth did these tourists choose Pla des Porxo? It's off the beaten track.'

'I agree, but there are some interesting ruins there and of course they might have gone further and climbed Puig de Moncaire. It has great views.'

'I suppose you've climbed it?' he drawled.

'A few times. It's quite an arduous route for novices. Will you start at the Moncaire Estate?'

'It'll prove fastest. I will inform the staff.'

'I'll join you on the search.'

'Is that really necessary, Bel?'

'Yes, I'd like to support your operation, and I'm quite familiar with the area. Besides, they are my clients and I want to know that they're okay.'

There was silence for a second. 'Always so thoughtful, Bel,' Capitán Gómez replied in a sarcastic tone.

'It's serendipitous that we're due to meet later today with Llorenç too.'

He grunted. 'A whole day together, Bel. How fortunate am I.'

The line went dead. Isabel shrugged and headed with Pep via the cut-through close to the church. As they turned right into Calle Pastor, Señora Coll appeared before them.

'Ah, Bel, I've just been collecting my special pills from Doctor Ramis. They are a lifesaver.'

Isabel exhaled deeply. 'Marvellous. How lovely you look today. What a pretty shawl.'

The elderly matron leant forward confidentially.

'To be honest, I have an ugly plaster on my neck where the cat scratched me this morning. A shawl hides it perfectly.'

As Señora Coll headed off, Isabel stared thoughtfully after her before taking out her mobile and leaving a hurried message on Llorenç's phone.

'He'll want to know about this latest hiker episode.'

Pep nodded. 'You bet. He'll be grumpy that he's not here to share the drama even though the zone where the couple have gone missing is far more relevant to the mayors of Fornalutx and Escorca.'

Isabel shot him a warning look.

'You may joke, but Llorenç really cares about the village and the welfare of its visitors. They are staying in Sant Martí so of course he needs to be involved.'

Duly chastised, Pep nodded. 'Fair enough, but you've got to admit that he does love a crisis.'

Isabel conceded the point and winked. 'It's probably the adrenalin rush, which as we know is a rare sensation for residents of our sleepy village.'

They arrived back at Ca'n Moix and Isabel went upstairs and changed into her hiking gear. She gathered together her GPS device, dynamic rope, carabiners, harness and *cinta* Americana – always good for fixing broken items temporarily – and hastily packed them in a rucksack. Pep popped his head around the door and raised an eyebrow at the pile of items on Isabel's bed. There was a woolly hat and gloves, compass, small hammer, knife, space blankets, head torch and walking pole.

'Are you taking all that clobber to Pla des Porxo?'

'The mountain rescue team will hopefully have all the necessary gear, but I like to be prepared.'

Pep inspected a whistle attached to a carabiner on her rucksack and chuckled. 'I doubt this will be much use.'

'It's old school, but whistles can save lives when technology fails. It's the same with compasses and this.' Isabel held out a wind-up torch that required no batteries.

'You could survive in a jungle with all this.'

Isabel smiled. 'I have.'

In the kitchen she tucked some tasty treats into the side pockets of her rucksack along with energy bars and water. Furó eyed her keenly and began whining and chasing his tail.

'Calm down. I've packed your supplies too. Come on.'

At the front door, Pep touched her arm. 'Don't take any risks.'

'As if.'

'By the way, is the windscreen wiper holding out after Bernat fixed it?'

Isabel grinned. 'If I get back, I'll let you know.'

The mountain road to Lluc was fairly quiet, though Isabel imagined that the rescue and Guardia teams would already have arrived at the nearest point to explore the area. Singing loudly, she coursed along the road, breathing in the fresh cool air. Meanwhile, Furó snuggled inside his comfy blanket on the passenger seat, occasionally peering out of the open window to enjoy the forest views, his glossy fur rippling in the breeze. At the sign for the Moncaire Estate, Isabel took a left turn. The owners would be away at this time of the year, but the manager would already be apprised of the situation. To prove the point, a Guardia officer stood at the entrance to the track. He inspected Isabel's police badge and waved her through. Pequeñito bumped along the track, a little out of sorts when Isabel swung a fast left and then a sharp right. A Guardia van and two abandoned mountain rescue vehicles were parked up on a verge ahead of her. Her chum, Enric, was standing alone on the track, staring intently at a map. He looked up and smiled as she approached.

'It's not going to be easy to find this pair. It's a large area, as you know. The team has just set off in two parties to Puig de Moncaire and Pla des Porxo. Capitán Gómez said you were on your way, so I waited for you.'

'Thanks. And where is he?'

'As soon as he got here he headed over to the Moncaire Estate and hasn't returned. One of his officers is waiting for him in that van.'

She grinned. 'Probably having a coffee with the staff. Well, shall we head off towards Pla des Porxo?'

He nodded. 'Let's go. I think we should perhaps scour forestland east of Porxo away from the other search parties. Without a map, it's easy to get disorientated there on the way to the Puig. Did they have one?'

Isabel shrugged. 'Who knows. They and their two friends who stayed behind are regular hikers, though, and pretty fit.'

Enric heaved on his backpack and donned his warm gloves. 'There's a huge estate towards the east on the edge of dense forestland. We could pop by and ask if they've had sight of them.'

Isabel frowned. 'It's called the Voin estate. Isn't it owned by a Russian billionaire?'

'Apparently so, but I heard the guy only visits about once a month. He's got his own private jet and staff running the place. It's alright for some.'

Isabel suddenly smiled. 'Isn't that near the place some walkers thought they'd seen a lynx or a leopard a year ago?'

Enric nodded and laughed. 'That's right. Perhaps we'll get lucky today. We all reckon they saw a fast-moving hunter's dog or genet.'

'Probably.' She offered a teasing grin. 'I remember once seeing what I thought was a huge log in the Amazonas, but in reality it was an anaconda.'

He pulled a face. '*Que susto!*'

Having coordinated their GPS devices, Isabel left the Guardia officer a handwritten note with a smiley face for Capitán Gómez which outlined their proposed route and cheekily instructed him to get a move on. The young man chuckled but looked doubtful.

'He won't like that. I'll just give it to him and pretend I haven't read it.'

As they walked briskly along the stony footpath flanked by tough *càrritx*, prickly junipers and wild olive trees, Isabel scanned the grey, craggy mountains and karst landscape around them. It would be like looking for a needle in a haystack.

After a few hours, they stopped for a snack and took in their surroundings. It had become a ghostly lunar landscape of fine mist, limestone boulders, deep hill caves and slopes of scree. In the distance, Isabel could see a dense forest of Holm oaks and an unending pewter sky. Enric chomped on his chorizo baguette. Dusting crumbs from his mouth, he pointed to one of several leathery shrubs nearby.

'*Pistacia terebinthus*. It's everywhere up here.'

Isabel munched on handful of cashew nuts. 'It's so unworldly in winter and yet these hardy little fellows always survive.'

'True, and look at that shaggy rosemary bush over there. Another resilient mountain resident.'

They each had a good draught of water and ploughed on, keeping a beady eye out for any signs that the hiking couple had walked in the same direction. A few hours passed by and the overgrown path became harder to locate. Enric studied his GPS and mobile and indicated to keep climbing up the steep limestone slope.

'We're on course. Soon we'll descend on the other side into the forest. That's where the Voin estate is located.' He looked at his mobile. 'I've just had a text from one of the rescue team. They're scouring the area around the ruins now and have found a biscuit wrapper. It could be theirs.'

'Well, whoever it belonged to should have taken it with them.' Isabel wiped her brow and panted. 'Come on, let's keep up the pace.'

An hour later, they arrived at high walls and an austere metal gate. A sign indicated that it was private property and the domain of hunters. Isabel pressed the intercom, aware that on one of the stone pillars a video camera was coolly observing them.

A disembodied, gruff voice filled the still air. 'What do you want?'

'Police.'

Moments later the gate slid open. Isabel and Enric walked along a well-maintained and winding asphalt track bordered by lavender and hibiscus shrubs.

'How far is the property?' Isabel asked.

'I only came here once years ago. It's a good five minutes' walk to the main house. I seem to remember that at the back of the property there are several outbuildings and a cottage where the estate manager and his son live. They kept a fair few animals here when I visited.'

As the roof of the house came into view, a jeep hurtled along the track towards them. A burly man with a heavy beard dressed in a hunting jacket and woolly cap leant out of the window.

'Hop in. I'll take you to the house.'

Settled in the back of the vehicle, Isabel flicked open her police badge. The man grinned at her in the mirror.

'I don't need to see that. I can smell an officer a mile away.'

He looked over at Enric.

'You're a local guide, aren't you? I've seen you with groups. They're always tramping about where they shouldn't.'

'And who are you?' Isabel asked.

'Pistola. It's a nickname.'

'I'd never have guessed. What do you do here?'

'Look after the estate when my boss is away.'

'What's his name?'

'Nikolai Petrov. He's not here very often and since we're in a remote area we need to keep vigilant.'

The vehicle passed a perfectly manicured lawn and rose garden and parked by the front door of a substantial stone property. Isabel stepped out onto the paved courtyard where an old collie welcomed them with a wagging tail. She bent down and stroked his muzzle while he licked her hand.

'Why do you need to be vigilant here? It looks like a fortress. Have you had break-ins?'

The man tutted. 'Several. That's why we keep geese on the north side of the property and have high walls and CCTV.' He glanced at the dog. 'Brut is old and no threat to a burglar, so we're getting a Rottweiler soon. A mate of mine breeds them. That'll be a good deterrent for intruders.'

'Have you reported the break-ins to the police?' she asked.

'We've called the Guardia and cops often enough, but they never do anything.'

Enric chimed in. 'A wild and uninhabited area of terrain like this isn't easy to police.'

Pistola offered an indifferent sniff and led them into a palatial drawing room.

'Take a seat.'

'We can't stay long,' Isabel replied, perching on an armchair. 'We just need to ask a few questions.'

'About those injured hikers? The mayor of Fornalutx told me about it.'

'Have you any idea who might be involved?'

He gave a shrug. 'All I know is that lunatic, Frans Bordoy, should be a prime suspect. We have a few hunts here on our land and he's often come up to protest at the gate. Once he managed to climb over a wall and let loose some goats.'

'What animals do you keep here?'

'Domestic animals – sheep, goats and pigs and a few cows.'

'Do you ever get hikers coming by?'

He scowled. 'We have signs all around our land warning that it's private and the site of *la caza*, but they still come. My son, Ariel, is a groundsman and he sees them off. Until now it's not been illegal for them to pass close to the estate.'

Enric frowned. 'They probably just get lost on their way to Puig de Moncaire and the forest is free for everyone to roam.'

'Well, in the light of all these hiker accidents, the mayors of Fornalutx and Escorca have agreed that we can completely block anyone entering the nearby forests. It's for their own safety. We have dangerous cliffs, caves and sinkholes around here and we don't want anyone to get hurt on our land or in the surrounding forestland.'

Isabel laughed. 'So, what are you proposing? That every landowner should now be allowed to stop all hikers from crossing their land in the Tramuntanas?'

'Absolutely. We should stop hikers and groups completely. It's not wise for them to be out walking while some madman is on the loose.'

'I'm sure the tourism department would have a view on that,' she said witheringly. 'And the mountain guides.'

Enric looked out of the window and gave an impatient sigh. 'I think there's more danger of hikers being attacked by a leopard or lynx than a madman.'

The man gave a snort. 'At least that yarn gave us a laugh. What I'd give to see a leopard in the wild.'

Isabel stood up and placed her hands on her hips. 'Did you see a German couple here yesterday morning? They were hiking to the Pla des Porxo ruins and possibly Puig de Moncaire. Neither has returned to their rental property in Sant Martí and they can't be reached by phone.'

Pistola threw out his hands. 'That's my point. It's dangerous for hikers up here. Who knows what might happen next? This guy could have a weapon.'

'Or guys,' Isabel mooted. 'This is unlikely to be the work of one person.'

'I don't agree. I think it's Frans Bordoy leading you cops a merry dance. Anyway, in answer, no, we haven't seen anyone here. Ariel patrols our land every few hours. If he'd seen them, he would have offered help.'

The door opened and a young man entered wearing a black leather jacket, jeans and a slouch beanie. He looked over at Pistola.

'What's going on?'

'These people are asking if we've seen a missing German couple. Went walking near here yesterday morning.' He turned to Isabel. 'This is Ariel.'

'No one came this way,' Ariel replied in a surly manner. 'We don't want any hikers or groups nosing around here. The boss doesn't like it.'

Isabel gave him a sharp look. 'Why?'

'For one thing, Mr Petrov's house is full of valuable antiques and paintings and they could be thieves, and there are also hunters about. We don't want anyone to get hurt.'

'You have a hunter's licence?' asked Enric.

'Of course,' Pistola replied. 'Quite a few locals use the surrounding land in the hunting season too.'

'Did you have any hunts going on yesterday?' Isabel asked.

'No,' Ariel replied. 'But there are hunters all over the hills. We just control our own boundaries.'

'How much land does Mr Petrov have?' she asked.

Pistola yawned.

'Aside from the estate, Mr Petrov owns a substantial area of forestland right up to the eastern ridge. From this weekend, though, it too is going to be completely out of bounds to all walkers. You can ask for verification at the ajuntament in Fornalutx.'

'Thanks. We'll check. Can you give me your contact details too, please?' Isabel asked.

The man walked over to an ornate desk and pulled a pristine card from a holder and handed it to her. 'Here are the estate details with my mobile number too.'

Isabel examined the gold-embossed lettering, noting that the name of the estate was written in Cyrillic as ВОИН. 'How do you pronounce that?'

Pistola gave a hoarse laugh. 'That's Russian for warrior. You pronounce it *voyeen*.'

Isabel nodded and tucked the card in her pocket. 'And where do you two live?'

'We've got a small cottage in the back garden,' Pistola replied. 'It's enough for us.'

'I'd imagine it's a blissfully quiet place to live,' she said.

'That's how we like it here.' The man sniffed. 'With this recent spate of hiker accidents, we've had a lot of disruption. It's best to keep walkers away from the Trams for all our sakes.'

Ariel exchanged a furtive glance with his father and pulled his beanie down over his ears. He turned to Isabel.

'That creepy Frans Bordoy, with his long greasy hair and tats, is always hanging around our woods and stalking the hills, and of course he hates tourists. He's definitely your man. Anyway, if we hear anything, we'll let you know.'

Isabel surveyed the sallow youth for a few moments and passed one of her own cards to Pistola.

He drove them back to the front gate.

'Be careful out there and watch your back,' he said with a sour grin. 'Many have come a cropper in these hills.'

As they walked through the forest, Enric turned to her.

'What a hostile pair. Do you think they really can block hikers and groups entering this land? If this goes on, we guides could lose our livelihoods.'

Isabel frowned. 'We'll check with the local councils. It's probably just a temporary measure.'

Twenty minutes later, Isabel bent down and with a gloved hand picked up various spent cartridge shells that glinted among mulchy leaves. As they walked on, she discovered a few more and some of the bright red plastic variety. She examined each carefully and popped them in a clear bag in the side pocket of her backpack.

'Several people have been hunting here and this isn't the Russian's jurisdiction.'

'Some rogue hunters?' asked Enric.

Isabel stopped abruptly and put a finger to her lips. Enric stood still and looked about him as the silence was suddenly broken by a low murmur. It sounded like someone in pain. Isabel pointed to the right of her and silently they cut a path in the direction of the sound. As they drew closer, Enric whispered to her, 'There's a cave in among all those shrubs.'

Isabel called out, 'Is anybody there? Police!'

For a moment there was silence and then a bedraggled young woman with wild eyes emerged from the cave, her face and hiking gear covered in grime.

'Thank God you've come. Is that you, Isabel? We got completely lost yesterday afternoon. None of the cairns and signs made sense and it grew dark. We found ourselves in these strange woods and suddenly people began shooting at us. Somehow we stumbled across this cave and have been too frightened to come out. Klaus has twisted his ankle and can't walk.'

Enric looked askance. 'Shots? But there is no hunting here at night.'

She nodded frantically. 'We heard voices and people shooting so we ran in blind panic. That's when Klaus took a bad tumble. We crept around in the dark and found this small cave where we've been hiding ever since.'

Isabel and Enric tramped through the wild foliage to the cave and opened their rucksacks. Both pulled out head lamps, water bottles, space blankets and snacks.

'Here, wrap this around you, Susanne,' said Isabel.

While she offered the woman a foil blanket, Enric provided her with fresh water. Inside the cave, Isabel found Klaus stretched out on the ground with one hiking boot removed. He eyed her with relief and confusion.

'You're the rentals agent. How come you're here?'

Isabel smiled. 'I do a little of everything. Are you cold? Take this space blanket.'

He wrapped it around his shaking body and grimaced. 'I think I could get up with the help of a stick. My ankle is bruised and swollen so I can't put weight on it. My ribs hurt too.'

Isabel gently pulled down his sock and inspected the damage by the beam of her headlight.

'I think you've most likely fractured this. Enric is radioing for help. We'll see if the nearby estate can bring a vehicle as close as possible.'

Susanne and Klaus tucked into the snacks inside the cave. They appeared ravenous and there was loud chatter interspersed with tears and nervous laughter. Meanwhile, Enric rang through to the mountain rescue team to call off the hunt and arrange a rescue vehicle to come to the estate. Enric beckoned to Isabel and she followed him outside.

'They seem delirious. The woman didn't make any sense. There are no night hunts anywhere around here.'

Isabel pushed out her bottom lip. 'I know, and yet we found a lot of shell cases. They're probably old, but it's worth checking. Any luck with Pistola and his charming son?'

He raised an eyebrow. 'They're on their way now and even have a stretcher.'

Isabel winked. 'Maybe this happens a lot around here.'

'All I know is that there's something a bit creepy about these woods. I don't feel comfortable. It's as if we're being watched.'

Isabel nodded. 'Ditto. I feel a sense of foreboding.'

They turned at the sound of a vehicle approaching. Pistola and Ariel parked some way off as there was no access by car. Together they trudged through the shrubs and bracken carrying a stretcher between them. Isabel greeted them with a smile.

'Thanks for your support.'

Ariel gave a terse nod. 'Glad they've been found, but frankly they should never have been here in the first place.'

Isabel sat in the mayoral office, tucking into a hefty slice of *gató de almendras*. Maria, Llorenç's trusty secretary, stood nearby, a radiant smile on her face.

'You like it?'

'It's superb. I love the citrus ice topping and the crunchy pieces of candied orange.'

'It's based on my grandma's recipe, but I've added my own twist.'

Isabel nodded enthusiastically while Llorenç and Capitán Gómez looked on in some bemusement.

'Thank you, Maria,' said Llorenç. 'I'm sure the cake's delicious but we have serious matters to discuss.'

The cheery soul blushed pink and nodded. 'Of course. I'll leave you to it.'

She hastily retreated to the outer office. Llorenç ran a weary hand over his forehead.

'If she's not chattering about cake recipes, she's hiding under her desk afraid of non-existent phantoms! Honestly.'

'Blame Josep for that,' Isabel retorted.

Llorenç nodded. 'I've already had stern words with him. So, my friends, what are we to do following this latest hiking crisis? How is the young couple?'

'They're both okay, although Klaus has a broken ankle and cracked rib. It was a frightening experience for them,' she replied.

He shook his head despairingly. 'I take it we're no further down the line in discovering the culprits?'

Capitán Gómez tapped his knee with a gloved hand. As usual his green uniform was pristine, with creases in all the right places.

'I have maintained for some time now that Frans Bordoy is behind all this.' He turned to Isabel. 'I also accept that we have no hard evidence, despite questioning the rogue several times. Various landowners have confirmed that he has proven himself quite a pest over the years.'

'Odd that he should go from being a pest to a potential murderer overnight,' Isabel muttered.

'Not odd at all, Bel. Think about serial killers. They usually start by torturing amphibians and mammals before moving on to humans. I imagine this menace and his deranged eco-warriors have been building up to this.'

Isabel frowned and looked across at Llorenç.

'What do you know about the estate owned by the Russian billionaire? The estate manager claims they have been given permission to stop all walkers entering adjoining land indefinitely. It covers a massive area.'

Llorenç nodded. 'That's correct. Nikolai Petrov has owned it for a few years and made many structural improvements. He is on very good terms with the mayors of Escorca and Fornalutx and is a generous donor to local charitable causes.'

'That's what I feared,' Isabel replied.

'Whatever do you mean?' asked Capitán Gómez sharply. 'I wish we had more responsible landowners like Petrov around here. Those foolish hikers who got lost near his land yesterday have proven the point. Why should his people have to put up with the constant disruption? These hikers are a danger to themselves, and that's without a mountain stalker on the loose.'

'The couple claimed that they got lost and as night fell, shots were fired at them. This is why they sought safety in that cave. I found some shells close by, which I'm going to get analysed.'

Capitán Gómez gave a winnowing laugh. 'What utter nonsense. As for those spent bullets, you will find many in the hills left by hunters.'

'I know that, but I'd like confirmation from forensics as to their vintage.'

'Very well, Bel. Have it your own way.'

Llorenç gave an impatient sigh. 'I have decided to convene an urgent meeting here tomorrow afternoon with the mayors of Fornalutx and Escorca and local landowners and guides. We must glean as much information as we can about any trespassers or suspicious characters that any of them may have seen recently. I know you can't make it, Alvaro, but how about you, Bel?'

'Sure. I'm at the precinct in the morning, but I'll be back in the afternoon.'

Isabel turned to Capitán Gómez. 'Are you happy for me to talk to Frans Bordoy?'

He shrugged. 'You won't get anything out of him, but by all means go ahead. It might convince you of his madness.'

Isabel smiled and hooked the pannier over her shoulder. 'Have a good afternoon, gentlemen.'

As Isabel strode into her *entrada*, loud music was booming from the upstairs office. Before she'd reached the landing, the door shot open and Pep gave a small screech.

'*Que susto*! I was just popping down to the kitchen for some coffee.'

'Good timing. You can make me one too. Do we need this volume?'

He turned tail and switched the music off.

'My bluetooth speaker's really cool, isn't it? It's so small, but the sound is really big.'

'So I've noticed,' she replied with narrowed eyes. 'How's my whiskery boy?'

'Sleeping in his basket as ever. By the way, the Sunflower King called. He says to ring him back soonest.'

Isabel groaned. 'Josep Casanovas. That's all I need today.'

She walked into her office and smiled to see Furó twitching in his dreams. Steeling herself, she phoned the ingratiating editor.

'Bel, so glad you called. I have news. A male reader contacted the newspaper an hour ago to report seeing a grubby white van outside Silvia Porres's home in the early hours of Monday. He'd read about the murder in the newspaper this morning and remembered seeing something suspicious. Much as I am still furious about my treatment at the hands of Cabot, I felt it was my duty to let you know.'

Isabel flicked her eyes to the ceiling. 'Have you his details?'

'Afraid not. He refused to call the police. Few locals want any kind of interaction with the local police and authorities these days.'

'Did he say when he saw the vehicle?'

'Apparently he was having a late dinner with a friend in Palmanyola and left his home around one o'clock. The reason he noticed the white van is because the streets were empty and it screeched out of the drive of Silvia Porres's house in front of him and sped off in the direction of Palma. About twenty minutes later, he spotted it again on the MA-30 heading in the direction of Son Ferriol. It had evidently got delayed behind a slow lorry or stopped somewhere en route. The last he saw of it was turning onto the MA-15, which as you know leads to Algaida, Montuïri and Porreres.'

'He gave you a lot of detail,' said Isabel, a tad suspiciously.

'Probably bored and looking for a bit excitement on his way home. Not everyone leads as fascinating a life as you, beautiful Bel.'

'Okay, Josep. That's really helpful. I owe you.'

'How about dinner some time?'

'When life's less frantic, that would be great.'

'So you're running this case?'

'I'm just lending a hand where I can.'

Josep gave a hearty laugh. 'Always so modest. That oaf, Cabot, doesn't deserve you.'

Isabel killed the call and bashed the mobile against her head.

'Ah, the sign of true love,' said Pep with a grin as he placed a *cortado* on her desk.

'Oh, be quiet. By the way, did you have any luck at the Chinese store identifying that wooden butterfly sign I gave you?'

He nodded. 'I nearly forgot. The owner's son told me that they are very common and can be bought in bulk from China. They don't sell them at the shop in Soller but at some of the other island stores run by Chinese families. He offered to call round for me.'

'Brilliant. There's the vaguest chance that our mountain menace or menaces might have placed an order locally.'

He nodded enthusiastically. 'I'm on the case.'

'Just one thing. Did he think the butterfly motif was significant in any way?'

Pep shook his head. 'He thought the symbol was a standard motif stamped on this kind of sign along with the likes of flowers, bees and birds.'

'I thought as much.' She took a sip of coffee. 'Llorenç and the other local mayors are holding a meeting with all the landowners and guides tomorrow afternoon. I'd like you to be there.'

Pep beamed. 'I wouldn't miss it for the world.' He hovered in the doorway. 'I'm heading off to see Susanne and Klaus now, so I'll see you tomorrow.'

She smiled. 'Do send them my best.'

When he'd left, Isabel made a quick call to Tolo with the update from Josep Casanovas. Despite his loathing for the editor, he welcomed the new information. Isabel hung up and approached her whiteboard, where she had scribbled names, notes and symbols with interconnecting lines. With a heavy black marker, she had divided the board into two with the headings SEBI MURDER and MOUNTAIN MENACE. She began jotting down thoughts.

The outer office door banged open and Florentina stalked in.

'Bel, are you there?'

Isabel heard her mother's voice as if in a dream. She must have been at the whiteboard for three hours by now.

'I'm in here, thinking.'

'You do far too much thinking, my girl. Time to eat. Look at poor Furó. He must be famished.'

Isabel bit her lip. 'I've come up with a terrible notion and if I'm proven correct, it will seem almost preposterous.'

'Is this to do with Sebi Vives?'

Isabel felt suddenly clammy and ran a hand over her face. 'It's all too abhorrent for words. I'm not sure I want to dig further.'

Her mother stepped forward and embraced her.

'Bel, you are stronger than you know, and you won't rest until you have answers. I wish you hadn't got involved with any of this police work, but you are your father, so just follow your nose and instincts and clarity will come.' She paused. 'But first let's eat.'

Isabel smiled. 'You're the best mother in the world. So what's for dinner?'

Florentina tousled her hair and laughed. 'Come downstairs to the kitchen where poor Miguel and Idò are patiently waiting for us, and you'll find out.'

SIXTEEN

As Isabel emerged from the lift, she was greeted by an excitable Corc. His dark hair had been cropped short and he was wearing an oversized blue suit and tie. There was a sheen to his ruddy face and his hands shook, possibly in excitement.

'Ah, Señorita Flores, I mean, Bel. How lucky is that? Tolo sent me off to get coffees and here you are, standing like an angel before me. Otherwise, I'd have had to guess what you might want.'

'Well, Corc. I nearly always have the same.'

'That's true. So, you want a *cortado* and *bocadillo de jamón* as usual?'

Isabel frowned. 'I never have ham rolls.'

Corc threw his head back and howled with laughter. 'Got you! That was a joke.'

Several officers looked up as they walked along the long, white-walled corridor, but seeing the source of merriment they shook their heads and strode on.

'Very funny. You caught me,' Isabel replied.

She watched in bemusement as he disappeared into the lift, chortling merrily to himself. In Tolo's office, he and Gaspar were huddled over a report at his desk. Tolo smiled and kissed her on the cheeks.

'We're just going through Nacho's findings. He's on his way up.'

Gaspar grinned and gave her a hug. 'Hey, two kisses for me too, please.'

'You're both in a suspiciously good mood,' she replied.

Gaspar shrugged. 'A small breakthrough. We've discovered substantial payments made from Sebi Vives to an obscure Liechtenstein bank account held by Silvia Porres. Better still, we've also traced hefty payments made from Marc Castell to Sebi Vives.'

'When Sebi died, no further payments were made, but then, of course, you discovered cash hidden at Silvia's house. Nacho has found a single print on one of the bank notes, evidently a careless mistake.'

'Marc Castell's, presumably?' she prompted.

'Don't spoil it.' Gaspar tutted. 'But yes, it is Castell's print.'

Isabel shook her head. 'So, we might assume that Sebi used regional government funds to give the Mestres a big backhander for arranging the crooked motorway contract with Castell. With the fat sum he himself creamed off from the contract, Sebi was able to pay off his multiple gambling debts to them. Meanwhile, Marc Castell got a ludicrously good deal for constructing the motorway. So, where does Silvia Porres fit in? I'm guessing that Sebi couldn't push through the contract tender to the finishing line without her involvement, so he was forced to give her a cut.'

Gaspar nodded. 'But then Sebi was killed and suddenly Silvia no longer received her regular lucrative monthly instalments at the Liechtenstein bank. Maybe she got greedy and blackmailed Castell and the Mestres?'

Tolo rubbed his chin. 'That would explain the multiple hidden bank notes you found in her garden, Bel. She had them all over a barrel.'

'Didn't do her much good in the end,' Isabel replied. 'I suppose they got bored with her demands and bumped her off.' She frowned. 'All the same, it doesn't add up.'

'What doesn't?' asked Gaspar.

'Silvia evidently lived a simple existence. She was dowdy, as was the home she inherited from her mother. It needed a good deal of work. So what was she doing with the money?'

'Maybe she was going to do a runner to Liechtenstein and was just biding her time,' replied Gaspar with a smirk.

Tolo jumped up from his chair and paced about the office. 'This is all well and good, but we still don't know who killed Sebi. The only decent suspect we had was Pablo Pons, but still there's not a single shred of hard evidence to convict him.'

There was a knock on the door and Nacho walked in. He saw Isabel and smiled.

'I've got good and bad news, Bel.'

'Oh?'

No sooner had he joined them at the meeting table than Corc barged through the open door and smashed a tray of drinks, croissants and *ensaïmadas* down beside him.

'Hi, Doctor Blanco. I got you a *café con leche*.'

'Perfect. Thanks, Corc.'

He scuttled out, banging the door behind him, causing Tolo to curse.

'So, Nacho, take us through the results,' said Gaspar.

He turned to Isabel. 'As you know, we have successfully identified a fingerprint on one of the bank notes you found at Silvia Porres's home. It irrefutably belongs to Marc Castell. Also, the partially burnt red matchbook you discovered in her barbecue is offered free to clients at Gran Casino Atlántico. The figure nine is the second to last digit in the casino's phone number.'

Isabel nodded. 'Of course Silvia had visited the casino before, despite her protestations to the contrary.'

He pulled his long mane of hair back. 'One more key piece of evidence is the fag end you found in Silvia Porres's garden. It is a close match to the DNA of Rocci Mestre held on our central database.'

Tolo clapped his hands together. 'Spectacular. And what about the timeline? Any chance of it proving conclusively that Rocci Mestre was at Silvia's house the night she was abducted?'

He shook his head. 'That's not so easy to prove as the sample had badly deteriorated, but it's possible.'

Gaspar gnawed on a biro. 'The point is that we now have proof that both he and Castell had visited Silvia's home. It's another step forward and offers us a direct connection between Silvia and the Mestres.'

Tolo gave a grunt of acknowledgement. 'True.'

Nacho raised an eyebrow. 'The pieces are gradually falling into place, but we've still a long way to go. For example, the chewing gum found by Furó at S'Albufera and the wrapper he discovered at the site in Llucmajor where Sebi was abducted have a DNA match but are invisible on every police database. Disappointingly, we have no idea who it belongs to, but it's a major development. We've analysed the DNA swab from Pablo Pons and there's no match. How about getting swabs from the Mestres?'

'Without hard evidence against them, that'll be tricky, but it's something we'll do as soon as the opportunity arises,' Tolo replied. 'And your ferret deserves a medal, Bel.'

Isabel gave him a smile. 'He's certainly proven himself an important team player.'

'We also have a potential breakthrough regarding the vehicle used to run over Silvia Porres. We discovered a microscopic smear of green paint on the victim's clothing. In addition, we found a tiny chip of yellow paint underneath the body. We checked back with the PDQ DB...'

'What's that?' asked Gaspar.

'The Paint Data Query database. You can cross reference samples and check the OEM, the original equipment manufacturer. We are now confident that the corpse of Silvia Porres was run over multiple times by a John Deere 6155M tractor, series 6M.'

'That means nothing to me,' Gaspar replied. 'But, wow, great work.'

'Are those the brightly coloured green and yellow big beasts I see in the agricultural heartland here?' asked Isabel.

'Spot on. It's a hugely popular brand here in Spain. We found microscopic soil samples, too, that hail from around Es Pla.'

'So all we need to do is locate the agricultural land or farm where this atrocity occurred,' replied Tolo.

'The Mestres own rural properties, don't they?' asked Isabel.

'Several,' Gaspar replied.

Isabel tapped her chin. 'And thanks to Casanovas we now know that a white van was seen by one of his readers leaving Silvia's home around one o'clock on Monday morning heading in the direction of Algaida and Montuïri.'

Tolo growled. 'Please try not to mention Casanovas in my office.'

'He has his uses, boss,' Gaspar replied with a wink. 'We've identified a particularly large and remote rural property in Montuïri owned by Rocci Mestre so have requested a search warrant for that, and for all of the other properties owned by the brothers.'

'What about Marc Castell?' asked Isabel.

Gaspar consulted his notes. 'He has a pile in Santa Ponsa and a substantial builder's yard and depot in Inca, but we're checking to see if he has land anywhere else.'

Nacho nodded enthusiastically. 'If we find the exact location where Silvia Porres's body was run over and stored, we may be lucky enough to find enough DNA to convict her killers.'

'What about that white van? Doesn't Pablo Pons own one?' asked Tolo.

Isabel nodded. 'True, but so does Castell and just about every other worker on the island. Remember that Sara Vives also claimed that a white van shunted her vehicle the week before Sebi's death.'

Gaspar interrupted. 'The Guardia checked over Pons's vehicle. It was clean.'

'That's as may be, but he's still not out of the woods yet, despite your instincts about the guy, Bel. He still sent hate mail and attacked Sebi Vives physically,' Tolo replied.

Isabel offered him an inscrutable look. 'It still doesn't prove anything. Meanwhile, did the note left by Silvia's corpse on the motorway yield any DNA?'

Nacho shook his head. 'Frustratingly, it was as clean as a whistle. A dead end.'

Isabel shrugged. 'Anything more on those footprints down at the Canal in S'Albufera?'

He pulled a face. 'Still baffling. I sought the help of the forensic podiatrist in Barcelona who has helped us before. She offered an interesting perspective. Her view is that two athletic, lightweight men with foot sizes forty-three and forty-four carried Sebi in the body bag to the canal and once there, they were joined by a tall male with a foot size of forty-six. You'll recall that after Sebi's body was thrown into the canal only two sets of prints – size forty-four and forty-six – were visible heading back up the bank. That means that the assailant with size forty-three prints who'd come down to the canal simply disappeared into thin air. We also have no idea where the individual with forty-six prints came from. One possibility is that he came in a small motorboat via the canal and waited for the others to arrive on the bank with the body bag. He then swapped places with the guy with forty-three prints who got into the boat, perhaps to guide the body bag along the canal into open water. I appreciate that the weather would have made it a precarious exercise.'

Isabel suddenly smiled and shook her head. 'It's a nice little theory, but it still doesn't hold water for me.'

'Very funny,' cried Tolo.

Nacho continued. 'The podiatrist maintains that the tall guy had a malformed right foot. She analysed the tread and found that he walked heavily on that side and in a wholly unnatural way. She also believed him to be a very malnourished individual with a light, weak gait. Her conclusion was that the taller of the three might have a serious wasting disease such as cancer.'

'Any thoughts on the ages of the abductors?' asked Gaspar.

Nacho shrugged. 'The jury's out, but she thought between thirty-five and fifty given their athletic ability and body strength. The encouraging news is that the three shoeprints are quite distinctive. They are all from Caucho, a well-known, upmarket Spanish brand of rubber boot that hails from Murcia.'

Isabel took a bite from her *ensaïmada*. 'Great progress, Nacho. Well done. Any thoughts on their colour?'

He turned to her. 'They come in yellow, red and black.'

'What next?' said Tolo.

Nacho cleared his throat. 'We're in touch with Caucho and hoping that its client database for Mallorca might throw up some clues.'

Isabel raised an eyebrow. 'Meanwhile, we're on the lookout for a malnourished giant of a man with a foot deformity. Bit of a tall order.'

Tolo threw out his hands. 'What is it with you and these awful puns today?'

'Just can't help it,' she replied with a roguish grin. Fumbling in her pannier she pulled out a small polythene bag. 'Nacho, I found these spent cartridges in forestland in the Tramuntanas yesterday. Any chance of giving me a steer on their vintage and provenance?'

He held them up to the light and stared at her. 'The plastic ones are from a typical rifle, but this brass cartridge is a bad boy.'

'My thinking too. I'd hazard it's from a Lapua Magnum or similar.'

Tolo eyed her in alarm. 'Impossible, Bel. You know that's a high-profile military spec rifle. You'd only use it for big game hunting.'

'Precisely, that's why I urgently need to know how long that casing has been knocking around the woods.'

Tolo ran a fretful hand through his hair. 'Is this connected with the mountain stalker case?'

'Everything's connected in the end,' she replied enigmatically. 'How long before I can have the results, Nacho?'

'We're up against it but hopefully Monday.'

Gaspar sighed. 'If you're right, Bel, we'll need to get Interpol involved. Surely this is Gómez's call?'

'He's still in denial and fixated with his one suspect, Frans Bordoy, but if I can give him some hard evidence, he'll soon come round.'

Tolo drummed his fingers impatiently on his desk. 'The government will go into overdrive if we've got some rogue sniper loose in the Trams. Both cases are growing more complicated by the day.'

'I always find the tighter the knot, the more thrilling it is to unravel. Everything is coming to a head.'

The three men observed her quietly with sceptical eyes.

Isabel dusted crumbs from her lips and smiled. 'Well, I don't know about you lot, but I have a pressing engagement at the gourmet department at El Corte Inglés.'

Tolo tutted. 'Always thinking about food.'

'Olives, to be precise.'

And with a cheeky smile, she wished them all farewell and set off in the direction of Jaume III.

Isabel inspected the shelves of gourmet fare on the upper level of El Corte Inglés, Mallorca's only department store. The brand had two branches in Palma, but Isabel preferred to shop at the least crowded, more intimate of the two. As she hungrily eyed the exclusive international products, an assistant caught her eye.

'Can I help you with anything?'

Isabel nodded. 'I'm looking for *olives cassées de la vallée des Baux de Provence*.'

The woman tapped her lip. 'You've stumped me. I don't think we've ever carried such a product, but let me check with a colleague who has been here longer than me.'

A few minutes went by and a stout older lady headed towards her.

'You have good taste, *señorita*. I know those French olives well. We used to have a buyer here who insisted on stocking them, but when she left, they were never re-ordered. I think they were a bit too rarefied.'

'Would you remember the buyer's name?'

She smiled sadly. 'Silvia Porres. She left for a well-paid job as head of food and beverage at the Gran Casino Atlántico and soon after entered the world of local politics. We were close colleagues but lost touch over the years. Then, only yesterday, I read in the newspapers that she had been found murdered. I was horrified.'

Isabel offered her a sympathetic nod. 'It is indeed tragic. The newspapers are full of it.'

'What a coincidence that you should come here today asking for those olives. She was such a quiet soul who wouldn't hurt a fly. Poor Silvia, she had a sad life.'

'Really?'

'She'd been estranged from her mother since her late teens. The woman apparently neglected Silvia as a child and became an alcoholic after she was widowed. Then she became seriously ill. Despite an acrimonious relationship, Silvia continued to pay all the nursing fees at her mother's exclusive private home.'

'Where was it?'

She shrugged. 'Near Santa Ponsa, I think. The reason why Silvia left here was to earn more money to keep her old mother at the home. She herself lived a simple life with her cat. And now she's dead.'

The woman's colleague appeared.

'Are you free to take over at the till?'

'Just coming.' She turned to Isabel. 'Let's hope Silvia can now rest in peace.'

Isabel left the shop, her mind whirring. It seemed likely that Silvia Porres had been tempted to break the law in order to financially support her ailing mother at her home. Maybe she had been desperate and lonely and simply took a wrong turn in life.

Crossing Jaume III, Isabel made her way to the Pilates studio of Fran Grau just a few streets away. The chic and luxurious white premises looked very welcoming and Isabel momentarily lamented the fact that she had never sampled such an exercise in her life. The receptionist offered her a menu of classes, treatments and therapies, and allowed her to watch a class in progress through a glass door.

'It looks very relaxing,' Isabel said.

The woman laughed. 'Appearances can be deceptive. It gets to the core muscles, I can tell you!'

'Do you offer physiotherapy and podiatry?' Isabel asked. 'I am always looking for good practitioners.'

She nodded. 'Fran Grau, our founder, is a first-rate podiatrist and reflexologist and we have an excellent physio and chiropractor. Please take a card too.'

Isabel smiled. 'One day I might spoil myself and book a few treatments.'

The woman frowned. 'It shouldn't be a treat. It's about looking after your health. You owe it to yourself.'

Isabel breezed off along the street, inspecting the price menu as she walked. She let out an expletive and laughed to herself as she contemplated how the other half lived. One thing was certain, she would not be splashing out at Fran Grau's exclusive studio anytime soon.

About to cross Passeig de Mallorca, Isabel suddenly stopped in her tracks. Standing by the stone bridge that crossed Torrent de Sa Riera were Jaume Perez, his husband Eli Castano and Mateu having a heated discussion. She held back and observed them from a distance. Sara's son puffed urgently at a cigarette while Eli attempted to placate him by putting his arm around his shoulder. The youth stepped back and stalked off shaking his head angrily while the two men looked on miserably.

When they had gone, Isabel crossed the bridge and headed for the precinct where she had left Pequeñito. Her mind was working on overtime and her heart raced as she unwrapped a Chupa Chup and popped it in her mouth. Immediately she began to breathe more easily. At the precinct, she rummaged in her pannier. Earlier she had forgotten to give Nacho another sample for analysis. But where had she put it? She would have to search the car and her home in case it had slipped out of her bag, but first she needed to ring Agila, the carer of Martín Vives, to arrange a visit. Once she was through Llorenç's meeting with the local landowners later in the afternoon, she intended to drive over to Colonia San Jordi to speak with the elderly man. There was something she urgently needed to know and somehow she felt he would hold the answer.

As Isabel approached Café Jordi, she heard raised voices and the clinking of glasses. With a grin, she threw open the door. A swell of men were packed at small tables, pontificating loudly as the diminutive Llorenç attempted to maintain order in front of the bar. He was flanked by the mayors of Escorca and Fornalutx, both of whom wore serious expressions, and Jordi, the owner of the café, who was gesticulating wildly at his customers. He clapped his hands together.

'Can you lot be quiet for one moment. We are in the presence of a lady, so show some manners.'

A curvy waitress emerged from the back of the bar with a tray of beers and glared at him.

'Are you referring to Bel or me?'

Jordi winced. 'Both of you, of course, Dolores. I didn't see you there. Can I get you a drink, Bel?'

'A *cortado*, thanks.'

Isabel nodded to various landowners and mountain guides and greeted the mayors.

'I apologise for being late, but I've only just returned from the Palma precinct. What have I missed?'

Llorenç patted her arm.

'I know how busy you are, Bel. We have reached a slight impasse. Many here are calling for all hiking in the Tramuntanas to be suspended until the culprit is found. The consensus is that Frans Bordoy is the most likely suspect and should be arrested and interrogated.'

There were nods and murmurs of approval from the attendees. Isabel addressed them all.

'This isn't the Spanish Inquisition and thankfully neither the Guardia nor National Police make arrests based on rumour or suspicion. There is no evidence against Señor Bordoy. He has been questioned on several occasions by Capitán Gómez and the Guardia team and denies any involvement in the recent spate of accidents involving hikers.'

'Well of course he would! Perhaps we need to do your job for you and get a confession.'

Isabel stared at Ariel, the accuser, who, sullen as ever, stood with his arms tightly folded, wearing his slouch beanie and jeans.

'Ariel, we meet again. You'd be wise to remember that anyone suspected of a crime is innocent until proven guilty. One day, you might find yourself grateful for that legal principle.'

A hush fell over the room. Ariel stormed out of the café, throwing a thunderous glance in her direction. His father looked unsettled and hastily followed in his footsteps. Isabel remained composed while Pep and Enric stood up at the back of the room and applauded her loudly. Others slowly joined in. Isabel waited for the clamour to die down.

'There is no room in our valley for vigilantes and lynch parties, and stopping responsible guides and hikers from roaming the hills is not the long-term solution.'

The mayor of Fornalutx offered a puzzled expression. 'Well, what is?'

She turned to him. 'In a short while we will have answers, but until then, let's keep alert and always with perspective.'

At six-thirty, the communal office door banged open and Idò's deep, gravelly voice filled the air.

'Still working?' he said to Pep as he came into the office, raising his eyebrows at Isabel. 'I thought you knocked off in the early afternoon.'

Pep issued a grunt. 'Always so funny, Idò. Actually, your kind sister is bringing round a plate of food for me before I go home.'

'Florentina feeds everyone around here. Don't tell me that Llorenç and Angélica are still on that crazy diet?'

'I don't think they'll keep it up for much longer,' Isabel said. 'I was at Café Jordi earlier and Dolores told me that Llorenç's wife has given up on the diet already.'

Pep shrugged. 'That's true, but Angélica is still fanatical about it. It's making her so bad-tempered too. She's irritable all the time. It can't be good in her job and she doesn't seem to be losing any weight.'

Idò slapped his big, bear-like hand down on Pep's desk. 'It's not surprising. She's probably craving proper food.'

Isabel gave a hearty yawn. 'I need to get going. Agila, the carer for Sebi Vives's father, called earlier and asked me to pop by around eight o'clock after his supper.'

'You're going all the way to Colonia San Jordi?' Idò exclaimed.

'Why not? I want to give Boadicea a good run,' she replied. 'I'll leave Furó to slumber here.'

A voice called from the *entrada*, 'Cooeee! I've brought food.'

Pep's eyes lit up. 'I'm coming, Florentina. Hey Bel, have something to eat before you leave. It'll only take you an hour to get there.'

'I saw my sister making *tumbet* and *porc amb coll* earlier,' said Idò. 'Don't miss out.'

Isabel hesitated for a moment and then with a determined nod of the head, jogged down the stairs to join her mother in the kitchen.

By the time Isabel arrived on the outskirts of Colonia Sant Jordi, the heavens were already peppery and thunder grumbled in the distance. As she manoeuvred Boadicea into a parking space on the drive, flashes of buttery light streaked the dark sky. She sniffed the salty air. The sea would soon be seething and writhing in rage. As she approached the porch, the front door opened and a petite, elderly woman with keen dark eyes peered out.

'Señorita Flores?'

Isabel shook her hand.

'Just call me Bel. I take it you're Agila?'

Politely the woman nodded and welcomed her into the softly lit *entrada*.

'The sea is angry tonight,' she observed. 'It's the first storm here for many months. Bad weather unsettles Martín, so I apologise if he acts strangely.'

'It's fine. Let's just play it by ear. I won't stay long.'

'Can I get you a glass of wine or Salabat?'

'Salabat?' Isabel asked.

Agila smiled. 'It's a popular warming drink in my country. Fresh ginger tea with honey and lemon.'

'That sounds heavenly. Thanks.'

Isabel followed the woman into a large elegant sitting room crammed with artworks, where a crackling fire glowed in the grate. In the subdued light, Isabel could just about make out the bucolic scenes on the canvasses, many showcasing the island's fauna and flora. Agila offered her a chair.

'I will fetch Martín for you. He is calm and has had his dinner and medication. I have told him that you are one of Sara's friends. If he becomes distressed, it is best to leave.'

Isabel nodded. 'Understood.'

Moments later, a tall and wiry elderly man appeared in the doorway. He was dressed in pyjamas and a blue woollen dressing gown and leant on a stylish, gilt-headed walking stick. Isabel was struck by his fine features, calm expression and bright, intelligent eyes. Such a face belied the turmoil within.

She smiled. 'Good evening, Señor Vives.'

Martín Vives frowned and looked about him. He fixed his gaze on her.

'I recognise you. You are Lucy, my darling Margalida's agent and close friend.'

He paused and pointed to a window whose external shutters screeched and flapped in the moaning wind. Flashes of lightning illuminated the room.

'Listen to the storm. It is speaking to us.'

Isabel approached him and took his hand. 'Yes, we should listen to the sea and the skies and the call of the wind. They always teach us something.'

As if breaking from a reverie, he smiled broadly and hugged her. 'I'm overjoyed to see you again, Lucy. It's been so long. Come, let me show you Margalida's latest pieces here. She is working like a beaver in her studio so we can't disturb her, but I can show you Gabriel's new sketches in his room. He is showing such promise.'

Agila entered, bearing a gilt tray with two cups. 'Here is your tea, Martín.'

'Ah, Agila. Silly you! This is Lucy, Margalida's art dealer friend from Madrid. She is nothing to do with Sara.'

The woman patted his arm and winked at Isabel. 'Of course. I am getting old and my memory isn't so good these days.'

'Lucy wants to see Gabriel's new artworks.'

The woman frowned. 'I think he's gone to bed, so we shouldn't disturb him.'

'Nonsense!' he cried, taking a sip of his tea. 'He is still hiking in the mountains. Let's show Lucy his works.'

Isabel picked up her cup of Salabat and offered him an encouraging nod.

'That would be fantastic. He has a studio here?'

'Of course. It is where he works and sleeps, but most of the day he is studying at the university, as you know. Come.'

Agila shot Isabel a concerned glance and with a philosophical shrug led them down a flight of stairs to a small basement. Above them, as the wild storm raged, came the sudden sound of breaking glass. Isabel stopped in her tracks.

Agila tutted. 'The gardener left some old glass panes propped up against the garage wall. I fear they have fallen over and broken. Here, let me open the door for you.'

She produced a key that hung on a chain about her waist and turned the lock. A musty aroma seeped from the door as she entered. As the woman switched on a light, Isabel pondered when the room had last been occupied.

Agila smiled politely. 'I'll be back shortly.'

Isabel walked into the cosy space and gasped to see so many vibrant artworks adorning the walls. One large canvass in particular caught her eye. It was of a beautiful, unworldly butterfly, its iridescent wings spread out, its body a myriad of shimmering colours.

'The mighty mountain meh,' cried Martín, in delight. 'Have you heard of it?'

Isabel slowly nodded and turned to him. With some vigour, the elderly man joined her at the picture.

'It's my favourite of all his works. Such a talented boy, isn't he?'

Isabel blinked as a flash of lightning glinted from a far-off window. She looked beyond the room to a darkened annexe with large French windows. Martín smiled.

'Those doors lead to a flight of stone steps carved into the rock face that take you right down to a rocky cove. It is inspirational for Gabriel and he goes down there often to paint.'

Isabel followed him into the room and switched on a light. A single bed was covered in a beautiful crimson quilt, while an old wooden desk groaned under the weight of a stack of framed works. An easel was set up next to a table on which pens and paintbrushes were neatly displayed, and next to it, a large bookcase cluttered with art tomes. She examined its contents and smiled when she saw a familiar spine. It was an old and well-thumbed copy of *One Hundred Years of Solitude*. She turned the pages, revealing an elegantly inked inscription on the title page which read: "To G, forever CC". She held the page up to Martín.

'Who is CC?'

He examined the page and whispered conspiratorially, 'Seeing is believing.'

Isabel replaced the book and offered him an encouraging nod. She looked around her and sniffed the air. It was stale and musty and yet everything in the room had been polished and perfectly preserved, as if Gabriel might appear at any moment.

'What a treasure trove this is.'

Martín laughed. 'He's a great collector. I was only saying the same to Mateu the other day.'

'Mateu came by?'

'Yes. My grandson is a dear boy, but he doesn't swim well so he should be careful of water. It's evidently a family trait. All the same he is stubborn, just like Gabriel, and doesn't always listen.'

A crash of thunder made Isabel start. Her heart thumped.

'Did Mateu collect something important when he was here?'

Absentmindedly, Martín walked towards the French windows, his nose against the icy glass pane.

'Shall we go down there now, Lucy? Perhaps we could swim? The sea is calling.'

Isabel gave a sigh.

'It's a lovely thought, but I must be on my way soon. I have a long journey home and the storm is growing fierce.'

He gave a sad shake of the head and followed her meekly to the bedroom door.

'I hope Gabriel will be safe. He's a good walker but not a confident swimmer and the lake is dangerous and full of sharks.'

Isabel patted his arm and turned off the lights. She guided him up the steps to the ground floor.

Agila rushed to greet them.

'Is everything alright?'

'We're fine. Were the glass panes broken?' Isabel replied.

The woman nodded. 'It's okay. The gardener can clear up the mess in the morning. Are you leaving?'

'Yes, I think I'd better go before the weather worsens. It's been a fascinating visit.'

Agila pushed a strand of pewter hair from her eyes and smiled.

'Let me fetch your leather jacket, gloves and bike helmet. I left them on a chair in the kitchen.'

Isabel followed her into the warm room where another fire burnt. Her eyes wandered to what she assumed was a pantry with a rustic, wood-latticed door. Amber light shone from within and Isabel was immediately transported back to her childhood and the rickety old confessional box of the church of Sant Antoní. As instructed by her mother, she would dutifully kneel behind a black curtain and whisper her transgressions through a shady latticed window where in the dim light only the profile of Padre Agustí could be seen. For the price of a Hail Mary, the slate would be wiped clean for another day in the eyes of God. Confession and absolution of mortal sin. Was it ever really possible to return to purity of soul, however heinous the crime? As she fastened up her jacket on the blustery porch, Martín Vives smiled from behind the front door.

'Safe journey back to Madrid, Lucy, and don't forget to send Sebi my love.'

Isabel winced and felt a stab of sorrow. In the driving rain, she fired up Boadicea and switched on the headlights, contemplating a wet and precarious ride back to Sant Martí. She was about to set off when Martín dashed towards her, hotly pursued by Agila. He stood like a ghost in front of the glaring headlights, tears of rain rolling down his cheeks.

'I gave it to Mateu. Pandora's box of secrets. Alas, one day we all must learn the truth.'

SEVENTEEN

After a refreshing early morning swim with Furó, Isabel returned to Ca'n Moix clutching a bag of freshly baked croissants from Bon Día. Pep smiled as she walked into the office.

'You're going to be pleased with me,' he said.

'Really? But aren't I always pleased with you, dear Pep?'

He laughed. 'I think we both know the answer to that.'

'I've bought us croissants and Mama left some of her homemade *mora* jam yesterday. Coffee time?'

Pep stroked Furó's damp and gleaming fur. 'I'll go and put a brew on. By the way, how was your meeting with Sebi's old man last night?'

Isabel exhaled deeply. 'It was unsettling and sad. He became very confused and thought I was his wife's art dealer from Madrid. He also seemed to think Sebi was still alive. Interestingly, he confirmed that Mateu had paid him a visit and mentioned that whatever was in the box would reveal a truth.'

Pep rubbed his eyes and yawned. 'What truth?'

'That's what we need to discover, though I think I have an idea.'

'Oh?'

She shook her head. 'Not yet. I need to clarify a few final things first to make sure I'm not off track.'

He headed for the stairs. 'Always the woman of mystery.'

Isabel settled Furó in his basket and made a call to Professor Vilalba to arrange another visit. To her delight he agreed to meet at the university the next morning in spite of it being a Saturday. As she stood in front of her whiteboard scribbling some notes, her door banged open and Idò bounced in.

'Morning Bel, a bit of intel for you.'

She smiled. 'I like intel.'

'I was talking to one of the landowners over a coffee at Café Jordi's this morning and he told me something interesting. He said that there had been a lot of strange sightings around Pla des Porxo.'

She grinned. 'I heard the rumours about exotic creatures on the loose. Who is this landowner?'

'Old Xim Basa. He has a strip of land that backs onto the Russian's place. He said that a month ago he was up there very late because one of his sheep was giving birth and he heard a right hullabaloo and multiple shots being fired. He reckons there were lots of folk hunting in forestland directly around the estate.'

'Hm, intriguing, and backs up what the lost German hikers maintained. I think I'll call Xim, if that's okay?'

'Be my guest. I'll text you his number now.'

'When did you become so savvy with your smartphone?' teased Isabel.

Pep walked into the room and offered them both coffees. 'I taught him. Come on, give me some credit, Idò.'

The older man winked at him. 'Well, nipper, you've got to have some use in this office. Otherwise you're just dancing at your desk or throwing balls to Furó every day.'

With a guffaw, Isabel nudged her uncle and offered them both croissants.

'So, Pep, you said I was going to be pleased with you. Care to elaborate?'

He sat on the edge of her desk, sipping his coffee.

'My first bit of news is that I have finally checked all the shoe sizes and profiles of the key members and volunteers of TAA on that list that you gave me and only two men had relevant shoe sizes. I called Pablo Pons's assistant, who sent me their profiles. One is eighty-two years old and the other was on the mainland at the time of the killing of Sebi Vives. So all clean.'

'Great work, Pep,' said Isabel.

'And now for the best bit. The local Chinese family who own the Soller store called me this morning. Apparently, those wooden signs are sold at an elderly friend's store near Inca. So I called him and guess what?'

Isabel gave him a sly grin. 'He said that a woman with long dark hair had bought some.'

'How did you know that?' said Pep. 'She'd visited about two months ago and bought up his shop's supply of about a hundred signs.'

'Excellent, Pep. Now I need you to pop by his store. Find out every detail about the woman, her physique, clothes, attitude and whether she disclosed anything to the owner.'

Pep flushed with excitement. 'Right away!'

Idò gleefully clapped his hands together. 'So now we've got that lout, Frans Bordoy, good and proper. It's got to be one of his eco-mob.'

Isabel polished off her croissant, threw her mobile into her pannier and headed for the door. She kissed her uncle on the cheek.

'He is just the man I'm about to visit, but dear uncle, I believe you may be wide of the mark.'

And with that she whistled to Furó and together they set off at speed down the stairs.

The casita belonging to Frans Bordoy sat on a peaceful stretch of mountainside overlooking Fornalutx. Isabel stood admiring the mountain views, and the healthy woodland and grove of olive trees in front of the tiny stone house. Frans had created a thriving vegetable patch flanked by lemon trees bursting with fruit. Several hens and scrawny cockerels stalked about the nearby scrubland, while a family of guinea fowl and two imperious-looking peacocks made themselves at home in the front garden. Solar panels had been fitted on a sloping roof of rusty-coloured terracotta tiles, partially masked by bushy shrubs.

The front door opened and Frans, his long dark hair falling about his shoulders, observed Isabel with a lazy expression.

'Come in. Make yourself at home. Or are you here to arrest me?'

She winked at him. 'Up to you. If you've got anything to confess, just let me know. Any chance of a coffee first?'

He laughed and beckoned her inside the cosy house, stopping momentarily to admire Furó.

'I had a ferret named Bonnie as a child. My father found a few abandoned young ones in woodland and we looked after them.'

'That's unusual.'

He shrugged. 'He reckoned they'd been dumped there. Maybe a commercially bought pet that had given birth and the owner wanted rid of them.'

Isabel frowned. 'That kind of irresponsible behaviour makes me mad.'

'Me too. So how do you like your coffee?'

'A *cortado*, please, with a little sugar. I like your tattoos. Quite a selection.'

He stretched out his arms. On the right arm were woodland images and on the other oceanic scenes. 'They bear testimony to my manifesto about protecting Mother Nature.'

'It's reflected in your artworks too, if I recall. I remember attending one of your exhibitions in Soller some years ago.'

He handed her a small cup of piping coffee and gestured for her to follow him. Isabel found herself in a surprisingly spacious studio with large windows that looked out on Aleppo pines and a mountainside dotted with lentic bushes. The walls were covered with huge canvasses of an eclectic nature, most bearing activist slogans. In one, a male hiker appeared to lose his balance and was falling backwards from a cliff edge into an abyss, his face a picture of abject terror. Another showed two female hikers studying a map, oblivious to a vulture with a cruel expression about to strike them with its beak.

'These are cheery,' remarked Isabel. 'A case of art imitating life, or maybe the other way round?'

Frans squatted on a stool and lit himself a cigarette.

'Who knows? I like to think it's divine intervention.'

'Presumably you know that the Guardia and just about every landowner here thinks you are responsible for the hiker accidents? These canvasses don't help your case.'

'I know that, but I've had nothing to do with what happened. You don't have to believe me. If I go to jail, so be it.'

'That's a bit defeatist.'

He puffed out a plume of smoke. 'Sometimes, life is stacked against you. I just wait for the universe to see justice done.'

Furó leapt onto his lap and nuzzled his shirt.

'Actually, I do believe you and it seems that Furó does too. He is an excellent judge of character. I have a theory and I need your help.'

The man stroked Furó's head. 'Go on.'

'I need some information about the Russian estate at Pla des Porxo.'

He chuckled. 'So finally someone is asking the right questions. How long have you got?'

Isabel drew up in front of Ca'n Moix. Señora Coll was talking with Doctor Ramis by his gate. Evidently, the postmistress had some new malady or had popped by for some of his efficacious 'magic pills', in reality a placebo, but happily she never knew. Isabel banged open the car door.

'Señora Coll! Can I have a word?'

The old lady offered the doctor a kiss on both cheeks and walked slowly over to Isabel. Doctor Ramis winked at his neighbour and pottered back along his path.

'That man is a saint,' declared Señora Coll. 'I'd have died many years ago had it not been for those magic pills.'

Isabel nodded encouragingly. 'Indeed. How lucky we are to have him here in Sant Martí. Now, I need to ask you something important about Frans Bordoy.'

'Ah, that dear boy. I wish he'd get a haircut and have a good bath, but he has a heart of gold.'

Isabel smiled. 'I have just been speaking with him and he told me that last Tuesday he spent the whole afternoon and evening with you. Is that correct?'

She laughed. 'There are no secrets around here! Yes, he came over to clean out my corral and do some gardening and later I cooked him dinner and we watched a wonderful documentary about the highest peaks in the world. Who'd have known?'

'What was the film called?'

'That's easy. It was called *Mountain* and one of those Hollywood actors did the commentary, but surprisingly, he was very good.'

Isabel stifled a smirk. 'What time did Frans go home?'

She offered a coy grin. 'To be honest, he didn't. We'd had a nice supper and I'd opened a bottle of wine so suggested he stay overnight. I have a lovely spare bedroom. He left at first light as he didn't want neighbours talking. Such a considerate young man.'

Isabel gave a sigh. 'Would you be happy to give a statement to the police?'

Señora Coll's expression turned anxious. 'Frans isn't in any trouble, is he?'

'Some hikers went missing on Tuesday and the Guardia believe Frans could have been involved given that he is vehemently against visitors to the Tramuntanas. He refused to give his whereabouts that day or night so he's a suspect. I managed to get the truth out of him, but I needed you to verify his story. In reality, he was protecting your reputation.'

She shook her head sorrowfully. 'As if my reputation needed protecting at my age, *reina*. What a thoughtful lad, though. I had heard some nasty talk about him in the village recently. Ignorance breeds malice. When do you need the statement?'

'Could you come with me to meet Capitán Gómez in Palma tomorrow?'

'Of course. Just say the word.'

Isabel gave her a hug and whistled to Furó, who remained in his cosy basket on the passenger seat. Yawning, he stretched and joined her on the pavement. Together, they watched as Señora Coll walked laboriously along Calle Pastor. Isabel smiled.

'Come on, my little friend. We have urgent work to do, but I feel that we are now on the last lap.'

Isabel held the mobile away from her ear and closed her eyes momentarily. She had endured half an hour of stilted conversation with Capitán Gómez and was in need of a strong drink. Her eyes flicked open when she heard an urgent voice.

'Bel, are you still there?'

'Sorry, Alvaro, my office phone was bleating and Pep isn't in the office.'

'Do you want to call me back?'

She groaned inwardly. 'No, that's okay. Let's just agree a time to meet tomorrow with Señora Coll. How about ten o'clock at your office?'

'Fine. And what about this old chap Xim Basa you mentioned? I'm still sceptical about these tales of nighttime hunts near Pla des Porxo.'

'I'll call him to find out more. Meanwhile, we'll need to wait until Monday for forensics to identify the age and rifle models of those casings I found.'

He breathed heavily down the line. 'I'm confident that will prove a red herring, Bel.'

'But if my hypothesis is backed up by forensics, you'll act quickly?'

He tutted. 'I respect you, Bel, but what you've suggested is completely outlandish. All the same, pending the forensic report on Monday, I will ensure that all units are on standby and will inform my superiors in Madrid.'

'Even you have superiors, Alvaro?' Isabel goaded.

He tittered. 'Indeed, Bel, I do.' He hesitated. 'It's also important that I apprise the local mayors of a potential new lead. In the meantime, please don't think about taking any impetuous actions without my direct order.'

Isabel said her goodbyes, ended the call and looked out of the window at the darkening sky. It had been a long day and she had spent the afternoon trying to make sense of the many strands of the case forming a cat's cradle in her head. She was tempted to potter downstairs to the kitchen for a glass of wine and a plate of food, but seeing that she was running low on Chupa Chups and sunflower seeds, she decided she would pop by Bon Día for more supplies. First, though, she needed to make a call to a leading Palma clinic.

Tolo had been summoned urgently to Madrid and she was disappointed that they would not now be seeing one another until his return on Sunday evening. Still, she would buy *gambas rojas al ajillo* from her most trusted local fisherman and select one of Tolo's favourite red wines. Leaving Furó slumbering in his basket, she jogged along Calle Pastor to the *plaça*, stopping briefly to pass the time of day with her neighbour, Juliana. As she browsed the shelves of Bon Día, clutching a family-size pack of Chupa Chups, she turned to find Ariel hovering behind her. He was wearing his customary beanie and sardonic sneer.

'Those lollipops have plastic sticks. Not great for the environment.'

She turned to face him. 'Actually, you're wrong. They are now made of paper and the company are using recycled plastics.'

'Still, not good for your teeth.'

'You and your father use guns. They're not so great for the environment or the health. Talking of which, I found a lot of spent cartridges littering the forest near your land the other day.'

He offered an insolent shrug. 'Not ours.'

At the counter, Jesus gave him a wary glance.

'I heard your boss was flying in next week? If you want supplies, let me know soonest.'

Ariel nodded. 'Sure. We'll confirm the order tomorrow. Can I have my usual?'

Jesus reached for a packet of cigarettes from a glass cabinet behind the counter. Isabel tutted.

'Now those aren't great for your health, Ariel.'

'We've all got to die sometime.'

'Some sooner than others,' she replied.

Isabel followed him out into the dark, cool *plaça* and suddenly reached for his beanie. The youth sprang backwards.

'What the hell are you doing?'

'I just wanted to see the brand name. I think my brother in San Sebastian might like one for the cold winters there.'

He scowled. 'Just ask next time. It's Running Man. It's not a cheap brand.'

Isabel pulled up her jacket collar. 'I'm sure it isn't. I'll see you around.'

Back home in the warmth of her kitchen, Isabel heated her mother's homemade aubergine, tomato and parmesan bake in the oven and opened a bottle of Myotragus. She needed the fortification of a glass of robust, local red wine. With her jacket still on and glass in hand, she slipped outside into the silky darkness and stood on the patio listening to the distant clucks of her hens and the whispering of the leaves. A barn owl called from a far-off garden and a dog barked urgently. With a slight shiver, she lit the candles on the table and turned on the patio heater she had been gifted by Tolo. The warm glow embraced her and she immediately relaxed and sat back in her wicker chair, relishing the peace and shadowy darkness beyond. He was forever spoiling her with indulgent and thoughtful gifts that she would never think to purchase for herself. Isabel wondered whether he had created a list of items that he felt sure she must have in order to be happy. In truth, she was happy just as she was with Tolo in her life, and hanging out in the mountains with Furó and her loving family, friends and neighbours. No material goods could ever match all that, though she freely admitted that Pequeñito and now Boadicea had added a certain *joie de vivre* to her life.

She estimated that it was about eight-thirty. Tolo would be dining with the head of the Ministry of the Interior and elite members of the National Police in Madrid and was unlikely to be free to talk with her before eleven o'clock. As agreed, he would call her later from his hotel room. They would have much to discuss, not least her encounter with Martín Vives and her findings about Silvia Porres and her mother. And then there was the strange altercation between Eli, Jaume and Mateu that she'd witnessed in Palma. It would be a long call. She sighed and relished her first few sips of wine.

Her mobile's harsh ring ripped through the calm night, making her flinch. The name Emilio Navarro flashed up on her screen, increasing her agitation.

'Bel, I'm sorry to disturb you on a Friday night, but I have just received some intel about Hugo that is quite compelling and bizarre.'

Isabel blinked hard. 'Whatever do you mean?'

'The National Central Bureau and Interpol in Mexico have just sent me some images that are indisputably your uncle. He is still alive.'

Isabel gulped. Her mouth was dry and her body shook. Quickly she took a long sip of wine.

'Mexico?'

'It seems that Hugo has been living in Mexico for some months. He has been spotted at the *hacienda* of one of the country's leading drug lords.'

'How can that be?' Isabel whispered. She thought of her fearless, investigative journalist uncle, a man who had always upheld strong and noble values. How could he have turned to crime? It simply made no sense.

'Interpol admits that there is more to the story. Their agents are monitoring the situation closely to ensure his safety.'

Isabel felt bewildered. 'I don't understand.'

'It's complicated and I know little other than that your uncle appears to have been part of an undercover operation known to Interpol. I have been asked to step aside from the investigation.'

'But I need to know what's happening.'

He gave a nervous cough. 'I assume Interpol will make contact with you at some stage. In the meantime, no one must get wind of this, including Tolo, I'm afraid.'

Isabel felt a flash of anger. 'Why ever not?'

'The order is from the minister of the interior in Madrid. No Spanish force is to be informed or involved. This is classified information, Bel. Hugo may be alive, but his life has never been in such mortal danger.'

EIGHTEEN

Isabel sat next to Señora Coll in the bland, pristine office occupied by Capitán Gómez and Tricia, his long-suffering and loyal secretary. There was a strong aroma of furniture polish in the air and not a file, paper or pen seemed out of place. Tricia looked up wearily from her computer.

'Sorry to keep you, Bel. He'll be back any minute.'

Isabel smiled over at her. 'I know the drill.'

The door swung open and the Guardia chief strode over to his desk. His green uniform seemed particularly stiff and unyielding. Isabel pondered whether he starched it every morning. He addressed Señora Coll with zealous eyes.

'Your statement is ready so all you have to do is read it over carefully and sign it. Here's a pen.'

He buffed the shiny metal instrument on his sleeve and handed it to her.

The elderly woman nodded. 'Give me a moment. I need my reading specs.'

As she sifted through the contents of her handbag, Capitán Gómez leant forcefully on the desk, a sneer planted on his lips.

Isabel detected a sharp, regular inflection in his jaw and deduced that he must be chewing gum. If it was supposed to have a soothing effect on him, it didn't appear to be working.

'I would just remind you, Señora Coll, that should it be discovered that you have committed perjury in any way, you can expect a long and uncomfortable prison term.'

Isabel rolled her eyes impatiently. 'Alvaro, is that really necessary?'

'But I am telling the truth, sir,' Señora Coll whispered croakily. 'Why would I lie?'

'A good question, *señora*, but every day criminals sit before me and like you, they plead that their statements are honest only to be exposed later as complete frauds!'

Isabel puffed out her cheeks. 'I need a Chupa Chup.'

'Urgh. I wish you wouldn't eat those ghastly things,' he grumbled.

'My choice. Besides, chewing gum isn't so great for you.'

'All the same, it's been used by humans for thousands of years so it can't be so harmful.'

'That's as may be, but it's full of sugar. In Iran and Saudi Arabia, they can't get enough of the stuff and they both have a serious problem with tooth decay.'

He offered a pert smile. 'You have quite a curious and eclectic bank of knowledge, Bel.'

She nodded. 'Chewing gum is interesting, particularly used gum. You know, it has a typical bacteriome worldwide, and although a lengthy process, you can extract DNA and perform 16S rRNA sequencing on it even if quite degraded.'

'Really? I shall remember that when I discard my gum.'

'You should, Alvaro. If accused of a crime, it could be your undoing.'

He laughed. 'Hopefully I shall continue to stay within the confines of the law.'

Señora Coll eyed them both in confusion.

'Can we go now, Bel? I need to open shop.'

Isabel rose swiftly. 'Of course.'

At the door, the captain gave a small salute and fixed his lizard green eyes on Isabel.

'We'll be in touch, Bel. As discussed yesterday, please don't do anything impulsive or take the law into your own hands.'

She laughed. 'Of course not. It's simply not in my nature.'

Isabel dropped the postmistress back in Sant Martí and returned home to Ca'n Moix. She needed to do some online investigative research and to make some calls. One was to her uncle's friend, Xim Basa, who owned land near Pla des Porxo, while another was to Victor, a former police chum now working in security at the small private aerodrome of Palma Son Bonet. Although the airport served mostly helicopters and recreational and training aircrafts, it did accommodate private international flights. It was located eight kilometres north-east of the capital and had officially become a national and international customs airport back in 1946.

Having successfully finished her tasks, Isabel immediately sped off on Boadicea to the university, where she spent an hour in deep conversation with Professor Vilalba. On her return to the village, she was ravenous and popped into Bar Castell for a coffee and *bocadillo*. Rafael stood behind the counter with his arms folded, wearing a lopsided smile.

'Llorenç is on the terrace. He's getting himself wound up about the mountain falls and he's just broken his diet. Knew it wouldn't last long.'

Isabel winked. 'It must be all the stress.'

She wandered through the tables inside, greeting various locals on the way, and found the mayor on the tail end of a phone call, an anxious expression planted on his face. He finished the call and popped the mobile into his jacket pocket.

'Are you okay, Llorenç?'

He emitted a sigh. 'I have just had a long conversation with Capitán Gómez and he tells me that based on a testimony from Señora Coll, Frans Bordoy may no longer be our chief suspect. That means we are back to square one with no leads whatsoever.'

Isabel pulled out a chair and yawned.

'Oh, I wouldn't say that.'

She leant over and examined his empty plate and bread bowl. 'Do I detect that you've been eating bread?'

He regarded her with a scowl. 'I haven't got time to follow Angélica's diet. I can resume it as soon as this worrying mountain matter is behind us.'

'Of course,' Isabel replied soothingly. 'Now, on that subject, I have some thoughts that I'd like to share with you, but they may not bring you much comfort.'

Llorenç gaped at her. 'Well, don't leave me in suspense.'

Isabel smiled as Rafael approached the table with a tray. 'Let me enjoy my coffee and food first and of course, your sparkling company, and then I'll tell you all.'

As Isabel arrived back at Ca'n Moix having apprised an increasingly agitated and disapproving Llorenç of her plans for later that day, she spied Doctor Ramis cutting his hedgerow of oleander. He looked up and waved his secateurs in her direction.

'What ho! How's my beautiful and talented neighbour?'

She cocked her head to the side. 'I don't know. I haven't met her yet.'

'Oh, you're a wag.'

Isabel laughed. 'How's life? Is my mother luring you to yet another exercise class today?'

He rubbed his whiskery chin. 'As it happens, we're off to a salsa class later at the community hall. Juliana is in charge and promises it'll be fun. She's serving caipirinhas afterwards.'

'Mightn't it be better to have them first to loosen you all up?'

'I might suggest it, dear girl.' He paused to blow his nose. 'It's been a long morning.'

'Tell me about it. Difficult patients?'

'One of Bernat's wealthy Swedish expat clients from Deià had only just collected his car from his depot when he was involved in a nasty shunt near the petrol station in Soller. A young driver was speeding down the hill and simply didn't have time to break at the roundabout. The car is back at Bernat's workshop and his poor client is left with severe whiplash. I took a good look at his neck and packed him straight off to Clinica Rotger in Palma for an MRI.'

Isabel listened keenly. 'Did you prescribe a cervical collar?'

He shook his head. 'These days it's not really recommended. I placed ice on his neck and suggested a course of gentle physiotherapy.'

'Did he have a lot of bruising?'

Doctor Ramis placed his hands in the small of his back and stretched. 'No, with whiplash it's more about discs, muscles and tendons being jolted. He'll be fine, just a bit of a shock to the system.'

'I'm pleased to hear it. Enjoy your class. Tell Mama that I'll be out tonight, so no need to leave me kitchen supplies.'

'Going anywhere interesting?'

She raised an eyebrow. 'Actually, it is interesting in a macabre sort of way.'

'I'm guessing a horror movie?'

She eyed him in some bemusement. 'In a manner of speaking, you could be right.'

Pep turned off his music as soon as Isabel walked into the office and jumped up from his seat.

'How was your morning?'

Isabel yawned heavily. 'It's been pretty hectic for a Saturday. And what, may I ask, are you doing in at the weekend?'

'I popped by that Chinese store near Inca yesterday afternoon and was leaving you an update.'

He wafted a neatly typed piece of paper under her nose.

'Pep, you really are becoming an excellent investigator.'

She grasped the sheet and, sitting on the edge of his desk, read it thoroughly.

'So the elderly owner thought that the client who bought the wooden signs was in her twenties? You say here that she came in alone late one afternoon.'

Pep shrugged. 'Apparently she was wearing large sunglasses and a heavy coat with a hood, but he could see that she had long brown hair. To be honest, he's very old and was a bit vague.'

'Odd to be wearing shades in the middle of dark January, wouldn't you say?'

'That's why the old man remembered her.' Pep shrugged. 'Hollywood actors wear shades all the time. Mind you, I doubt she's one.'

'Oh, I don't know,' Isabel replied with a grin. 'Her acting skills might be first class.'

Pep chewed on his lip. 'Who do you think she is?'

Isabel sprang up and was about to speak when her mobile rang. It was Enric, the mountain guide. She listened carefully. The call ended and she tapped the phone against her chin.

'What's up?' asked Pep.

'Enric is in the *plaça* and wants a quick word. I won't be long.' Isabel turned to him at the door. 'Are you busy later tonight? I'm planning a small reconnaissance mission.'

'Is it risky?' he asked suspiciously.

'It involves a nighttime mountain adventure. There will be risks.'

There was a glimmer in Pep's eye. 'Count me in. Angélica is at a birthday party and sleepover with her girlfriends tonight.'

'Excellent. I'll explain everything later. Meet me back here at eleven tonight.'

'Will Furó be joining us?'

Isabel hesitated. 'On this occasion, I think not. We'll leave him to have a good night's kip.'

And with a smile, she set off down the stairs.

Enric was waiting for Isabel by the fountain. He had his hands in his jacket pockets and wore a troubled expression. Isabel kissed him on both cheeks.

'You must be psychic. You're just the man I wanted to see.'

He looked surprised. 'Really?'

'So what did you want to talk with me about? It sounded important.'

He looked about him. 'This village has ears. Can we talk down by the *torrente*?'

They walked in companionable silence along Carrer del Bisbe and followed the road to the fast-running *torrente*. On the bridge, they looked down at the rushing water.

'It's so different in winter, isn't it?'

Isabel smiled. 'Yes, you can't believe it's the same place. Hopefully, with all the rain we've had the last few months, the reservoirs will be full.'

'I took a hiking group to Gorg Blau yesterday and the water's nice and deep.'

'I thought hiking had been temporarily banned?'

He nodded. 'It's banned for lone walkers and we guides are restricted to certain popular and easy hikes, mostly around the reservoir. All of us have already lost loads of bookings.'

'All the more reason to find the culprits as soon as possible.'

'Did you have any luck identifying those cartridge casings you found in the forest last week?'

'Steady on,' she replied. 'Forensics can't work miracles. Still, I should hear back on Monday, with any luck.'

'Good. You see I've learnt that the Russian owner is back at Pla des Porxo tomorrow night.'

Isabel smiled. 'Yes, I know. His flight gets in to Son Bonet airport late afternoon.'

'You already know?'

She nodded. 'I've a good contact at the airport.'

Enric continued. 'Some other guides and I were discussing the situation with the injured hikers. We feel something odd is going on at that estate.'

Isabel listened attentively. 'Care to elaborate?'

He shrugged. 'In all honesty, we've no idea, but something bad. Maybe Nikolai Petrov is an arms dealer and trialling ammo up there. That would explain all those cartridges and why Pistola doesn't want any of us near the estate.'

'And who is stalking the hills and misdirecting hikers?'

'We've drawn a blank on that one. None of us can identify the woman that hikers mentioned, but we all want to help catch the criminals. That's why I've come to you.'

He threw her a miserable look. 'If this goes on, I'll have no income and nor will the other guides.'

Isabel gave him a reassuring hug.

'Thank you for sharing your thoughts in confidence with me but please listen. I think I know who is behind the hiker accidents and the Guardia will be taking action soon. In the meantime, don't discuss the matter with your colleagues.'

'Can't you tell me more than that?'

Isabel led him back towards Carrer del Bisbe. 'I'm afraid not but have faith. Soon, you'll be hiking those hills with wild abandon. Until then, mum's the word.'

When Isabel returned to Ca'n Moix, her head was brimming with untamed thoughts, so much so that she rushed upstairs and immediately called Gaspar.

'Are you in the office?'

He sniggered. 'What do you think? The boss has given me about a million tasks to get done by end of play.'

'And there he is having fun in Madrid.'

Gaspar let rip a deep hoot of laughter. 'I can't imagine anything worse than being grilled over dinner by the director general of police.'

'True, but at least he's seeing his son, Fabio, for lunch tomorrow. Vinegar before sugar.'

'And then dinner over at yours. I'm happy for you lovebirds. So what can I do for you?'

Isabel rapped her fingers on her desk. 'Would you be able to get me an appointment to speak with Sebi and Sara Vives' private doctor? Isn't it the illustrious Dr Sánchez?'

'That's him. Doctor to the *politicos* and stars. I'd say there's zero chance of him seeing you without a warrant.'

'I'd rather not get heavy. Let me find another way.'

'What are you going to do, hijack him on his way to work?' asked Gaspar.

'If it comes to it.' Isabel chuckled. 'So, any more news?'

'Forensics has confirmed that the binding used on the drug haul you discovered in that old Lada parked in Palma is a direct match to the one on the cocaine package found in Sebi's abandoned car. The drug dealer is a stooge of Rocci Mestre, so we can safely assume that he got him to plant the gun and drugs in Sebi's vehicle at some stage.'

Isabel nodded. 'I thought as much. Sebi would have remained blissfully ignorant of the fact. It was a little insurance policy should he ever try to pull a fast one or expose the Mestres in any way over the motorway deal. I wonder if Rocci acted alone or his brothers were also in on it.'

'Hard to say, but he's definitely the rotten apple in the pile. It would help too if we had the brothers' DNA, but without proof we can't take that path yet. It could be a match with those used gum samples Furó found.'

Isabel frowned. 'No, I don't think so. I have another idea floating in my mind.'

'In more good news,' Gaspar continued, 'we've just heard that on Monday we'll get the warrant to search Rocci Mestre's property in Montuïri and also the main homes of all three brothers and that of Marc Castell.'

'Fantastic. That'll keep the forensics team busy. Do you think Nacho will still find time to get the results back on those bullets I found at Pla des Porxo? The timing's critical.'

'He knows. You'll have the report early Monday morning.'

Isabel breathed a sigh of relief.

'I'll get to the precinct early. Are any of the other rural properties owned by the Mestres of interest?'

'David Mestre has a *casita* in an area of the Tramuntanas that is fairly inaccessible. One of the team did a recce yesterday. It would be impossible to get any kind of tractor up there as it's a precarious single track and the land is made up of *bancales*. Not the best place to flatten a corpse. The other properties are quite exposed and have neighbouring land backing onto them. Still, we'll be carrying out forensics at them all.'

Isabel winced. 'I hope we can catch Silvia's perpetrators. She might have been on the wrong side of the law, but she didn't deserve such a grisly fate. One last thing. Any chance of tracking down her mother at a private nursing home in Santa Ponsa?'

'Nothing in our findings has shown up about any living relatives. Where did you get that intel?'

'On my shopping trip to the gourmet department of El Corte Inglés. Silvia and her mother were estranged for some years, it seems. I also discovered that she'd worked for the Mestres at Gran Casino Atlántico some years back. That doesn't appear on her official CV.'

He gave a low whistle. 'Good sleuth work. We checked her work history with the regional government's HR department and nothing showed up about either El Corte Inglés or the casino. They confirmed that she had inherited her mother's property and lived alone.'

'I imagine that Sebi had all that erased from her file. Now we know how she got the job with Sebi Vives, given his close ties with the Mestres. Quite a web.'

'She would have proven the perfect stooge for Vives, rubber-stamping corrupt contracts and being paid handsomely for her silence.' He sighed. 'If her mother's still alive and kicking, we'll find her. Leave it with me.'

Moments later, Isabel sat at her desk cracking open sunflower seeds with Furó curled up on her knee. She smoothed the fur on the top of his head and smiled when his paw touched her hand.

'Tonight, Pep and I will be away for some time, but I'll make sure that you have a bowl of Mama's tasty snacks awaiting you in the kitchen.'

His eyes popped open and he nuzzled her hand.

'I'd take you with us, but it's just too risky.'

She was suddenly distracted by a huge basket of ironed white sheets left, most likely by the cleaning team, in the corner of her office. How had she not noticed them before? Since working with Tolo, she had increasingly neglected the day-to-day running of the rentals business, leaving much of it to Pep and her loyal support system of family and friends. Did she miss it? Part of her still enjoyed the buzz of meeting clients of different nationalities and she took great satisfaction in maintaining her position as the highest-rated holiday rentals agent by visitors to the Soller valley. And yet, the lure of police work was so compelling and addictive. Furó had his serious coffee-bean coloured eyes fixed on her.

'For now I can juggle both,' she told him. 'Besides, as the dictum goes, variety is the spice of life, don't you agree?'

Furó jumped impatiently off her lap, yawned and scampered over to the door. Isabel laughed and accompanied him downstairs to the kitchen. As far as her ferret was concerned, philosophising could wait, because food always came first.

Somewhere in the sooty darkness a scops owl emitted a regular, hypnotic sonic beep. Scores of tiny silvery bats flitted across the night skies. Deep thunder echoed in the mountains, but it was a dry and brittle night that accentuated the creaking and snapping of twigs and the rustle of leaves. Isabel and Pep crouched low by a wall, listening to the sounds of the forest as they gulped from water bottles. They'd parked their motorbikes among trees some distance from the winding, rocky track that led directly to the Russian's estate, scaled a metal fence and walked the last few kilometres on foot shielded by forestland. Isabel had used a powerful LED flashlight to blind the camera lens on the first gate and would be doing the same on the main gate to the house. She extracted a bar of nut chocolate and offered it to Pep.

'How can you eat? My stomach is churning.'

Isabel shrugged. 'Relax. Victor, my contact at Son Bonet airport, said that Pistola and Ariel always hang out in Palma the night before Nikolai Petrov flies in. They go to flashy bars and stay at a nice hotel on the pretext that they're picking up last-minute supplies for his visit.'

'But what if they have guard dogs, searchlights and barbed wire fences?'

'This isn't Colditz, Pep,' Isabel replied, as she bit off a lump of chocolate.

'What's Colditz?' he hissed at her.

'A Renaissance castle in Germany that once served as a World War Two prisoner-of-war camp. Have you never seen that British black and white movie with the actor John Mills? It was made in the fifties and is quite a classic thriller.'

'You sound just like Doctor Ramis. This old movie obsession must be catching!'

She tittered. 'Okay, let's get going. First, let me disable the camera and then we can scale the gate. Here are your thermal night-vision goggles. They were expensive, so don't lose them.'

Pep looped the strap of the gadget around his neck. 'What if there are dogs?'

'We run unless you brought juicy bones.' She nudged him. 'There's only an elderly collie named Brut who wouldn't hurt a fly. Mind you, they said they'd be buying a Rottweiler soon.'

Pep shook his head and, mumbling, followed her to the gate. She lobbed some rocks over the wall onto the driveway and several sensor lights pinged on. They waited a few minutes until there was darkness once more. Flashing her strong light at the gate camera, she swung a foot at the metal bars and with gloved hands hoisted herself up and over. She jumped down onto the other side and beckoned to Pep. He scaled the gate and they took cover in nearby trees and waited. She gave an indignant sniff.

'That was far too easy. You'd think they'd have made it a bit harder for all the thieves purportedly trying to penetrate their land.'

Pep fixed her with an anxious expression. 'There may be guards with rifles near the house.'

Isabel grinned. 'Let's find out.'

Keeping to the shadows, they crept along the track until the main building came into view. Sensors suddenly lit up the grounds, causing Pep to start, but Isabel didn't react. As agreed prior to their arrival, Isabel stole along the hedgerows to the nearside of the building and, using her night-vision goggles, searched for alarm sensors and entry points. Pep kept close to her, his eyes constantly roving the sombre grounds. Not far off came the sound of agitated geese and the call of a barn owl, and closer to hand, the panting of a dog. Isabel reached out and felt the warm fur of the resident collie. She nuzzled him and spoke soothingly.

'Here, Brut. I've brought you a present.'

Reaching into her rucksack, she withdrew a plastic bag and let loose a hunk of meat. The dog hungrily set to work on it. Isabel headed for an arched wooden door set back in a high stone wall adjacent to the front porch. Having disabled an electric control panel close by, she got down on her haunches and pulled a set of skeleton keys from her rucksack. She worked on the lock until it clicked open and indicated to Pep to follow her as she made her way soundlessly into the vast, walled garden beyond. A manicured lawn flanked by neat gravel paths stretched out before them, surrounded by mature shrubs, extravagant water features and marble and bronze sculptures. Pep nudged her and pointed to a stone cottage and a series of large well-constructed wooden buildings on the other side of the garden.

Isabel turned to him and whispered, 'The main house seems to have quite a sophisticated alarm system, but the garden and grounds only have sensors. Let's be careful now because I'm not sure what we'll find over there.'

He nodded and gave her the thumbs-up. The cottage was veiled in darkness, but an eerie violet light shone from the larger of the three wooden buildings. A loud humming sound came from within, which Isabel thought might indicate an electrical device or air-cooling system. Cautiously, the pair crept around the environs of the garden until they'd reached the buildings.

'A – are we going to break in?' asked Pep.

Isabel frowned. 'I'm not interested in the cottage. That's obviously where Pistola and his son, Ariel, live. I want to take a look at the other blocks.'

'What do you think might be inside?'

'I have an idea.' She halted and sniffed the air. 'There's a strong smell of livestock and muffled animal sounds. Surely that's a clue?'

Pep puffed out his lower lip. 'If you say so. Let's hope they haven't bought that Rottweiler yet.'

Isabel stopped to collect her thoughts and then headed for the larger of the wooden blocks. She wandered around the perimeter until she'd detected the flicker of a dull LED light and an external alarm panel. Next, she inspected the metal door.

'This is operated by a wireless security system, which is impressive given that we're in the middle of nowhere,' she said quietly. 'I brought my frequency jammer so we should be okay.'

'Is that legal?' asked Pep.

Isabel rolled her eyes in the silky darkness and grinned. Unearthing the small and effective device which she'd bought cheaply off a Chinese website some years before, she set about disarming the alarm.

'How does that work?' asked Pep in wonderment.

'It blocks the cellular signals of a wireless security system, but it's not foolproof. Some systems are quite stubborn.'

His eyes opened wide. 'How often have you done this sort of thing?'

'Once or twice,' she whispered.

Minutes later, she used her trusty set of skeleton keys to open the door. A lean corridor greeted them, and another metal door, but its key remained in the lock. Isabel examined the walls and ceilings.

'Looks like this building is sealed and soundproofed. Be prepared.'

Pep's eyes bulged and he grabbed her shoulder. 'Prepared for what?'

Isabel sighed. 'Come on, grow some, as they say in the American movies.'

She turned the key in the lock and tentatively pushed open the door just as loud animal cries erupted from within. Before her were numerous pens, each one holding a large number of domestic animals. She and Pep looked around them in some amazement. Each pen was fitted with heating lamps and a dim violet light penetrated the gloom.

'The room is climate-controlled and that whirring sound is an extraction fan,' Isabel commented.

'Why are they all locked in here?' asked Pep.

'Why indeed?' she replied.

She led Pep around the different animal stalls. There were donkeys, cows, bulls and deer and smaller mountain species such as goats, sheep, hares and rabbits. Wild black pigs and hogs were kept in separate pens, while a series of large cages housed birds of prey and fowl of different varieties. Isabel used her night goggles to record what she saw, commenting on her findings as she went. When she'd finished recording, she headed for the door.

'Did you notice that each animal had a specific-coloured tag stapled in its ear with a number? The hogs have blue tags and the donkeys have red, for example.'

He nodded. 'It's bizarre. Are they rearing and selling them?'

'No, I don't think so. I believe they have a more sinister purpose. Come on, let's explore the next two huts.'

Pep followed her outside and nervously looked about him.

'It's eerily quiet. What if someone turns up unexpectedly?'

Isabel shrugged. 'Hopefully we'd hear the vehicle some distance away.'

After a struggle with the lock, Isabel entered the adjoining wooden building. This one was empty save for a dozen wooden chairs and two robust oak hunting tables with brass brace-bar supports. Running along one side of the room, with its bland concrete floor, was a row of large metal cupboards. Isabel found that all were secured with locks and heavy-duty padlocks.

'This is going to take a little time.'

'Maybe we should go now,' Pep replied. 'I feel uneasy.'

Isabel offered him a reassuring smile.

'Listen, why don't you act as sentry on the front door while I crack these locks?'

He nodded and walked slowly back to the entrance, a frown on his face.

Isabel toiled for another fifteen minutes until she was finally able to penetrate the first cupboard. Inside, she discovered a wall of powerful hunting rifles, each secured with chains and bolts. She gave a low whistle as she filmed the contents and examined each of the models. If the other cupboards contained similar high-spec rifles, there'd be enough for a fully-fledged battle. Sitting back on her heels, Isabel bit her lip hard. Her instincts had been right, but she still needed proof of one final element in the puzzle. Carefully she closed the cupboard and clicked the padlock back into place. She set to work on the next lock. This time she discovered hunting tackle and row upon row of gleaming knives of different sizes. A shelf was stacked with leather gloves and hunting jackets, while on a higher level she spied something orange and luminous. She reached up and pulled down an item on the top layer, jumping back in alarm when she realised what it was. As she stood there, fumbling with her video camera, Pep burst through the door and ran towards her.

'I can hear a car in the distance. Someone's coming.'

Isabel raised her eyebrows in alarm.

'Okay. Quickly put this back on that shelf for me. You're taller than me.'

Pep picked up the fluorescent body bag and eyed her in terror.

'What are they doing with one of these?'

'There are more piled up. Hurry. I need to secure the place. No one can know we were here. Go and keep a lookout until I return.'

Pep jogged back to the entrance. Isabel took deep breaths and hastily secured the cupboard and replaced the padlock. As she was heading for the door, her attention fell on a silky-black fur rug in a corner of the room that seemed out of place in the stark space. Curiosity got the better of her and she flipped it over at one edge. It was a real pelt and smelt musty and savage. What animal had it belonged to? Not one from around the local woods, she surmised. Underneath, sunken in the concrete floor, was a large steel trapdoor secured with metal bolts and a combination padlock. In dismay, Isabel realised that a special set of tools, gun or even dynamite would be needed to crack it. She sat back on her heels and surveyed it in frustration until Pep reappeared.

'I can hear a vehicle. Hurry!'

'Damn. We haven't seen inside the third building yet. Okay, I'm coming.'

Using her night-vision goggles to reach the entrance, Isabel locked the door and hastily reactivated the alarms. There was the distant sound of a throbbing engine and tyres on gravel. A vehicle was fast approaching the house.

'You said they'd be staying in Palma overnight,' he said accusingly. 'How do we get out now?'

Isabel put a finger to her lips and, beckoning to him, ran beyond the huts. To her relief, she discovered a garden shed. Grabbing a rock from a border of shrubs, she lobbed it through the window and cleared the broken glass with the sleeve of her jacket. Pep opened his mouth in surprise as Isabel hitched herself up on the frame with gloved hands and propelled herself through the open window. Moments later, she hoisted herself up from inside and climbed out with a bulging rucksack on her back. Grabbing the shadows, she directed Pep along the back wall of the house towards the arched side door from which they had entered and gestured to him to crouch low behind trees.

'Have you lost your mind?' he hissed.

Isabel whispered in his ear, 'Just keep still and be ready to run.'

The house was suddenly illuminated and a few minutes later was once more enveloped in darkness. Isabel waited. Sure enough, there was a rattle at the wooden door followed by heavy footsteps, and Ariel and his father burst through. The sensors activated and the garden was flooded with golden light.

Ariel swayed slightly on his feet and slurred his words. 'Someone has definitely been here, snooping around. The alarm at the front of the house was deactivated.'

His father gave a grunt. 'No one has been in the house. The alarm system's faulty. It happened before.'

Ariel shook his head. 'I think we should check out the buildings. Something doesn't feel right.'

The two tramped off, arriving at the shed first. Isabel heard Ariel cursing and shouting. She grabbed Pep's arm. 'Go!'

They slid out from behind the trees and made for the open wooden door. Without stopping for breath or looking back, they ran along the track, keeping to the bushes. All the same, they disturbed the sensors and bright lights illuminated the road. Cursing, Isabel forged on with Pep following behind. At the gate, she hurled her heavy rucksack onto the other side and levered herself up using her upper-body strength. As she reached the summit, Pep did likewise, casting a glance back over his shoulder. There came the sound of jingling and Brut appeared, tongue wagging, the small metal discs on his collar chafing one another. He looked through the metal bars and whimpered.

'We'll be back, old chap,' said Isabel and hastily joined Pep as he disappeared into nearby woodland. After a while, they stopped to catch their breath in the darkness. Isabel scrunched her nose and playfully punched Pep's arm.

'I'm sorry. I took a risk and got caught out. For some reason, they must have changed their plans. Still, the garden shed should keep them busy until we reach the next gate.'

She opened her voluminous rucksack and old tools spilled out, including a cordless drill.

'Why the heck did you take those?'

'We need Pistola and Ariel to think that whoever broke in was an amateur after a quick steal. Mind you, I think I'll hang onto this lightweight DeWalt drill. They cost a small fortune.'

He tutted. 'That's stealing.'

'I'll bring it back to the estate once we're through this.'

'Through what?'

Isabel gave a sigh. 'I'll explain everything when we get back to Sant Martí. For now, let's just get away from here.'

Forty minutes later, they arrived at a small clearing close to where they had hidden their bikes. Pep looked back twitchily at the second gate they had just scaled and briefly at his watch.

'It's four o'clock in the morning.'

Isabel straddled her bike. 'Time flies when you're enjoying yourself, Pep.'

'No one seems to be coming after us,' he said in some relief.

'Ariel looked the worse for wear and both will hopefully reach the conclusion that some chancer broke into the shed to steal some tools. The alarms were reactivated and I left nothing out of place, so they shouldn't suspect anything more sinister.'

Pep sat astride his bike, its lights piercing the narrow and gloomy track ahead.

'But why did they come back if they were supposed to be staying in Palma?'

'Who knows, Pep, but as they say, there's no place like home.'

Isabel pushed down her helmet and revved Boadicea's engine. Ten minutes later they arrived at the mouth of the track that led onto the MA-10. The silent and winding mountain road stretched out before them, flanked on either side by dark, impenetrable forestland. Isabel lifted up the visor of her helmet and called to Pep.

'Come back to the house and we can warm up with coffee and brandy.'

He nodded. 'And what about a slice of Florentina's plum cake?'

She gave the thumbs-up and with a roar of the engine, sped off into the sooty night.

NINETEEN

A lazy sun stretched its rays slowly over the bay, casting golden light on the rows of small fishing boats and gleaming yachts that shimmied on the jostling waves. Isabel yawned and threw a pebble into the sea from her favourite eyrie, an imposing lump of grey limestone rock on the far side of Can Repic beach. It was late morning on Sunday and a handful of joggers and dog walkers were coursing along the beach's pedestrianised walkway. Isabel loved the winter months when the port was calm and free of bustle and the hotels went into hibernation.

Some longed for hot sunshine, but Isabel preferred the gentle temperatures and the local, intimate *fiestas* that were the hallmark of January and February. Soon it would be the *fiesta* of Sant Antoni, a particularly important event in January for Sant Martí as the revered Egyptian was its patron saint. Of course, Sant Antoni was often confused with that more famous saint of the same name who hailed from Portugal, the finder of lost things, but the villagers were proud of their lesser-known saint. For one thing, he was a devotee of animals and purportedly loved pigs; he was often accompanied by one on his travels in the Egyptian desert. On this expanse of parched sandy terrain, the saint endured supernatural temptation by all manner of demons, which is why the *fiesta* involved barbecues and demon dances around a huge wood pyre in the village *plaça*. The saint was celebrated throughout the Soller valley, but the inhabitants of Sant Martí jealously guarded him as their own.

Florentina revered the village's patron saint but also had a soft spot for his Portuguese namesake, proving a firm believer in his magical powers as the finder of lost things. She would regularly invoke the saint's spiritual aid whenever she lost her reading glasses. When they appeared sometime later, more often than not attached to the top of her head, she would offer him grateful thanks and many a devout prayer.

Normally, Isabel would be feeling excited about the forthcoming village celebrations, but she had too much weighing on her mind. She was agitated about her findings at the Voin estate and frustrated that she wasn't able to investigate what lay beyond the trapdoor in the larger of the wooden buildings. Sweeping back her mane of wet hair, she whistled to Furó. He hurtled towards her from the waves. He jumped up on the towel that covered her legs and shook the water from his fur. Isabel giggled.

'Yuk! Come on, *amigo mío*. Let's go home.'

As she squeezed out her swimming costume, her mobile rang. It was Victor, her security contact at Son Bonet airport.

'I have an update for you, Bel. Petrov and his associates will now be arriving at Son Bonet at 17:00 in two light cabin jets. Apparently, he's flying into Zaragoza from Monaco in his Gulfstream 200 and then transferring to two smaller Citation Ultras for the last leg. The Gulfstream will arrive much later at Son Sant Joan airport.'

'I wonder why,' Isabel mused. 'How many people do the Citations accommodate?'

'Six pax and the midsize Gulfstream up to ten, but I understand it will just be carrying cargo. This has become quite a pattern with Petrov of late. The passengers arrive first and the cargo plane lands at night at Son Sant Joan airport.'

'That's very useful information, Victor.'

He continued, 'Pistola, Petrov's estate manager, came by this morning to check everything was in order. He wasn't in the best of moods. Apparently, his boss called him late last night from Monaco and demanded he bring a much larger vehicle to the airport today. Pistola told me that he and his son returned to the estate in the early hours to get the vehicle and discovered they'd had a burglary.'

'What bad luck,' Isabel replied.

'He said only petty stuff was taken so he seemed relieved.'

'I bet he was. So what about checks on the incoming passengers at Son Bonet, and the cargo later at Son Sant Joan?'

'Nikolai Petrov doesn't hang about,' he replied. 'He pays for premium, fast-track service and is on his way shortly after arrival. I think there's a lot of imbibing on the flight as one of his guests was out cold last month. They had to carry him into the car.'

'Do you remember his nationality?'

'Same as the others. They all have Russian passports.'

'Are the cargo checks very thorough at Son Sant Joan?'

He issued a tut. 'Hand on heart, not so hot late at night. Petrov is a well-known and liked figure and he rarely has a hard time with cargo. It's nearly always large crates of beluga caviar, Russian vodka or valuable artefacts and paintings for his estate.' He paused. 'So what do you want from us?'

'Nothing. Don't raise any suspicions that he's under surveillance. Just keep a close eye on anything unusual. Please call me if any of his passengers are blind drunk this time around.'

'Will do. I'll keep you posted.'

Isabel put her mobile back in her pannier and shook her head. 'Just our luck, Furó. Those blockheads only returned to the estate last night to pick up a larger vehicle.'

The ferret whined and hung his head.

'Never mind. All is on course. Let's have a fortifying breakfast before I meet with Llorenç and Capitán Gómez. At least we have something to look forward to as Tolo is coming for dinner.'

She picked up the bag of fresh *gambas rojas* that she'd bought an hour earlier from the local fisherman she knew. She would pan fry them in olive oil with plenty of *ajo* and *perejil*, just how Tolo liked them. Isabel breathed in the salty air and smiled broadly at the azure sea. Life had its challenges, but everything was passing and sooner or later a sublime and golden orb would dance across the horizon once more.

Jesus stood outside Bon Día with a scowl on his face. He was wearing a striped apron that just about covered his large girth.

'Anything wrong?' asked Isabel as she and Furó headed for Bar Castell.

He gave a sigh. 'It's Sunday and I've been up since five o'clock, as usual, baking bread. I'm tired.'

'Aren't you shutting up soon for lunch?'

He nodded. 'And this morning that arrogant young pup, Ariel, rang, demanding I organise an extra delivery of groceries to the estate later today.'

'With no warning?'

'That's my point. It's always last minute with that lot. The Russian seems to be coming over every month now and is quite demanding. Mind you, he and his rich chums don't stay long. Apparently, they arrive today and are off on Wednesday. So I told Ariel he'd have to fetch the order himself early tomorrow morning. I'm not his slave.'

Isabel patted his shoulder. 'Good for you. Sunday should be a day of rest.'

He lowered his voice. 'Any progress on the mountain villain?'

'I'm confident that we'll have answers this week.'

Jesus nodded and rubbed his chin. 'It's not been good for business, Bel. We rely on hikers and groups during the winter months and it's all stopped, just like that. Ridiculous of the Guardia to overreact and ban all the hikers from the Trams.'

Isabel shrugged. 'Better safe than sorry. I'm sure everything will be back to normal soon.'

He smiled at her. 'You always look on the bright side, Bel. A ray of sunshine around here.'

He began to pull down his metal shutters. Isabel wished him a relaxing afternoon. As she walked into Bar Castell, Rafael greeted her from behind the counter.

'A bit late for breakfast, isn't it?'

'I had a long night.'

He chuckled. 'Best not to ask questions, then, and by the way, Llorenç told me that this afternoon you're both having a private meeting here with that miserable Guardia captain. He even got me to close off the balcony for the meeting as if you were VIPs.'

'Outrageous.' Isabel grinned. 'I mean I am, but the others?'

Llorenç whisked his damp tea towel in her direction as she pottered over to a table.

'How about scrambled eggs, and my special today, which is grilled artichokes with *jamón*?'

'Perfect, and a side order of raw meat for Furó too.'

The ferret sneezed heavily and began chasing his tail.

'He's doing his happy dance for you.'

'Much obliged, Furó, a plate of minced lamb coming up,' Rafael replied and disappeared into the depths of his aromatic kitchen.

Isabel arrived back at Ca'n Moix and inspected the front garden and porch. Long tendrils of forest-green ivy had curled around several large terracotta pots of flowers and the soft and wispy grass on the lawn needed a cut. The recent rains had saturated the soil and the potent aroma of rosemary and lavender hung in the air day and night. Isabel was about to head up to her office when she remembered something. She turned tail and, beckoning to Furó, entered Doctor Ramis's garden and rang the bell. Moments later, his cheery, whiskery visage appeared at the door.

'Bel, what a marvellous surprise. Is this a social call?'

The doctor was in his nightshirt, a sure sign that he was about to have his lunchtime *siesta*.

'I need some advice. It relates to the Sebi Vives case, but I don't want to disturb your nap.'

Doctor Ramis welcomed her inside.

'My dear girl, that can wait. I have the whole afternoon. How can I help?'

'I wondered whether you might know Doctor Sánchez.'

He gave a sniff. 'You mean *the* Doctor Sánchez?'

She nodded. 'He's the family doctor of the Vives family and could provide me with some crucial information. However, my police colleague, Gaspar, feels he will only cooperate with a search warrant, but time is not on our side.'

He patted his bushy moustache and led her into the kitchen.

'As it happens, I know him very well. We both studied medicine in Barcelona and Navarra and meet up once or twice a year for dinner.'

Isabel studied his face with bright eyes. 'Would it be an imposition to intervene on my behalf?'

'What exactly do you want to know?'

Isabel clicked her teeth. 'I have a few questions to ask about Sara Vives' well-being.'

He grasped his mobile. 'I'm not sure what he might say, but I'll call him.'

'What, now?'

'No time like the present.'

He bounded over to the back door and stepped into his garden while Isabel sat at the table, drumming her fingers on the wood. Some time elapsed before he reappeared.

'You're in luck. It took some persuading and he is adamant that you respect patient confidentiality by signing something. He will only answer questions critical to the investigation but appears keen that Sebi's killer is brought to justice.'

'Shall I call him to confirm?' Isabel asked.

'No need. He has agreed to see you tomorrow at his surgery in Palma at eleven o'clock.'

'That's very specific.'

'He's a busy man. I suggest you fall in line. Also, I'd advise bringing him a large *ensaïmada* with *crema* from Morells bakery. He's a devil for them.'

Isabel offered him a hug. 'I can't thank you enough.'

'My pleasure. I just hope that he can help. And now, I think I will take that *siesta*. Florentina and I are off to Can Busquets for supper tonight with the other *salsa* students, so this way I'll be on sparkling form.'

As she and Furó set off along the garden path, the doctor called after them.

'Good luck, Bel, and give my best to Tolo.'

Back at the house, Isabel toiled at her whiteboard while Furó slept soundly in his basket. When she was satisfied with her machinations, she set off for Bar Castell for her meeting with Llorenç and Capitán Gómez.

On their return from the Voin estate in the early hours of the morning, she and Pep had knocked back a warming brandy and coffee and wished each other goodnight. First thing in the morning before her swim, she had called the police chief to apprise him of her findings at the estate. Although furious that she had broken into the property, he conceded that they should convene urgently with Llorenç to discuss a plan of action. As Isabel walked across the *plaça*, she was flagged down by Padre Agustí. Breathing deeply, Isabel stopped to greet the elderly priest.

'Ah Bel, just the person. As the *fiesta* of Sant Antoni begins on Friday in the village, I wanted to check that you're still available to read a prayer at the service on Sunday morning.'

'Of course,' Isabel replied. 'It's in the diary. Eleven o'clock.'

The priest eyed her in dismay. 'No, nine o'clock!'

Isabel tutted. 'Yes, that's right. I am helping with the children's parade at eleven. Don't fret, Padre.'

'I was sorry that you missed the *fiesta* committee meeting yesterday.'

'It's been a busy time. Rest assured, I will be there. And now, if you'll excuse me, I have an important meeting with Llorenç.'

As she ran up the stairs to Bar Castell, Isabel made a mental note not to forget the following weekend's Sunday service. If she was counting on a little divine intervention in the challenging week ahead, the least she could do would be to turn up to support the elderly priest in church.

Two hours later, Isabel emerged from her meeting with Llorenç and Capitán Gómez. They stood in a huddle by the front steps, deep in conversation. Finally, the Guardia chief gave a long sigh.

'This is one of the most troubling cases of my career, Bel. I am now convinced by your findings and video footage, but I'd like the reassurance of corroborative evidence from the precinct's forensics team. I want to know about the provenance of those rifle cartridges that you found. Meanwhile, my team will be conducting further tactical planning before we stage the operation tomorrow night.'

'The National Police team at the airport office are already apprised?'

'Naturally, Bel. Our own operatives and those of the airport authority in Palma will be closely monitoring the arrival of Nikolai Petrov and his associates at Son Bonet. Later, they will also be tracking the arrival of his luggage at Son Sant Joan Airport. An observation unit will be stationed close to the estate tonight, so we are well prepared. Let's convene at my offices at nine tomorrow morning.'

She nodded. 'I'll pop by the precinct first thing to pick up the ammunitions report.'

Llorenç stood silently by, a sad expression on his face. 'If what you say is true, this is indeed a calamitous day in the history of our valley. As agreed, I will speak with the mayors of Fornalutx, Escorca and Soller following the mission tomorrow evening. Let us pray all goes according to plan.'

Isabel breathed heavily. 'There's only so much intelligence we can gather in advance, but as discussed, we all know the drill.'

'Indeed we do, Bel,' replied Llorenç.

As he took his leave, Capitán Gómez spun around on his shiny black heels and fixed Isabel with a bleak smile.

'And when this unpleasant event is over, I shall be expecting you to return that power drill to its rightful owner.'

Isabel returned to Ca'n Moix and made a quick call to Tolo. He had already arrived at Madrid airport.

'I had a light lunch with Fabio and now I'm reading through some reports before my flight. I'll be with you by eight.'

'I can't wait,' said Isabel. 'By the way, I've been with Llorenç and Gómez for the last few hours. You and I have a lot to catch up on.'

'This morning, Gómez actually had the courtesy to alert my department as well as the airport team about the proposed operation,' he replied. 'He called me to discuss your findings and frankly, I'm incredulous. Neither of our two forces could ever have imagined such a scenario. Do you think it's wise to wait until tomorrow?'

'I advised Gómez to hold fire as we need to catch the culprits in the act. It's highly unlikely that things will kick off tonight when they've just flown in. Besides, there is a covert Guardia team in situ should that happen. Let's discuss it all later. How was your meeting with the director general?'

'Quite amicable, given the circumstances. The minister wants closure on the Sebi Vives case as soon as possible.'

'Don't we all? We need a few more days.'

'The DG is patient. He knows what is at stake here politically and is being supportive. Let's talk through next steps over supper.'

The call ended and Isabel hugged the mobile in her hands. She and Tolo had so much to catch up on, and yet she wasn't sure how he'd react to some of her thoughts on the Sebi Vives case. There were still huge question marks in her mind and she lacked vital evidence. She called her mother's close friend, Juana Ripoll, owner of the Morells Bakery, and ordered an *ensaïmada de crema* for pick-up early the following morning and settled down to revisit her notes again.

Isabel sat at her desk and stared out of the window until her thoughts were interrupted by the bleeping of her mobile. When she saw that Josep Casanovas was ringing, she almost killed the call.

'Josep, what a surprise.'

'Bel, I know it's Sunday, but I had to call you with some intel. Naturally, it's always a pleasure to hear your voice, but...'

'Intel? Of what kind, Josep?'

Sounding slightly deflated, he continued, 'One of my investigative reporters has been keeping an eye on Marc Castell's movements ever since Silvia Porres's body was discovered on the site of the new motorway near Búger.'

Isabel interrupted. 'Isn't that the job of Tolo's department?'

'Sure, Bel, but don't be alarmed. We just wanted to get the measure of the man and to report back anything to the police that we found suspicious. We're just reporters at the end of the day.'

Isabel grabbed a pencil and involuntarily snapped it in two.

'So what did you want to tell me?'

'Well, my reporter happened to follow Marc Castell the other day to a new location. It was a piece of land on the outskirts of Porreres. He drove there in an old white van and spent a long time locking the metal gate when he left.'

Isabel sat up in her chair. 'Thank you, Josep. I appreciate your calling with this info, but it isn't your place to be interfering in such a delicate police matter.'

A long sigh filled the line. 'All I want is to help you on this case, Bel. I suppose you haven't any updates you'd like to offer? And what about the Tramuntana Terror?'

Isabel chuckled. 'Is that what you're calling it? Look, Josep, when we've wrapped up both cases, I'll offer you a line.'

'So are any arrests imminent?' he persisted.

'Stop fishing. I'll be in touch.'

Isabel ended the call and gave a long groan. She turned to Furó as he pattered across to her.

'You know, I might be needing a glass of wine earlier than I thought.'

No sooner had she spoken than her mobile rang again. Impatiently, Isabel picked it up but answered quickly when she saw the name of the caller.

'Victor, what news?'

'Petrov and his boozy cronies arrived on cue and set off hastily in awaiting vehicles with Pistola and his son. Just like last time, another legless Russian guest had to be bundled into one of the cars.'

'How would you describe him?'

'Expensive clothes and shoes. He was a lot thinner than the rest, which might explain why he couldn't hold his liqueur.'

When she'd finished the call, Isabel grabbed a Chupa Chup and swivelled it in the air with a grim expression. 'As the *dicho* goes, eat, drink and be merry, for tomorrow you die.'

At eight o'clock, Isabel stood stirring aromatic rice on the stove while she sipped a glass of deep red wine. She savoured a mouthful. There was a rat-a-tat-tat at the front door. Furó raced into the *entrada*, his mouth open and tail wagging happily. Isabel smiled and her heart fluttered. Tolo stood before her, a lopsided smile on his face, his eyes sparkling. The crescent of an early moon rested on his shoulders and his silhouette was framed by the distant, shadowy mountains. Before she could speak, he had wrapped her in a bear hug and rested his head on her shoulder. The spell was broken when Furó began dancing impatiently about his feet and sneezing loudly. Stroking the ferret's head, Tolo picked him up and placed an arm around Isabel's waist. Together, they walked into the warm *entrada*, old friends turned lovers, for whom words could wait.

TWENTY

Isabel sat in the driver's seat of Pequeñito and looked up at the pewter sky. It had just gone seven-thirty and unsurprisingly at such an early hour she had easily found a space in the precinct's cramped car park. She was on the point of leaving the vehicle when there was a rumble from the heavens shortly followed by the pitter-patter of heavy rain.

Tolo had set off earlier from Sant Martí for a briefing with the regional president, so she didn't expect him to join her at her meeting with Gaspar Fernandez and Nacho Blanco. They would be able to debrief one another later in the day. Throwing on her jacket, Isabel jumped out of Pequeñito and poked her tongue out at the scowling sky.

'Go on, give me your best,' she said out loud.

Even though she ran quickly, by the time she reached the entrance she was soaked. Wiping droplets of rain from her face, she took the lift to the homicide department and walked towards Corc's desk. He had his back to her and was speaking fulsomely to someone on the phone. She stood and waited for him to finish the call, a slight frown crossing her brow as she eavesdropped. As he replaced the receiver, she touched his shoulder.

'Bel, *que susto*! There's hardly anyone around at this time of the day. You gave me a fright.'

'Sorry to have frightened you,' Isabel replied. 'Do members of the public call this early?'

'Not usually. That wasn't a member of the public, though. It was a local official wanting some information.'

Isabel nodded. 'I see.'

A door opened close by and Gaspar emerged from his office wearing his habitual wide smile.

'Bel, come in. Nacho and I have just been discussing logistics for the searches at the Mestres' properties. Our response task force is on standby for eleven o'clock this morning.'

Isabel listened intently. 'What about the intel that Casanovas gave me yesterday about Marc Castell? Can we get a search warrant quickly?'

'We're on the case, Bel. As soon as you called me yesterday with the information, I got in touch with the presiding judge. Hopefully, we'll have news later today from the *comisión judicial*.'

'Casanovas is proving quite an asset,' she replied.

Nacho smirked. 'Don't let Tolo hear you say that, but you're right. Maybe he's trying to make amends for his behaviour at the motorway crime scene.'

Corc bustled in and offered them all coffees. For a moment, he stood in the doorway, listening to their conversation, until Isabel turned to him.

'Don't let us keep you, Corc.'

He nodded and quickly turned tail. Gaspar chuckled.

'Don't be too harsh on him, Bel. He's harmless enough.'

She cocked her head on one side. 'So, Nacho, I have another sample for you. I'd placed it in my jacket pocket and only found it by luck last night.'

Nacho took the clear plastic bag from her and, laughing, inspected the screwed-up piece of silver foil.

'Please don't tell me this is more used gum? Where did you find this?'

'Just in a place of potential interest. If you get any results, let me know. It's a bit of a long shot.'

'Will do.' He coughed. 'So, regarding the rifle cartridges. Not good news. I'm in communication with the Interpol and Guardia teams which, as you know, have firearms reference tables. Those cartridges are from four different weapons: there's a 300 Winchester Magnum, 338 Lapua Magnum and a TOZ-17 hunting rifle.'

Isabel ran a hand through her hair. 'The TOZ-17 was produced back in the fifties at the Tula Arms Plant in Russia. It's part of a family of bolt-action repeating rifles used mostly by the Russian military and paramilitary. Not the sort of gun you'd choose for shooting goats and rabbits,' she said.

Gaspar whistled. 'Is someone trying to start a war over here? Gómez didn't expand on his thoughts when he called through to the precinct yesterday. He just spoke of concerning irregularities up at the Russian estate.'

Nacho looked tense. 'More concerning to Interpol is that one of the samples recovered is from a standard AK-12 assault rifle. That Kalashnikov model has a range of at least three hundred metres.'

Isabel folded her arms tightly. 'Seven hundred rounds a minute.'

Gaspar gasped. 'How is Interpol and the Guardia handling this?'

Isabel took a sip of coffee and began pacing around Gaspar's office.

'I've a meeting over at the Guardia offices shortly. Trust me, Gómez has everything in hand. He's got the backing of the UCE-1 unit and central ops in Madrid, who are closely monitoring the situation.' She offered a pert smile. 'This is when you want a military unit with a hundred and seventy years of history on your side. The Guardia has its international security service agents on the case, but we won't know how bad the situation is until the special ops unit springs into action tonight.'

'Are you accompanying them?' asked Gaspar in alarm.

'What do you think? Pep and I are the only ones who have penetrated the buildings of interest. I think I know where the bodies are buried.'

'Figuratively speaking, Bel, I hope.'

Isabel massaged her forehead. 'Sadly, there's nothing figurative about this case.'

It was nearly eleven o'clock and Isabel and Capitán Gómez stood chatting in hushed, tense tones at the entrance of the Palma Command Centre of the Guardia Civil. They had endured a protracted meeting with seasoned officers from the Special Intervention Unit, the Guardia's highly specialised military task force, discussing the imminent nighttime operation that would take place at the Voin estate. As they confirmed tactics for the delicate mission, they were joined in a video conference call by a commander of the Grupo de Acción Rapida, the central tactical unit of the Guardia, based in Logroño on the mainland. The director general of the Guardia in Madrid had taken Isabel's written assessment of the situation sufficiently seriously to give the go-ahead on the operation. The video footage taken on her illicit undercover visit to the Voin estate had further convinced him of the urgency of the matter. There were still unanswered questions, but his view was that the stakes were too high for the armed response unit to delay action. As Isabel took her leave, anxious not to be late for her next meeting, Capitán Gómez eyed her dejectedly.

'Until tonight. Pray God you are right, Bel. This could end very badly for you and me career-wise if your evaluation of the situation is flawed.'

Isabel raised an eyebrow. 'Have faith, Alvaro. I may lack a few pieces of the jigsaw, but instinctively I feel that we're on track. And remember, those spent cartridges alone offer sufficient reason for grave concern.'

He folded his arms tightly. 'Well, let's hope your instincts are right once more or we're both in the mire.'

Isabel walked towards Pequeñito, her stomach tightening and her heart fluttering. She stood for a few minutes by the car, taking long, deep breaths, and forced herself to focus on the few forlorn trees nearby. A bird's sweet call assailed her ears and her body relaxed. Jumping into the driver's seat, she revved the engine and selected 'Everybody Hurts' by R.E.M., one of her favourite songs, and turned it up loud. Now was not the time to allow fear and self-doubt to have the upper hand.

Isabel parked close by the pristine offices of Doctor Sánchez, squirrelled away in an exclusive and discreet area of Calatrava, in the old quarter of Palma. She was on a yellow line, so she made a quick call to one of her long-suffering Palma traffic warden colleagues and asked for clemency. The woman tutted but promised to alert the warden for that zone. Isabel dashed into the surgery. The receptionist greeted her warmly and offered her a coffee. She sat down heavily on the chocolate-hued leather sofa to wait and examined the alabaster sculptures, modern artworks and costly, contemporary furniture in the room. It was beyond her comprehension that anyone would waste money on such boring and soulless pieces. She adored vintage furniture and items that bore the scars of time, love and loss, rather than the assortment of bland cream and beige furnishings that adorned the room.

Brisk footsteps approached and a slightly built man with bushy, silver hair and an ironic smile appeared.

'Isabel Flores?' he said, extending his hand. 'Famed neighbour of my famed friend Doctor Ramis?'

Isabel grinned. 'You may be disappointed.'

'Never!' He looked about the room. 'You hate it. I can see it in your eyes. Cultural disgust. I agree with you entirely, but my spoilt and entitled clients love it and frankly I am a medical man, not an interior designer, so I leave it to others to deck out my lair. Come, you have questions and I have limited time.'

Once seated in his office, Isabel leant forward confidentially.

'I appreciate your seeing me without a warrant and so I'll be as transparent as possible.'

He smiled. 'I trust my old friend Miguel. I will hold him to account if you ruin my day. How can I help?'

'It's about your patients Sebi and Sara Vives.'

He nodded. 'A terrible business. I have been the family doctor for Sebi's family for years. Sara, Martín and Mateu, of course, remain clients.'

'A few weeks ago, Sara was shunted in her car and was forced to wear a neck brace due to whiplash. Did you prescribe that?'

He frowned. 'Indeed, Sara came to see me with a severe neck bruise. She told me about the shunt. I did not prescribe a neck brace, but she may have sought some kind of neck support.'

FALLEN BUTTERFLY

Isabel observed his face carefully. 'The injuries that she sustained were severe and perhaps unusual for a car shunt?'

'I concur.' He fiddled with a pen. 'She showed evidence of petechial haemorrhage of the left eye and ecchymosis and erythema – or in layman's terms, severe bruising and a skin rash caused by inflamed capillaries – but it was difficult to know how that was triggered.'

Isabel nodded.

'In truth, she was traumatised and monosyllabic. I suggested she have X-rays and tests at Clinica Rotger, but she refused.'

'So what did you prescribe?'

'Frankly, painkillers, rest and physiotherapy. You have to understand that Sara is a highly emotional individual. She is also notoriously clumsy and accident-prone. For example, a few years ago, she broke an ankle getting off her horse. Another time, she slipped in the kitchen and cut her eye and had a concussion, and quite recently, she burnt her hand badly in the oven. Poor Sebi was frantic and brought her here in the middle of the night.'

'Does she drink?'

He tutted. 'Don't we all? Okay, so maybe she enjoys a tipple now and then, but she's not an alcoholic. Living with Sebi couldn't have been easy. I imagine she sought comfort in the odd glass over the years.'

'What about Mateu?'

He shrugged. 'A brilliant boy. He won a scholarship to his university and frankly could have done any course he'd fancied. He is a first-class student and his mother worships him.'

'How do you think he is dealing with his father's death?'

'Badly. I wouldn't say they were close, but all the same, there was a deep fondness.'

Isabel rose from her seat. 'You've been more than kind.'

'Is that it? I have at least one minute more to give you.'

She laughed and pulled a stiff white cardboard box out of her pannier and placed it on his desk.

'Miguel told me that this was your Achilles heel.'

His eyes lit up as he examined the logo on the carton. 'Surely not a morsel of heaven from my favourite bakery in Morells?'

'You could be right.'

He grinned. 'I'm indebted.'

As he showed her to the front door, he leant forward and kissed her lightly on both cheeks.

'I trust you'll use that information wisely, Señorita Flores. Years gallop by and we personal physicians arrogantly assume that we know our clients inside out, but we're wrong. You see, in the end, none of us know a damn thing about one another. Everything is a just a mirage.'

Isabel had arranged to have lunch with one of her very favourite judges. Margarita Subirán was a woman of sixty-five with sharp, intelligent blue eyes and a cynical air. They had been friends ever since Isabel had arrived on the island and had sought the judge's wise counsel in a troubling case involving international organised crime. Now Isabel needed her advice again. She arrived early at the tribunal offices and waited in the nearby *plaça* for her friend to finish her session in court. Her meeting with Doctor Sánchez had confirmed her suspicions, but it didn't mean that she felt any happier about it. As she walked slowly about the square, her mind a maelstrom of hurried thoughts, Margarita appeared before her with a concerned expression on her face.

'What's going on, Bel?'

Isabel gave her a hug.

'I need some help.'

'What's new?' She smiled. 'But first, let's eat. I know just the place.'

A full moon hung low in the sky as Isabel crouched in dark woodland close to the entrance to the Voin estate. It was eleven in the evening and she was cold and stiff. Capitán Gómez and his special ops team were her silent companions as they all waited patiently in the darkness for any signs of movement. A hand tapped her leg and Pep hissed in her ear.

'What are you waiting for?'

Isabel leant close to him and whispered, 'As I explained earlier, we need to catch them in the act.'

'But say nothing happens?'

She shrugged in the chill. 'Then I'm wrong and we all go home.'

Isabel knew that Pep was ecstatic to have been allowed to accompany her and the Guardia on the dangerous mission. Capitán Gómez had given him strict instructions to stay with the observation crew by the vehicles once the special op crew had penetrated the interior of the estate. With no firearms or police training, it would be his safest and only option once the circus began.

All of a sudden, the driveway was flooded with golden light and loud raucous voices sounded in the distance. The special ops commander turned to his officers.

'Take up position. They're coming.' He turned to Bel. 'Please accompany my deputy, Andreu, and unit one, as planned.'

Isabel squeezed Pep's arm and nodded to Capitán Gómez, who hung back with his own team. Soon she fell into line behind the heavily armed and equipped men from unit one as they soundlessly took position closer to the perimeter. The rest of the units, led by Capitán Gómez, fanned out seamlessly into the surrounding forest. Before long came the growl of engines and excited male laughter. As the stream of jeeps and animal carriers approached, their lights illuminating the front gates, Isabel felt for the Heckler & Koch at her waist. She hoped that it wouldn't be needed. The gates rolled back and the caravan of vehicles lumbered along the track towards the surrounding woodland. From her hideaway, Isabel heard Russian and Arabic words drifting from the open windows and the anxious cries of animals emanating from the various trucks. The last vehicle was a specialist carrier with two large open metal cages. The distinctive face of a noble wild cat stared out. Her eyes widened. What was it? A lynx?

Andreu patted her back hard and their team of eight was off, running low through the open gates and into the bushy shrubs to the side of the track. She jogged next to Andreu, using her night-vision glasses to find her way. When they came in sight of the *finca*, she signalled to him to wait. They conferred in hurried whispers. Three of the team broke off and headed towards the *finca*, while she and the others made for the wooden side door that she and Pep had used previously to enter the gardens. To Isabel's surprise, one of the officers used a tiny gadget to break open the heavy new lock effortlessly and soon they were running through the gardens. Two of the officers headed for the cottage and kicked down the front door, while Isabel directed Andreu and the remaining officer to the wooden buildings.

The door of the first building was unlocked and the animal pens and cages empty. Only a few random white feathers lay beneath the bird cages. Isabel turned tail and directed Andreu and his officer to the second hut. The front door was closed, but it didn't take long for Isabel to open it with her set of skeleton keys. Andreu smirked.

'Those things actually work. Impressive. But what's wrong with good old brute force?'

Once inside, Isabel headed for the cupboards where she had discovered the body bags and hunting tackle. She wasn't surprised to find their doors wide open and empty.

Isabel turned to Andreu with a grim expression. 'It's as I thought. They've taken the body bags with them. Let me show you the trap door.'

They rolled back the heavy black fur rug and Andreu inspected the steel trap door imbedded in the cement floor. He called to his officer, who efficiently broke the bolts and padlock with heavy bolt cutters. The door still wouldn't budge. He turned to Isabel.

'Stand back. We're going to have to breach the door.'

He took out his handgun and aimed at the hinges and lock. Smoke rose in the air and Isabel discerned the sharp aroma of cordite. The officer kicked at the steel door and it crashed some feet below. They looked at one another.

'I'll go down first,' Andreu said.

Isabel nodded. 'I'll cover you.'

Andreu turned to his officer. 'Keep alert. We'll do a quick recce.'

He quickly radioed through to the nearest team and discovered that they had found the cottage empty. They were already on their way to penetrate the third wooden building and to rejoin their colleagues at the *finca*. The first response team confirmed that at the *finca* they had only encountered a team of serving staff and an old collie. They reported shooting resonating from the outlying woodland. Andreu gave them instructions to secure the premises and await further orders.

Tentatively, he began his descent via a lengthy steel ladder. He gave a signal that he'd reached secure ground, and Isabel followed in his wake. They stood in a large and dusty empty space that possessed just one metal door. The air was cool and musty and a dank, rotten smell hung in the air.

Andreu spoke quietly. 'Do you want to give it a try?'

Isabel took out her keys and worked at the lock for a few minutes. She shook her head.

'This is reinforced on the inside. We'll need to blow it.'

Andreu aimed at the lock, fired two shots and kicked back the heavy door. They stood with guns cocked, looking ahead into the gloom. Before them stretched a long concrete corridor on either side of which were row upon row of deep cages. In the hot and sticky atmosphere, the stench of sweat, rotting animal flesh and scat made Isabel gag. As Andreu walked slowly ahead, Isabel reached out to the wall on one side and identified a switch. She called to him. 'There's a light.'

He turned to her. 'There's no one here. Turn it on.'

Within seconds the area was filled with fluorescent light. Isabel looked around in horror. The floor-to-ceiling cages were filled with wild animals: roe and musk deer and two wild cats surrounded by carrion. The creatures began roaring and crying out, disturbed by the noise and light. A sophisticated heating and oxygen system appeared to be installed above each cage.

'What is this horror chamber?' Andreu asked.

'The playroom of rich and vile people who think it's okay to extinguish endangered species for sport.'

She bent down to examine a small, brown-eyed deer in a cage, its body shaking in terror. A sudden rage gripped her and she had to fight to control her emotions. If Nikolai Petrov were to appear, it would take all her strength not to shoot him dead.

Andreu yelled to her, 'Bel, come here. This is too much.'

Isabel ran along the corridor and discovered Andreu peering into a cage separated from the rest where an emaciated, dazed and clearly sedated man lay filthy and naked on the bare floor. In horror, Isabel shone her torch on the figure and flinched. His ear was punctured with a gold tag that bore the number one.

Andreu stared at her. 'How did you envision this?'

Isabel stared at him, her eyes filling with tears. 'It is human depravity at its worst. I didn't want to believe my own thoughts, but the evidence became overwhelming. Let's get help.'

Andreu urgently radioed his colleagues but got no response.

'We're perhaps too deep down here. Let's head back up.'

They reached the foot of the ladder and heard a cold voice from above their heads.

'Welcome to my zoo. I see that you have found the jewels of my enterprise.'

High above them, a man's face loomed large. It was Nikolai Petrov. Isabel and Andreu shared a hurried glance as the man stared down at them, a menacing grin on his face.

'You have ruined my hunt and now you have violated sacred space. For that you will both pay with your lives.'

Andreu beckoned to Isabel to step backwards as the Russian aimed a high-calibre rifle at them.

'Where are my men?' Andreu called up.

'Where indeed? This one is as dead as a dodo.' He laughed hysterically. 'The others are all still at war in the woods, but Ariel and I slipped back undetected. There is another entrance to the gardens that your foolish colleagues will not know about. Your unit has returned to the *finca* and you are alone. Now you will die down there with my treasured pet creatures for company. This is the price you pay for interfering.'

'Ariel, are you there?' Isabel shouted.

A familiar head appeared. He wore a nervous expression.

'Maybe it's time to remove that ridiculous beanie,' she said.

With an insouciant shrug, Ariel plucked the soft hat from his head, allowing a mane of dark hair to flood around his shoulders.

'I knew you were onto me when you reached for my beanie outside Bon Día the other day.'

'I was onto you long before that,' she replied witheringly. 'Better to give yourselves up. There's nowhere to hide.'

'You're quite wrong,' interjected Nikolai Petrov. 'We have false passports and a vehicle at the back of the estate. We're leaving now. As they say in Mallorca, *adeu*!'

He raised his hand. In horror, Isabel saw that he was holding a grenade. Andreu's mouth fell open and together they ran towards the corridor, just managing to slam the battered metal door behind them. There was a large boom and the sound of falling masonry and then silence.

Isabel opened her eyes. A hazy Capitán Gómez stared earnestly into her face. She felt groggy and wasn't sure whether she was experiencing a nightmare or reality. She let her lids close again in the hope that the apparition would go away. She had no such luck. Capitán Gómez was shaking her violently.

'Bel! Wake up!' he commanded as he yelled to his various lackeys.

With effort she focused on his face and licked her lips, tasting something metallic on her tongue. Her left arm throbbed and there was a searing pain in her ribcage. Gradually, she was able to raise herself onto her right elbow. The police captain reached forward and poured cold water into her mouth. She spluttered and coughed.

'Where are we?'

'In a wretched and stinking underground corridor used by a madman to incarcerate animals and humans. Happily, he is dead and you are alive.'

Isabel blinked hard. 'Petrov is dead?'

He sat back on his heels. 'He hurled a grenade at you and Andreu but somehow the blast knocked him off his feet and he fell to his death. You were saved by the metal door, but it fell on top of you both.'

Isabel winced in pain. 'Is Andreu alive?'

He nodded. 'He took the full brunt of the door and is in a bad way, but he'll recover. The medics are with him now.'

Isabel shook her head miserably. 'As I had suspected, Petrov was a monster.'

Capitán Gómez offered a ghost of a smile. 'Thankfully for you and me, he was. Imagine if you'd been proven wrong? My reputation would have been in tatters. As it is, the operation has been deemed a huge success and the director general of the Guardia in Madrid is delighted. I take my hat off to you again, Bel.'

Isabel felt a sudden panic. 'What happened to the others? Did Ariel get away? He's got a false passport and is posing as a woman.'

'We'll put out an alert. He won't get far.' He stood up and stretched his back. 'We had a short battle out there, but mercifully no one was killed and the felons were quickly arrested. The animals have been recovered and in some cases needed to be tranquilised. We have a team of vets and animal behaviourists arriving to deal with the poor creatures down here. Many are very sick. The human victim is in a critical state.'

Pain ripped through Isabel's ribcage. She gasped.

'What about the other victim that arrived on the flight yesterday?'

'We discovered him sedated and locked in a room in the main house. He's being taken to hospital.' He patted her arm and sighed. 'You are in no shape to take all this on board, so let's talk when you're back on your feet. The medical team is here to take you to hospital. You're concussed and appear to have broken ribs.'

Isabel protested weakly. She had the sensation of being grasped by strong hands and whisked into the air. She struggled and voices reverberated around her. Soon everything dulled and she returned to the land of troubled dreams.

TWENTY-ONE

Sun poured into the kitchen from the walled aromatic garden where Isabel stood with her mobile to her ear. As she paced about the patio, she caught a glimpse of Florentina bustling about inside, preparing coffees, cakes and croissants for the lively group chatting around her table. Despite protestations from the medical team and Tolo, Isabel had discharged herself from hospital first thing in the morning, stubbornly resolved to tie up loose ends on the Sebi Vives case. Tolo had reluctantly driven her back to Sant Martí and insisted that he provide her with a driver and unmarked police car until her return to full health. As soon as she'd arrived at Ca'n Moix, she had called Capitán Gómez, keen to discuss the previous night's operation. She finished the call and walked slowly over to the open doorway, smiling as she listened, undetected, to the lively conversation taking place within the kitchen.

'Fancy Gómez disturbing Bel after such a night. The poor girl needs to recover,' protested Idò.

Pep laughed. 'Bel called him as soon as she got here. You can't blame him.'

Tolo tutted. 'It's true. I told her to wait until she'd at least had breakfast, but she insisted on calling him. She's as stubborn as a *burro*.'

'Am I?' Isabel asked as she strode into the kitchen. She made a baying sound and they all grinned.

'That sounds more like a cow than a donkey,' said Florentina.

'So give us the heads-up,' said Pep. 'Have they caught Ariel yet, and what happened to Pistola?'

'What about the poor man chained in the basement?' asked Idò as he helped himself to a sugared croissant.

Isabel laughed and pulled out a chair next to Tolo. 'Give me a coffee, Mama, and I'll fill you all in.'

Florentina passed her a *cortado* and orange juice while Pep placed a plate of pastries and cakes in front of her. Isabel took a long sip of coffee and laughed as Llorenç leant forward and grabbed a large piece of walnut cake.

'Steady on,' growled Idò. 'You'll be putting all that weight back on if you keep this up.'

Pep smirked. 'Don't listen, Llorenç. You need to keep up your strength as mayor of Sant Martí.'

Llorenç gave him a wink and savoured a mouthful of cake.

'In truth, I always eat too much when I'm stressed and this mountain menace case has been a horror.'

Florentina made the sign of the cross.

'All I can say is thank heavens that our Bel is still in one piece. It's a miracle no one got hurt.'

Pep frowned. 'Not quite, Florentina. Nikolai Petrov perished.'

She shrugged. 'He only had himself to blame, though God rest his soul.'

'I hope he rots in hell,' said Idò, sniffing. 'I still can't get my head round how he could get away with such horrible things for so long, and I don't know the half of it.'

Tolo let out a long sigh. 'Often people can never contemplate the unimaginable until it happens.' He turned to Isabel. 'So, *cariño*, don't keep us in suspense.'

She scrunched his hand. 'You'll all remember that I first met Ariel and Pistola when Enric and I were looking for my missing renters and ended up at the Voin estate?'

They all nodded.

'At the time, I found it odd how vehemently Ariel tried to lay the blame for the misplaced signs and cairns firmly at Frans Bordoy's door, homing in on his long hair, tattoos and eco-activist stance. I noticed that he wore a slouch beanie. They are particularly useful for accommodating man buns.'

'What the heck is one of those?' spluttered Idò.

Pep grinned. 'A lot of guys have ponytails and buns these days, Idò.'

The elderly man mumbled and rolled his eyes.

'That aside, I found his father, Pistola, very defensive and thought his and Ariel's attitude to hikers was quite offensive and frankly weird. Just after we met them, I discovered cartridges in nearby woodland from various potent Russian rifles. That led me to believe that we were dealing with something far more sinister than local illegal hunters.'

'So the woman with long brown hair that the hikers reported seeing was in fact Ariel?' asked Llorenç.

Isabel nodded and chomped on a morsel of croissant. 'I saw Ariel again at the meeting held at Café Jordi for local landowners and guides. The room was quite hot, but Ariel stubbornly kept his slouch beanie on and fretfully pulled it down over his ears. It struck me that his slim physique matched the description given by the hikers, and of course, he would know the mountains like the back of his hand. Instinct told me that he was our suspect.

When I bumped into him again outside Bon Día, I pretended to grab at his beanie and he went into a blind panic. That confirmed my suspicions.'

'And what about the wooden signs bought at the Chinese owned store near Lloseta?' asked Pep.

'Yes, thanks to your excellent sleuthing, Pep, it was clear that Ariel had bought them from that store. He had masqueraded as a woman and allowed his long hair to show, although he wore shades, an oddity during the darkness of winter but crucial for his disguise.'

Pep nodded. 'Presumably Ariel and Pistola came up with the plan to disorientate hikers and to prevent them entering the land around their estate.'

'Exactly. Their intention wasn't to kill anyone but to cause fear and injury so that hikers would be banned from the Tramuntanas or severely restricted from wandering off safe guided routes. Pistola would randomly choose a local peak and target lone hikers, effortlessly getting ahead of them to plant the false signs and cairns. Nikolai Petrov wanted the vast woodland around the Voin estate to become a playground for international amateur bounty hunters. This was all confirmed by Capitán Gómez this morning in my call with him.'

'Do they have hard evidence?' asked Llorenç.

'When Pep and I stole into the estate late at night last Saturday, we managed to investigate two of the wooden outbuildings but not the third. Capitán Gómez's officers were able to explore it last night. It was the office of the operation, and computer records clearly illustrated that for the past year Nikolai Petrov had been bringing exotic species to his estate as hidden cargo on his private jets. Fortunately, only four endangered cats had been transported here thus far and three remain alive. Two of them were the ones I encountered in captivity below ground.'

Tolo touched her hand. 'The cartridges that Isabel brought to our forensics team for analysis proved that deadly assault weapons were being used, the kind that might be used to hunt down big game and even humans.'

Florentina gasped. 'It's unthinkable.'

'Over the past year, hikers have reported hearing shots being fired and strange sightings such as big cats prowling about Pla des Porxo late at night. Everyone treated it as a joke, but it was all true. These were rare creatures like the Siberian lynx and the Amur leopard which were let loose to be hunted by Nikolai Petrov and his dubious big buck international clients,' Isabel replied.

'So old Xim Basa was right about hearing shots in the night up there?' asked Idò.

'Indeed he was. After I spoke with him, I was convinced that we had bounty-style hunters on our hands,' Isabel replied.

'So how did it work?' asked Idò.

Isabel shifted in her seat and winced as pain shot through her broken ribs.

'Petrov would invite his rich, bloodthirsty chums to pay astronomical sums for a hunt involving animals, and on the last two occasions, human beings. The animals would be sedated and placed in crates with hidden compartments below expensive paintings, caviar and vodka bottles. Victor, my contact at Son Bonet airport, offered me useful intel on this. Usually Petrov and his guests would travel in one or two smaller jets that would touch down at Son Bonet, but for cargo, he'd arrange another larger jet that arrived at the private terminal of Son Sant Joan airport at night.'

'Were the security teams in the loop?' asked Llorenç in horror.

'Not at all. The security teams had no idea that any live creatures were being transported over here. Petrov and his hand-picked air crew were always charming and friendly with the airport teams and so they suspected nothing.'

'How did the animals stay alive during the flight?' asked Florentina.

Isabel stretched out her arms. 'According to Capitán Gómez, his officers found evidence on Petrov's computer to show that a sophisticated oxygen supply system was added to the crates to keep the sedated creatures alive. The crates had false bases that went undetected by the late-night security teams.'

'Did they do the same for the human beings?' asked Llorenç.

Isabel got up to make herself another coffee, but Florentina jumped to her feet.

'Stay where you are, my girl.'

'That was the clever part,' said Isabel, sitting back down. 'There is evidence from records kept on Petrov's computer that there have so far been two human victims used for these hunts, both of whom are mercifully still alive, though the man I discovered in the basement is in intensive care in Palma. My contact at Son Bonet airport told me that recently one of the guests on Petrov's flight was blind drunk and had to be carried into a car. He also noted that the drunken guest who arrived on Sunday was much thinner than the others, though dressed in expensive clothing. It occurred to me that the so-called guest might in fact be a victim, maybe a kidnapped, ill-nourished beggar from the streets of Russia that had been drugged and brought over to be hunted. A human being was the ultimate prize, which would carry the highest bounty for hunters of the game.'

'Who could do such a thing?' asked Florentina, placing another coffee in front of Isabel.

Llorenç shook his head sorrowfully. 'When Bel suggested this to Capitán Gómez and me before we had hard evidence, I honestly thought she'd lost the plot.'

Isabel ran a hand over her forehead.

'I don't blame you. It must have sounded preposterous, like something from a horror film. Capitán Gómez just told me that they interrogated Pistola in the early hours of this morning after they had successfully rounded up the foreign hunters and animals at the estate. He confirmed that Petrov and his thugs had so far kidnapped two male down-and-outs on the streets in Moscow. The first survived a previous hunt but developed a serious fever and had been languishing underground. That is where Andreu, from the Guardia's special ops team, and I discovered him. The second arrived this Sunday on Petrov's private flight and was to be the top target in the group's last hunt at the estate. Thanks to the Guardia, he's safe.'

'How did they transport them here without raising suspicion at the airports?' asked Llorenç.

'That was easy. The two men were cleaned up and fed well over a few weeks, so that they didn't appear too emaciated. Before setting off for Mallorca, they were dressed in expensive clothes and given false passports. Petrov presumably assured them both that he had work for them on his estate. During the flights to Son Bonet airport, the victims were sedated and alcohol was spilled on their clothes to suggest they were inebriated. It would no doubt have been passed off as a joke at security. Then they were bundled into the awaiting vehicle and ferried to the estate.'

'What about the animals?' asked Tolo.

Isabel sighed. 'All of them were given colour-coded tags and numbers according to their species and considered worth in the hunting game. When I discovered the animal pens at the estate during my recce with Pep, this became apparent. The more exotic the animal, the higher its worth in the game. The nightly hunt would run for a set time and if any of the bigger game had survived, they'd be sedated in the underground lair and kept for the following month's event.'

'It's totally grotesque,' muttered Tolo.

'What's concerning is that the hunts were stepping up. They were soon planning to introduce three a month. Film footage was also discovered on the computer of the sickening award ceremonies that they staged here before the hunters were flown back to Moscow or international airports.'

'Is there any chance of catching up with these other murderers?' asked Llorenç.

'All Petrov's clients had code names and false passports, but Capitán Gómez believes Interpol and their affiliated agents will find them. At least those currently being held in custody by the Guardia will get their comeuppance.'

'And what about that little rat, Ariel?'

Isabel clapped her hands together. 'Capitán Gómez told me he'd been arrested trying to board a plane to Madrid with a false Russian passport. Apparently, he passed off brilliantly as a woman.'

Tolo looked across at Pep. 'While Isabel went off with one of the special ops units last night, what were you doing?'

'Capitán Gómez insisted I stay with the stationary team, but I was given night-vision glasses and saw how quickly the Guardia captured all the culprits and brought the animals to safety. It was like a Hollywood movie.'

Tolo laughed. 'No criminal should mess with the Guardia's elite military units. We're lucky to have them.'

'How could this happen here?' protested Llorenç. 'We live in a veritable paradise. Is this how some foreign residents reward us?'

Isabel rolled her eyes. 'There are good and bad people everywhere, Llorenç, and thanks to some of our local foreign residents and their efforts, we are working towards cleaner air, beaches and oceans.'

Pep laughed. '*Touché*. You've got to move with the times, Llorenç.'

Idò bit his lip. 'I feel sorry for Frans Bordoy in all this. He was innocent all along.'

'Yes, he was,' Isabel replied. 'He cares passionately about protecting the Tramuntanas and although a little vociferous and eccentric at times, he has a heart of gold. He has been so caring of Señora Coll.'

'He deserves a medal just for that!' laughed Idò.

'And of course, he is half German and half mainlander,' she quipped.

Llorenç held up his hands in defeat and laughed. 'Okay, I stand corrected. Some of our foreign residents are very nice people.'

'Talking of which, you need to organise that town hall meeting to discuss their complaints about air quality.'

He laughed. 'Fair enough, Bel. Let's do it once we've got the Sant Antoni celebrations over with and you can be my translator.'

She smiled. 'You're on.'

'So what happens next?' asked Pep.

'The animals will be identified and the exotic species repatriated to Russia via specialist agencies. As for the two Russian victims, they will be returned to the motherland when they've recovered,' Isabel replied.

'To become beggars again?' he quizzed.

'Capitán Gómez is hopeful that those who inherit the Voin estate will make amends and show publicly their opprobrium for Nikolai Petrov's actions. The Russian beggars will no doubt be paid off handsomely and have bright futures wherever they want.'

Llorenç rose. 'Let's hope so. Now I must get back to the office. You too, Pep.'

'I'll ditto that,' said Tolo.

As Llorenç and the others made their way into Florentina's *entrada*, Tolo hung back.

He turned to Isabel. 'Any chance of you resting here a while?'

She tutted. 'Of course not. I need to revisit S'Albufera briefly and then the house of Martín Vives, and what about the raid on Marc Castell's estate? Should I accompany you there later?'

Tolo eyed her in despair. 'You have cracked ribs and a badly bruised left arm and you may still be concussed.' He paused. 'Don't roll your eyes. I'll arrange for an officer to pick you up now and take you to S'Albufera and the Vives house, but you are not joining us on Castell's land. Please leave it to Gaspar, Nacho and me.'

Isabel frowned. 'You will find DNA from Silvia Porres.'

'So you believe.'

'Might the Mestres have got wind that you've a warrant for Castell's properties?'

'It's likely, given that we've searched their own homes. They'll assume Castell is next.'

'That's my worry.'

Tolo stared at her. 'What do you mean?'

Isabel felt butterflies pirouetting in her stomach and shook her head. 'Never mind. When are you going?'

He looked at his watch. 'Gaspar and forensics are on their way. I'm joining them now.'

While he strode outside to arrange a car for Isabel, she searched out Furó, who was curled up in a box in her mother's pantry. He yawned and crawled up her jumper, placing his head on her shoulder. Isabel felt a jolt of pain from her ribcage and sat down again.

'Everything is coming to a head, my little friend. I hope I can stay the course.'

As if understanding her every word, he gave a bark and began squealing excitedly. Isabel laughed.

'I'll take that as a vote of confidence.'

Tolo returned.

'I'm off and your car is en route here. Are you really sure you need to return to S'Albufera?'

'Yes,' she replied decisively. 'Earlier I rang the admin office to speak briefly with one of the workers there, so they are expecting me.'

'But can't your visit to Martín Vives's house at least wait?'

'I'm afraid not. I'm following an important hunch.'

'Just please be careful and get my officer to bring you straight back here when you're done.'

Isabel nodded as he bent and kissed her head and hurriedly left the house.

The rain had started to fall as Isabel stepped out of the unmarked police car. The officer offered a complicit nod and parked in a space on the drive. Isabel had to admit that it had been relaxing to let someone else do the driving, and she had enjoyed the pastoral scenes as they got closer to S'Albufera. As planned, she had strolled along the quiet gravel track to the park's reception and spoken at some length with some of the team members, including the worker that she'd originally questioned. She had hoped to jog their memories with some images that she'd found online. Half an hour later, she returned to the car to find her patient driver reading *El Periódico*. He quickly started the engine and they set off in the direction of Colonia Sant Jordi. She had mixed feelings about revisiting the house and an overwhelming feeling of guilt and betrayal. Martín was a gentle and honourable man who had been dealt such cruel blows in life. He had trusted her and now she was about to abuse that trust. Standing on the doorstep, she suddenly felt muzzy and gripped the pillar. Rain splashed on her face and revived her just as the door sprung open. Agila smiled at her.

'I was so pleased when you called to say you were in the area. Are you just popping by to see Martín? It's just that he's having his nap.'

Isabel forced a smile. 'Actually, I'm not here to see him.'

Agila ushered her inside. 'Look at that rain. I fear it's in for the rest of the day. The sea is so restless.'

Isabel followed her into the kitchen. 'Any chance of you making me that special tea of yours?'

'Of course. I always have it on the boil in this weather. So how is the case going? Any further progress on finding Sebi's killer?'

'It's coming to a head.'

The woman bit her lip. 'I appreciate that you can't tell me much during an ongoing investigation.'

Isabel gratefully accepted the tea. 'The truth is, Agila, that I need to see the garage.'

'The garage?' She tittered. 'I'm afraid it's a mess. It's full of old crates, paintings and boxes of books and home to two old dusty vehicles. I never set foot in the place.'

Isabel sipped thoughtfully. 'I'm searching for something important connected with Sebi and I feel it might possibly be there.'

Agila shrugged. 'I should ask Martín's permission, but presumably you won't be too long?'

Isabel shook her head. 'Do any family members use the garage?'

'None that I know of. Martín's van hasn't been driven since he became ill and there's a Fiat without tyres that's been rotting in there for years. Only Sebi used to come here now and then but Sara hardly at all. She hasn't been back since Sebi's death, but she's fragile and this must have been such a shock for her.'

Isabel drained her cup as the woman sifted delicately through a mugful of keys with labels.

'Here are the garage keys. Let me show you.'

Agila put on a mac and the two walked beneath a large black umbrella to the garage. She spotted Isabel's car and smiled.

'You have your own driver? You must be important.'

'Not at all. I just had a small accident and driving isn't easy currently.'

'I'm so sorry to hear that. Here we are.'

Agila unlocked the garage door and rolled it back. 'Can I leave you here? I just don't like to be away from Martín for too long.'

Isabel nodded. 'Of course. I'll return the key as soon as I'm done.'

Agila left and Isabel stepped into the large space. Putting on her latex gloves, she cast an eye over the messy contents. One side of the garage was stacked with high shelves groaning with cardboard boxes, while on the far wall there was a series of worn and broken wooden cupboards, their contents spilling onto the ground. A tangle of gilt and wood frames, tennis rackets, baskets, vintage clothes and old children's toys had been dumped on top of them, some of which had fallen onto the garage floor. An ancient, grubby white Fiat Panda without wheels stood forlornly in a corner, covered in dust, and yet sporting a huge love heart on the windscreen. Isabel pondered who the artist might have been. The doors opened easily enough, if a tad creakily, but the interior exhibited little of interest, having been gutted like a fish.

She wandered over to the larger vehicle hidden under a voluminous black plastic cover which, with difficulty, she managed to pull off. Isabel stared sombrely at the grey van for a few minutes. She attempted to open the doors, but they were all closed fast. She walked slowly around the room in search of the keys. An acute pain in her ribcage forced her to double up and she cursed, leaning against a brick wall. Beads of sweat broke out on her forehead. Crouching down, she took long breaths and put her hands on the ground to support herself, listening to the methodical pitter-patter of the falling rain. Carefully, she extracted a bottle of water and a painkiller from her pannier and glugged it down. After a while, her head stopped swimming and once again she was able to take stock of her surroundings. She scanned the room, homing in on the front right tyre of the grey van. Something glinted in the gloom.

Isabel got up slowly and placed a gloved hand on top of the tyre. A car key on a fob was tucked inside. She took her time opening the van because, with a heavy heart, she was sure of what she'd find. She slid open the side door and issued a heavy sigh. Facing her were three pairs of dark red rubber boots.

Isabel sat talking at length with Tolo in the back of the car while her driver stood discreetly under the porch with a mug of coffee provided by an agitated Agila. Tolo gave a cough.

'I have a unit on its way to you now. The team will take charge and secure the garage and premises until the forensics team arrives. You've done a great job. Now go home.'

Isabel cleared her throat. 'How much longer will you be at Marc Castell's place?'

'Forensics have been beavering away, but it's slow going. It's a big parcel of land and we've also still got to investigate a few old outhouses. All the same, everyone's in good cheer following the discovery of the John Deere tractor. We're on track.'

'So still no sign of Marc Castell?'

'We're urgently trying to locate him. The Mestre brothers are being questioned again at the precinct by members of my team, but as you'd expect, they're being tight-lipped. They've got their lawyers swarming the place.'

Shortly after she'd finished the call, two police cars arrived, a welcome cue for Isabel to take her leave. After briefing the officers and reassuring Agila, she and her driver set off. The rain had stopped and Isabel felt a sudden surge of energy and hope as bright sunlight spread its rays across forestland and fields of dormant vines. Aromatic air wafted through the open window, bristling with the fragrance of pine and rosemary.

'Back to Sant Martí?' her driver asked politely, as he caught her eye in the central mirror.

She shook her head. 'Change of plan. We're going to Porreres.'

Isabel arrived at the gate to Marc Castell's land and smiled at the officers on duty. She knew them both well.

'Where will I find Tolo?'

'Aren't you supposed to be resting after your adventure with the Guardia last night?' one of them asked.

'Word gets around fast.'

He laughed. 'No secret's safe with the force.'

She winked. 'I'll remember that.'

'Give us a sec and we'll call the guv. He could be anywhere.'

Moments later, he directed her driver to follow the rough track for one kilometre and to look out for a series of dilapidated outhouses. The terrain was densely forested on one side while fields of olive, algaroba and almond trees dominated the other. Soon they reached a muddy clearing where a line of police vehicles were parked. Tolo was leaning against a tree, speaking on his mobile with a stern expression on his face. When he saw Isabel peering out of the open window of the car, his face lightened and he ended the call.

He opened her door. 'So you specifically ignored my instructions to go home?'

'*Claro*. What did you think I'd do?'

'But how are you feeling?'

She shrugged. 'So any progress here?'

He nodded.

'Nacho and the team have found evidence of miniscule dried blood and paint smears in soil samples close to a stretch of newly ploughed land, so hopefully we're going to be able to gather sufficient DNA to prosecute Marc Castell at least.'

Isabel nodded. 'But Marc Castell is just the stooge. The Mestres are calling the shots and Rocci is the loose cannon.'

'I know. Although we have evidence of dubious bank transfers between Sebi Vives, Marc Castell and the brothers, it's not enough to support a firm conviction. Hopefully we'll track down Castell and extract a confession.'

Isabel shook her head. 'That's not going to happen, Tolo. I believe Rocci Mestre will have made sure that Castell wouldn't squeak. I'm not sure how far David and Toni were embroiled, but certainly Rocci used Castell as his pimp, first to plant cocaine and a gun in Sebi Vives' car for insurance purposes, and secondly to get rid of Silvia Porres. We have evidence that they were both at Silvia's premises. Her mistake was in attempting to blackmail them all.'

He looked alarmed. 'You think he's dead?'

Isabel rubbed her forehead. 'Put it this way, Marc Castell was never going to make old bones.'

At gone eight in the evening, Isabel and Nacho heard shouting and a whistle blow. They were sitting under strong portable lights in one of the old outhouses, sifting through sealed bags of various finds and the miniscule samples of dried blood that Nacho believed would offer crucial DNA. They both jumped up and made their way outside, where Tolo was speaking urgently with a group of officers. The tense conversation ended and he turned and beckoned to Isabel and Nacho to follow. They caught up and he looked at Isabel.

'They've found a male corpse buried under loose soil near a disused water cistern. It appears that he was shot at close range. Let's go.'

The small group made their way quietly through thick undergrowth, following the lead officer until they arrived at the old cistern. A short distance beyond, an officer stepped forward and directed them to the muddy inert form. The man was curled in a foetal position surrounded by mulch and silt. Part of the cranium and nasal bone were missing and dried blood had stained the pale cheeks.

Isabel stared down at Marc Castell for a few seconds and spoke softly.

'Dog eat dog.'

Tolo cursed. 'We were so close. I'm damned if we'll let the Mestres walk away.'

Isabel patted his shoulder. 'It's late. Let's wrap up here tonight and leave our fight for another day.'

TWENTY-TWO

Isabel walked into the smart premises of Santa Margalida, the private nursing home for the elderly, and was greeted at the front desk by a cheery woman in white overalls.

'Señora Porres is expecting you. She gets a little confused, so best to speak slowly. I'll get a nurse to show you to her room.'

The woman made a brief call and moments later a nurse appeared. She wore a wan smile as she reached forward to shake Isabel's hand.

'Your colleague, Gaspar Fernandez, said that you might have some questions. I am a senior nurse here and have tended to Señora Porres since she arrived about five years ago. How can I help?'

They walked along a white-walled corridor flanked by a pretty courtyard.

'Would you know where she was living before she arrived here?'

The woman nodded. 'Her daughter, Silvia, had her transferred here from a state home, but she never visited, sadly. She told me that she and her mother had been estranged for years.'

'So what motivated Silvia to look after her mother?'

'Silvia had apparently heard from her mother's lawyer out of the blue. He informed her that her mother was in a nursing home in Palma and had assigned her home in Palmanyola to her daughter. Señora Porres has an untreatable heart condition and Parkinson's disease and was no longer able to look after herself. I think Silvia felt a sense of duty to her mother.'

'I imagine the fees here aren't cheap.'

The woman's kindly eyes settled on Isabel's face. 'It's very expensive, but Silvia moved out of a rented flat into her mother's house and was offered a new job at a casino. Before long she became a highflyer in a regional government job. She never seemed to have a care about the fees.'

'What will happen to Señora Porres now that her daughter is dead?'

'It's a terrible tragedy. Obviously, we will keep her mother here for now and until we hear from Silvia's lawyer. Hopefully, the eventual sale of the house and Silvia's disposable assets will enable her to remain with us.' She spoke quietly. 'Frankly, she has little time left, so I doubt the owners would remove her anyway.'

'How did Señora Porres react to news of her daughter's death?'

They arrived at a white door with a gold number seven inscribed on it. The nurse shook her head. 'She hasn't cried or said a word about it, but her health has rapidly declined.'

The nurse paused at the door.

'Is ten minutes enough? She gets exhausted easily.'

Isabel nodded and stepped inside the gloomy room. A thin, elderly woman wearing a floral nightdress and shawl observed her with sharp eyes. Her hands shook as she grasped fretfully at the sheet.

'Come and sit with me. You are the policewoman they told me about?'

Isabel pulled up a metal chair and took the woman's hand.

'My name is Bel and I met your daughter, Silvia.'

The woman was silent for a second. 'I was a terrible mother and I failed her. My daughter led a miserable life because of me and now she's dead.'

Isabel chose her words carefully. 'Life is all about making mistakes, some small, some big, but acknowledging them and trying to make amends is what matters.'

She eyed Isabel with watery eyes. 'But she never, ever forgave me. That's why she never visited.'

'Perhaps she felt it best to lay the past to rest and not to unsettle old ghosts. But Silvia never stopped caring about you. She worked hard to pay for your fees here and she moved into your house, which proves to me that she still cherished memories of home.'

'Did she live alone?'

Isabel smiled. 'She had a lovely old Persian cat named Lobo.'

'That was my cat. He must be nearly twenty years old. When I got ill, my neighbour fed him at my house every day.'

'Then it must be the same neighbour who has adopted him.'

The woman offered a fleeting smile and stared at Isabel for a long time until she began to cough violently. Her hands trembled violently as she sought to sit upright. Isabel gently lifted her into a sitting position and passed her a glass of water with a straw. When she was calm, she grasped Isabel's hand tightly.

'I have little time left, Bel. All I ask is that you find my daughter's killer, then I can be set free.'

Isabel's eyes filled with tears and she nodded. 'Señora Porres, you have my word.'

Nacho sat munching on a large *bocadillo* of *jamón* Serrano and cheese on the sofa in Tolo's office. He was in good spirits, convinced that the forensic evidence his team had found on Marc Castell's land the previous day would seal the dead man's guilt. He smiled when Isabel walked in holding a coffee-to-go and a paper bag.

'Snacking as ever!'

Isabel kicked his outstretched foot.

'You're a fine one to talk.'

She sat down heavily next to him and pulled a large slice of *coca con acelgas* out of the bag.

'I'm absolutely starving. It's been non-stop this morning.'

Tolo and Gaspar were huddled over notes at a table on the other side of the room and observed them both in bemusement.

Gaspar grinned. 'Don't mind us, you two, although the precinct cafeteria is just one floor down. So, how did your meeting with Señora Porres go?'

Isabel placed her coffee cup on the small table at her side.

'It filled in some gaps. We owe it to her to nail her daughter's killer.'

Gaspar nodded. 'From what Nacho has told us, we'll have more than enough to prove Marc Castell's guilt, posthumously at least.'

'That's not enough. We know from the cigarette stub I discovered in the garden at Silvia's house that Rocci Mestre was probably at her house on the night she was abducted. He is a known bloodthirsty thug, the worst of the Mestre brothers, and most likely had a hand in Silvia's death and the murder of Marc Castell.'

Tolo offered her a sympathetic glance. 'I agree, Bel, but we have zero proof at this stage. Those brothers are as slippery as eels.'

'There must be a way,' Isabel replied. 'Meanwhile, are we still on course for tomorrow night?'

'Absolutely. I will have the warrant. All units are on standby. Mateu Vives is definitely still here?' asked Tolo.

Isabel nodded. 'He won't return to Barcelona until he thinks his mother is able to cope.'

She looked at Nacho. 'When might you get forensics back from the garage at Martín Vives' place? We need those results before we can act.'

Nacho wiped his mouth with his hand and stared at her with a broad smile.

'What are you so cheerful about?' she asked.

'I've kept the best till last.'

Tolo smiled. 'Tell her.'

'As you know, our forensic team worked tirelessly yesterday and all through the night on the finds at the garage. We were also given excellent support from colleagues at the European Network of Forensic Science Institutes. Two of their DNA experts even flew in yesterday to assist. Just an hour ago, we had the preliminary results. Your investigating skills and shrewd instincts have paid off again.'

Isabel eyed him impatiently. 'Don't keep me in suspense.'

'We now have solid proof of who killed Sebi Vives. Furthermore, the DNA from the used gum sample you gave me yesterday is a direct match to samples found by Furó at the Llucmajor crime scene and S'Albufera. That, dear Bel, is the final piece in this complex jigsaw.'

The car park of the Gran Casino Atlántico was surprisingly quiet, although Isabel sniffed in disapproval as she passed a row of Maseratis, Ferraris and Aston Martins. Several of the owners would be local drug dealers still touting their killer wares on the streets of Mallorca. As she entered the casino, a stork-like hostess tottered over on precarious heels to greet her. Isabel was in no mood for niceties. She nodded, flicked her badge and stalked into the bar, unannounced. The same young barman was drying glasses behind the glitzy counter and offered her a full-teeth smile.

'I remember you. Couldn't keep away?'

'It was those olives. They're quite addictive.'

'What can I get you?'

Isabel smiled. '*Agua con gas*, thanks.'

He headed for the shelf of glasses and she heard footsteps close by.

David Mestre offered her a charming smile.

'Señora Flores. Back again? I'm flattered that you are growing to like my second home so much. You should have called in advance and we could have had lunch together.'

'It's just a flying visit. Do you have a moment?'

'Of course. In fact, opportunely, my brother is here. I don't believe you've met him?'

Isabel turned, her stomach churning at the thought of coming face to face with Rocci Mestre again, but another man nodded to them from one of the alcove tables.

'Toni is my younger brother, though Rocci is of course the baby of the family. Come, let me introduce you to him.'

Lean and fit with pronounced muscles, Toni Mestre stood up and offered Isabel his hand. As Isabel took a seat, the waiter bustled over with drinks and bowls of snacks and olives.

'So Señorita Flores, we hear that our dear friend, Marc Castell, has been found dead.'

'Well, you're certainly ahead of the game. It's not even been reported yet.'

Toni flicked a quick look at his older brother. 'We have contacts everywhere. After your people raided our homes and took our fingerprints and found nothing, you went for poor Marc. He couldn't handle the pressure and went completely off the grid.'

'That would imply that he had something to hide, wouldn't you agree?'

David shook his head. 'He was a sensitive soul. The death of Sebi and then Silvia affected him greatly. Then the motorway project was halted, costing him thousands. He was becoming desperately depressed. Taking his own life was probably the only way out that he could see.'

Isabel chewed on an olive and observed him carefully.

'You could have been an actor, David. You said that without a hint of irony.'

Toni breathed heavily and knocked back a shot of clear liquid.

'Marc was a close friend of the family and a key business associate, so please don't make implications,' he replied heatedly.

David patted his arm. 'It's okay, Toni. Señorita Flores is only doing her job.'

Isabel felt she had nothing left to lose. Life was a gamble and this was one of those moments.

'Let's not play games anymore. We know that Marc and your brother Rocci were both involved in the abduction of Silvia Porres from her home in Palmanyola. Carelessly, your brother even left a cigarette butt with plenty of DNA at the scene, another of which we discovered close to the body of Marc Castell in Porreres. The pair asphyxiated Silvia Porres and transported her body first to Marc's land, where they callously ran over it several times with a tractor, and then to the motorway site. It was a clumsy and, frankly, naïve attempt to frame local environmentalists.'

Toni Mestre's eyes bulged. 'That's a lie.'

Isabel plucked a salted pecan nut from one of the bowls, crunched hard on it and grinned.

'You're not so good an actor as David. The problem for you both is that Rocci will bring you down if you continue to protect him. He is lawless and a liability, as you know. Like a house of cards, your empire will come toppling down at his hands sooner rather than later.'

Toni Mestre pushed back his chair and stood up. 'I don't want to hear any more of this crap.'

His brother placed a steely hand on his arm. 'Sit down.'

Isabel continued. 'So, help me out. Naturally, when your homes were raided by the police, you knew Castell would be next and that his little slice of bloodied paradise in Porreres would be discovered, DNA from Silvia and all. You panicked and arranged for Rocci to kill him so that he wouldn't squeak, or maybe Rocci took matters into his own hands. Am I warm?'

'Squeak about what?' shouted Toni.

David frowned. 'Calm down, Toni. Can we not have a civilised discussion?'

'The homicide department has a trail of paperwork with proof of offshore payments that connect you to Silvia Porres, Sebi Vives and Marc Castell. We know that you all scratched each other's backs with the motorway contract and that Silvia began blackmailing you when Sebi died. In your eyes, she became greedy and had to be silenced. It wasn't a bright idea to try and blame her death on eco-warriors.'

David observed her closely. 'Do go on. This is fascinating.'

She turned to him. 'I know that Silvia left her job in the gourmet department of El Corte Inglés to work for you. She introduced you to the olives cassées de la vallée des Baux de Provence, which are fabulous, by the way.'

Toni Mestre began cackling menacingly. 'This woman is deranged. What is all this tosh about olives?'

Isabel raised a hand and continued. 'Poor Silvia led a very unhappy life. She was estranged from her abusive mother but five years ago learnt through the woman's lawyer that she was dying and had left Silvia her house and cat in Palmanyola. Working here at the casino offered her a chance of a higher salary, which she used to fund care for her mother. Silvia had her moved to a private nursing home in Santa Ponsa and when, through your string-pulling, she got a job working for Sebi Vives, she hit the jackpot. You planted her there in order to administer and facilitate the movement of funds between all parties without suspicion in his department. She was paid handsomely, which ensured that her mother could remain at her private home. When Sebi died, your lucrative scheme had to be disbanded rapidly as the police investigated and Silvia was forced to erase as much evidence as possible. Her revenue stream was cut off, but she hit on the plan to blackmail you all. She needed to keep up the payments at the home.' She took a sip of water. 'So you decided to eliminate her.'

The two men said nothing for a few seconds. David formed a pyramid with his slender fingers and suddenly looked up.

'This is an imaginative and terrible tale, Señorita Flores, but total fabrication. My brothers and I would never condone murder. We are businessmen, not killers.'

Isabel stared him down. 'Maybe not, but your brother is.'

She got up to leave.

Toni eyed her furiously. 'Is that it? You come in here and accuse us of all kinds of crime without a shred of evidence and then just walk out?'

She shrugged. 'I just want you to know that I know the truth. It may take time, but I promise you this: I will avenge Silvia's death.'

David stood up and walked with her to the entrance of the casino.

'What will become of Silvia's mother?'

Isabel folded her arms. 'What do you care? She'll be out on the street, of course, without funds to pay for the nursing home. Extreme guilt about her past deeds and grief at her daughter's death will take its toll.'

He offered her an inscrutable look. 'One thing you did say is true. My brother Rocci is a law unto himself and at times a huge disappointment to me.'

He walked briskly back through the doors.

Isabel sat in Pequeñito for a few minutes and rubbed her tired eyes. The pain in her ribcage returned and she quickly knocked back a painkiller with water. Had she achieved anything from her dramatic little stunt? Time would tell.

It was early evening and Tolo sat on Isabel's patio sipping a glass of *cava*. Isabel paced about the nearby orchard, talking confidentially to Sara Vives on her mobile.

The long conversation ended and she tucked the mobile back in her pocket.

'You sounded so sincere,' he said with a wry grin.

'But I am, Tolo. I'm no actor.'

He gave a snort. 'You could win an Oscar. What about your performance with the Mestres today?'

'That's different.'

He gave her a wink. 'So everything's under control?'

Isabel took a seat next to him and nodded.

'Sometimes I hate our job. We just pick over broken lives and destroy them completely.'

He grabbed her hand. 'No, we don't destroy them. We bring people to justice for destroying the lives of others. If they self-destruct in the process, that is not our fault.'

Isabel curled her feet up under her and snuggled into a blanket.

'But what about mitigating circumstances?'

He spoke gently. 'I understand that, but we have a job to do. There are nearly always mitigating circumstances, but people need to be held to account. We owe it to those both living and dead, as you well know.'

Isabel picked up her glass and clinked it against his. 'To ghosts past and present, let justice be done.'

TWENTY-THREE

A knot of coppery-brown storm clouds sat broodingly on the horizon as Isabel drove along the quiet rural roads towards Llucmajor. She had left Furó in the care of her mother. Pep had left early to sort out a problem with the heating at one of the rental properties. After a sleepless night, Isabel had risen early and taken Furó for his habitual swim. She had returned to the office and with a strong coffee by her side, had calmly re-read her notes on the Vives case. Despite her feelings of anxiety at what lay ahead, Isabel had persuaded Tolo and Gaspar to allow her to drive to the Vives residence alone in order to talk through her findings with those assembled in a civilised manner. Tolo and his units would be close at hand and Manel, the protection officer, would be on duty, and had been apprised of the situation.

With the car windows wide open, Isabel shivered as a cool breeze tickled her neck and shoulders and played with the open notebook on the passenger seat. Splashes of rain began to hit the windscreen and she reluctantly wound up the front windows.

'Still no other car on the road though, Pequeñito, and unlike Boadicea, you'll make sure I stay dry.'

She grinned and tapped the steering wheel.

'What's that you say? Motorbikes are dangerous in wet weather. You have a point, but they are still fun to ride.'

She tutted to herself. Was she alone in talking to her car? Hopefully so. Pep found it quite unnerving, while Tolo would just laugh and tell her that he could recommend a good psychologist. As she drew closer to the *finca*, she took deep breaths and braced herself for the encounter. Everything was passing and at least now there would be resolution, however sad and messy that might be. She took a sharp left turn onto the rainy track leading to the home of the Vives. Manel offered her a nod and sympathetic smile as she parked near the porch. Isabel put her notebook and mobile in her pannier. She would hopefully need neither, but it was always best to be prepared.

Grabbing a bright orange umbrella, she ran towards the front steps. Sara was already there to greet her with a tense smile.

'A bright yellow car and an orange umbrella! Thank you for bringing a slice of sunshine with you, Bel.'

Isabel felt wooden inside but attempted levity.

'I always like to look on the bright side of life. Thank you for arranging our get-together now that we have completed the investigation.'

'As agreed by phone, we're all here and keen to hear what you have to say. Come inside and I'll get you a warming coffee.'

Isabel left her jacket and brolly by the front door and followed Sara into the kitchen. Beyond, she saw the concerned faces of Mariana and Fran as they sat together on one of the cream sofas. Isabel went to greet them and Sara busied herself in the kitchen, making coffee.

'So the investigation is complete?' asked Mariana. 'You are certain of Sebi's killer?'

Isabel sighed. 'Let's discuss our findings when Sara has joined us. Where is Mateu?'

Fran frantically chewed at a piece of gum. 'In his room, listening to music.'

Isabel sat in an upright chair and gratefully accepted her coffee from Sara.

'We felt it better to discuss your findings before inviting Mateu to join us,' blurted Sara. 'He has already gone through so much. It will be easier for us to explain things to him later.'

Isabel eyed her curiously. 'Well, let us begin and we can call Mateu when the time is right.'

Fran gave a hoarse laugh. 'That's an odd thing to say.' She took a sip of her coffee. 'I heard off the record from my husband that Marc Castell, the motorway contractor, has been found dead, and is implicated in this whole sorry business along with Silvia Porres.'

Mariana offered her a well-staged look of surprise. 'But surely Pablo Pons, who sent Sebi death threats and most likely shunted Sara's car was also embroiled in the mess?'

Isabel shot Fran an icy stare. 'I'm not sure where your husband received that intelligence, but any information pertaining to this case remains classified.'

Fran tutted impatiently. 'He is the regional president and as you'd expect, he has a line to important contacts here on the island. Naturally, he wouldn't breathe a word about this to anyone.'

'I'm presuming that the Mestres count as important contacts?' Isabel replied.

Fran shrugged. 'I believe my husband did speak to David Mestre yesterday.'

Isabel turned to her. 'I popped by your Pilates studio the other day. It proved that you're a woman of many talents.'

The woman tittered. 'I'm not sure about that. I would have shown you around if I'd known.'

'I was just passing by.' Isabel paused. 'Aside from your impressive level of fitness, I discovered online that you studied podiatry and reflexology for many years.'

Fran tutted. 'That's no secret. Forgive me, but I'm not sure where this is heading.'

Isabel looked across at Mariana. 'You too are a highly regarded medical practitioner at your clinic and a very fit cycling enthusiast.'

She nodded. 'Well, we girls all have to watch our weight.'

Isabel leant forward in her chair and eyed them all. 'Weight is a choice word. You see, it took me a while to work out how you and Fran were able to carry Sebi Vives in a body bag for quite some distance along the path in S'Albufera.'

'What on earth are you talking about?' said Sara in a faint voice.

'This is absurd,' yelled Fran.

Isabel held up a hand. 'Humour me for a few more minutes, ladies. You see, to all intents and purposes, Sebi's death appeared to have been the work of zealous environmentalists opposed to the new motorway. It would have destroyed part of the valuable wetlands of S'Albufera Natural Park, a catastrophe for local fauna and flora. Pablo Pons, a hot-headed and passionate eco-warrior, was a perfect fit for the crime. He had already attacked Sebi physically and sent him death threats.'

Sara held a hand to her chest, a look of terror in her eyes.

'He attempted to kill me too when he shunted my car.'

'No, he didn't, Sara,' Isabel replied. 'Your car was never shunted, which is why when I asked to see it in case of evidence you told me that it had already been repaired. The truth is that some nights previously, Sebi, in one of his drunken and abusive rages, attempted to strangle you. It followed a pattern of abuse that had been going on for years.'

Sara sat bewitched, her hands trembling, while the other two women looked on with a mixture of fury and disbelief.

'I discovered that you had suffered numerous accidents and broken limbs over the years that your doctor put down to clumsiness, but your abusive husband was to blame. A few years ago, no doubt encouraged by your two loyal girlfriends here, you bravely reported Sebi's abuse to the authorities. Sadly, the case was thrown out of court due to lack of evidence, or perhaps Sebi's VIP status afforded him some kind of protection. I spoke with a judge who was familiar with the case and she remembered being outraged by the outcome.'

'Outrage wasn't enough,' spat Fran. 'Sebi was a monster and should have been locked up.'

Mariana eyed Isabel evenly. 'Do carry on.'

Isabel gave a sigh. 'So now we need to step back in time because the past inevitably impacts the present and future. Sara, when you were a nineteen-year-old student, you and Sebi's younger brother, Gabriel, were childhood sweethearts. He was a budding artist and a sensitive soul who devoted himself to his art and you. But on a fateful weekend hiking expedition with Sebi and your mutual friends, Jaume and Eli, he drowned. I have trawled through old cuttings and media and police reports of that night, but my understanding is that the manner of Gabriel's death was never conclusive. Purportedly, after imbibing heavily, you all went to sleep in small tents while Sebi and Gabriel, bizarrely, untethered a small boat on the banks of Gorg Blau and took it out into the dark, freezing cold waters. They were both drunk, and as Gabriel leant over the side, he fell in. Sebi apparently dived in and tried to find his brother, but he had disappeared under the water. He then returned to the bank to raise the alarm and Gabriel's body was dredged up the next day. I think there was probably another version to events, but I can only speculate.'

Sara began to cry and hung her head. 'Sebi forced him into that little fishing boat. It was just sitting by the bank and he untethered it. He was a bully and knew that Gabriel couldn't swim. He plied him with alcohol all night and then marched him to the bank and told him to go for a sail with him. The rest of us were drunk and tired. We left them to it and went to sleep. I remember waking to hear Sebi screaming hysterically. He was a coward and a murderer. He left his brother, my love, to die.'

As she burst into hysterical tears, Mariana turned on Isabel.

'What right have you to bring up the past so cruelly?'

'Because it is the reason we are all sitting together here now. The truth is that a heartbroken Sara soon after discovered that she was pregnant with Gabriel's child. I'm not sure why, but Sara and Sebi married.'

Mariana stood up and checked that the door was closed.

'Have you no heart? Mateu will be devastated when he does find out about all this but now is not the right moment.'

Isabel took out a Chupa Chup and unwrapped it slowly.

'I am certain that Mateu already knows. He recently visited his grandfather, who gave him a box of memorabilia. I believe that it contained love letters between Sara and Gabriel. A few days ago, I witnessed Mateu arguing with his godparents, Eli and Jaume, and I strongly believe that he was challenging them about what he had discovered and about his parentage. I imagine that all of you, including your families, were in on the secret, but of course the marriage could never have worked because Sara had been in love with Gabriel and blamed Sebi for his death.'

Sara wiped her eyes. 'What you have said is true, but you cannot know everything. When I found out that I was pregnant, our two grief-stricken families got together and demanded Sebi and I marry. Sebi had always seemed jealous of Gabriel's relationship with me and was insistent that we could have a good life together and bring up his brother's child in a loving home. I could never forgive him for what happened to Gabriel, but I was very young and in deep shock. Foolishly, under extreme parental pressure, I did as I was told.'

Fran gave an exasperated sigh. 'When Mariana and I got to know Sara in the early days as all our husbands climbed the political ladder, we saw how abusive and vile Sebi had become. It was obvious that he resented Sara's lack of affection for him and her closeness to Mateu. That was the reason he sent him away to boarding school and that's also when he became physically violent. At first Sara didn't want to report it, but yes, as you suggested, we stepped in to help, as did Eli and Jaume. Not that any of us were taken seriously in court, and it made our husbands angry. They buried the whole episode.'

Isabel nodded and sucked thoughtfully on her Chupa Chup.

'So the three of you resolved to dispense with Sebi but waited for the perfect moment and a time when Mateu would be away at university. The universal hatred directed at Sebi over the motorway offered the ideal opportunity to act. You also wanted the death to have meaning, while at the same time hopefully framing someone else.'

The three women, as if mesmerised, listened in silence.

Isabel continued. 'A professor and lepidopterist at the University of the Baleares showed me some beautiful watercolours of butterflies that, on a subsequent visit, I discovered were painted by Gabriel, then a student at the university. There was one of a multi-coloured butterfly called the mighty mountain meh that particularly captured my imagination. When I visited Sebi's family home, I saw a painting of the very same magnificent butterfly. So, I revisited the professor and he confessed to me that the butterfly had never existed but was the brainchild of Gabriel. They had both christened it the mighty mountain meh and it became their little joke and they would tell people that it had harked back to Moorish times. That is how I guessed that all the paintings that the professor had originally shown me were by Gabriel. He also told me of his love for the clouded yellow, and when I visited Sebi's family home, I found many paintings of it as well as a copy of *One Hundred Years of Solitude* in Gabriel's bookcase. It is a masterful tale which I have been reading myself. Yellow butterflies are an important symbol in the book, and you, Sara, were Gabriel's yellow butterfly. The book had been dedicated to him by someone with the initials CC. I believe it was you. It stands for *Colias croceus*, does it not?'

'How can you possibly know that?' asked Sara faintly.

'When I last popped by here, your bare feet were on display and I noticed a tattoo of a yellow butterfly on the inside of your ankle with the initials CC and GV intertwined.'

'What does any of this prove in relation to Sebi's death?' asked Fran.

'I will explain. The three of you plotted to terminate Sebi some time ago and hit on a plan. You ordered clouded yellow pupae online and bred them here. I'm guessing in your garage, Sara?'

She looked away.

'You planned to dispose of Sebi at S'Albufera. You believed it would point the finger at activists such as Pablo Pons and his associates. You used an Australian-branded body bag which is particularly robust with strong handles. It's a rare brand, and after contacting Clinica del Rey, I discovered from its director that the clinic has a contract with the company.'

She turned to Mariana. 'I'm guessing you just helped yourself to one of the body bags at the clinic.'

The surgeon observed her with pursed lips.

Isabel continued. 'Once you had the body bag, you decided to give Sebi some company in the form of insects, fish and soil relating to S'Albufera to push the environmental angle. You also wanted to terrify Sebi. You knew he had a lifelong hatred of eels and insects. I learnt that from Mateu when we chatted. The inclusion of clouded yellow butterflies was in memory of Gabriel. In effect, you were avenging his death.'

Mariana clasped her hands together. 'This is madness. How could we have lured Sebi to voluntarily get inside a body bag?'

Isabel crunched on her lollipop. 'I'm getting to that. Sebi was spending an increasing amount of time at the Gran Casino Atlántico. He had gambling debts and was in a mess. Something happened as a trigger a few nights before the shunt that you feigned. Whatever it was persuaded you to accelerate your plans. As I have suggested, I believe that Sebi tried to strangle you, Sara, and that was the trigger. Sara, you wore a neck brace when I first visited and invented the shunt story, but I knew from your bloodshot eyes that you had suffered physical violence. You showed signs of petechial haemorrhage and erythema and you were agitated and had a raspy voice. I was sure that you had suffered from traumatic asphyxia. Now is the really clever part. On the night of Sebi's death—'

'Wait!' Sara looked at her with sad eyes. 'The trigger for Sebi's rage, three nights before his death, was because I again accused him of being responsible for Gabriel's death. We had both drunk a lot and things got heated. Finally, he blurted out that he had always resented Gabriel and had been jealous of his talent. He had wanted me for himself and hoped that Gabriel and I would split up. That night, he had wanted to frighten and bully Gabriel into submission, but when he fell overboard, instead of trying to save him, he allowed him to drown. In fury, I attacked Sebi with my bare hands, but I was quickly overpowered and he began to throttle me in earnest. Eventually, I passed out and woke up in severe pain. I was unable to speak so texted Mariana and she came over and tended to me. That was when we dreamt up the story of the car shunt.'

'Thanks for filling me in,' Isabel replied. 'As I presumed, on the night of Sebi's death, you made sure that, as usual, he would be drinking at the casino. Close to eight o'clock, you called him while he was at the bar. You told me that you wanted to find out what time he'd be home, but I believe that was a lie. I think you told him that either Fran or Mariana had a problem with their car and asked him to make a detour on the way home in order to go and help. Conveniently, you sent him to a remote road in rural Llucmajor, but of course you'd meticulously planned all this long before. Sebi arrived at the location you gave him and discovered both Fran and Mariana by the car on the side of the road. He must have been a bit surprised. While Fran presumably distracted him with the fictitious tyre or engine problem, Mariana, using her medical skills, knocked him out with propofol, a powerful anaesthetic. That would have been easy to procure at her clinic too. Our forensic team found the puncture wound in the right arm. Then the two of you carried Sebi into the vehicle and drove his car into woodland. The car was locked and I've still no idea what you did with the key.'

The door banged open and a wired-looking Mateu appeared.

'I know exactly what happened to it. I was looking for the key to the garage a few days ago and discovered the key to my father's Audi R8 along with the duplicate in my mum's bedside table.'

He dropped them on the table in front of Isabel. 'I've been outside the door listening to all this. It's surreal.'

'Mateu, what were you doing looking for the garage key?' Sara cried.

'I'm not stupid. A lot of things didn't add up when I got home. You kept huddling with Fran and Mariana and all of you would stop speaking when I appeared. The garage door was locked and you told me you'd lost the key. I didn't believe you. I knew something was going on. Were Eli and Jaume in on this?'

Sara shook her head emphatically. 'They know nothing.'

Isabel turned to him. 'The box your grandfather gave you late one night confirmed your paternity?'

He nodded. 'I don't know how you know about that, but Grandad told me it was full of family secrets that needed airing. I know he's not quite right in the head now, but what I discovered all made sense. There were loads of love letters and images of Mum with Gabriel. I realised that I looked just like him.'

Isabel smiled sadly. 'Yes, you are the spitting image of him and exactly the same age as he was when he died. Eli and Jaume showed me an old photograph of all of them when they were young and I knew then that he had to be your father.'

Sara sobbed quietly. 'I'm so sorry for everything, Mateu, but I could never forgive Sebi for causing your father's death.'

Isabel stood up and walked over to the garden window. The skies had cleared and rain dripped steadily from the eaves while white light shone in the sky.

Mateu sat next to his mother and placed a tentative arm around her shoulder. He looked at them all.

'So, how did you kill him, exactly?'

Fran rubbed her forehead. 'Let's see whether clever little Miss Detective can enlighten you.'

Isabel returned to her seat. 'Once you'd hidden Sebi's car in woodland, you took him back here, and while he was still sedated, you removed his clothes, gagged and bound him and placed him in the body bag. I'm guessing you burnt the clothes?'

Sara nodded slowly.

'One thing I'm curious about is where you got hold of the eel and other creatures?'

Fran gave a cackle. 'Easy. We bought them from an island supplier and kept the fish in a tank in the garage. The same applied to the insects, which we nurtured there. It became quite a lab.'

'But you didn't include birds. Why was that?' asked Isabel.

Sara fretfully twisted her damp tissue. 'I love birds. I couldn't allow any to be killed.'

Isabel continued. 'Next you transported Sebi's body into the grey van that belonged to his father, Martín. It was in the garage at the Vives family home and hadn't been used since he became ill with Alzheimer's. I discovered from Jaume Perez that Martín and his carer, Agila, would visit a care centre twice a week. On the evening of Sebi's death, neither was at the house because Monday was Agila's night off and Martín was accommodated at a private clinic in Palma. Sara would have been able to remove the van undetected on one of those days and to return it to the garage in the early hours of the Tuesday following Sebi's death.'

'I've got to hand it to you, Isabel, you're good,' said Fran with a cold smile.

Isabel held her gaze. 'On the Monday night, Sara drove both of you in the van to S'Albufera. Once she'd dropped you and

Mariana off, she drove away, ready to return when you'd done the deed. You are both extremely fit and sporty women so were highly capable of carrying Sebi along the gravelled track to the Gran Canal. I imagine you used head torches and knew the route well. Actually, you were quite ingenious.'

'How?' demanded Mariana.

'You wore men's rubber boots from a company called Caucho in Murcia. They must have been hard to walk in, but presumably you and Fran had done some practice runs of carrying a heavy weight between you for that distance while wearing them. I assume you did this in a quiet, rural area undetected.'

'Why wear outsized boots?' asked Mateu.

Isabel eyed him steadily. 'They wore sizes forty-three and forty-four to appear as men, but when they'd descended the muddy bank and disposed of Sebi in the canal, Fran swapped her pair of boots for a larger pair that she'd carried in a rucksack. They were size forty-six. It was a brilliant ruse because as an experienced podiatrist, she knew how to throw a forensic podiatrist off the scent. She put the original boots into her rucksack and donned the larger ones and returned up the muddy bank, leaning heavily on one side and distributing the weight in such a way that led our police podiatrist off track. The forensic report indicated that a third malnourished and tall male was present, possibly suffering from a terminal illness.'

Fran gave a cocky smile. 'All true. I have studied feet for many years and know how to create false profiling. How did you work it out?'

Isabel shrugged. 'Logic, really. There couldn't have been a third person waiting on the bank when you both arrived. It would neither have been possible to steer a vessel or swim along the canal in that atrocious weather, nor could a male with large feet have been lying in wait by the bank. If that had been the case, the forensic team would have discovered more of his footprints. Besides, where could the apparent third person have gone?'

'We just wanted to cause confusion,' said Fran somewhat proudly.

'Unfairly, you also wanted to implicate Pablo Pons and his close associates. Pons even had a forty-six shoe size which matched a print at the crime scene.'

'Pure serendipity,' she replied. 'But he's a tall man, so I assumed that would be about right.'

'You also used bright orange floats on the body bag, presumably because you wanted the body found quickly so that it would be most likely connected to the recent controversial environmentalist demos.'

'True.' Mariana shrugged.

'I showed the park wardens images of you and Fran and one of them confirmed seeing you both walking through the park some days earlier and in previous weeks. Presumably these were test runs.'

Fran wore a bitter expression. 'You're thorough, I'll give you that.'

'I also believe I saw you, Mariana, standing on the bridge in a black-hooded coat the day after Sebi's body was discovered.'

'I felt compelled to revisit, but I was careful.'

Isabel tutted. 'For future reference, it's never wise to return to a crime scene. To continue, after you had left Sebi to his fate, you both walked back to the park's entrance where Sara picked you up. No doubt you cleaned up back here, after which Sara returned the van to Martín Vives's garage and left the clean boots inside. It was naïve to think someone wouldn't discover them sooner or later and make connections.'

Fran chewed on her piece of gum and slow-clapped. 'Well, aren't you a canny sleuth.'

'Actually, I shouldn't take all the credit. You helped me out with your love of gum.'

The woman gawped at her. 'How?'

'I have a pet ferret who cleverly found some used gum both at S'Albufera and later at the crime scene in Llucmajor. The two samples had the same DNA, but there was no match on the criminal database. The second time I visited you all here, I noticed that you were chewing gum and had discarded it in an ashtray in the kitchen. Before I left the house, I popped into the kitchen to retrieve it.'

Mariana tutted. 'I remember you taking your glass into the kitchen that day. We all thought you very sweet and polite. In reality, it was a devious move.'

'I'm a detective – it's my job to look for clues and to follow my instincts. Anyway, when the forensic team analysed the new gum sample, your guilt was confirmed. It proved that you had been present at both locations at the time of Sebi's killing.'

Fran held her head in her hands and groaned. 'I've never liked ferrets.'

'Neither does Furó like criminals,' Isabel retorted. 'Another thing: I believe it was you who was observing me when I visited the Llucmajor crime scene one night and who also broke into my house last Friday.'

Fran nodded. 'Yes, that was me. I saw you picked something up and thought it was some kind of evidence. I drove to your home and had an excuse at the ready in case I was spotted, but it was so easy. When you left your home, I tried the front door and found it unlocked. There wasn't even a need to search for a key under a pot.'

Isabel raised an eyebrow. 'You're right. Slack personal security on my side. Still, you didn't find anything.'

Fran let out a frustrated sigh. 'No, I didn't.'

'I'm grateful, because the piece of chewing gum my ferret found proved irrefutably that you were at the crime scene that night.'

Mateu turned to his mother. 'But did you intend for Dad to die? He was still alive when he was thrown into the water. Maybe someone could have dragged the bag to shore.'

There was menace in Fran's reply. 'No one could have rescued him on such a freezing night and in such wild waters. We knew he'd die of hypothermia, be smashed on rocks or be overcome by water, but most of all, we wanted him to have a slow and meaningful death.'

'Meaningful?' quizzed Isabel.

'We hoped that as he approached his last moments, he'd have time to think about his miserable life and the cruelty he'd inflicted on others and understand why he'd ended up there.'

'I guess we'll never know,' Isabel replied.

There was loud knocking at the front door. Isabel stood up.

'My police colleagues have arrived, I'm afraid to say. You will be cautioned and taken to the precinct for questioning. Mateu, please come with me. We will need to let the forensics team do their job.'

He rose numbly and, with tears in his eyes, hugged his mother tightly.

'I can't condone what you all did, but I think I understand why. I knew that things between you and Dad weren't right for a long time, but I didn't know the whole story.' He wiped his eyes. 'All the same, Sebi might not have been my biological father but he was still my father. I'll be haunted by thoughts of his fear and suffering in those last minutes of life.'

Sara clung to him, sobbing heavily, as Tolo and several officers entered the property.

'Know this, Mateu. I have never stopped loving your father. Gabriel was my world and the pain of losing him was unbearable. But then you came along and gave me renewed hope. You are the reason I get up every day. I hope in time you will find it in your heart to forgive me. Sebi was not your father. He was always an imposter in our lives.'

Fran and Mariana rose stiffly and wrapped their arms around Sara and Mateu. Isabel watched at a discreet distance until the huddle broke up and the three women allowed themselves to be handcuffed.

Mariana offered Isabel a defiant stare as they departed. 'We have no regrets. Sebi Vives was an abomination and we're all glad he's dead.'

Isabel stood in Calle Sant Feliu stretching her arms to the heavens with eyes closed while a few passers-by eyed her curiously. She and Gaspar had spent several hours interviewing Mateu and allowing him to ask leading questions. Although still a young man, he had a maturity and sensibility that convinced Isabel that he would be okay despite the confusion and intense sorrow he was currently feeling. With love and guidance from his godfathers, she hoped that he would thrive until the day he was reunited with his mother.

Now she was on her way to discuss Mateu's future with Eli and Jaume. She strolled along the street, peering into the window of the stylish Rialto Living store. She arrived at the polished wooden door of their stylish dwelling and paused. The two men were expecting her and it was with a heavy heart that she pressed the buzzer. Thinking back to their earlier encounter, she wished that they had been more open with her about the Vives's family's swag bag of secrets and the failed domestic violence court case against Sebi. It would have cut corners and speeded up the investigation considerably, but on the other hand, police work was all about putting in the spadework, analysing data and evidence and not reaching hasty conclusions. There was a crackle on the intercom and a voice, clearly Jaume's, welcomed her inside.

Late that afternoon, Isabel drove over to Muro to visit Pablo Pons. It had been a long day and she was keen to tie up some loose ends on the case. Formerly a prime suspect, the leader of Terra: Acció Ara was now no longer under investigation, much to Isabel's satisfaction. As she approached the porch, the burly gym owner strode over to greet her.

'Dead on five o'clock. You operate on British military lines.'

Isabel laughed. 'I don't wear a watch, but I had a feeling I'd be on time.'

They settled with coffees in one of the consulting rooms. Pablo smiled.

'I'm guessing you're here to tell me that the case is solved and that you've found Sebi's killer.'

Isabel sat back in her chair and grinned. 'I don't think I'm at liberty to discuss the outcome of the case, but I'm happy to tell you that you are officially no longer a suspect.'

He nodded. 'Tolo Cabot implied that when I visited the precinct to give a statement. He and his sharp-dresser deputy are actually good guys.'

'That's Gaspar. He is a bit of a style icon at the precinct. Mind you, there's not a lot of competition. They're good eggs and I'm lucky to work with them.'

'So what next? Will the motorway be shelved?'

Isabel gave him a wink. 'Put it this way, in the next week or so, I think there'll be a government announcement that might make a lot of people happy. Of course, this is just pure speculation on my side.'

Pablo Pons grinned. 'I so hope you're right. Mind you, if the motorway no longer goes ahead, my members will be twiddling their thumbs.'

'I very much doubt that. There are environmental issues island-wide that need policing from groups like yours.' She hesitated. 'Just one thing: no more death threats and punch-ups, please, however tempting. You know where that leads.'

He nodded. 'After this experience, I'm going to be stepping back on the campaigning front and spending more time on helping to create coherent and positive environmental policies that can be adopted by the local government. I'm open to having a conversation when the time comes.'

Isabel smiled. 'I'm sure Tolo would put in a good word along the line.'

The front doorbell rang. Isabel sprung from her seat.

'And you have a successful gym to run, so get back to work!'

Pablo welcomed a local client into the reception and accompanied Isabel to her car.

'If ever you want to have a gym session, it's on the house,' he said, giving her a bear hug.

Isabel revved the engine. 'I fear that time won't permit, but never say never.'

As she reached the road, she smiled at the brilliant blue sky above. Winter was waning and in the twinkling of an eye, it would be spring.

After a long catch-up with Tolo by phone, Isabel raided her fridge and whooped with joy at her mother's sumptuous offerings.

There was a large dish of *fideua* crammed with fish and seafood, aubergine pâté, *tumbet* and *pica pica*. Her mother had also left a specially prepared bowl of mashed meat for Furó. The ferret was already dancing at Isabel's heels as she pulled out a few dishes for inspection. Next, she peeked into the pantry and discovered a freshly baked apple tart and *gató de almendras* decorated with slices of candied orange and lemon and drizzled with icing. In the wooden bread bin was a fresh *masa madre* loaf and another with green olives.

'What a feast, Furó. I'd better not be too greedy as it's the beginning of Sant Antoni tomorrow, and there'll be many hungry mouths to feed here during the day.'

He stood eyeing her expectantly until she warmed his dish and settled it in front of him. Opening a bottle of red wine, she breathed in the rich and earthy aroma and poured herself a big glass. She was relieved that the case was reaching its conclusion but was still unhappy that there was insufficient evidence to charge Rocci Mestre with the murders of Marc Castell and Silvia Porres. She knew that Marc Castell, though murdered himself, was his co-conspirator, but it would be a travesty of justice if Rocci were to slip the net. She hoped that forensics might find DNA or something crucial to connect him with the crime on Castell's land.

With a frustrated sigh, she took a long sip from her glass and pottered off to the patio, where she read until her dinner had heated in the oven. It was late by the time she rose wearily, and yawning, wished the stars and moon a very good night. She switched off the kitchen lights and was on the point of plodding up the stairs to bed when she heard a knock at the front door. Isabel frowned. Who might be calling at this time of night? It never boded well. As a precaution, she called out *'Quien es?'*

No one answered. She turned on the lights in the front garden and opened the door. There was no one about. A small padded envelope left on the porch caught her eye. She strode along her path and looked right and left along Calle Pastor, but its only visitor was a nimble-footed black cat. She stepped back into the *entrada* where an anxious Furó awaited her and ripped open the blank envelope. A black USB flash drive dropped into her hands. There was no note and no clue as to the sender. Despite her exhaustion, she gripped it tightly and headed upstairs to her office. Her beauty sleep would have to wait.

TWENTY-FOUR

A s council workers in the *plaça* began setting up a stage and microphone in anticipation of the *fiesta*, a bright sun spread its golden tentacles across the terracotta roof tiles of Sant Martí. Isabel emerged smiling from Bon Día, her pannier crammed with bags of sunflower seeds and fresh croissants, and stood to inspect the work in hand. Llorenç sidled up to her.

'Padre Agustí will be doing his address at seven o'clock, but I've told him to keep it brief.'

Isabel laughed. 'Good luck with that one.'

She heard her name being called and turned. Enric was kitted out in his mountain guide gear and was surrounded by expectant hikers.

'Where are you heading?' she asked.

'Massanella, but first we're stocking up on goodies at Bon Día.' She gave him the thumbs-up.

'It's great to see guides back working in the Trams, isn't it?'

Llorenç offered an enthusiastic nod. 'Thank heavens. And I see from *El Periódico* that a number of arrests have been made in the Sebi Vives case. Congratulations.'

'Thanks, but it's all about team effort and Furó is officially on the taskforce now.'

He laughed. 'He's a canny little ferret. So when will more details about the case be released?'

'Soon. I have given Casanovas a small scoop on condition that he plays ball following Tolo's press conference this afternoon.'

'Then I shan't pry any further, dear Bel. I shall see you later.'

Isabel strode through the square and along Calle Pastor, grinning as she caught sight of Señora Coll at her neighbour's gate. She reminded herself that the elderly matron had unwittingly helped in her in the Vives case when she'd bumped into her wearing a shawl to hide a cat scratch on her neck. It had reminded Isabel that Sara Vives had also been wearing a scarf, which she later deduced could have been used to hide her bruised neck. The postmistress was wafting a small bottle of pills in the air and talking animatedly to Doctor Ramis. He looked relieved to see Isabel.

'Ah, just the person I wanted to see. If you'll excuse me, Señora Coll.'

She nodded politely, popped her medication into a shopping bag and pottered off towards the *plaça*.

Doctor Ramis sighed. 'Heaven forbid she discovers one day that I'm merely feeding her sugar pills!'

Isabel giggled. 'Your secret is safe with me. You wanted a word?'

'Yes, indeed. I spoke with my old chum Ignacio Sánchez yesterday. He was quite taken with you and has invited us both for lunch in Palma.'

'That would be fun. Doctor Sánchez was a great help with the Sebi Vives case.'

'So you have caught the killer?'

Isabel cocked her head on one side. 'Tolo will be making a press announcement later today, but the case will soon be closed.'

'Soon?'

'By good fortune, I had a little helping hand with one aspect of the investigation last night. It has proven the final piece in a complex jigsaw.'

He clapped her on the back. 'Well done. Now I must attend to a patient, but I look forward to seeing you tonight. Your mother says that you will be helping her with the barbecue. She has prepared enough food for a team of *castellers*.'

Isabel groaned. 'No change there. Of course, Tolo is an expert with barbecues. Maybe I'll leave them both to it.'

He ambled along his path. 'Good plan.'

Isabel entered Ca'n Moix and opened the door to the office. Balls of screwed-up newspaper were everywhere. Pep jumped up from his seat.

'Furó and I were just mucking about. I'll clear them up.'

She grinned. 'First let's have our breakfast.'

'Great, but don't keep me in suspense. I want to know the upshot of the investigation. There's not much meat in Casanovas' news report online today.'

'It was a gesture of goodwill. I had suspicions about who the departmental mole was at the precinct and earlier this morning called Casanovas and insisted he confirm the identity of the culprit or I'd never give him another scoop.'

'He agreed?'

'Yes, but it is a delicate matter that I will need to discuss with Tolo alone. So, Pep, as my unofficial deputy sleuth, let me show you some video footage from a USB stick left in an envelope at my front door last night. I immediately downloaded it to Tolo and the team and an arrest was made in the early hours.'

She ushered him into her office and sat him down at the computer while she selected the correct file.

'Before you watch, prepare yourself. The two brief films don't make for pleasant viewing. I'll play the first.'

Pep nodded but gave a gasp as he watched the grainy film, his eyes on stalks. At the end, he winced and shot a look at Isabel.

'Who are these men? Is this shot at Silvia Porres's house? There's a fluffy cat on the porch. You told me about it.'

'Well remembered, Pep. Yes, the first film is from Silvia's porch. It shows two men clearly entering the property and leaving the house with what appears to be a body bag. Although they are both wearing dark hoodies and attire, we have some clues to their identities. What do you see?'

He played it back and froze one of the images. 'One of them has a tattoo on his neck.'

'Excellent, and what else?'

He shrugged. 'The other one is holding a cigarette as he enters.'

'Very good, but there's one more crucial item on display.'

Pep replayed the video a few times and then banged his fist down on the desk. 'The man with the tattoo is wearing a watch.'

Isabel nodded. 'It's not just any watch. It's a Rolex Cosmograph Daytona, according to Gaspar and the team. It has a customised white dial featuring eight diamonds framed in platinum. It's one of a kind. Now watch the second video.'

Pep stared at the screen. 'Where is this?'

'It's the strip of land near Porreres owned by Marc Castell. This is the plot where forensics discovered traces of Silvia Porres's blood in soil samples and where they also discovered Castell's body.'

'The same man is in this video too. He's wearing a hoodie again, but you can still see the watch and tattoo. Is that Marc Castell with him? Oh no, the man with the Rolex has a gun.'

Isabel played the video again and froze it. 'Yes, the man holding the gun is our killer. Tolo called me this morning to say that it is without doubt Rocci Mestre. He owns a customised Rolex, one of a kind, and the tattoo on his neck is of a dragon.'

'So he killed Silvia Porres and Marc Castell?'

'Correct, but we believe that Marc Castell assisted him with the murder of Silvia. His reward was his own death.'

'But why did Rocci kill him?'

'Because he knew far too much. It was easiest to dispose of him. Without any hope of a testimony or confession from Castell, we had precious little evidence to convict him, but this footage has changed all that.'

'I suppose having a distinctive tattoo isn't a great idea for a criminal.'

'Nor is wearing a customised Rolex. The same goes for getaway cars with personalised number plates.'

'Was someone filming them? Why give you the evidence?'

'That is the question, dear Pep. I strongly believe that someone decided that Rocci was uncontrollable and had set up cameras at both places to implicate him.'

'Do you know who?'

She tapped her nose. 'I have an inkling, but in truth we may never know.'

The front door banged open and Florentina's voice floated up the stairs.

'Have you had breakfast?'

Isabel closed the file, grabbed the bag of fresh croissants from her pannier and hot-footed it downstairs with Pep in tow.

Isabel was in the kitchen surrounded by bags of food ready to be transported to the *plaça* when Tolo arrived. It was nearly six-thirty and the oompah band had already struck up, the loud music weaving its way through the streets of the village and along Calle Pastor. Llorenç, perhaps overcome with joy that the mountain menaces had recently been captured, had provided the entertainment and drinks free of charge to the residents of Sant Martí. Communal barbecues had been set up around the square on which locals could grill their meat, vegetables and fish, and trestle tables were provided around a central log fire. The jolly event would mark the beginning of the week-long *fiesta* of Sant Antoni and was the envy of other villages in the valley.

Isabel stood in deep concentration in the kitchen. She made a snap decision. Grabbing her mobile and David Mestre's card, she strode into the garden and called him on his private line. He answered in three rings.

'Isabel Flores, what a lovely surprise.'

She hesitated a moment. 'Is it? I imagined that a call from a police detective might not fill you with joy.'

'Firstly, you are an independent operator, which I admire, and secondly, I'm a great believer in forgive and forget. It was regrettable that the National Police felt it necessary to raid our homes, but at least no evidence was discovered and we have been proven completely innocent of any connection to the tragic death of Sebi Vives and Silvia Porres.'

Isabel's lips creased into a smile. 'You and Toni might be in the clear, but Rocci appears to be in a spot of bother.'

David Mestre issued a long sigh. 'Rocci likes to paddle his own canoe, and so if he has foolishly entered choppy waters, Toni and I will not be offering a lifebuoy.'

'So it seems. I heard from the chief of police that despite not being close to Rocci, you bought him a special watch for his last birthday.'

'Indeed I did. After all, he is my brother. It is a one-off and there isn't another like it in the world. It is unique to Rocci.'

Isabel shook her head. 'Smart move, David. I doubt our paths will cross again, but thank you for doing the decent thing.'

'And what could that possibly be?'

'I think you know.'

He was silent for a moment and then replied in a steelier voice. 'And now I hope we can all put this sorry episode behind us. Toni and I would appreciate being left to run our business without police intervention.'

'Just keep on the right side of the law, and I'm sure my colleagues will keep off your back.'

He issued a snort of amusement. Isabel ended the call.

She walked into the kitchen and helped herself to a bowl of black olives on the table. She had bought them from Agromart, a store that specialised in local products, and although her mother and Idò prepared their own tart, green variety in brine, she secretly preferred the sweeter flavour of those prepared in olive oil. She thought of ill-fated Silvia Porres and her love for olives cassées de la vallée des Baux de Provence. The woman had broken the law, but she had been a dutiful daughter, and now Isabel would be able to assure her dying mother that justice had been done.

There was a sharp knock at the front door and Tolo walked into the kitchen and wrapped his arms around her.

'Am I late?'

She kissed him. 'For once, no. You are on barbecue duty with Mama tonight.'

'*Vale*, and what about you?'

'I'm helping with the wine and *cava*.'

He laughed. 'I always pick the short straw.'

She eyed him seriously. 'How did the press conference go?'

He popped an olive into his mouth. 'A lot of questions but all good. Even Casanovas towed the line, but then you did give him a scoop with the arrests. Now he's got the whole story, so hopefully he'll get off our backs.'

'I've just spoken with David Mestre. I thanked him for the video footage. Well, not in so many words.'

He folded his arms. 'Was that wise?'

She shrugged. 'Without it, we'd never have been able to convict Rocci.'

'True, but he and Toni Mestre are now free of a rogue brother and there's not enough evidence to implicate either in the shady business of the motorway contract.'

Isabel nodded. 'But importantly, we have our killers and hopefully, the motorway will now never happen.'

He licked an oily finger. 'The regional president is resigning tomorrow and the motorway project is dead and buried. I believe Mariana Blasi's husband will follow suit. You can't really serve in government when your wife is in the clink.'

'But in fairness, neither Felip Blasi nor Teo Grau knew anything about their wives' nocturnal activities.'

'I agree, but that's life. Harsh lessons all round.'

'Do you think the three women will receive long prison sentences?'

Tolo shrugged. 'I'm not sure about Sara, given Sebi's history of abuse, but the others should expect hefty prison terms. Mind you, they have powerful connections, of course, so who knows whether their sentences will eventually be reduced.' He raised an eyebrow. 'Shall we go? I'm starving.'

Isabel hesitated. 'One other thing. I've discovered who the departmental mole is. It's Corc.'

He stared at her in disbelief. 'What? Impossible!'

'I forced Casanovas to tell me the truth. I've had my suspicions for a while. I overheard Corc passing sensitive information to a caller when I popped into the precinct early one morning. Casanovas admitted it was him. Corc has been played by a cynical media.'

'He'll be out on his ear when the commissioner gets wind of this.'

'Don't tell him, Tolo. Corc is a simple, trusting soul and I don't believe he had any idea that talking to the press was wrong. Be kind. He can be trained.'

Tolo frowned. 'I'll think about it.' He paused. 'Any more news about Uncle Hugo?'

Isabel stiffened. 'Not really.'

He eyed her quizzically. 'What aren't you telling me? What's wrong?'

'Oh, this is hopeless. The truth is that Emilio called me last Friday and swore me to secrecy.'

'About what?'

'There are developments, but he said no one can know, and that apparently includes you.'

He ran a hand through his hair. 'In that case, the National Police is implicated in some way. Don't tell me any more. You mustn't be compromised. I think this might herald good news if it is what I'm thinking. Let's put this aside for tonight.'

Isabel nodded in relief while he gathered the food bags and playfully bashed her with one. 'Care to help?'

They arrived in the crowded *plaça* just as Padre Agustí was finishing his speech.

'And so remember that our patron saint, Antoni Abad, must never be confused with Antoni of Padua, not that he wasn't a holy man too, of course. Our Antoni loved animals and particularly pigs...'

There were sniggers from the crowd.

'And why not? They are intelligent and complex sentient beings. This is why at the animal blessing this Sunday we will celebrate all animals, but pigs above all. Blessed be our *fiesta* and may you drive the demons away, just as Sant Antoni did in that vast Egyptian desert.'

There was thunderous applause, and laughter as a group of demons danced about the crowds, poking them with their forks.

Isabel greeted her mother and Doctor Ramis, as Pep and Angélica wove through the crowd to reach them. With an encouraging nod from Pep, Isabel smiled at the mayor's beloved daughter.

'How slim you look, Angélica!'

The girl looked at her for a moment in some confusion and then laughed heartily.

'*Que va*! Since going on that stupid diet, I put on more weight. I'm going to eat exactly what I want from now on, starting with the biggest prawns on the grill tonight.'

Isabel laughed and in surprise turned to see Señora Coll dancing the *cucaracha* with a smartly dressed Frans Bordoy. As they passed round drinks and chatted with neighbours and friends, Isabel felt a tap on her shoulder. Capitán Gómez fixed his beady green eyes on her.

'A moment, Bel.'

Isabel reluctantly followed him to the edge of the *plaça*.

'I thought you should know, Bel, that the two Russian victims of Nikolai Petrov and his monstrous associates are recovering well in hospital. Petrov's sister, appalled at the goings-on, will donate the *finca* to our regional government to be turned into a nature and conservation centre for schools.'

'That's good news, Alvaro. Congratulations on an excellent outcome.'

He tutted. 'But the success of the mission was also thanks to your rather eccentric yet effective policing methods.'

'Thanks. Do you know what will happen to Brut, the old collie?'

'Xim, the farmer with land next to the Voin estate, has adopted him.'

Isabel smiled. 'I'm pleased. Well, let's get back to the *fiesta*.'

He shook his head. 'Not so fast, Bel. I still have a grave matter to discuss with you.'

'Whatever do you mean?'

'You'll recall that you absconded with a power drill when you broke into Petrov's shed. You have still not returned it. This will have consequences.'

Isabel's eyes widened in disbelief. 'Are you serious? For heaven's sake. I never wanted the wretched drill. I had to make it appear like a burglary.'

Capitán Gómez frowned, then threw his head back and laughed manically. 'Can't you take a joke, Bel? As if I care about the drill. Now, I must be off to police this event. You can never trust the reckless behaviour of locals.'

He slithered through the crowds and disappeared from view. Would she ever truly get the measure of the man? With a smile, she made her way back to the merry throng and laughed at the sight of Tolo in a chef's hat and apron performing the conga with Florentina, Pep, Llorenç and a host of other giggling locals. Even Jesus from Bon Día was shaking his hips. Her heart melted. Nothing in the world could ever beat the power of community and there was nowhere else she'd rather be.

Acknowledgements

Once again, my sincerest thanks go to my partner in crime, illustrator, Chris Corr, talented designers, Chris Jones and Ben Ottridge, and editors Lucy York and Laura Burge. A special mention to my agent, Francine Fletcher of Fletcher Associates, for her continued friendship and guidance.

It goes without saying that big hugs are due to my hugely supportive husband, Alan, son Ollie, sister, Cecilia and nephew, Alex, for their constant cheerleading and encouragement.

Finally, immeasurable thanks to you, my readers, for having supported me thus far on my publishing journey. Without you, it simply wouldn't have been possible.

THE DEVIL'S HORN

AN ISABEL FLORES MALLORCAN MYSTERY

ANNA NICHOLAS

THE DEVIL'S HORN
An Isabel Flores Mallorcan Mystery

Anna Nicholas

Paperback: 978-1-9996618-4-7
Ebook: 978-1-9996618-5-4

When 33-year-old Isabel Flores Montserrat quits her promising career with the Spanish police to run her mother's holiday rentals agency in rural Mallorca, her crime-fighting days seem far behind.

Basking in the Mediterranean sunshine with pet ferret Furó, she indulges her passion for local cuisine, swimming in the sea and raising her pampered hens.

However, in just a few days, the disappearance of a young British girl, violent murder of an elderly neighbour, and discovery of a Colombian drug cartel threaten to tear apart Isabel's idyllic life.

Together with local chief inspector Tolo Cabot, an old admirer of her unorthodox methods, Isabel must race against the clock to untangle a sinister web of crime and restore peace to the island once more.

HAUNTED
MAGPIE

AN ISABEL FLORES MALLORCAN MYSTERY

ANNA NICHOLAS

HAUNTED MAGPIE
An Isabel Flores Mallorcan Mystery

Anna Nicholas

Paperback: 978-1-9996618-6-1
Ebook: 978-1-9996618-7-8

Eccentric, headstrong and engaging, Isabel Flores Montserrat is a cross between a highly charged Precious Ramotswe (*The No.1 Ladies' Detective Agency*) & Phryne Fisher (*Miss Fisher's Murder Mysteries*).

When 33-year-old Isabel Flores Montserrat quits a promising career with the Spanish police to run her mother's holiday rentals agency in rural Mallorca, it seems that her crime-fighting days are far behind. Basking in the Mediterranean sunshine with pet ferret, Furo, she indulges her passion for local cuisine, swimming in the sea and raising her pampered hens.

However, when a young florist goes missing, Isabel is once again seconded by the National Police to help solve the mystery. Meanwhile, trouble is brewing in her own village with a sinister spate of animal disappearances. When another islander vanishes, Isabel and the local police chief, Tolo Cabot, must hunt a potential serial killer using their unorthodox investigative skills. With the clock ticking, they urgently need to find answers and restore harmony to the island once more.

A FLIGHT OF FANCY AROUND MALLORCA
PEACOCKS IN PARADISE
ANNA NICHOLAS

PEACOCKS IN PARADISE
A Flight of Fancy Around Mallorca

Anna Nicholas

Paperback: 978-1-8383110-0-1
Ebook: 978-1-8383110-1-8

The long-awaited seventh title in Anna Nicholas's humorous travel series about how to live the dream in a Mediterranean country. The author explores different local cultural themes in each title.

Anna delves into the island's authentic heartland, exploring nature reserves, bird sanctuaries and paprika, fruit and almond farms. On her travels, she meets the makers of siurell whistles, palm leaf baskets, hot sauces and ensaïmada pastries, and revels in visiting local producers of wine, craft beer, gin and brandy – and Mallorca's famed herbes liqueur.

Meanwhile, she and chum, Alison, are tackling all 54 Tramuntana peaks over 1,000m, enduring the arduous overnight Guell hike to Lluc Monastery along the way.

Back home in Soller, new kittens and abandoned ducks abound and just as peacock, Jeronimo, swoops in, Anna hears of Josephine, a lonely peahen. Could love be in the air?

A Lizard in my Luggage
MAYFAIR TO MALLORCA IN ONE EASY MOVE

ANNA NICHOLAS

PB: 9781999661700
EB: 9781999661717

CAT ON A HOT TILED ROOF
Mayhem in Mayfair and Mallorca

ANNA NICHOLAS

PB: 9781999661724
EB: 9781999661731

GOATS FROM A SMALL ISLAND
GRABBING MALLORCAN LIFE BY THE HORNS

ANNA NICHOLAS

PB: 9781999661748
EB: 9781999661755